VIOLA GWYN

VIOLA GWYN

By GEORGE BARR McCUTCHEON

AUTHOR OF

"Quill's Window," "West Wind Drift," "Sherry," "Black is White," "The City of Masks," "Mr. Bingle," "The Rose in the Ring," etc.

A. L. BURT COMPANY

Publishers   New York

Published by arrangement with Dodd, Mead & Company

Printed in U. S. A.

CONTENTS

VIOLA GWYN

PROLOGUE

THE BEGINNING

KENNETH GWYNNE was five years old when
his father ran away with Rachel Carter, a
widow. This was in the spring of 1812, and
in the fall his mother died. His grandparents brought
him up to hate Rachel Carter, an evil woman.

She was his mother's friend and she had slain her
with the viper's tooth. From the day that his questioning intelligence seized upon the truth that had
been so carefully withheld from him by his broken-
hearted mother and those who spoke behind the hand
when he was near,—from that day he hated Rachel
Carter with all his hot and outraged heart. He came
to think of her as the embodiment of all that was evil,
—for those were the days when there was no middle-
ground for sin and women were either white or scarlet.

He rejoiced in the belief that in good time Rachel
Carter would come to roast in the everlasting fires of
hell, grovelling and wailing at the feet of Satan, the
while his lovely mother looked down upon her in pity,
—even then he wondered if such a thing were possible,
—from her seat beside God in His Heaven. He had
no doubts about this. Hell and heaven were real to
him, and all sinners went below. On the other hand,

1

his father would be permitted to repent and would instantly go to heaven. It was inconceivable that his big, strong, well-beloved father should go to the bad place. But Mrs. Carter would! Nothing could save her! God would not pay any attention to her if she tried to repent; He would know it was only "make-believe" if she got down on her knees and prayed for forgiveness. He was convinced that Rachel Carter could not fool God. Besides, would not his mother be there to remind Him in case He could not exactly remember what Rachel Carter had done? And were there not dozens of good, honest people in the village who would probably be in Heaven by that time and ready to stand before the throne and bear witness that she was a bad woman?

No, Rachel Carter could never get into Heaven. He was glad. No matter if the Scriptures did say all that about the sinner who repents, he did not believe that God would let her in. He supported this belief by the profoundly childish contention that if God let *everybody* in, then there would be no use having a hell at all. What was the use of being good all your life if the bad people could get into Heaven at the last minute by telling God they were sorry and never would do anything bad again as long as they lived? And was not God the wisest Being in all the world? He knew *everything!* He knew all about Rachel Carter. She would go to the bad place and stay there forever, even after the "resurrection" and the end of the world by fire in 1883, a calamity to which he looked forward with grave concern and no little trepidation at the thoughtful age of six.

At first they told him his father had gone off as a soldier to fight against the Indians and the British.

He knew that a war was going on. Men with guns were drilling in the pasture up beyond his grandfather's house, and there was talk of Indian "massacrees," and Simon Girty's warriors, and British redcoats, and the awful things that happened to little boys who disobeyed their elders and went swimming, or berrying, or told even the teeniest kind of fibs. He overheard his grandfather and the neighbours discussing a battle on Lake Erie, and rejoiced with them over the report of a great victory for "our side." Vaguely he had grasped the news of a horrible battle on the Tippecanoe River, far away in the wilderness to the north and west, in which millions of Indians were slain, and he wondered how many of them his father had killed with his rifle,—a weapon so big and long that he came less than half way up the barrel when he stood beside it.

His father was a great shot. Everybody said so. He could kill wild turkeys a million miles away as easy as rolling off a log, and deer, and catamounts, and squirrels, and herons, and everything. So his father must have killed heaps of Indians and red-coats and renegades.

He put this daily question to his mother: "How many do you s'pose Pa has killed by this time, Ma?"

And then, in the fall, his mother went away and left him. They did not tell him she had gone to the war. He would not have believed them if they had, for she was too sick to go. She had been in bed for a long, long time; the doctor came to see her every day, and finally the preacher. He hated both of them, especially the latter, who prayed so loudly and so vehemently that his mother must have been terribly disturbed. Why should every one caution him to be quiet and not make a noise because it disturbed mother, and yet say nothing when that old preacher went right into her room and yelled same as he always did in church? He was very bitter about it, and longed for his father to come home with his rifle and shoot everybody, including his grandfather who had "switched" him severely and unjustly because he threw stones at Parson Hook's saddle horse while the good man was offering up petitions from the sick room.

He went to the "burying," and was more impressed by the fact that nearly all of the men who rode or drove to the graveyard down in the "hollow" carried rifles and pistols than he was by the strange solemnity of the occasion, for, while he realized in a vague, mistrustful way that his mother was to be put under the ground, his trust clung resolutely to God's promise, accepted in its most literal sense, that the dead shall rise again and that "ye shall be born again." That was what the preacher said,—and he had cried a little when the streaming-eyed clergyman took him on his knee and whispered that all was well with his dear mother and that he would meet her one day in that beautiful land beyond the River.

He was very lonely after that. His "granny" tucked him in his big feather bed every night, and listened to his little prayer, but she was not the same as mother. She did not kiss him in the same way, nor did her hand feel like mother's when she smoothed his rumpled hair or buttoned his flannel nightgown about his neck or closed his eyes playfully with her fingers before she went away with the candle. Yet he adored her. She was sweet and gentle, she told such wonderful fairy tales to him, and she always smiled at him. He wondered a great deal. Why was it that she did not *feel* the same as mother? He was deeply puzzled. Was it because her hair was grey?

His grandfather lived in the biggest house in town. It had an "upstairs,"—a real "upstairs,"—not just an attic. And his grandfather was a very important person. Everybody called him "Squire"; sometimes they said "your honour"; most people touched their hats to him. When his father went off to the war, he and his mother came to live at "grandpa's house." The cabin in which he was born was at the other end of the street, fully half-a-mile away, out beyond the grist mill. It had but three rooms and no "upstairs" at all except the place under the roof where they kept the dried apples, and the walnuts and hickory nuts, some old saddle-bags and boxes, and his discarded cradle. You had to climb up a ladder and through a square hole in the ceiling to get into this place, and you would have to be very careful not to stand up straight or you would bump your head,—unless you were exactly in the middle, where the ridge-pole was.

He remembered that it was a very long walk to "grandpa's house"; he used to get very tired and his father would lift him up and place him on his shoulder; from this lofty, even perilous, height he could look down upon the top of his mother's bonnet,—a most astonishing view and one that filled him with glee.

His father was the biggest man in all the world, there could be no doubt about that. Why, he was bigger even than grandpa, or Doctor Flint, or the parson, or Mr. Carter, who lived in the cabin next door and was Minda's father. For the matter of that, he was, himself, a great deal bigger than Minda, who was only two years old and could not say anywhere near as many words as he could say—and did not know her A B C's, or the Golden Rule, or who George Washington was.

And his father was ever so much taller than his mother. He was tall enough to be her father or her grandfather; why, she did not come up to his shoulder when she walked beside him. He was a million times bigger than she was. He was bigger than anybody else in all the world.

The little border town in Kentucky, despite its population of less than a thousand, was the biggest city in the world. There was no doubt about that either in Kenneth's loyal little mind. It was bigger than Philadelphia—(he called it Fil-*lef*-ily),—where his mother used to live when she was a little girl, or Massashooshoo, where Minda's father and mother comed from.

He was secretly distressed by the superior physical proportions of his "Auntie" Rachel. There was no denying the fact that she was a great deal taller than his mother. He had an abiding faith, however, that some day his mother would grow up and be lots taller than Minda's mother. He challenged his toddling playmate to deny that his mother would be as big as hers some day, a lofty taunt that left Minda quite unmoved.

Nevertheless, he was very fond of "Auntie" Rachel. She was good to him. She gave him cakes and crullers and spread maple sugar on many a surreptitious piece of bread and butter, and she had a jolly way of laughing, and she never told him to wash his hands or face, no matter how dirty they were. In that one respect, at least, she was much nicer than his mother. He liked Mr. Carter, too. In fact, he liked everybody except old Boose, the tin pedlar, who took little boys

out into the woods and left them for the wolves to eat
if they were not very, very good.

He was four when they brought Mr. Carter home
in a wagon one day. Some men carried him into the
house, and Aunt Rachel cried, and his mother went
over and stayed a long, long time with her, and his
father got on his horse and rode off as fast as he could
go for Doctor Flint, and he was not allowed to go outside the house all day,—or old Boose would get him.

Then, one day, he saw "Auntie" Rachel all dressed
in black, and he was frightened. He ran away crying.
She looked so tall and scary,—like the witches Biddy
Shay whispered about when his grandma was not
around,—the witches and hags that flew up to the sky
on broomsticks and never came out except at night.

His father did the "chores" for "'Auntie" Rachel
for a long time, because Mr. Carter was not there to
attend to them.

There came a day when the buds were fresh on the
twigs, and the grass was very green, and the birds
that had been gone for a long time were singing again
in the trees, and it was not raining. So he went down
the road to play in Minda's yard. He called to her,
but she did not appear. No one appeared. The house
was silent. "Auntie" Rachel was not there. Even the
dogs were gone, and Mr. Carter's horses and his
wagon. He could not understand. Only yesterday
he had played in the barn with Minda.

Then his grandma came hurrying through the trees
from his own home, where she had been with grandpa
and Uncle Fred and Uncle Dan since breakfast time.
She took him up in her arms and told him that Minda
was gone. He had never seen his grandma look so stern
and angry. Biddy Shay had been there all morning

too, and several of the neighbours. He wondered if it could be the Sabbath, and yet that did not seem possible, because it was only two days since he went to Sunday school, and yesterday his mother had done the washing. She always washed on Monday and ironed on Tuesday. This must be Tuesday, but maybe he was wrong about that. She was not ironing, so it could not be Tuesday. He was very much bewildered.

His mother was in the bedroom with grandpa and Aunt Hettie, and he was not allowed to go in to see her. Uncle Fred and Uncle Dan were very solemn and scowling so terribly that he was afraid to go near them.

He remembered that his mother had cried while she was cooking breakfast, and sat down a great many times to rest her head on her arms. She had cried a good deal lately, because of the headache, she always said. And right after breakfast she had put on her bonnet and shawl, telling him to stay in the house till she came back from grandpa's. Then she had gone away, leaving him all alone until Biddy Shay came, all out of breath, and began to clear the table and wash the dishes, all the while talking to herself in a way that he was sure God would not like, and probably would send her to the bad place for it when she died.

After a while all of the men went out to the barn-lot, where their horses were tethered. Uncle Fred and Uncle Dan had their rifles. He stood at the kitchen window and watched them with wide, excited eyes. Were they going off to kill Indians, or bears, or catty-munks? They all talked at once, especially his uncles, —and they swore, too. Then his grandpa stood in front of them and spoke very loudly, pointing his finger at them. He heard him say, over and over again:

"Let them go, I say! I tell you, let them go!"

He wondered why his father was not there, if there was any fighting to be done. His father was a great fighter. He was the bestest shot in all the world. He could kill an Injin a million miles away, or a squirrel, or a groundhog. So he asked Biddy Shay.

"Ast me no questions and I'll tell ye no lies," was all the answer he got from Biddy.

The next day he went up to grandpa's with his mother to stay, and Uncle Fred told him that his pa had gone off to the war. He believed this, for were not the rifle, the powder horn and the shot flask missing from the pegs over the fireplace, and was not Bob, the very fastest horse in all the world, gone from the barn? He was vastly thrilled. His father would shoot millions and millions of Injins, and they would have a house full of scalps and tommyhawks and bows and arrers.

But he was troubled about Minda. Uncle Fred, driven to corner by persistent inquiry, finally confessed that Minda also had gone to the war, and at last report had killed several extremely ferocious redskins. Despite this very notable achievement, Kenneth was troubled. In the first place, Minda was a baby, and always screamed when she heard a gun go off; in the second place, she always fell down when she tried to run and squalled like everything if he did not wait for her; in the third place, Injins always beat little girls' heads off against a tree if they caught 'em.

Moreover, Uncle Dan, upon being consulted, declared that a good-sized Injin could swaller Minda in one gulp if 'he happened to be 'specially hungry,—or in a hurry. Uncle Dan also appeared to be very much surprised when he heard that she had gone off to the war. He said that Uncle Fred ought to be ashamed of himself; and the next time he asked Uncle Fred about Minda he was considerably relieved to hear that his little playmate had given up fighting altogether and was living quite peaceably in a house made of a pumpkin over yonder where the sun went down at night.

It was not until sometime after his mother went away,—after the long-to-be-remembered "fooneral," with its hymns, and weeping, and praying,—that he heard the grown-ups talking about the war being over. The redcoats were thrashed and there was much boasting and bragging among the men of the settlement. Strange men appeared on the street, and other men slapped their backs and shook hands with them and shouted loudly and happily at them. In time, he came to understand that these were the citizens who had gone off to fight in the war and were now home again, all safe and sound. He began to watch for his father. He would know him a million miles off, he was so big, and he had the biggest rifle in the world.

"Do you s'pose Pa will know how to find me, grandma?" he would inquire. " 'Cause, you see, I don't live where I used to."

And his grandmother, beset with this and similar questions from one day's end to the other, would become very busy over what she was doing at the time and tell him not to pester her. He did not like to ask his grandfather. He was so stern,—even when he was sitting all alone on the porch and was not busy at all.

Then one day he saw his grandparents talking together on the porch. Aunt Hettie was with them, but she was not talking. She was just looking at him as he played down by the watering trough. He distinctly heard his grandma say:

"I think he ought to be told, Richard. It's a sin to let him go on thinking—" The rest of the sentence was lost to him when she suddenly lowered her voice. They were all looking at him.

Presently his grandfather called to him, and beckoned with his finger. He marched up to the porch with his little bow and arrow. Grandma turned to go into the house, and Aunt Hettie hurried away.

"Don't be afraid, Granny," he sang out. "I won't shoot you. 'Sides, I've only got one arrer, Aunt Hettie."

His grandfather took him on his knee, and then and there told him the truth about his father. He spoke very slowly and did not say any of those great big words that he always used when he was with grown-up people, or even with the darkies.

"Now, pay strict attention, Kenneth. You must understand everything I say to you. Do you hear? Your father is never coming home. We told you he had gone to the war. We thought it was best to let you think so. It is time for you to know the truth. You are always asking questions about him. After this, when you want to know about your father, you must come to me. I will tell you. Do not bother your grandma. You make her unhappy when you ask questions. You see, your Ma was once her little girl and mine. She used to be as little as you are. Your Pa was her husband. You know what a husband is, don't you?"

"Yes, sir," said Kenneth, wide-eyed. "It's a boy's father."

"You are nearly six years old. Quite a man, my lad." He paused to look searchingly into the child's face, his bushy eyebrows meeting in a frown.

"The devil of it is," he burst out, "you are the living image of your father. You are going to grow up to look like him." He groaned audibly, spat viciously over his shoulder, and went on in a strange, hard voice. "Do you know what it is to steal? It means taking something that belongs to somebody else."

"Yes, sir. 'Thou shalt not steal.' It's in the Bible."

"Well, you know that Indians and gipsies steal little boys, don't you? It is the very worst kind of stealing, because it breaks the boy's mother's heart. It sometimes kills them. Now, suppose that somebody stole a husband. A husband is a boy's father, as you say. Your father was a husband. He was your dear mother's husband. You loved your mother very, very much, didn't you? Don't cry, lad,—there, there, now! Be a little man. Now, listen. Somebody stole your mother's husband. She loved him better than anything in the world. She loved him, I guess, even better than she loved you, Kenneth. She just couldn't live without him. Do you see? That is why she died and went away. She is in Heaven now. Now, let me hear you say this after me: My mother died because somebody stole her husband away from her."

" 'My mother died because somebody stoled her husband away from her,' " repeated the boy, slowly.

"You will never forget that, will you?"

"No,—sir."

"Say this: My mother's heart was broken and so she died."

"'My mother's heart was broken and she—and so she died.'"

"You will never forget that either, will you, Kenneth?"

"No, sir."

"Now, I am going to tell you who stole your mother's husband away from her. You know who your mother's husband was, don't you?"

"Yes, sir. My Pa."

"One night,—the night before you came up here to live,—your Auntie Rachel,—that is what you called her, isn't it? Well, she was not your real aunt. She was your neighbour,—just as Mr. Collins over there is my neighbour,—and she was your mother's friend. Well, that night she stole your Pa from your Ma, and took him away with her,—far, far away, and she never let him come back again. She took him away in the night, away from your mother and you forever and forever. She—"

"But Pa was bigger'n she was," interrupted Kenneth, frowning. "Why didn't he kill her and get away?"

The old Squire was silent for a moment. "It is not fair for me to put all the blame on Rachel Carter. Your father was willing to go. He did not kill Rachel Carter. Together he and Rachel Carter killed your mother. But Rachel Carter was more guilty than he was. She was a woman and she stole what belonged in the sight of God to another woman. She was a bad woman. If she had been a good woman she would not have stolen your father away from your mother. So now you know that your Pa did not go to the war. He went away with Rachel Carter and left your mother to die of a broken heart. He went off into the wilderness with that bad, evil woman. Your mother was unhappy. She died. She is under the ground up in the graveyard, all alone. Rachel Carter put her there, Kenneth. I cannot ask you to hate your father. It would not be right. He is your father in spite of everything. You know what the Good Book says? 'Honour thy father and—' how does the rest of it go, my lad?"

" 'Honour thy father and thy mother that thou days may be long upon thou earth,' " murmured Kenneth, bravely.

"When you are a little older you will realize that your father did not honour his father and mother, and then you may understand more than you do now. But you may hate Rachel Carter. You *must* hate her. She killed your mother. She stole your father. She made an orphan of you. She destroyed the home where you used to live. As you grow older I will try to tell you how she did all these things. You would not understand now. There is one of the Ten Commandments that you do not understand,—I mean one in particular. It is enough for you to know the meaning of the one that says 'Thou shalt not steal.' You must not be unhappy over what I have told you. Everything will be all right with you. You will be safe here with granny and me. But you must no longer believe that your father went to the war like other men in the village. If he were *my* son, I would—"

"Don't say it, Richard," cried Kenneth's grandma, from the doorway behind them. "Don't ever say that to him."

CHAPTER I

NIGHT was falling as two horsemen drew rein in front of a cabin at the edge of a clearing in the far-reaching sombre forest. Their approach across the stump-strewn tract had been heralded by the barking of dogs,—two bristling beasts that came out upon the muddy, deep-rutted road to greet them with furious inhospitality. A man stood partially revealed in the doorway. His left arm and shoulder were screened from view by the jamb, his head was bent forward as he peered intently through narrowed eyes at the strangers in the road.

"Who are you, and what do you want?" he called out.

"Friends. How far is it to the tavern at Clark's Point?"

"Clark's Point is three miles back," replied the settler. "I guess you must have passed it without seein' it," he added drily. "If it happened to be rainin' when you come through you'd have missed seein' it fer the raindrops. Where you bound fer?"

"Lafayette. I guess we're off the right road. We took the left turn four or five miles back."

"You'd ought to have kept straight on. Come 'ere, Shep! You, Pete! Down with ye!"

The two dogs, still bristling, slunk off in the direction of the squat log barn. A woman appeared behind the man and stared out over his shoulder. From the

15

tall stone chimney at the back of the cabin rose the blue smoke of the kitchen fire, to be whirled away on the wind that was guiding the storm out of the rumbling north. There was a dull, wavering glow in the room behind her. At one of the two small windows gleamed a candle-light.

"What's takin' you to Clark's Point? There ain't no tavern there. There ain't nothin' there but a hitch-post and a waterin'-trough. Oh, yes, I forgot. Right behind the hitch-post is Jake Stone's store and a couple of ash-hoppers and a town-hall, but you wouldn't notice 'em if you happened to be on the wrong side of the post. Mebby it's Middleton you're lookin' fer."

"I am looking for a place to put up for the night, friend. We met a man back yonder, half an hour ago, who said the nearest tavern was at Clark's Point."

"What fer sort of lookin' man was he?"

"Tall fellow with red whiskers, riding a grey horse."

"That was Jake Stone hisself. Beats all how that feller tries to advertise his town. He says it beats Crawfordsville and Lafayette all to smash, an' it's only three or four months old. Which way was he goin'?"

"I suppose you'd call it south. I've lost my bearings, you see."

"That's it. He was on his way down to Attica to get drunk. They say Attica's goin' to be the biggest town on the Wabash. Did I ask you what your name was, stranger?"

"My name is Gwynne. I left Crawfordsville this morning, hoping to reach Lafayette before night. But the road is so heavy we couldn't—"

"Been rainin' steady for nearly two weeks," interrupted the settler. "Hub-deep everywhere. It's a

good twenty-five or thirty mile from Crawfordsville to
Lafayette. Looks like more rain, too. I think she'll
be on us in about two minutes. I guess mebby we c'n
find a place fer you to sleep to-night, and we c'n give
you somethin' fer man an' beast. If you'll jest ride
around here to the barn, we'll put the hosses up an'
feed 'em, and—Eliza, set out a couple more plates,
an' double the rations all around." His left arm and
hand came into view. "Set this here gun back in the
corner, Eliza. I guess I ain't goin' to need it. Gimme
my hat, too, will ye?"

As the woman drew back from the door, a third
figure came up behind the man and took her place.
The horseman down at the roadside, fifty feet away,
made out the figure of a woman. She touched the
man's arm and he turned as he was in the act of step-
ping down from the door-log. She spoke to him in a
low voice that failed to reach the ears of the travellers.

The man shook his head slowly, and then called out:
"I didn't jist ketch your name, mister. The wind's
makin' such a noise I— Say it again, will ye?"

"My name is Kenneth Gwynne. Get it?" shouted
the horseman. "And this is my servant, Zachariah."

The man in the door bent his head, without taking
his eyes from the horseman, while the woman murmured something in his ear, something that caused him
to straighten up suddenly.

"Where do you come from?" he inquired, after a
moment's hesitation.

"My home is in Kentucky. I live at—"

"Kentucky, eh? Well, that's a good place to come
from. I guess you're all right, stranger." He turned
to speak to his companion. A few words passed be-

tween them, and then she drew back into the room. The woman called Eliza came up with the man's hat and a lighted lantern. She closed the door after him as he stepped out into the yard.

"'Round this way," he called out, making off toward the corner of the cabin. "Don't mind the dogs. They won't bite, long as I'm here."

The wind was wailing through the stripped trees behind the house,—a sombre, limitless wall of trees that seemed to close in with smothering relentlessness about the lonely cabin and its raw field of stumps. The angry, low-lying clouds and the hastening dusk of an early April day had by this time cast the gloom of semi-darkness over the scene. Spasmodic bursts of lightning laid thin dull, unearthly flares upon the desolate land, and the rumble of apple-carts filled the ear with promise of disaster. The chickens had gone to roost; several cows, confined in a pen surrounded by the customary stockade of poles driven deep into the earth and lashed together with the bark of the sturdy elm, were huddled in front of a rude shed; a number of squealing, grunting pigs nosed the cracks in the rail fence that formed still another pen; three or four pompous turkey gobblers strutted unhurriedly about the barnlot, while some of their less theatrical hens perched stiffly, watchfully on the sides of a clumsy wagon-bed over against the barn. Martins and chimney-swallows darted above the cabin and out-buildings, swirling in mad circles, dipping and careening with incredible swiftness.

The gaunt settler conducted the unexpected guests to the barn, where, after they had dismounted, he assisted in the removal of the well-filled saddle-bags and rolls from the backs of their jaded horses.

"Water?" he inquired briefly.

"No, suh," replied Zachariah, blinking as the other held the lantern up the better to look into his face. Zachariah was a young negro,—as black as night, with gleaming white teeth which he revealed in a broad and friendly grin. "Had all dey could drink, Marster, back yander at de crick."

"You couldn't have forded the Wea this time last week," said the host, addressing Gwynne. "She's gone down considerable the last four-five days. Out of the banks last week an' runnin' all over creation."

"Still pretty high," remarked the other. "Came near to sweeping Zack's mare downstream but—well, she made it and Zack has turned black again."

The settler raised his lantern again at the stable door and looked dubiously at the negro.

"You're from Kentucky, Mr. Gwynne," he said, frowning. "I got to tell you right here an' now that if this here boy is a slave, you can't stop here,—an' what's more, you can't stay in this county. We settled the slavery question in this state quite a spell back, an' we make it purty hot for people who try to smuggle niggers across the border. I got to ask you plain an' straight; is this boy a slave?"

"He is not," replied Gwynne. "He is a free man. If he elects to leave my service to-morrow, he is at liberty to go. My grandfather freed all of his slaves shortly before he died, and that was when Zachariah here was not more than fifteen years of age. He is as free as I am,—or you, sir. He is my servant, not my slave. I know the laws of this state, and I intend to abide by them. I expect to make my home here in Indiana,—in Lafayette, as a matter of fact. This boy's name is Zachariah Button. Ten years ago he was a slave. He has with him, sir, the proper credentials to support my statement,—and his, if he chooses to make one. On at least a dozen occasions, first in Ohio and then in Indiana, I have been obliged to convince official and unofficial inquirers that my—"

"That's all right, Mr. Gwynne," cried the settler heartily. "I take your word for it. If you say he's not a slave, why, he ain't, so that's the end of it. And it ain't necessary for Zachariah to swear to it, neither. We can't offer you much in the way of entertainment, Mr. Gwynne, but what we've got you're welcome to. I came to this country from Ohio seven years ago, an' I learned a whole lot about hospitality durin' the journey. I learned how to treat a stranger in a strange land fer one thing, an' I learned that even a hoss-thief ain't an ongrateful cuss if you give him a night's lodgin' and a meal or two."

"I shall be greatly indebted to you, sir. The time will surely come when I may repay you,—not in money, but in friendship. Pray do not let us discommode you or your household. I will be satisfied to sleep on the floor or in the barn, and as for Zachariah, he—"

"The barn is for the hosses to sleep in," interrupted the host, "and the floor is for the cat. 'Tain't my idee of fairness to allow human bein's to squat on proppety that rightfully belongs to hosses an' cats,— so I guess you'll have to sleep in a bed, Mr. Gwynne." He spoke with a drawl. "Zachariah c'n spread his blankets on the kitchen floor an' make out somehow. Now, if you'll jist step over to the well yander, you'll find a wash pan. Eliza,—I mean Mrs. Striker,—will give you a towel when you're ready. Jest sing out to her. Here, you, Zachariah, carry this plunder over an' put it in the kitchen. Mrs. Striker will show you.

Be careful of them rifles of your'n. They go off mighty sudden if you stub your toe. You'll find a comb and lookin' glass in the settin' room, Mr. Gwynne. You'll probably want to put a few extry touches on yourself when I tell you there's an all-fired purty girl spendin' the night with us. Go along, now. I'll put the feed down fer your hosses an' be with you in less'n no time."

"You are very kind, Mr.— Did you say Striker?"

"Phineas Striker, sir,—Phin fer short."

"I am prepared and amply able to pay for lodging and food, Mr. Striker, so do not hesitate to—"

"Save your breath, stranger. I'm as deef as a post. The storm's goin' to bust in two shakes of a dead lamb's tail, so you'd better be a leetle spry if you want to git inside afore she comes."

With that he entered the barn door, leading the horses. Gwynne and his servant hurried through the darkness toward the light in the kitchen window. The former rapped politely on the door. It was opened by Mrs. Striker, a tall, comely woman well under thirty, who favoured the good-looking stranger with a direct and smileless stare. He removed his tall, sorry-looking beaver.

"Madam, your husband has instructed my servant to leave our belongings in your kitchen. I fear they are not overly clean, what with mud and rain, devil-needles and burrs. Your kitchen is as clean as a pin. Shall I instruct him to return with them to the barn and—"

"Bring them in," she said, melting in spite of herself as she looked down from the doorstep into his dark, smiling eyes. His strong, tanned face was beardless, his teeth were white, his abundant brown hair tousled and boyishly awry,—and there were mud splashes on his cheek and chin. He was tall and straight and his figure was shapely, despite the thick blue cape that hung from his shoulders. "I guess they ain't any dirtier than Phin Striker's boots are this time o' the year. Put them over here, boy, 'longside o' that cupboard. Supper'll be ready in ten or fifteen minutes, Mr. Gwynne."

His smile broadened. He sniffed gratefully. A far more exacting woman than Eliza Striker would have forgiven this lack of dignity on his part.

"You will find me ready for it, Mrs. Striker. The smell of side-meat goes straight to my heart, and nothing in all this world could be more wonderful than the coffee you are making."

"Go 'long with you!" she cried, vastly pleased, and turned to her sizzling skillets.

Zachariah deposited the saddle-bags and rolls in the corner and then returned to the door where he received the long blue cape, gloves and the towering beaver from his master's hands. He also received instructions which sent him back to open a bulging saddle-bag and remove therefrom a pair of soft, almost satiny calfskin boots. As he hurried past Mrs. Striker, he held them up for her inspection, grinning from ear to ear. She gazed in astonishment at the white and silver ornamented tops, such as were affected by only the most fastidious dandies of the day and were so rarely seen in this raw, new land that the beholder could scarce believe her eyes.

"Well, I never!" she exclaimed, and then went to the sitting-room to whisper excitedly to the solitary occupant, who, it so chanced, was at the moment busily and hastily employed in rearranging her brown, windblown hair before the round-topped little looking-glass over the fireplace.

"I thought you said you wasn't goin' to see him," observed Mrs. Striker, after imparting her information. "If you ain't, what are you fixin' yourself up fer?"

"I have changed my mind, Eliza," said the young lady, loftily. "In the first place, I am hungry, and in the second place it would not be right for me to put you to any further trouble about supper. I shall have supper with the rest of you and not in the bedroom, after all. How does my hair look?"

"You've got the purtiest hair in all the—"

"How does it look?"

"It would look fine if you *never* combed it. If I had hair like your'n, I'd be the proudest woman in—"

"Don't be silly. It's terrible, most of the time."

"Well, it's spick an' span now, if that's what you want to know," grumbled Eliza, and vanished, fingering her straight, straw-coloured hair somewhat resentfully.

Meanwhile, Kenneth Gwynne, having divested himself of his dark blue "swallow-tail," was washing his face and hands at the well. The settler approached with the lantern.

"She's comin'," he shouted above the howling wind. "I guess you'd better dry yourself in the kitchen. Hear her whizzin' through the trees? Gosh all hemlock! She's goin' to be a snorter, stranger. Hurry inside!"

They bolted for the door and dashed into the kitchen just as the deluge came. Phineas Striker, leaning his weight against the door, closed it and dropped the bolt.

"Whew! She's a reg'lar harricane, that's what she is. Mighty suddent, too. Been holdin' back fer ten minutes,—an' now she lets loose with all she's got. Gosh! Jest listen to her!"

The hiss of the torrent on the clapboard roof was deafening, the little window panes were streaming; a dark, glistening shadow crept out from the bottom of the door and began to spread; the howling wind shook the very walls of the staunch cabin, while all about them roared the ear-splitting cannonade, the crash of splintered skies, the crackling of musketry, the rending and tearing of all the garments that clothe the universe.

Eliza Striker, hardy frontierswoman though she was, put her fingers to her ears and shrank away from the stove,—for she had been taught that all metal "drew lightning." Her husband busied himself stemming the stream of water that seeped beneath the door with empty grain or coffee bags, snatched from the top of a cupboard where they were stored, evidently for the very purpose to which they were now being put.

Gwynne stood coatless in the centre of the kitchen, rolling down his white shirt-sleeves. Behind him cringed Zachariah, holding his master's boots and coat in his shaking hands, his eyes rolling with terror, his lips mumbling an unheard appeal for mercy.

The sitting-room door opened suddenly and the other guest of the house glided into the kitchen. Her eyes were crinkled up as if with an almost unendurable pain, her fingers were pressed to her temples, her red lips were parted.

"Goodness!" she gasped, with a hysterical laugh, not born of mirth, nor of courage, but of the sheerest dismay.

"Don't be skeered," cried Phineas, looking at her over his shoulder. "She'll soon be over. Long as the roof stays on, we're all right,—an' I guess she'll stay."

Kenneth Gwynne bowed very low to the newcomer. The dim candle-light afforded him a most unsatisfactory glimpse of her features. He took in at a glance, however, her tall, trim figure, the burnished crown of hair, and the surprisingly modish frock she wore. He had seen no other like it since leaving the older, more advanced towns along the Ohio,—not even in the thriving settlements of Wayne and Madison Counties or in the boastful village of Crawfordsville. He was startled. In all his journeyings through the land he had seen no one arrayed like this. It was with difficulty that he overcame a quite natural impulse to stare at her as if she were some fantastic curiosity.

The contrast between this surprising creature and the gingham aproned Eliza was unbelievable. There was but one explanation: She was the mistress of the house, Eliza the servant. And yet, even so, how strangely out-of-place, out-of-keeping she was here in the wilderness.

In some confusion he strode over to lend a hand to Phineas Striker. The rustle of silk behind him and the quick clatter of heels, evidenced the fact that the girl had crossed swiftly to Eliza's side.

Later on he had the opportunity to take in all the details of her costume, and he did so with a practised, sophisticated eye. It was, after all, of a fashion two years old, evidence of the slowness with which the modes reached these outposts of civilization. Here was a perfect fitting blue frock of the then popular changeable *gros de zane*, the skirt very wide, set on the body in large plaits, one in front, one on each side and two behind. The sleeves also were wide from shoulder to elbow, where they were tightly fitted to the lower arm. The ruffles around the neck, which was open and rather low, and about the wrists were of plain bobinet quilling. Her slippers were black, with cross-straps. He had seen such frocks as this, he was reminded, in fashionable Richmond and New York only a year or so before, but nowhere in the west. Add a Dunstable straw bonnet with its strings of satin and the frilled pelerine, and this strange young woman might have just stepped from her carriage in the most fashionable avenue in the land.

Zachariah, lacking his master's good manners, gazed in open-mouthed wonder at the lady, forgetting for the moment his fear of the tempest's wrath. Only the most hair-raising crash of thunder broke the spell, causing him to close his eyes and resume his supplication.

"Now's your chance to get at the lookin' glass, Mr. Gwynne," said Striker. "Right there in the sittin'-room. Go ahead; I'll manage this."

Muttering a word of thanks, the young man turned to leave the room. He shot a glance at his fellow guest. Her back was toward him, she had her hands to her ears, and something told him that her eyes were tightly closed. A particularly loud crash caused her to draw her pretty shoulders up as if to receive the death-dealing bolt of lightning. He heard her murmur again:

"Goodness—gracious!"

Eliza suddenly put an arm about her waist and drew the slender, shivering figure close. As the girl buried her face upon the older woman's shoulder, the latter cried out:

"Land sakes, child, you'll never get over bein' a baby, will ye?"

To which Phineas Striker added in a great voice: "Nor you, neither, Eliza. Ef we didn't have company here you'd be crawlin' under the table or something. She ain't afraid of wild cats or rattlesnakes or Injins or even spiders," he went on, addressing Gwynne, "but she's skeered to death of lightnin'. An' as fer that young lady there, she wouldn't be afeared to walk from here to Lafayette all alone on the darkest night,—an' look at her now! Skeered out of her boots by a triflin' little thunderstorm. Why, I wouldn't give two—"

"My goodness, Phin Striker," broke in his wife, a new note of alarm in her voice, "I do hope them chickens an' turkeys have got sense enough to get under something in this downpour. If they ain't, the whole kit an' boodle of 'em will be drownded, sure as—"

"I never yet see a hen that liked water," interrupted Phineas. "Er a turkey either. Don't you worry about 'em. You better worry about that side-meat you're fryin'. Ef my nose is what it ort to be, I'd say that piece o' meat was bein' burnt to death,—an' that's a lot wuss than bein' drownded. They say drowndin' is the easiest death—"

"You men clear out o' this kitchen," snapped Eliza. "Out with ye! You too, Phin Striker. I'll call ye when the table's set. Now, you go an' set over there in the corner, away from the window, deary, where the lightnin' can't git at you, an'— You'll find a comb on the mantel-piece, Mr. Gwynne, an' Phineas will git you a boot-jack out o' the bedroom if that darkey is too weak to pull your boots off for you. Don't any of you go trampin' all over the room with your muddy boots. I've got work enough to do without scrubbin' floors after a pack of— My land! I do believe it's scorched. An' the corn-bread must be—"

Phineas, after a doubtful look at the stopped-up door-crack, led the way into the sitting-room. Zachariah came last with his master's boots and coat. He was mumbling with suppressed fervour:

"Oh, Lord, jes' lemme hab one mo' chaince,—jes' one mo' chaince. Good Lord! I been a wicked, ornery nigger,—only jes' gimme jes' one mo' chaince. I been a wicked,—Yassuh, Marster Kenneth, I got your boots. Yassuh. Right heah, suh. Oh, Lordy-Lordy! Yassuh, yassuh!"

Seated in a big wooden rocker before the fireplace, Gwynne stretched out his long legs one after the other; Zachariah tugged at the heavy, mud-caked riding-boots, grunting mightily over a task that gave him sufficient excuse for interjecting sundry irrelevant appeals for mercy and an occasional reference to his own unworthiness as a nigger.

The tempest continued with unabated violence. The big, raw-boned Striker, pulling nervously at his beard, stood near a window which looked out upon the barn and sheds, plainly revealed in the blinding, almost uninterrupted flashes of lightning. Such sentences as these fell from his lips as he turned his face from the bleaching flares before they ended in mighty crashes: "That struck powerful nigh,"—or "I seen that one runnin' along the ground like a ball of fire," or "There goes somethin' near," or "That was a tree jest back o' the barn, you'll see in the mornin'."

"Dere won't never be any mo'nin'," gulped the unhappy Zachariah, bending lower to his task, which

now had to do with the boot-straps at the bottoms of
his master's trouser-legs. Getting to his feet, he proceeded, with a well-trained dexterity that even his terror failed to divert, to draw on the immaculate calfskin boots with the gorgeous tops. Then he pulled
the trouser-legs down over the boots, obscuring their
upper glory; after which he smoothed out the wrinkles
and fastened the instep straps. Whereupon, Kenneth
arose, stamped severely on the hearth several times to
settle his feet in the snug-fitting boots, and turned to
the looking-glass. He was wielding the comb with
extreme care and precision when his host turned from
the window and approached.

"Seems to me you're goin' to a heap o' trouble,
friend," he remarked, surveying the tall, graceful
figure with a rather disdainful eye. "We don't dress
up much in these parts, 'cept on Sunday."

"Please do not consider me vain," said the young
man, flushing. He smarted under the implied rebuke,
—in fact, he was uncomfortably aware of ridicule.
"My riding-boots were filthy. I—I— Yes, I know,"
he broke in upon himself as Phineas extended one of
his own muddy boots for inspection. "I know, but,
you see, I am the unbidden guest of yourself and Mrs.
Striker. The least I can do in return for your hospitality is to make myself presentable—"

"You'll have to excuse my grinnin', Mr. Gwynne,"
interrupted the other. "I didn't mean any offence.
It's jest that we ain't used to good clothes an' servants
to pull our boots off an' on, an'—butternut pants an'
so on. We're 'way out here on the edge of the wilderness where bluejeans is as good as broadcloth or doe-
skin, an' a chaw of tobacco is as good as the state
seal fer bindin' a bargain. Lord bless ye, I don't keer

how much you dress up. I guess I might as well tell
ye the only men up at Lafayette who wear as good
clothes as you do are a couple of gamblers that work
up an' down the river, an' Barry Lapelle. I reckon
you've heerd of Barry Lapelle. He's known from one
end of the state to the other, an' over in Ohio an'
Kentucky too."

"I have never heard of him."

Striker looked surprised. He glanced at the closed
sitting-room door before continuing.

"Well, he owns a couple steamboats that come up
the river. Got 'em when his father died a couple o'
years ago. His home used to be in Terry Hut, but
he's been livin' at Bob Johnson's tavern for a matter
of six months now, workin' up trade fer his boats, I
understand. He's as wild as a hawk an'—but you'll
run across him if you're goin' to live in Lafayette."

"By the way, what is the population of Lafayette?"

Phineas studied the board ceiling thoughtfully for
a moment or two. "Well, 'cordin' to people who live
in Attica she's got about five hundred. People who
live in Crawfordsville give her seven hundred. Down
at Covington an' Williamsport they say she's got about
four hundred an' twelve. When you git to Lafayette
Bob Johnson an' the rest of 'em will tell you she's over
two thousand an' growin' so fast they cain't keep track
of her. There's so much lyin' goin' on about Lafayette
that it's impossible to tell jest how big she is. Countin'
in the dogs, I guess she must have a population of
between six hundred and fifty an' three thousand. You
see, everybody up there's got a dog, an' some of 'em
two er three. One feller I know has got seven. But,
on the whole, I guess you'll like the place. It's the
head of navigation at high water, an' if they ever build

the Wabash an' Erie Canal they're talkin' about she'll
be a regular seaport, like New York er Boston. 'Pears
to me the worst is over, don't you reckon so?"

Kenneth, having adjusted his stock and white roll-
over collar to suit his most exacting eye, slipped his
arms into the coat Zachariah was holding for him, settled the shoulders with a shrug or two and a pull at
the flaring lapels, smoothed his yellow brocaded waistcoat carefully, and then, spreading his long, shapely
legs and at the same time the tails of his coat, took a
commanding position with his back to the blazing logs.

"Are you referring to my toilet, Mr. Striker?" he
inquired amiably.

"I was talkin' about the storm," explained Phineas
hastily. "Take the boots out to the kitchen, Zachariah. Eliza'll git into your wool if she ketches you
leavin' 'em in here. Yes, sir, she's certainly lettin' up.
Goin' down the river hell-bent. They'll be gettin' her
at Attica 'fore long. Are you plannin' to work the
farm yourself, Mr. Gwynne, or are you goin' to sell
er rent on shares?"

Gwynne looked at him in surprise. "You appear to
know who I am, after all, Mr. Striker."

Striker grinned. "I guess everybody in this neck
o' the woods has heerd about you. Dan Bugher,—
he's the county recorder,—an' Rube Kelsey, John
Bishop, Larry Stockton, an' a lot more of the folks
up in town, have been lookin' down the Crawfordsville
road fer you ever since your father died last August.
You 'pear to be a very important cuss fer one who
ain't never set foot in Indianny before."

"I see," said the other reflectively. "Were you acquainted with my father, Mr. Striker?"

"Much so as anybody could be. He wasn't much

of a hand fer makin' friends. Stuck purty close to the farm, an' made it about the best piece o' propetty in the whole valley. I was jest wonderin' whether you was plannin' to live on the farm er up in town."

"Well, you see, I am a lawyer by profession. I know little or nothing about farming. My plans are not actually made, however. A great deal depends on how I. find things. Judge Wylie wishes me to enter into partnership with him, and Providence M. Curry says there is a splendid chance for me in his office at Craw-fordsville. I shall do nothing until I have gone thor-oughly into the matter. You know the farm, Mr. Striker?"

"Yes. It's not far from here,—five or six mile, I'd say, to the north an' east. Takes in some of the finest land on the Wea Plain,—mostly clear, some fine timber, plenty of water, an' about the best stocked farm any-wheres around. Your father was one of the first to edge up this way ten er twelve year ago, an' he got the pick o' the new land. He came from some'eres down the river, 'bout Vincennes er Montezuma er some such place. I reckon you know that he left another passel of land over this way, close to the Wabash, an' some propetty up in Lafayette an' some more down in Crawfordsville."

"I have been so informed," said his guest, rather shortly.

"I bought this sixty acre piece offen him two year ago. All timber when I took hold of it, 'cept seven-teen acres out thataway," jerking his thumb, "along the Middleton road." He hesitated a moment. "You see, I worked for your father fer a considerable time, as a hand. That's how he came to sell to me. I got married an' wanted a place of my own. He said he'd sooner sell to me than let some other feller cheat the eye-teeth outen me, me bein' a good deal of fool when it comes to business an' all. Yep, I'd saved up a few dollars, so I sez what's the sense of me workin' my gizzard out fer somebody else an' all that, when land's so cheap an' life so doggoned short. 'Course, there's a small mortgage on the place, but I c'n take keer of that, I reckon."

"Ahem! The mortgage, I fancy, is held by—er—the other heirs to his property."

"You're right. His widder holds it, but she ain't the kind to press me. She's purty comfortable, what with this land along the edge o' the plain out here an' a whole section up in the Grand Prairie neighbourhood, besides half a dozen buildin' lots in town an' a two story house to live in up there. To say nothin' of—"

"Come to supper," called out Mrs. Striker from the doorway.

"That's somethin' I'm always ready fer," announced Mr. Striker. "Winter an' summer, spring an' fall. Step right ahead, Mr.—"

"Just a moment, if you please," said the young man, laying his hand on the settler's arm. "You will do me a great favour if you refrain from discussing these matters in the presence of your other guest to-night. My father, as you doubtless know, meant very little in my life. I prefer not to discuss him in the presence of strangers,—especially curious-minded young women."

Phineas looked at him narrowly for an instant, a queer expression lurking in his eyes.

"Jest as you say, Mr. Gwynne. Not a word in front of strangers. I don't know as you know it, but up to the time your father's will was perduced there wasn't a soul in these parts as knowed such a feller as you wuz on earth. He never spoke of a son, er havin' been married before, er bein' a widower, er anything like—''

"I am thoroughly convinced of that, Mr. Striker," said Kenneth, a trifle austerely, and passed on ahead of his host into the kitchen.

"Bring in them two candlesticks, Phin," ordered Mrs. Striker. "We got to be able to see what each other looks like, an' goodness knows we cain't with this taller dip I got out here to cook by. 'Tain't often we have people right out o' the fashion-plates to supper, so let's have all the light we kin."

CHAPTER II

T HE tempest by now had subsided to a distant, rumbling murmur, although the rain still beat against the window-panes in fitful gusts, the while it gently played the long roll on the clapboards a scant two feet above the tallest head. Far-off flashes of lightning cast ghastly reminders athwart the windows, fighting the yellow candle glow with a sickly, livid glare.

Kenneth's fellow-guest was standing near the stove, her back toward him as he entered the kitchen. The slant of the "ceiling" brought the crown of her head to within a foot or so of the round, peeled beams that supported the shed-like roof, giving her the appearance of abnormal height. As a matter of fact, she was not as tall as the gaunt Eliza, who, like her husband and the six-foot guest, was obliged to lower her head when passing through the kitchen door to the yard.

The table was set for four, in the middle of the little kitchen; rude hand-made stools, without backs, were in place. A figured red cloth covered the board, its fringe of green hanging down over the edges. The plates, saucers and coffee-cups were thick and clumsy and gaudily decorated with indescribable flowers and vines done entirely in green—a "set," no doubt, selected with great satisfaction in advance of the Striker nuptials. There were black-handled case-knives, huge four-tined forks, and pewter spoons. A blackened cof-

fee-pot, a brass tea-kettle and a couple of shallow skillets stood on the square sheet-iron stove.

"Come in and set down, Mr. Gwynne," said Mrs.
Striker, pointing to a stool. With the other hand she
deftly "flopped" an odorous corn-cake in one of the
skillets. There was a far from unpleasant odor of
grease.

"I can't help thanking my lucky stars, Mrs. Striker,
that I got here ahead of that storm," said he, moving
over to his appointed place, where he remained standing. "We were just in time, too. Ten minutes later
and we would have been in the thick of it. And here
we are, safe and sound and dry as toast, in the presence
of a most inviting feast. I cannot tell you how much
I appreciate your kindness."

"Oh, it's—it's nothing," said she, diffidently. Then
to Striker: "Put 'em here on the table, you big lummix. Set down, everybody."

The young lady sat opposite Gwynne. She lowered
her head immediately as Phineas began to offer up his
established form of grace. The unhappy host got himself into a dire state of confusion when he attempted
to vary the habitual prayer by tacking on a few words
appertaining to the recent hurricane and God's goodness in preserving them all from destruction as well as
the hope that no serious damage had been done to other
live-stock and fowls, or to the life and property of
his neighbours,—amen!

To which Zachariah, seated on a roll of blankets in
the corner, appended a heartfelt amen, and then sank
back to watch his betters eat, much as a hungry dog
feasts upon anticipation. He knew that he was to
have what was left over, and he offered up a silent

prayer of his own while wistfully speculating on the prospects.

The two colonial candlesticks stood in the centre of the table, a foot or two apart. When Gwynne lifted his head after "grace," he looked directly between them at his vis-à-vis. For a few seconds he stared as if spell-bound. Then, realizing his rudeness and conscious of an unmistakable resentment in her eyes, he felt the blood rush to his face, and quickly turned to stammer something to his host,—he knew not what it was.

Never had he looked upon a face so beautiful, never had he seen any one so lovely as this strange young woman who shared with him the hospitality of the humble board. He had gazed for a moment full into her deep, violet eyes,—eyes in which there was no smile but rather a cool intentness not far removed from un- friendliness,—and in that moment he forgot himself, his manners and his composure.

The soft light fell upon warm, smooth cheeks; a broad, white brow; red, sensitive lips and a perfect mouth; a round firm chin; a delicate nose,—and the faint shadows of imperishable dimples that even her unsmiling expression failed to disturb.

Not even in his dreams had he conjured up a face so bewilderingly beautiful.

Her hair, which was puffed and waved over her ears, took on the shade of brown spun silk on which the light played in changing tones of bronze. It was worn high on her head, banded à la grecque, with a small knot on the crown from which depended a number of ringlets ornamented with bowknots. Her ears were completely hidden by the soft mass that came down over them in shapely knobs. She wore no earrings,—for which he was acutely grateful, although they were the fashion of the day and cumbersomely hideous,—and her shapely throat was barren of ornament. He judged her to be not more than twenty-two or -three. A second furtive glance caught her looking down at her plate. He marvelled at the long, dark eyelashes.

Who was she? What was she doing here in the humble cot of the Strikers? Certainly she was out of place here. She was a tender, radiant flower set down amongst gross, unlovely weeds. That she was a person of consequence, to whom the Strikers paid a rude sort of deference, softened by the familiarity of long association but in no way suggestive of relationship, he was in no manner of doubt.

He was not slow to remark their failure to present him to her. The omission may have been due to ignorance or uncertainty on their part, but that was not the construction he put upon it. Striker was the free-and-easy type who would have made these strangers known to each other in some bluff, awkward manner,— probably by their Christian names; he would never have overlooked this little formality, no matter how clumsily he may have gone about performing it. It was perfectly plain to Gwynne that it was not an oversight. It was deliberate.

His slight feeling of embarrassment, and perhaps annoyance, evidently was not shared by the young lady; so far as she was concerned the situation was by no means strained. She was as calm and serene and impervious as a princess royal.

She joined in the conversation, addressed herself to him without constraint, smiled amiably (and adorably) upon the busy Eliza and her jovial spouse, and even laughed aloud over the latter's account of Zachariah

and the silver-top boots. Gwynne remarked that it was
a soft, musical laugh, singularly free from the shrill,
boisterous qualities so characteristic of the backwoods-
woman. She possessed the poise of refinement. He had
seen her counterpart,—barring her radiant beauty,—
many a time during his years in the cultured east: in
Richmond, in Philadelphia, and in New York, where
he had attended college.

He was subtly aware of the lively but carefully
guarded interest she was taking in him. He felt
rather than knew that she was studying him closely,
if furtively, when his face was turned toward the talk-
ative host. Twice he caught her in the act of averting
her gaze when he suddenly glanced in her direction,
and once he surprised her in a very intense scrutiny,—
which, he was gratified to observe, gave way to a swift
flush of confusion and the hasty lowering of her eyes.
No doubt, he surmised with some satisfaction, she was
as vastly puzzled as himself, for he must have appeared
equally out-of-place in these surroundings. His
thoughts went delightedly to the old, well-beloved story
of Cinderella. Was this a Cinderella in the flesh,—and
in the morning would he find her in rags and tatters,
slaving in the kitchen?

He noticed her hands. They were long and slim
and, while browned by exposure to wind and sun, bore
no evidence of the grinding toil to which the women
and girls of the frontier were subjected. And they
were strong, competent hands, at that.

The food was coarse, substantial, plentiful. (Even
Zachariah could see that it was plentiful.) Solid food
for sturdy people. There were potatoes fried in grease,
wide strips of side meat, apple butter, corn-cakes piping hot, boiled turnips, coffee and dried apple pie. The

smoky odor of frying grease arose from the skillets
and, with the grateful smell of coffee, permeated the
tight little kitchen. It was a savoury that consoled
rather than offended the appetite of these hardy eaters.

Striker ate largely with his knife, and smacked his
lips resoundingly; swigged coffee from his saucer
through an overlapping moustache and afterwards hiss-
ingly strained the aforesaid obstruction with his nether
lip; talked and laughed with his mouth full,—but all
with such magnificent zest that his guests overlooked
the shocking exhibition. Indeed, the girl seemed quite
accustomed to Mr. Striker's table-habits, a circumstance which created in Kenneth's questing mind the
conviction that she was not new to these parts, despite
the garments and airs of the fastidious East.

They were vastly interested in the account of his
journey through the wilderness.

"Nowadays," said Striker, "most people come up
the river, 'cept them as hail from Ohio. You must ha'
come by way of Wayne an' Madison Counties."

"I did," said his guest. "We found it fairly comfortable travelling through Wayne County. The roads
are decent enough and the settlers are numerous. It
was after we left Madison County that we encountered
hardships. We travelled for a while with a party of
emigrants who were heading for the settlement at Strawtown. There were three families of them, including a
dozen children. Our progress was slow, as they travelled by wagon. Rumours that the Indians were threat-
ening to go on the warpath caused me to stay close by
this slow-moving caravan for many miles, not only for
my own safety but for the help I might be able to
render them in case of an attack. At Strawtown we
learned that the Indians were peaceable and that there

was no truth in the stories. So Zachariah and I
crossed the White River at that point and struck off
alone. We followed the wilderness road,—the old Indian trace, you know,—and we travelled nearly thirty
miles without seeing a house. At Brown's Wonder we
met a party of men who had been out in this country
looking things over. They were so full of enthusiasm
about the prairies around here,—the Wea, the Wild
Cat and Shawnee prairies,—that I was quite thrilled
over the prospect ahead, and no longer regretted the
journey which had been so full of privations and hardships and which I had been so loath to undertake in
the beginning. Have you been at Thorntown recently?"

"Nope. Not sence I came through there some years
ago. It was purty well deserted in those days. Nothin'
there but Injin wigwams an' they was mostly run to
seed. At that time, Crawfordsville was the only town
to speak of between Terry Hut an' Fort Wayne, 'way
up above here."

"Well, there are signs of a white settlement there
now. Some of the old French settlers are still there
and other whites are coming in. I had heard a great
deal about the big Indian village at Thorntown, and
was vastly disappointed in what I found. I am quite
romantic, Miss—ahem!—quite romantic by nature,
having read and listened to tales of thrilling adventures
among the redskins, as we call them down my way,
until I could scarce contain myself. I have always
longed for the chance to rescue a beautiful white captive from the clutches of the cruel redskins. My
valour—"

"And I suppose you always dreamed of marrying
her as they always do in stories?" said she, smiling.

"Invariably," said he. "Alas, if I had rescued all the fair maidens my dreams have placed in jeopardy, I should by this time have as many wives as Solomon. Only, I must say in defence of my ambitions, I should not have had as great a variety. Strange as it may seem, I remained through all my adventures singularly constant to a certain idealistic captive. She looked, I may say, precisely alike in each and every case. Poor old Solomon could not say as much for his thousand wives. Mine, if I had them, would be so much alike in face and form that I could not tell one from the other,—and, now that I am older and wiser,—though not as wise as Solomon,—I am thankful that not one of these daring rescues was ever consummated, for I should be very much distressed now if I found myself married to even the most beautiful of the ladies my feeble imagination conceived."

This subtle touch of gallantry was over the heads of Mr. and Mrs. Striker. As for the girl, she looked momentarily startled, and then as the dimples deepened, a faint flush rose to her cheeks. An instant later, the colour faded, and into her lovely eyes came a cold, unfriendly light. Realizing that he had offended her with this gay compliment,—although he had never before experienced rebuff in like circumstances,—he hastened to resume his narrative.

"We finally came to Sugar River and followed the road along the southern bank. You may know some of the settlers we found along the river. Wischart and Kinworthy and Dewey? They were among the first to come to this part of the country, I am informed. Fine, brave men, all of them. In Crawfordsville I stopped at the tavern conducted by Major Ristine. While there I consulted with Mr. Elston and Mr. Wilson and others about the advisability of selling my land up here and my building lots in Lafayette. They earnestly advised me not to sell. In their opinion Lafayette is the most promising town on the Wabash, while the farming land in this section is not equalled anywhere else in the world. Of course, I realize that they are financially interested in the town of Lafayette, owning quite a lot of property there, so perhaps I should not be guided solely by their enthusiasm."

"They are the men who bought most of Sam Sargeant's lots some years back," said Striker, "when there wasn't much of anything in the way of a town,—them and Jonathan Powers, I think it was. They paid somethin' like a hundred an' fifty dollars for more'n half of the lots he owned, an' then they started right in to crow about the place. I was workin' down at Crawfordsville at the time. They had plenty of chance to talk, 'cause that town was full of emigrants, land-grabbers, travellers an' setch like. That was before the new county was laid out, you see. Up to that time all the land north of Montgomery County was what was called Wabash County. It run up as fer as Lake Michigan, with the jedges an' courts an' land offices fer the whole district all located in Crawfordsville. Maybe you don't know it, but Tippecanoe County is only about six years old. She was organized by the legislature in 1826. To show you how smart Elston and them other fellers was, they donated a lot of their property up in Lafayette to the county on condition that the commissioners located the county seat there. That's how she come to be the county seat, spite of the claims of Americus up on the east bank of the Wabash.

"Maybe you've heard of Bill Digby. He's the feller

that started the town o' Lafayette. Well, a couple o'
days after he laid out the town o' Lafayette,—named
after a Frenchman you've most likely heerd about,—
he up an' sold the whole place to Sam Sargeant fer a
couple o' hundred dollars, they say. He kept enough
ground fer a ferry landin' an' a twenty-acre piece up
above the town fer specolatin' purposes, I understand.
He afterwards sold this twenty-acre piece to Sam fer
sixty dollars, an' thought he done mighty well. When
I first come to the Wea, Lafayette didn't have more'n
half a dozen cabins. I went through her once on my
way up to the tradin' house at Longlois, couple a mile
above. You wouldn't believe a town could grow as
fast as Lafayette has in the last couple o' years. If
she keeps on she'll be as big as all get-out, an' Crawfordsville won't be nowhere. Tim Horran laid out
Fairfield two-three years back, over east o' here. Been
a heap o' new towns laid out this summer, all around
here. But I guess they won't amount to much. Jo-
siah Halstead and Henry Ristine have jest laid out
the town o' Columbia, down near the Montgomery line.
Over on Lauramie Crick is a town called Cleveland, an'
near that is Monroe, jest laid out by a feller named
Major. There's another town called Concord over
east o' Columbia. There may be more of 'em, but I
ain't heerd of 'em yet. They come up like mushrooms,
an' 'fore you know it, why, there they are.

"This land o' yours, Mr. Gwynne, lays 'tween here
an' this new settlement o' Columbia, an' I c'n tell you
that it ain't to be beat anywheres in the country. I'd
say it is the best land your fa—er—ahem!" The
speaker was seized with a violent and obviously unnecessary spell of coughing. "Somethin' must ha'
gone the wrong way," he explained, lamely. "Feller

ort to have more sense'n to try to swaller when he's talkin'."

"Comes of eatin' like a pig," remarked his wife, glaring at him as she poured coffee into Gwynne's empty cup. "Mr. Gwynne'll think you don't know any better. He never eats like this on Sunday," she explained to their male guest.

"I got a week-day style of eatin' an' one strickly held back fer Sunday," said Phineas. "Same as clothes er havin' my boots greased."

Kenneth was watching the face of the girl opposite. She was looking down at her plate. He observed a little frown on her brow. When she raised her eyes to meet his, he saw that they were sullen, almost un-pleasantly so. She did not turn away instantly, but continued to regard him with a rather disconcerting intensity. Suddenly she smiled. The cloud vanished from her brow, her eyes sparkled. He was bewildered. There was no mistaking the unfriendliness that had lurked in her eyes the instant before. But in heaven's name, what reason had she for disliking him?

"If you believe all that Phineas says, you will think you have come to Paradise," she said. At no time had she uttered his name, in addressing him, although it was frequently used by the Strikers. She seemed to be de-liberately avoiding it.

"It is a present comfort, at least, to believe him," he returned. "I hope I may not see the day when I shall have to take him to task for misleading me in so vital a matter."

"I hope not," said she, quietly.

As he turned to Striker, he caught that worthy gaz-ing at him with a fixed, inquisitive stare. He began to feel annoyed and uncomfortable. It was not the first time he had surprised a similar scrutiny on the part of one or the other of the Strikers. Phineas, on being detected, looked away abruptly and mumbled something about "God's country."

The young man decided it was time to speak. "By the way you all look at me, Mr. Striker, I am led to suspect that you do not believe I am all I represent myself to be. If you have any doubts, pray do not hesitate to express them."

Striker was boisterously reassuring. "I don't doubt you fer a second, Mr. Gwynne. As I said before, the whole county has been expectin' you to turn up. We heerd a few days back that you was in Crawfordsville. If me an' Eliza seem to act queer it's because we knowed your father an'—an', well, I can't help noticin' how much you look like him. When he was your age he must have looked enough like you to be your twin brother. We don't mean no disrespect, an' I hope you'll overlook our nateral curiosity."

Kenneth was relieved. The furtive looks were explained.

"I am glad to hear that you do not look upon me as an outlaw or—"

"Lord bless you," cried Striker, "there ain't nobody as would take you fer an outlaw. You ain't cut out fer a renegade. We know 'em the minute we lay eyes on 'em. Same as we know a Pottawatomy Injin from a Shawnee, er a jack-knife from a Bowie. No, there ain't no doubt in my mind about you bein' your father's son—an' heir, as the sayin' goes. If you turn out to be a scalawag, I'll never trust my eyes ag'in."

The young man laughed. "In any case, you are very good to have taken me in for the night, and I

shall not forget your trust or your hospitality. Wolves
go about in sheep's clothing, you see, and the smartest
of men are sometimes fooled."   He turned abruptly
to the girl.   "Did you know my father, too?"

She started violently and for the moment was speechless, a curious expression in her eyes.

"Yes," she said, at last, looking straight at him:
"Yes, I knew your father very well."

"Then, you must have lived in these parts longer
than I have suspected," said he. "I should have said
you were a newcomer."

Mrs. Striker made a great clatter of pans and skillets at the stove. The girl waited until this kindly
noise subsided.

"I have lived in this neighbourhood since I was eight
years old," she said, quietly.

Striker hastened to add: "Somethin' like ten or
'leven years,—'leven, I reckon, ain't it?"

"Eleven years," she replied.

Gwynne was secretly astonished and rather skeptical.
He would have taken oath that she was twenty-two
or-three years old, and not nineteen as computation
made her.

"She ain't lived here all the time," volunteered Eliza,
somewhat defensively. "She was to school in St. Louis
fer two or three years an'—"

The young lady interrupted the speaker coldly.
"Please, Eliza!"

Eliza, looking considerably crestfallen, accepted the
rebuke meekly. "I jest thought he'd be interested,"
she murmured.

"She came up the Wabash when she was nothin' but
a striplin'," began Striker, not profiting by his wife's
experience. He might have gone on at considerable

length if he had not met the reproving, violet eye. He changed the subject hastily. "As I was sayin', we've had a powerful lot o' rain lately. Why, by gosh, last week you could have went fishin' in our pertato patch up yander an' got a mess o' sunfish in less'n no time. I never knowed the Wabash to be on setch a rampage. An' as fer the Wild Cat Crick and Tippecanoe River, why, they tell me there ain't been anything like— How's that?"

"Is Wabash an Indian name?" repeated Kenneth.

"That's what they say. Named after a tribe that used to hunt an' fish up an' down her, they say."

"There was once a tribe of Indians in this part of the country," broke in the girl, with sudden zest, "known as the Ouabachi. We know very little about them nowadays, however. They were absorbed by other and stronger tribes far back in the days of the French occupation, I suppose. French trappers and voyageurs are known to have traversed and explored the wilderness below here at least one hundred and fifty years ago. There is an old French fort quite near here,—Ouia-tanon."

"She knows purty nigh everything," said Phineas, proudly. "Well, I guess we're about as full as it's safe to be, so now's your chance, Zachariah."

He pushed back his stool noisily and arose. Taking up the two candlesticks, he led the way to the sitting-room, stopping at the door for a word of instruction to the negro. "You c'n put your blankets down here on the kitchen floor when you're ready to go to bed. Mrs. Striker will kick you in the mornin' if you ain't awake when she comes out to start breakfast."

"Yassuh, yassuh," grinned the hungry darkey. "Missus won't need fo' to kick more'n once, suh,—

'cause Ise gwine to be hungry all over ag'in 'long about breakfus time,—yas-*suh!*"

"Zachariah will wash the dishes and—" began Kenneth, addressing Mrs. Striker, who was already preparing to cleanse and dry her pots and pans. She interrupted him.

"He won't do nothin' of the kind. I don't let nobody wash my dishes but myself. Set down here, Zachariah, an' help yourself. When you're done, you c'n go out an' carry me in a couple of buckets o' water from the well,—an, that's all you *can* do."

"I guess I'll go out an' take a look around the barn an' pens," said Phineas, depositing the candles on the mantelpiece. "See if everything's still there after the storm. No, Mr. Gwynne,—you set down. No need o' you goin' out there an' gettin' them boots o' your'n all muddy."

He took up the lantern and lighted the tallow wick from one of the candles. Then he fished a corncob pipe from his coattail pocket and stuffed it full of tobacco from a small buckskin bag hanging at the end of the mantel.

"He'p yourself to tobaccer if you keer to smoke. There's a couple o' fresh pipes up there,—jest made 'em yesterday,—an' it ain't ag'inst the law to smoke in the house on rainy nights. Used to be a time when we was first married that I had to go out an' git wet to the skin jest because she wouldn't 'low no tobaccer smoke in the house. Many's the time I've sot on the doorstep here enjoyin' a smoke with the rain comin' down so hard it'd wash the tobaccer right out o' the pipe, an' twice er maybe it was three times it biled over an'— What's that you say?"

"I did not say anything, Phineas," said the girl,

shaking her head mournfully. "I am wondering, though, where you will go when you die."

"Where I c'n smoke 'thout runnin' the risk o' takin' cold, more'n likely," replied Phineas, winking at the young man. Then he went out into the windy night, closing the door behind him.

CHAPTER III

SMILING over the settler's whimsical humour, Gwynne turned to his companion, anticipating a responsive smile. Instead he was rewarded by an expression of acute dismay in her dark eyes. He recalled seeing just such a look in the eyes of a cornered deer. She met his gaze for a fleeting instant and then, turning away, walked rapidly over to the little window, where she peered out into the darkness. He waited a few moments for her to recover the composure so inexplicably lost, and then spoke,—not without a trace of coldness in his voice.

"Pray have this chair." He drew the rocking-chair up to the fireplace, setting it down rather sharply upon the strip of rag carpet that fronted the wide rock-made hearth. "You need not be afraid to be left alone with me. I am a most inoffensive person."

He saw her figure straighten. Then she faced him, her chin raised, a flash of indignation in her eyes.

"I am not afraid of you," she said haughtily. "Why should you presume to make such a remark to me?"

"I beg your pardon," he said, bowing. "I am sorry if I have offended you. No doubt, in my stupidity, I have been misled by your manner. Now, will you sit down—and be friendly?"

His smile was so engaging, his humility so genuine, that her manner underwent a swift and agreeable change. She advanced slowly to the fireplace, a shy, abashed smile playing about her lips.

51

"May I not stand up for a little while?" she pleaded, with mock submissiveness. "I do so want to grow tall."

"To that I can offer no objection," he returned; "although in my humble opinion you would do yourself a very grave injustice if you added so much as the eighth of an inch to your present height."

"I feel quite small beside you, sir," she said, taking her stand at the opposite end of the hearth, from which position she looked up into his admiring eyes.

"I am an overgrown, awkward lummix," he said airily. "The boys called me 'beanpole' at college."

"You are not an awkward lummix, as you call yourself,—though what a lummix is I have not the slightest notion. Mayhap if you stood long enough you might grow shorter. They say men do,—as they become older." She ran a cool, amused eye over his long, well-proportioned figure, taking in the butter-nut coloured trousers, the foppish waistcoat, the high-collared blue coat, and the handsome brown-thatched head that topped the whole creation. He was almost a head taller than she, and yet she was well above medium height.

"How old are you?" she asked, abruptly. Again she was serious, unsmiling.

"Twenty-five," he replied, looking down into her dark, inquiring eyes with something like eagerness in his own. He was saying over and over again to himself that never had he seen any one so lovely as she. "I am six years older than you. Somehow, I feel that I am younger. Rather odd, is it not?"

"Six years," she mused, looking into the fire. The glow of the blazing logs cast changing, throbbing shadows across her face, now soft and dusky, like velvet, under the warm caress of the firelight. "Sometimes I

feel much older than nineteen," she went on, shaking
her head as if puzzled. "I remember that I was supposed to be very large for my age when I was a little
girl. Everybody commented on my size. I used to be
ashamed of my great, gawky self. But," she continued,
shrugging her pretty shoulders, "that was ages ago."

He drew a step nearer and leaned an elbow on the
mantel.

"You say you knew my father," he said, haltingly.
"What was he like?"

She raised her eyes quickly and for an instant studied
his face curiously, as if searching for something that
baffled her understanding.

"He was very tall," she said in a low voice. "As
tall as you are."

"I have only a dim recollection of him," he said.
"You see, I made my home with my grandparents after
I was five years old." He did not offer any further
information. "As a tiny lad I remember wishing that
I might grow up to be as big as my father. Did you
know him well?"

If she heard, she gave no sign as she turned away
again. This time she walked over to the cabin door,
which she opened wide, letting in a rush of chill, damp
air. He felt his choler rise. It was a deliberate, in-
tentional act on her part. She desired to terminate
the conversation and took this rude, insolent means of
doing so. Never had he been so flagrantly insulted,—
and for what reason? He had been courteous, defer-
ential, friendly. What right had she,—this insuffer-
able peacock,—to consider herself his superior? Hot
words rushed to his lips, but he checked them. He con-
tented himself with an angry contemplation of her slender, graceful figure as she poised in the open doorway,

holding the latch in one hand while the other was pressed against her bare throat for protection against the cold night air. Her ringlets, flouted by the wind, threshed merrily about the crown of her head. He noted the thick coil of hair that capped the shapely white neck. Despite his rancour and the glowering gaze he bent upon her, he was still lamentably conscious of her perfections. He had it in his heart to go over and shake her soundly. It would be a relief to see her break down and whimper. It would teach her not to be rude to gentlemen!

The two dogs came racing up to the threshold. She half-knelt and stroked their heads.

"No, no!" she cried out to them. "You cannot come in! Back with you, Shep! Pete! That's a good dog!"

Then she arose and quickly closed the door.

"The wind is veering to the south," she said calmly, as she advanced to the fireplace. She was shivering. "That means fair weather and warmer. We may even see the sun to-morrow."

She held out her hands to the blaze.

"Won't you have this chair now?" he said stiffly, formally. She was looking down into the fire, but he saw the dimple deepen in her cheek and an almost imperceptible twitching at the corner of her mouth. Confound her, was she laughing at him? Was he a source of amusement to her?

She turned her head and glanced up at him over her shoulder. He caught a strained, appealing gleam in her eyes.

"Please forgive me if I was rude," she said, quite humbly.

He melted a little. He no longer desired to shake

her. "I feared I had in some way offended you," he said.

She shook her head and was silent for a moment or two, staring thoughtfully at the flames. A faint sigh escaped her, and then she faced him resolutely, frankly.

"You have succeeded fairly well in concealing your astonishment at seeing me here in this hut, dressed as I am," she said, somewhat hurriedly. "You have been greatly puzzled. I am about to confess something to you. You will see me again,—often perhaps,—if you remain long in this country. It is my wish that you should not know who I am to-night. You will gain nothing by asking questions, either of me or of the Strikers. You will know in the near future, so let that be sufficient. At first I—"

"You have my promise not to disregard your wishes in this or any other matter," he said, bowing gravely. "I shall ask no questions."

"Ah, but you have been asking questions all to yourself ever since you came into this cabin and saw me—in all this finery—and you will continue to ask them," she declared positively. "I do not blame you. I can at least account for my incomprehensible costume. That much you shall have, if no more. This frock is a new one. It has just come up the river from St. Louis. I have never had it on until to-day. Another one, equally as startling, lies in that bedroom over there, and beside it on the bed is the dress I came here in this afternoon. It is a plain black dress, and there is a veil and a hideous black bonnet to go with it." She paused, a bright little gleam of mingled excitement and defiance in her eyes.

"You—you have lost—I mean, you are in mourning for some one?" he exclaimed. The thought rushed into his mind: Was she a widow? This radiantly beautiful girl a widow?

"For my father," she stated succinctly. "He died almost a year ago. I was in school at St. Louis when it happened. I had not seen him for two years. My mother sent for me to come home. Since that time I have worn nothing but black,—plain, horrible black. Do not misjudge me. I am not vain, nor am I as heartless as you may be thinking. I had and still have the greatest respect for my father. He was a good man, a fine man. But in all the years of my life he never spoke a loving word to me, he never caressed me, he never kissed me. He was kindness itself, but—he never looked at me with love in his eyes. I don't suppose you can understand. I was the flesh of his flesh, and yet he never looked at me with love in his eyes.

"As I grew older I began to think that he hated me. That is a terrible thing to say,—and you must think it vile of me to say it to you, a stranger. But I have said it, and I would not take it back. I have seen in his eyes,—they were brooding, thoughtful eyes,—I have seen in them at times a look—Oh, I cannot tell you what it seemed like to me. I can only say that it had something like despair in it,—sadness, unhappiness,— and I could not help feeling that I was the cause of it. When I was a tiny girl he never carried me in his arms. My mother always did that. When I was thirteen years old he hired me out as a servant in a farmer's family and I worked there until I was fourteen. It was not in this neighbourhood. I worked for my board and keep, a thing I could not understand and bitterly resented because he was prosperous. Then my mother fell ill. She was a strong woman, but she broke down in health. He came and got me and took me home.

I was a big girl for my age,—as big as I am now,—and strong. I did all the work about the house until my mother was well again. He never gave me a word of appreciation or one of encouragement.

"He was never unkind, he never found fault with me, he never in all his life scolded or switched me when I was bad. Then, one day,—it was three years ago,—he told me to get ready to go down to St. Louis to school. He put me in charge of a trader and his wife who were going down the river by perogue. He gave them money to buy suitable clothes for me,—a large sum of money, it must have been,—and he provided me with some for my own personal use. All arrangements had been made in advance, without my knowing anything about it.

"I stayed there until I was called home by his death. I expected to return to school, but my mother refused to let me go back. She said my place was with her. That was last fall. She is still in the deepest mourning, and I believe will never dress otherwise. I have said all there is to say about my father. I did not love him, I was not grieved when he passed away. It was almost as if a stranger had died."

She paused. He took occasion to remark, sympathetically: "He must have been a strange man."

"He was," she said. "I hope I have made you understand what kind of a man he was, and what kind of a father he was to me. Now, I am coming to the point. This finery you see me in now was purchased without my mother's knowledge or consent,—with money of my own. The box was delivered to Phineas Striker day before yesterday up in Lafayette. I came here to spend the night, in order that I might try them on. I live in town, with my mother. She left the farm after my father's death. She adored him. She could not bear to live out there on the lonely—but, that is of no interest to you. A few weeks ago I asked her if I might not take off the black. She refused at first, but finally consented. I have her promise that I may put on colours sometime this spring. So I wrote to the woman who used to make my dresses in St. Louis,—my father was not stingy with me, so I always had pretty frocks,—and now they have come. My mother does not know about them. She will be shocked when I tell her I have them, but she will not be angry. She loves me. Is your curiosity satisfied? It will have to be, for this is all I care to divulge at present."

He smiled down into her earnest eyes. "My curiosity is appeased," he said. "I should not have slept to-night if you had not explained this tantalizing mystery. Therefore, I thank you. May I have your permission to say that you are very lovely in your new frock and that you are marvellously becoming to it?"

"As you have already said it, I must decline to give you the permission," she replied, naïvely.

He thought her adorable in this mood. "As a lawyer," he said, "I make a practice of never withdrawing a statement, unless I am convinced by incontrovertible evidence that I was wrong in the first place,—and you will have great difficulty in producing the proof."

"Wait till you see me in my black dress and bonnet,—and mittens," she challenged.

He bowed gallantly. "Only the addition of the veil,—it would have to be a very thick one,—I am sure,—could make me doubt my own eyes. They are witnesses whose testimony it will be very hard to shake."

Her manner underwent another transformation, as swift as it was unexpected. A troubled, harassed expression came into her eyes, driving out the sparkle that had filled them during that all too brief exchange. The smile died on her lips, which remained drawn and slightly parted as if frozen; she seemed for the moment to have stopped breathing. He was acutely alive to the old searching, penetrating look,—only now there was an added note of uneasiness. In another moment all this had vanished, and she was smiling again,—not warmly, frankly as before, but with a strange wistfulness that left him more deeply perplexed than ever.

"I wonder,—" she began, and then shook her head without completing the sentence. After a moment she went on: "Phineas is a long time. I hope all is well."

They heard the kitchen door open and close and Striker's voice loudly proclaiming the staunchness of his outbuildings, a speech cut short by Eliza's exasperation.

"How many times do I have to tell you, Phin Striker, not to come in this here kitchen without wipin' your feet? Might as well be the barn, fer as you're concerned. Go out an' scrape that mud offen your boots."

Deep mumbling and then the opening and shutting of the door again.

"Sometimes, I fear, poor Phineas finds matrimony very trying," said the girl, her eyes twinkling.

Eliza appeared in the doorway. She was rolling down her sleeves.

"How are you two gettin' along?" she inquired, looking from one to the other keenly. "I thought Phin was in here amusin' you the whole time with lies about him an' Dan'l Boone. He used to hunt with old Dan'l when he was a boy, an' if ever'thing happened to them two fellers that he *sez* happened, why, Phin'd have to be nearly two hundred years old by now an' there

wouldn't be a live animal or Indian between here an'
the Gulf of Mexico." She seemed a little uneasy. "I
hope you two made out all right."

The girl spoke quickly, before her companion could
reply. "We have had a most agreeable chat, Eliza.
Are you through in the kitchen? If you are, would
you mind coming into the bedroom with me? I want
you to see the other dress on me, and besides I have
a good many things I wish to talk over with you. Good
night," she said to Gwynne. "No doubt we shall meet
again."

He was dumbfounded. "Am I not to see you in the
new dress?" he cried, visibly disappointed. "Surely
you are not going to deny me the joy of beholding you
in—"

She interrupted him almost cavalierly. "Pray save
up some of your compliments against the day when you
behold me in my sombre black, for I shall need them
then. Again, good night."

"Good night," he returned, bowing stiffly and in
high dudgeon.

Eliza, in hurrying past, had snatched one of the
candlesticks from the mantel, and now stood holding
the bedroom door open for the queenly young person-
age. A moment later the door closed behind them.

Gwynne was still scowling at the inoffensive door
when Striker came blustering into the room.

"Where are the women?" he demanded, stopping
short.

A jerk of the thumb was his answer.

"Gone to bed?" with something like an accusing
gleam in his eye as his gaze returned to the young
man.

"I believe so," replied Gwynne carelessly, as he sat

down in the despised rocker and stretched his long
legs out to the fire. "I fancy we are safe to smoke now,
Striker. We have the parlor all to ourselves. The
ladies have deserted us."

Striker took the tobacco pouch from the peg on the
mantel and handed it to his guest.

"Fill up," he said shortly, and then walked over to
the bedroom door. He rapped timorously on one of
the thick boards. "Want me fer anything?" he inquired
softly, as his wife opened the door an inch or two.

"No. Go to bed when you're ready an' don't ferget
to smother that fire."

"Good night, Phineas," called out another voice merrily.

"Good night," responded Striker, with a dubious
shake of his head. He returned to the fireplace.

"Women are funny things," said he, dragging up
another chair. " 'Specially about boots. I go out
'long about sun-up an' work like a dog all day, an'
then when I come in to supper what happens? First
thing my wife does is to look at my boots. Then she
tells me to go out an' scrape the mud off'm 'em. Then
she looks up at my face to see if it's me. Sometimes
I get so doggoned mad I wish it wasn't me, so's I could
turn out to be the preacher er somebody like that an'
learn her to be keerful who she's talkin' to. Supposin'
I do track a little mud into her kitchen? It's *our* mud,
ain't it? 'Tain't as if it was somebody else's land I'm
bringin' into her kitchen. Between us we own every
danged bit of land from here to the Middleton dirt-
road an' it ain't my fault if it happens to be mud once
in awhile. You'd think, the way she acts, I'd been out
stealin' somebody else's mud just for the sake of bringin'
it into her kitchen.

"An' what makes me madder'n anything else is the way she scolds them pore dogs when they come in with a little mud. As if a dog understood he had to scrape his feet off an' wash his paws an' everything 'fore he c'n step inside his master's cabin. Now you take cats, they're as smart as all get out. They're jist like women. Allus thinkin' about their pussonal appearance. Ever notice a cat walk across a muddy strip o' ground? Why, you'd think they was walkin' on a red hot stove, the way they step. I've seen a cat go fifty rods out of her way to get around a mud-puddle. I recollect seein' ole Maje,—he's our principal tom-cat,—seein' him creepin' along a rail fence nearly half a mile from the house so's he wouldn't have to cross a stretch o' wet ground jist outside the kitchen door. Now, a dog would have splashed right through it an' took the consequences. But ole Maje—*no, sir!* He goes miles out'n his way an' then when he gits home he sets down on the doorstep an' licks his feet fer half an hour er so before he begins to meow so's Eliza'll open the door an' let him in.

"Ever' so often I got to tie a litter of kittens up in a meal-bag an' take 'em over to the river an' drownd 'em, an' I want to tell you it's a pleasure to do it. You never in all your life heerd of anybody puttin' a litter of pups in a bag an' throwin' 'em in the river, did ye? No, sirree! Dogs is like men. They grow up to be useful citizens, mud er no mud. Why, if I had a dog what sat down on the doorstep an' licked his paws ever' time he got mud on 'em I'd take him out an' shoot him, 'cause I'd know he wasn't no kind of a dog at all. Now, Eliza's tryin' to make me act like a cat, an' me hatin' cats wuss'n pison. There's setch a thing as bein' too danged clean, don't you think so? Sort o' takes the

self-respect away from a man. Makes you feel as if
you'd ort to have petticoats on in place o' pants. How
do you like that terbaccer?"

Throughout the foregoing dissertation, Gwynne had
sat with his moody gaze fixed upon the flaring logs,
which Striker had kicked into renewed life with the
heel of one of his ponderous boots, disdaining the stout
charred poker that leaned against the chimney wall.
He was pulling dreamily at the corncob pipe; the fra-
grant blue smoke, drifting toward the open fireplace,
was suddenly caught by the draft and drawn stringily
into the hot cavern where it was lost in the hickory
volume that swept up the chimney.

He had taken in but a portion of his host's remarks;
his thoughts were not of dogs and cats but of the per-
plexing girl who eagerly gave him her confidence in
one moment and shrank into the iciest reticence the
next. Her unreserved revelations concerning her own
father, uttered with all the frankness of an intimate,
and the childish ingenuousness with which she accounted
for her raiment, followed so closely, so abruptly by the
most insolent display of bad manners he had ever
known, gave him ample excuse for reflection, and if
he failed to obtain the full benefit of Striker's discourse
it was because he had no power to command his addled
thoughts. As a matter of fact, he was debating within
himself the advisability of asking his host a few direct
and pointed questions. A fine regard for Striker's
position deterred him,—and to this regard was added
the conviction that his host would probably tell him
to mind his own business and not go prying into the
affairs of others. He came out of his reverie in good
time to avoid injury to his host's feelings.

"It is admirable," he assured him promptly. "Do

you cure it yourself or does it come up the river from Kentucky?"

"Comes from Kentucky. We don't have much luck tryin' to raise terbaccer in these parts."

Whereupon Mr. Striker went into a long and intelligent lecture upon the products of the soil in that section of Indiana; what to avoid and what to cultivate; how to buy and how to sell; the traders one could trust and those who could not be trusted out of sight; the short corn crop of the year before and the way he lost half a dozen as fine shoats as you'd see in a lifetime on account of wild hogs coming out of the woods and encin' 'em off. He interrupted himself at one stage in order to get up and close the door to the kitchen. Zachariah was snoring lustily.

"Whenever you feel like goin' to bed, jist say so," he said at last, as his guest drew his huge old silver watch from his pocket and glanced at it.

"I have been doing a little surmising, Mr. Striker," said the other. "You have only this sitting-room and one bedroom. The ladies are occupying the latter. My servant has gone to bed in the kitchen. I am wondering where you and I are to dispose ourselves."

"I could see you was doin' some figgerin', friend. Well, fer that matter, so was I. 'Tain't often she comes to spend the night here, an' when she does me an' Eliza give her our room an' bed an' we pull an extry straw tick out here in the room an' make the best of it. Now, as I figger it out, Eliza is usin' that straw tick herself, 'cause she certainly wouldn't ever dream of gettin' into bed with—with—er—her. Not but what she's clean an' all that,—I mean Eliza,—but you see, she used to be a hired girl once upon a time, an'—an'—well, that sort of makes a—"

"My fellow-guest confided to me a little while ago that she too had been a hired girl, Mr. Striker, so I don't see—"

"Did she tell you that?" demanded Phineas sharply.

"She did," replied Gwynne, enjoying his host's consternation.

"Well, I'll be tee-totally danged," exploded the settler. He got up suddenly and turning his back to his guest, knocked the burnt tobacco from his pipe against the stone arch of the fireplace. "I guess I better rake the ashes over these here coals," said he, " 'cause if I don't an' the cabin took fire an' burnt us all alive Eliza'd never git done jawin' me about it." Presently he stood off and critically surveyed his work. "I guess that'll fix her so's she won't spit any sparks out here an' set fire to the carpet. As I was sayin', I reckon I'll have to make up a bed here in front of the fireplace fer myself, an' let you go up to the attic. We got a—"

"I was afraid of this, Mr. Striker. You are putting yourselves out terribly on my account. I can't allow it, sir. It is too much to ask—"

"Now, don't you worry about us. You ain't puttin' us out at all. One night last winter,—the coldest night we had,—Eliza an' me slep' on the kitchen floor with nary a blanket er quilt, an' I had to git up every half hour to put wood on the fire so's we wouldn't freeze to death, all because Joe Wadley an' his wife an' her father an' mother an' his sister with her three children dropped in sort of unexpected on account of havin' their two wagons git stuck in a snow drift a mile er so from here. No, sirree, don't you worry. There's a spare tick up in the attic what we use fer strangers when they happen along, an' Zachariah has put your

blankets right here by the door,—an' your pistols, too,
I see,—so whenever you're ready, I'll lead the way up
the ladder an' show you where you're to roost. There's
a little winder at one end, so's you c'n have all the air
you want,—an', my stars, there's a lot of it to-night,
ain't there? Jist listen to her whistle. Sounds like
winter. She's changed, though, an' I wouldn't be surprised if we'd find the moon is shinin'."

CHAPTER IV

VIOLA GWYN

THEY stepped outside the cabin, into the fresh, brisk gale that was blowing. A gibbous moon hung in the eastern star-specked sky. Scurrying moonlit clouds off in the west sped northward on the sweep of the inconstant wind, which had shifted within the hour. A light shone dimly through the square little window of the bedroom. Kenneth's imagination penetrated to sacred precincts beyond the solid logs: he pictured her in the other frock, moving gracefully before the fascinated eyes of the settler's wife, proud as a peacock and yet as gay as the lark.

"Women like to talk," observed Striker, with a sidelong glance at the lighted window. He led the way to the opposite end of the cabin and pointed off into the night. "Lafayette's off in yan direction. There's a big stretch of open prairie in between, once you git out'n these woods, an' further on there's more timber. The town's down in a sort of valley, shaped somethin' like a saucer, with hills on all sides an' the river cuttin' straight through the middle. Considerable buildin' goin' on this spring. There's talk of the Baptists an' the Methodists puttin' up new churches an' havin' regular preachers instead of the circuit riders. But you'll see all this fer yourself when you git there. Plenty of licker to be had at Sol Hamer's grocery,—mostly Mononga-Durkee whisky,—in case you git the Wabash shakes or suddenly feel homesick."

67

"I drink very little," said Kenneth.

"Well, you'll soon git over that," prophesied his host. "Everybody does. A spell of aguer like we have along the river every fall an' winter an' spring will make you mighty thankful fer Sol Hamer's medicine, an' by the time summer comes you'll be able to stand more'n you ever thought you could stand. What worries me is how the women manage to git along without it. You see big strong men goin' around shakin' their teeth out an' docterin' day an' night at Sol's, but I'll be doggoned if you ever see a woman takin' it. Seems as if they'd ruther shake theirselves to death than tetch a drop o' whisky."

"You would not have them otherwise, would you?"

"Why, if I ever caught my wife takin' a swaller o' whisky, I'd—well, by gosh, I don't know what I *would* do. First place, I'd think the world was comin' to an end, and second place, I guess I'd be glad it was. No, sirree, I don't want to see whisky goin' down a woman's gullet. But that don't explain how they come to git along without it when they've got the aguer. They won't even take it when a rattlesnake bites 'em. Sooner die. An' in spite of all that, they bring he-children into the world that can't git over a skeeter bite unless they drink a pint or two of whisky. Well, I guess we better go to roost, Mr. Gwynne. Must be nine o'clock. Everything's all right out at the barn an' the chicken coops. Wolves an' foxes an' weasels visit us sometimes at night, but I got things fixed so's they go away hungry. In the day time, Eliza's got an ole musket o' mine standin' in the kitchen to skeer the hawks away, an' I got a rifle in the settin' room fer whatever varmint comes along at night,—includin' hoss-thieves an' setch-like."

"Horse-thieves?"

"Yep. Why, only last month a set of hoss-thieves from down the river went through the Wea plains an' stole sixteen yearlin' colts, drove 'em down to the river, loaded 'em on a flat-boat an' got away without losin' a hair. Done it on a Sunday night, too."

It was a few minutes past nine when Kenneth followed his host up the ladder and through the trap-door into the stuffy attic. He carried his rough riding-boots, which Zachariah had cleaned and greased with a piece of bacon-rind.

"I'll leave the ladder here," said Striker, depositing the candlestick on the floor. "So's I c'n stick my head in here in the mornin' an' rouse you up. There's your straw-tick over yander, an' I'll fotch your blankets up in a minute or two. I reckon you'll have to crawl on your hands an' knees; this attic wasn't built fer full-size men."

"I will be all right," his guest assured him. "Beggars cannot be choosers. A place to lay my head, a roof to keep the rain off, and a generous host—what more can the wayfarer ask?"

The clapboard roof was a scant three feet above the dusty floor of the attic. Stooping, the young man made his way to the bed-tick near the little window. He did not sniff with scorn at his humble surroundings. He had travelled long and far and he had slept in worse places than this. He was drawing off his boots when Striker again stuck his head and shoulders through the opening and laid his roll of blankets on the floor.

"Eliza jist stuck her head out to tell me to shut this trap-door, so's my snorin' won't keep you awake. I fergot all about my snorin'. Like as not if I left this door open the whole danged roof would be lifted right off'm the cabin 'fore I'd been asleep five minutes. Well, good night. I'll call you in the mornin' bright an' early."

The trap-door was slowly lowered into place as the shaggy head and broad shoulders of the settler disappeared. The young man heard the scraping of the ladder as it was being removed to a place against the wall.

He pried open the tight little window, letting a draft of fresh air rush into the stifling attic. Then he sat on the edge of the tick for a few minutes, ruminating, his gaze fixed thoughtfully on the sputtering, imperilled candle. Finally he shook his head, sighed, and began to unstrap his roll of blankets. He had decided to remove only his coat and waistcoat. The sharp, staccato barking of a fox up in the woods fell upon his ears. He paused to listen. Then came the faraway, unmistakable howl of a wolf, the solemn, familiar hoot of the wilderness owl and the raucous call of the great night heron. But there was no sound from the farmyard. He said his prayers—he never forgot to say the prayer his mother had taught him—blew out the candle, pulled the blankets up to his chin, and was soon fast asleep.

He did not know what time it was when he was aroused by the barking of Striker's dogs, loud, furious barking and ugly growls, signifying the presence in the immediate neighbourhood of the house of some intruder, man or beast. Shaking off the sleep that held him, he crept to the window and looked out. The moon was gone and the stars had almost faded from the inky black dome. He guessed the hour with the acute instinct of one to whom the vagaries of night have become fa-

miliar through long understanding. It would now
be about three o'clock in the morning, with the creeping dawn an hour and a half away.

Suddenly his gaze fell upon a light moving among
the trees some distance from the cabin. It appeared
and disappeared, like a jack o' lantern, but always it
moved southward, obscured every few feet by an intervening trunk or a clump of brush. As he watched
the bobbing light, he heard some one stirring in the
room below. Then the cabin door creaked on its rusty
hinges and almost immediately a jumble of subdued
hoarse voices came up to him. He felt for his pistols
and realized with something of a shock that he had
left them in the kitchen with Zachariah. For the first
time in his travels he had neglected to place them beside his bed.

The dogs, admonished by a sharp word or two, ceased
their barking. This reassured him, for they would
obey no one except Phineas Striker. Whoever was at
the cabin door, there was no longer any question in
his mind as to the peaceful nature of the visit. He crept
over to the trap-door and cautiously attempted to lift
it an inch or so, the better to hear what was going on,
but try as he would he could not budge the covering.
The murmur of voices went on for a few minutes longer,
and then he heard the soft, light pad of feet on the
floor below; sibilant, penetrating whispers; a suppressed feminine ejaculation followed by the low laugh
of a man, a laugh that might well have been described
as a chuckle.

For a long time he lay there listening to the confused sound of whispers, the stealthy shuffling of feet,
the quiet opening and closing of a door, and then there
was silence.

Several minutes passed. He stole back to the window. The light in the forest had vanished. Just as he was on the point of crawling into bed again, another sound struck his ear: the unmistakable rattle of wagon wheels on their axles, the straining of harness, the rasp of tug chains,—quite near at hand. The clack-clack of the hubs gradually diminished as the heavy vehicle made its slow, tortuous way off through the ruts and mire of the road. Presently the front door of the cabin squealed on its hinges, the latch snapped and the bolt fell carefully into place.

He could not go to sleep again. His brain was awake and active, filled with unanswered questions, beset by endless speculation. The first faint sign of dawn, creeping through the window, found him watching eagerly, impatiently for its appearance. The presence of a wagon, even at that black hour of the night, while perhaps unusual, was readily to be accounted for in more ways than one, none of them possessing a sinister significance. A neighbouring farmer making an early start for town stopping to carry out some friendly commission for Phineas Striker; a settler calling for assistance in the case of illness at his home; hunters on their way to the marshes for wild ducks and geese; or even guardians of the law in search of malefactors. But the mysterious light in the woods,—that was something not so easily to be explained.

The square little aperture was clearly defined against the greying sky before he distinguished signs of activity in the room below. Striker was up and moving about. He could hear him stacking logs in the fireplace, and presently there came up to him the welcome crackle of kindling-wood ablaze. A door opened and a gruff voice spoke. The settler was routing Zachariah out of his slumbers. Far off in some unknown, remote land a rooster crowed,—the day's champion, the first of all to greet the rising sun. Almost instantly, a cock in Striker's barnyard awoke in confusion and dismay, and sent up a hurried, raucous cock-a-doodle-doo, —too late by half a minute to claim the honours of the day, but still a valiant challenger. Then other chanticleers, big and little, sounded their clarion call,—and the day was born.

Kenneth, despite his longing for this very hour to come, now perversely wished to sleep. A belated but beatific drowsiness seized him. He was only half-conscious of the noise that attended the lifting of the trapdoor.

"Wake up! Time to git up," a distant voice was calling, and he suddenly opened his eyes very wide and found himself staring at a shaggy, unkempt head sticking up out of the floor, rendered grim and terrifying by the fitful play of a ruddy light from the depths below. For a second he was bewildered.

"That you, Striker?" he mumbled.

"Yep,—it's me. Time to git up. Five o'clock. Breakfass'll soon be ready. You c'n wash up out at the well. Sleep well?"

"Passably. I was awakened some time in the night by your visitors."

He was sitting up on the edge of the tick, drawing on his boots. Striker was silent for a moment.

"Thought maybe you'd be disturbed, spite of all we could do to be as quiet as possible. People from a farm 'tother side of the plains."

The head disappeared, and in a very few minutes Gwynne, carrying his coat and waistcoat, descended the ladder into the presence of a roaring fire. He shot a

glance at the closed bedroom door, and then hastily
made his way out of the cabin and around to the well.
Eliza was preparing breakfast. In the grey half-
light he made out Striker and Zachariah moving about
the barnlot. A rough but clean towel hung across
the board wall of the well, while a fresh bucket of water
stood on the shelf inside, its chain hanging limply from
the towering end of the "h'isting pole."

As he completed his ablutions, the darkey boy approached.

"Good morning, Zachariah," he spluttered, over the
edge of the towel. "Did you sleep well?"

"No, suh, Marse Kenneth, Ah slep' powerful porely.
Ah don't reckon Ah had mah eyes close' more'n fifteen
seconds all night long, suh."

His master peered at him. Zachariah's eyes were
not yet thoroughly open.

"You mean you did not have them open more than
fifteen seconds, you rascal. Why, you were asleep
and snoring by nine o'clock."

"Yas, suh, yas, suh,—but Ah done got 'em wide open
ag'in 'side o' no time. Ah jes' couldn't holp worryin',
Marse Kenneth, 'bout you all. Ah sez to mahself, ef
Marse Kenneth he ain' got no fitten place to lay his
weary haid—"

"Oh, then you were not kept awake by noises or—
by the by, did you hear any noises?"

"Noises? No, suh! Dis yere cabin hit was like a
grave. Thass what kep' me awake, mos' likely. Ah
reckon Ah is used to noises. Ah jes' couldn't go to
sleep widdout 'em, Marse Kenneth. Wuzzen't even a
cricket er a—"

His master's hearty laugh caused him to cut his
speech short. A wary glance out of the corner of his

eye satisfied him that it was now time to change the subject.

"Done fed de hosses, suh, an' mos' ready to packen up fo' de juhney, suh. Yas, *suh!* Ev'thing all hunky-dory jes' soon as Marse Kenneth done had his break-fuss. *Yas*, suh! Yas, *suh!*"

They ate breakfast by candle-light, Striker and Eliza and Kenneth. There was no sign of the beautiful and exasperating girl. Phineas was strangely glum and preoccupied, his wife too busy with her flap-jacks to take even the slightest interest in the desultory conversation.

"A little too early for my fellow-guest to be up and about, I see," ventured Kenneth at last, taking the bull by the horns. His curiosity had to be satisfied.

Striker did not look up from his plate. "She's gone. She ain't here."

"Gone?"

"Yep. Left jist a little while 'fore sun-up."

"Her ma sent for her," volunteered Eliza.

"Sent fer her to come in a hurry," added Striker, trying to be casual.

"Then it was she who went away in the wagon last night," said the young man, a note of disappointment in his voice.

"Airly this mornin'," corrected his host. "Jist half an hour or so 'fore sun-up."

"I trust her mother is not ill."

"No tellin'," was Striker's non-committal response.

It was quite apparent to Kenneth that they did not wish to discuss the matter. He waited a few moments before remarking:

"I saw a light moving through the woods above here,—a lantern, I took it to be,—just after I was awakened by the barking of the dogs. I thought at first it was that which set the dogs off on a rampage."

Striker was looking at him intently under his bushy eyebrows, his knife poised halfway to his lips. While he could not see Eliza, who was at the stove behind him, he was struck by the fact that there was a brief, significant suspension of activity on her part; the scrape of the "turnover" in the frying-pan ceased abruptly.

"A lantern up in the woods?" said Striker slowly, looking past Gwynne at Eliza.

"A light. It may not have been a lantern."

"Which way was it movin'?"

"In that direction," indicating the south.

The turning of the flap-jacks in the pan was resumed. Striker relaxed a little.

"Hunters, I reckon, goin' down stream for wild duck and geese this mornin'. There's a heap o' ducks an' geese passin' over—"

"See here, Phineas," broke in his wife suddenly, "what's the sense of sayin' that? You know it wasn't duck hunters. Nobody's out shooting ducks with the river as high as it is down this way, an' Mr. Gwynne knows it, if he's got half as much sense as I think he has."

"When I heard people out in front of the cabin shortly afterward, I naturally concluded that the lantern belonged to them," remarked the young man.

"Well, it didn't," said Striker, laying down his knife. "I guess it won't hurt you to know now somethin' that will be of considerable interest to you later on. I ain't betrayin' nobody's secret, 'cause I said I was goin' to tell you the whole story."

"Don't you think you'd better let it come from some-body else, Phin?" interposed his wife nervously.

"No, I don't, Eliza. 'Cause why? 'Cause I think he'd ort to know. Maybe he'll be able to put a stop to her foolishness. We didn't know until long after you went to bed that her real reason fer comin' here yester-day was to run off an' get married to Barry Lapelle. She didn't tell you no lies about her clothes an' all that, 'cause her ma had put her foot down on her takin' off black. They had it all planned out beforehand, her an' this Lapelle. He was to come fer her some time before daybreak with a couple of hosses an' they was to be off before the sun was up on their way to Attica where they was to be married, an' then go on down the river to his home in Terry Hut. Me an' Eliza set up all night in that bedroom, tryin' to coax her out of it. I don't like this Lapelle feller. He's a handsome cuss, but he's as wild as all get out,—drinks, gambles, an' all setch. Well, to make a long story short, that was prob'ly him up yander on the ole Injin trace, with his hosses, waitin' fer the time to come when they could be off. Her ma must have found out about their plans, 'cause she come here herself with two of her hired men an' old Cap'n Scott, a friend of the fam'ly, an' took her daughter right out from under Barry's nose. It was them you heared down here last night. I will say this fer the girl, she kinder made up her mind 'long about midnight that it was a foolish thing to do, run-nin' off like this with Barry, an' like as not when the time come she'd have backed out."

"She's a mighty headstrong girl," said Eliza. "Sot in her ways an' sp'iled a good deal by goin' to school down to St. Louis."

"Her mother don't want her to marry Lapelle. She's

dead sot ag'inst it. It's a mighty funny way fer the girl to act, when she's so fond of her mother. I can't understand it in her. All the more reason fer her to stick to her mother when it's a fact that the old woman ain't got what you'd call a friend in the whole deestrict. She's a queer sort of woman,—close an' stingy as all get out, an' as hard as a hickory log. Never been seen at a church meetin'. She makes her daughter go whenever there's a meetin', but as fer herself,—no, sirree. 'Course, I understand why she's so sot ag'inst Barry. She's purty well off an' the girl will be rich some day."

"Shucks!" exclaimed Eliza. "Barry Lapelle's after her 'cause she's the purtiest girl him or anybody else has ever seen. He ain't the only man that's in love with her. They *all* are,—clear from Lafayette to Terry Hut, an' maybe beyond. Don't you tell me it's her money he's after, Phin Striker. He's after *her*. He's got plenty of money himself, so they say, so why—"

"I ain't so sure about that," broke in her husband. "There's a lot of talk about him gamblin' away most everything his father left him. Lost one of his boats last winter in a poker game up at Lafayette, an' had to borrer money on some land he's got down the river to git it back. The packet *Paul Revere* it was. Used to run on the Mississippi. I guess she kinder lost her head over him," he went on musingly. "He's an awful feller with women, so good-lookin' an' all, an' so different from the farm boys aroun' here. Allus got good clothes on, an' they say he has fit a couple of duels down the river. Somehow that allus appeals to young girls. But I can't understand it in her. She's setch a level-headed girl,—but, then, I guess they're all alike

when a good-lookin' man comes along. Look at Eliza
here. The minute she sot eyes on me she—"

"I didn't marry you, Phin Striker, because you was
purty, let me tell you that," exclaimed Eliza, witheringly.

Gwynne, who had been listening to all this with a
queer sinking of the heart, interrupted what promised
to develop into an acrimonious wrangle over pre-con-
nubial impressions. He was decidedly upset by the
revelations; a vague dream, barely begun, came to a
sharp and disagreeable end.

"She actually had planned to run away with this
man Lapelle?" he exclaimed, frowning. "It was all
arranged?"

"So I take it," said Striker. "She brought some of
her personal trinkets with her, but Eliza never suspected
anything queer about that."

"The fellow must be an arrant scoundrel," declared
the young man angrily. "No gentleman would subject
an innocent girl to such—"

"All's well that ends well, as the feller says," interrupted Striker, arising from the table. "At least fer
the present. She seemed sort of willin' to go home with
her ma, so I guess her heart ain't everlastingly busted.
I thought it was best to tell you all this, Mr. Gwynne,
'cause I got a sneakin' idee you're goin' to see a lot
of that girl, an' maybe you'll turn out to be a source
of help in time o' trouble to her."

"I fail to understand just what you mean, Striker.
She is an absolute stranger to me."

"Well, we'll see what we shall see," said Striker,
cryptically. He opened the kitchen door and called
to Zachariah to hurry in and get his breakfast.

Half an hour later Kenneth and his servant mounted their horses in the barnyard and prepared to depart. The sun was shining and there was a taste and tang of spring in the breeze that flouted the faces of the horse-men.

"Follow this road back to the crossin' an' turn to your left," directed Striker, "an' 'fore you know it you'll be in Lay-flat, as they call it down in Crawfords-ville. Remember, you're allus most welcome here. I reckon we'll see somethin' of each other as time goes on. It ain't difficult fer honest men to be friends as well as neighbours in this part of the world. I'm glad you happened my way last night."

He walked alongside Gwynne's stirrup as they moved down toward the road.

"Some day," said the young man, "I should like to have a long talk with you about my father. You knew him well and I—by the way, your love-lorn friend knew him also."

The other was silent for half a dozen paces, looking straight ahead.

"Yes," said he, with curious deliberation. "She was sayin' as how she told you a lot about him last night,—what sort of a man he was, an' all that."

"She told me nothing that—"

"Jist a minute, Mr. Gwynne," said Striker, laying his hand on the rider's knee. Kenneth drew rein. "I guess maybe you didn't know who she was talkin' about at the time, but it was your father she was describin'. We all three knowed somethin' that you didn't know, an' it's only fair fer me to tell you the truth, now that she's out of the way. That girl was Viola Gwyn, an' she's your half-sister."

CHAPTER V

THE sun was barely above the eastward wall of
trees when Kenneth and his man rode away from
the home of Phineas Striker. Their progress
was slow and arduous, for the black mud was well up
to the fetlocks of the horses in this new road across
the boggy clearing. He rode ahead, as was the custom, followed a short distance behind by his servant
on the strong, well-laden pack-horse.

The master was in a thoughtful, troubled mood. He
paid little attention to the glories of the fresh spring
day. What he had just heard from the lips of the
settler disturbed him greatly. That beautiful girl his
half-sister! The child of his own father and the hated
Rachel Carter! Rachel Carter, the woman he had been
brought up to despise, the harlot who had stolen his
father away, the scarlet wanton at whose door the
death of his mother was laid! That evil woman, Rachel
Carter!

Could she, this foulest of thieves, be the mother of
so lovely, so sensitive, so perfect a creature as Viola
Gwyn?

As he rode frowningly along, oblivious to the low
chant of the darkey and the song of the first spring
warblers, he revisualized the woman he had known in
his earliest childhood. Strangely enough, the face of
Rachel Carter had always remained more firmly, more

81

indelibly impressed upon his memory than that of his own mother.

This queer, unusual circumstance may be easily, reasonably accounted for: his grandfather's dogged, almost daily lessons in hate. He was not allowed to forget Rachel Carter,—not for one instant. Always she was kept before him by that bitter, vindictive old man who was his mother's father,—even up to the day that he lay on his deathbed. Small wonder, then, that his own mother's face had faded from his memory while that of Rachel Carter remained clear and vivid, as he had known it now for twenty years. The passing years might perforce bring about changes in the face and figure of Rachel Carter, but they could not, even in the smallest detail, alter the picture his mind's eye had carried so long and faithfully. He could think of her only as she was when he last saw her, twenty years ago: tall and straight, with laughing eyes and white teeth, and the colour of tan-bark in her cheeks.

Then there had been little Minda,—tiny Minda who existed vaguely as a name, nothing more. He had a dim recollection of hearing his elders say that the babe with the yellow curls had been drowned when a boat turned over far away in the big brown river. Some one had come to his grandfather's house with the news. He recalled hearing the talk about the accident, and his grandfather lifting his fist toward the sky and actually blaming God for something! He never forgot that. His grandfather had blamed God!

He had thought of asking Striker about his father's widow, after hearing the truth about Viola, but a stubborn pride prevented. It had been on his tongue to inquire when and where Robert Gwynne and Rachel Carter were married,—he did not doubt that they had been legally married,—but he realized in time that in all probability the settler, as well as every one else in the community, was totally uninformed as to the past life of Robert and Rachel Gwynne. Besides, the query would reveal an ignorance on his part that he was loath to expose to speculation.

Striker had explained the somewhat distasteful scrutiny to which he had been subjected the night before. All three of them, knowing him to be Viola's blood relation, were studying his features with interest, seeking for a trace of family resemblance, not alone to his father but to the girl herself. This had set him thinking. There was not, so far as he could determine, the slightest likeness between him and his beautiful half-sister; there was absolutely nothing to indicate that their sire was one and the same man.

Pondering, he now understood what Striker meant in declaring that he ought to know the truth about the frustrated elopement. Even though the honest settler was aware of the strained relations existing between the widow and her husband's son by a former wife,—(the deceased in his will had declared in so many words that he owed more than mere reparation to the neglected but unforgotten son born to him and his beloved but long dead wife, Laura Gwynne),—even though Striker knew all this, it was evident that he looked upon this son as the natural protector of the wilful girl, notwithstanding the feud between step-mother and step-son.

And Kenneth, as he rode away, felt a new weight of responsibility as unwelcome to him as it was certain to be to Viola; for, when all was said and done, she was her mother's daughter and as such doubtless looked upon him through the mother's eyes, seeing a common enemy.

Still, she was his half-sister, and whether he liked it or not he was morally bound to stand between her and disaster,—and if Striker was right, marriage with the wild Lapelle spelled disaster of the worst kind. He had only to recall, however, the unaccountable look of hostility with which she had favoured him more than once during the evening to realize that he was not likely to be called upon for either advice or protection.

He mused aloud, with the shrug of a philosopher: "Heigh-ho! I fear me I shall have small say as to the conduct of this newly found relation. The only tie that bound us is gone. She is not only the child of my father, whom she feared and perhaps hated, but of mine enemy, whom she loves,—so the case is clear. There is a wall between us, and I shall not attempt to surmount it. What a demnition mess it has turned out to be. I came prepared to find only the creature I have scorned and despised, and I discover that I have a sister so beautiful that, not knowing her at all, my eyes are dazzled and my heart goes to thumping like any silly school boy's. Aye, 'tis a very sorry pass. Were it not so demned upsetting, it would be amusing. Fate never played a wilder prank. What, ho, Zachariah! Where are we now? Whose farm is that upon the ridge?"

Zachariah, urging his horse forward, consulted his memory. Striker had mentioned the farms they were to pass en route, and the features by which they were to be identified. Far away on a rise in the sweep of prairie-land stood a lonely cabin, with a clump of trees behind it.

"Well, Marse Kenneth, ef hit ain' de Sherry place hit shorely am de Sheridan place, an' ef hit ain't nuther one o' dem hit mus' belong to Marse Dimmit er—"

"It is neither of these, you rascal. We are to the north of them, if I remember our directions rightly. Mr. Hollingsworth and the Kisers live hereabouts, according to Phineas Striker. A house with a clump of trees,—it is Mr. Huff's farm. Soon we will come to the Martin and Talbot places, and then the land that is mine, Zachariah. It lies for the most part on this side of the Crawfordsville road."

"Is yo' gwine to stop dere, Marse Kenneth?"

"No. I shall ride out from town some day soon to look the place over," said his master with a pardonable lordliness of mien, becoming to a landed gentleman. "Our affairs at present lie in the town, for there is much to be settled before I take charge. Striker tells me the man who is farming the place is an able, honest fellow. I shall not disturb him. From what he says, my property is more desirable in every way than the land that fell to my father's widow. Her farm lies off to our left, it seems, and reaches almost to the bottomlands of the river. We, Zachariah, are out here in the fertile prairie land. Our west line extends along the full length of her property. So, you see, the only thing that separates the two farms is an imaginary line no wider than your little finger, drawn by a surveyor and established by law. You will observe, my faithful fellow,—assuming that you *are* a faithful fellow,—that as we draw farther away from the woods along the river, the road becomes firmer, the soil less soggy, the— If you will cast your worthless eye about you, instead of at these mud-puddles, you will also observe the vast fields of stubble, the immense stretches of corn stalks and the signs of spring ploughing on all sides. Truly 'tis a wonderful country. See yon pasture, Zachariah, with the cows and calves,—a good score of them. And have you, by the way, noticed what a glorious day it is? This is life!"

"Yas, suh, Marse Kenneth, Ah done notice dat, an' Ah done notice somefin ailse. Ah done notice dem buzzards flyin' low over yan way. Dat means death, Marse Kenneth. Somefin sho' am daid over yan way."

"You are a melancholy croaker, Zachariah. You see naught but the buzzards, when all about you are the newly come birds of spring, the bluebird, the robin, and the thrush. Soon the meadow lark will be in the fields, and the young quail and the prairie-hen."

"Yas, suh," agreed Zachariah, brightening, "an' de yaller-hammer an' de blue-jay an' de—an' de rattle-snake," he concluded, with a roving, uneasy look along the roadside.

"Do not forget the saucy parroquets we saw yesterday as we came through the forest. You went so far in your excitement over those little green and golden birds, with their scarlet heads, that you declared they reminded you of the Garden of Eden. Look about you, Zachariah. Here is the Garden of Eden, right at your feet. Do you see those plum trees over yonder? Well, sir, old Adam and Eve used to sit under those very trees during the middle of the day, resting themselves in the shade. And right over there behind that big rock is where the serpent had his nest. He gave Eve a plum instead of an apple, because Eve was especially fond of plums and did not care at all for apples. She—"

" 'Scuse me, Marse Kenneth, but dem is hawthorn trees," said Zachariah, grinning.

"So they are, so they are. Now that I come to think of it, it was the red-haw that Eve fancied more than any other fruit in the garden."

"Yas, suh,—an' ole Adam he was powerful fond ob snappin'-turtles fo' breakfas'," said Zachariah, pointing to a tortoise creeping slowly along the ditch. "An' lil Cain an' Abel,—my lan', how dem chillum used to gobble up de mud pies ole Mammy Eve used to make right out ob dish yere road we's ridin' on."

And so, in this sportive mood, master and man, warmed by the golden sun and cheered by the spring wind of an April morn, traversed this new-found realm of Cerus, forded the turbulent, swollen creek that later on ran through the heart of the Gwynne acres, and came at length to the main road leading into the town.

They passed log cabins and here and there pretentious frame houses standing back from the road in the shelter of oak and locust groves. Their passing was watched by curious women and children in dooryards and porches, while from the fields men waved greeting and farewell with the single sweep of a hat. On every barn door the pelts of foxes and raccoons were stretched and nailed.

Presently they drew near to a lane reaching off to the west, and apparently ending in a wooded knoll, a quarter of a mile away.

"There," said Kenneth, with a wave of his hand, "is where I shall some day erect a mansion, Zachariah, that will be the wonder and the envy of all the people in the country. For unless I am mistaken, that is the grove of oaks that Striker mentioned. Behold, Zachariah,—all that is mine. Four hundred acres of as fine farm-land as there is in all the world, and timber unparalleled. Yes, I am right. There is the house that Striker described, the place where my father lived when he first came to the Wea. Egad, 'tis not a regal palace, is it, Zachariah? The most imposing thing about it is the chimney."

They were gazing at a cabin that squatted meekly over against the wall of oaks. Its roof was barely visible above the surrounding stockade, while the barn and styes and sheds were hidden entirely beyond the slope. It was, in truth, the most primitive and insignificant house they had seen that day.

"He was one of the first to build in this virgin waste," mused the young man aloud. "Rough and parlous were the days when he came to this land, Zachariah. There was no town of Lafayette, no neighbours save the rude, uncultured trappers. Now see how the times have changed. And, mark my guess, Zachariah, there will be still greater changes before we are laid away. There will be cities and— Ha! Look, Zachariah,—to the right of the grove. It is all as Striker said. There is the other house,—two miles or more to the westward. That is *her* house. It is new, scarce two years old, built of lumber instead of logs, and quite spacious. There are, he tells me, two stories, containing four rooms, with a kitchen off the back, a smokehouse and a granary besides the barn,—yes, I see them all, just as he said we should see them after we rounded the grove."

He drew rein and gazed at the distant house, set on a ridge and backed by the seemingly endless forest that stretched off to the north and south. His face clouded, his jaw was set, and his eyes were hard.

"Yes, that would be Rachel Carter's house," he continued, harshly. "Her land and my land lying side by side, with only a fence between. Her grain and my grain growing out of the same soil. What an unholy trick for fate to play. Perhaps she is over there, even now. She and Viola. It is not likely that they would have started for town at an earlier hour than this. And to think of the damnable situation I shall find in town. She will be my neighbour,—just as she was twenty years ago. We shall live within speaking distance of each other, we shall see each other perhaps a dozen times a day, and yet we may neither speak nor see. Egad, I wonder what I'll do if she even attempts to address me! Heigh-ho! 'Tis the mischief of Satan himself. Come, Zachariah,—you lazy rascal! As if you had not slept soundly all night long, you must now fall asleep sitting bolt upright in the saddle."

And so on they rode again, at times breaking into a smart canter where the road was solid, but for the most part proceeding with irksome slowness through the evil slough. Ahead lay the dense wood they were to traverse before coming to the town. Soon the broad, open prairie would be behind them, they would be plunged into the depths of a forest primeval, wending their way through five miles of solitude to the rim of the vale in which the town was situated. But the forest had no terrors for them. They were accustomed to the long silences, the sombre shades, the seemingly endless stretches of wildwood wherein no mortal dwelt. They had come from afar and they were young, and hardy, and fearless. Beyond that wide wall of trees lay journey's end; a new life awaited them on the other side of the barrier forest.

Suddenly Zachariah called his master's attention to a horseman who rode swiftly, even recklessly across the fields to their left and well ahead of them. They watched the rider with interest, struck by the furious pace he was holding, regardless of consequences either to himself or his steed.

"Mus' be somebody pow'ful sick, Marse Kenneth, fo' dat man to be ridin' so fas'," remarked Zachariah.

"Going for a doctor, I sup— Begad, he must have come from Rachel Carter's farm! There is no other house in sight over in that direction. I wonder if—" He did not complete the sentence, but frowned anxiously as he looked over his shoulder at the distant house.

Judging by the manner and the direction in which he was galloping, the rider would reach the main road a quarter of a mile ahead of them, about at the point where it entered the wood. Kenneth now made out an unfenced wagon-road through the field, evidently a short-cut from Rachel Carter's farm to the highway. He permitted himself a faint, sardonic smile. This, then, was to be her means of reaching the highway rather than to use the lane that ran past his house and no doubt crossed a section of his farm.

Sure enough the horseman turned into the road some distance ahead of them and rode straight for the forest. Then, for the first time, Gwynne observed a second rider, motionless at the roadside, and in the shadow of the towering, leafless trees that marked the portal through which they must enter the forest. The flying horseman slowed down as he neared this solitary figure, coming to a standstill when he reached his side. A moment later, both riders were cantering toward the wood, apparently in excited, earnest conversation. A few rods farther on, both turned to look over their shoulders at the slow-moving travellers. Then they stopped, wheeled about, and stood still, awaiting their approach.

Kenneth experienced a poignant thrill of apprehension. What was he to expect: a friendly or a sanguinary encounter? He slipped his right hand into the saddle pocket and drew forth a pistol which he shoved

hastily inside his waistcoat, covering the stock with
the folds of his cape.

"Keep a little way behind me," he said to his servant,
a trace of excitement in his voice.

"Yas, suh," said Zachariah, with more alacrity than
valour, the whites of his eyes betraying something more
than a readiness to obey this conservative order. It
was a foregone conclusion that Zachariah would turn
tail and flee the instant there was a sign of danger.
"Slave hunters, Marse Kenneth, dat's what dey is," he
announced with conviction. "Ah c'n smell 'em five
miles away. Yas, suh,—dey's gwine a' make trouble
fo' you, Marse Kenneth, sho' as you is—" But by
this time he had dropped so far behind that his opinions
were valueless.

When not more than fifty yards separated the two
parties, one of the men, with a word and an imperative
jerk of the head to his companion, advanced slowly to
meet Kenneth. This man was the one who had waited
for the other at the edge of the wood.

Gwynne beheld a tall, strongly built young man who
rode his horse with the matchless grace of an Indian.
Although his companion was roughly dressed and wore
a coon-skin cap, this man was unmistakably a dandy.
His high beaver hat observed a jaunty, rakish tilt;
his brass-buttoned coat was the colour of wine and of
the latest fashion, while his snug fitting pantaloons
were the shade of the mouse. He wore no cumbersome
cape, but fashioned about his neck and shoulders was
a broad, sloping collar of mink. There were silver
spurs on his stout riding boots, and the wide cuffs of
his gauntlets were embroidered in silver.

He was a handsome fellow of the type described as
dashing. Dark gleaming eyes peered out beneath thick

black eyebrows which met in an unbroken line above his nose. Set in a face of unusual pallor, they were no doubt rendered superlatively brilliant by contrast. His skin was singularly white above the bluish, freshly shaven cheeks and chin. His hair was black and long and curling. The thin lips, set and unsmiling, were nevertheless drawn up slightly at one corner of the mouth in what appeared to be a permanent stamp of superiority and disdain,—or even contempt. Altogether, a most striking face, thought Gwynne,—and the man himself a person of importance. The very manner in which he jerked his head to his companion was proof enough of that.

"Good morning," said this lordly gentleman, bringing his horse to a standstill and raising his "gad" to the brim of his hat in a graceful salute.

Gwynne drew rein alongside. He had observed in a swift glance that the stranger was apparently unarmed, except for the short, leather gad.

"Good morning," he returned. "I am on the right road to Lafayette, I take it."

"You are," said the other. "From Crawfordsville way?"

"Yes. I left that place yesterday. I come from afar, however. This is a strange country to me."

"It is strange to most of us. Unless I am mistaken, sir, you are Mr. Kenneth Gwynne."

The other smiled. "My approach appears to be fairly well heralded. Were I a vain person I should feel highly complimented."

"Then you *are* Kenneth Gwynne?" said the stranger, rather curtly.

"Yes. That is my name."

"Permit me to make myself known to you. My name

is Lapelle,—Barry Lapelle. While mine no doubt is unfamiliar to you, yours is well known to me. In fact, it is known to every one in these parts. You have long been expected. You will find the town anxiously awaiting your appearance." He smiled slightly. "If you could arrange to arrive after nightfall, I am sure you would find bonfires and perhaps a torchlight procession in your honour. As it is, I rather suspect our enterprising citizen, Mr. William Smith, will fire a salute when you appear in view."

"A salute?" exclaimed Kenneth blankly.

"A joyful habit of his, but rather neglected of late. It used to be his custom, I hear, to put a charge of powder in a stump and set it off whenever a steamboat drew up to the landing. That was his way of letting the farmers for miles around know that a fresh supply of goods had arrived and they were to hurry in and do the necessary trading at the store. He almost blew himself and his store to Hallelujah a year or two ago, and so he isn't quite so enterprising as he was. I am on my way to town, Mr. Gwynne, so if you do not mind, I shall give myself the pleasure of riding along with you for a short distance. I shall have to leave you soon, however, as I am due in the town by ten o'clock. You are too heavily laden, I see, to travel at top speed,—and that is the way I am obliged to ride, curse the luck. When I have set you straight at the branch of the roads a little way ahead, I shall use the spurs,—and see you later on."

"You are very kind. I will be pleased to have you jog along with me."

CHAPTER VI

SO this was Barry Lapelle. This was the wild rake who might yet become his brother-in-law, and whose sprightly enterprise had been frustrated by a woman who had, herself, stolen away in the dark of a far-off night.

As they rode slowly along, side by side, into the thick of the forest, Kenneth found himself studying the lover's face. He looked for the signs of the reckless dissipated life he was supposed to have led,—and found them not. Lapelle's eyes were bright and clear, his skin unblemished, his hand steady, his infrequent smile distinctly engaging. The slight, disdainful twist never left the corner of his mouth, however. It lurked there as a constant reminder to all the world that he, Barry Lapelle, was a devil of a fellow and was proud of it. While he was affable, there was no disguising the fact that he was also condescending. Unquestionably he was arrogant, domineering, even pompous at times, absolutely sure of himself.

He spoke with a slight drawl, in a mellow, agreeable voice, and with meticulous regard for the King's English,—an educated youth who had enjoyed advantages and associations uncommon to young men of the frontier. His untanned face testified to a life of ease and comfort, spent in sheltered places and not in the staining open, where sun and wind laid bronze upon the skin. A lordly fellow, decided Kenneth, and forthwith took a keen dislike for him. Nevertheless, it was not difficult to account for Viola's interest in him; nor, to a certain extent, the folly which led her to undertake the exploit of the night before. Barry Lapelle would have his way with women.

"You come from Kentucky, Mr. Gwynne," Lapelle was saying. "I am from Louisiana. My father came up to St. Louis a few years ago after establishing a line of steamboats between Terre Haute and the gulf. Two of our company's boats come as far north as Lafayette, so I spend considerable of my time there at this season of the year. You will find, sir, a number of Kentucky and Virginia people in this part of the state. Splendid stock, some of them. I understand you have spent several years in the East, at college and in pursuit of your study of the law."

"Principally in New York and Philadelphia," responded the other, subduing a smile. "My fame seems to have preceded me, Mr. Lapelle. Even in remote parts of the country I find my arrival anticipated. The farmer with whom I spent the night was thoroughly familiar with my affairs."

"You are an object of interest to every one in this section," said Lapelle, indifferently. "Where did you spend the night?"

"At the farm of a man named Striker,—Phineas Striker."

Lapelle started. His body appeared to stiffen in the saddle.

"Phineas Striker?" he exclaimed, with a swift, searching look into the speaker's eyes. Suddenly a flush mantled his cheek. "You were at Phineas Striker's last night?"

"Yes. We had lost our way and came to his place

just before the storm," said Kenneth, watching his companion narrowly. Lapelle's face was a study. Doubt, indecision, even dismay, were expressed in swift succession.

"Then you must have met,—but no, it isn't likely," he said, in some confusion.

Kenneth hesitated a moment, enjoying the other's discomfiture. Then he said: "I met no one there except my sister, who also happened to be spending the night with the Strikers."

The colour faded from Lapelle's face, leaving it a sickly white. "Were you in any way responsible for— well, for her departure, Mr. Gwynne?" he demanded, his eyes flaming with swift, sudden anger.

"I was not aware of her departure until I arose this morning, Mr. Lapelle. Striker informed me that she went away before sunrise."

For a moment Lapelle glared at him suspiciously, and then gave vent to a short, contemptuous laugh.

"A thousand apologies," he said, shrugging his shoulders. "I might have known you would not be consulted."

"I never laid eyes on my half-sister until last night," said Kenneth, determined to hold his temper. "It is not likely that she would have asked the advice of a total stranger, is it? Especially in so simple a matter as going home when she felt like it."

Lapelle shrugged his shoulders again. "I quite forgot that you are a lawyer, Mr. Gwynne," he said, drily. "Is it your purpose to hang out your shingle in the town of Lafayette?"

"My plans are indefinite."

"You could do worse, I assure you. The town is bound to grow. It will be an important town in a very

few years." And so the subject uppermost in the minds
of both was summarily dismissed.

They came at last to the point where a road branched
off to the right. The stillness was intense. There was
no sign of either human or animal life in the depths
of this wide, primeval forest.

"Follow this road," said Lapelle, pointing straight
ahead. "It will take you into the town. You will find
the bridge over Durkee's Run somewhat shaky after
the rain, but it is safe. I must leave you here. I shall
no doubt see you at Johnson's Inn, in case you intend
to stop there. Good morning, sir."

He lifted his hat and, touching the spirited mare
with the gad, rode swiftly away. A few hundred feet
ahead he overtook his mud-spattered friend and the
two of them were soon lost to sight among the trees.

Kenneth fell into profound cogitation. Evidently
Lapelle had waited at the edge of the forest for a report
of some description from the farmhouse belonging to
Rachel Carter. In all probability Viola was still at
the farm with her mother, and either she had sent a
message to her lover or had received one from him.
Or, it was possible, Lapelle had despatched his man to
the farmhouse to ascertain whether the girl was there,
or had been hurried on into the town by her mother.
In any case, the disgruntled lover was not content to
acknowledge himself thwarted or even discouraged by
the miscarriage of his plans of the night just ended.
Kenneth found himself wondering if the incomprehensible Viola would prove herself to be equally determined.
If so, they would triumph over opposition and be married, whether or no. He was conscious of an astounding, almost unbelievable desire to stand with Rachel
Carter in her hour of trouble.

His thoughts went back, as they had done more than once that morning, to Viola's artful account of his own father. He had felt sorry for her during and after the recital and now, with the truth revealed to him, he was even more concerned than before,—for he saw unhappiness ahead of her if she married this fellow Lapelle. He went even farther back and recalled his own caustic opinions of certain young rakes he had known in the East, wherein he had invariably asseverated that if he "had a sister he would sooner see her dead than married to that rascal." Well,—here he was with a sister,—and what was he to do about it?

Zachariah, observing the dark frown upon his master's face, and receiving no answer to a thrice repeated question, fell silent except for the almost inaudible hymn with which he invited consolation.

From afar in the thick wood now came the occasional report of a gun, proof that hunters were abroad. Many times Kenneth was roused from his reverie by the boom and whiz of pheasants, or the ring of a woodman's axe, or the lively scurrying of ground squirrels across his path. They forded three creeks before emerging upon a boggy, open space, covered with a mass of flattened, wind-broken reeds and swamp grass, in the centre of which lay a wide, still bayou partially fringed by willows with the first sickly signs of spring upon them in the shape of timid mole-ear leaves. Beyond the bridge over the canal-like stream which fed the bayou was a ridge of hills along whose base the road wound with tortuous indecision.

The first log cabin they had seen since entering the wood nestled among the scrub oaks of the hill hard by. The front wall of the hut was literally covered with the pegged-up skins of foxes, raccoons and what were described to Kenneth as the hides of "linxes," but which, in reality, were from the catamount. A tall, bewhiskered man, smoking a corncob pipe, leaned upon the rail fence, regarding the strangers with lazy interest.

Kenneth drew rein and inquired how far it was to Lafayette.

" 'Bout two mile an' a half," replied the man. "My name is Stain, Isaac Stain. I reckon you must be Mister Kenneth Gwynne. I heerd you'd be along this way some time this mornin'."

"I suppose Mr. Lapelle informed you that I was coming along behind," said Kenneth, smiling.

" 'Twuzn't Barry Lapelle as told me. I hain't seen him to-day."

"Didn't he pass here within the hour?"

"Nope," was the laconic response.

"I met him back along the road. He was coming this way."

"Must 'a' changed his mind."

"He probably took another road."

"There hain't no other road. I reckon he turned off into the wood an' 'lowed you to pass," said Mr. Stain slowly.

"But he was in great haste to reach town. He may have passed when you were not—"

"He didn't pass this place unless he was astraddle of an eagle er somethin' like that," declared the other, grinning. "An' even then he'd have to be flyin' purty doggone high ef I couldn't see him. Nope. I guess he took to the woods, Mr. Gwynne, for one reason er 'nother,—an' it must ha' been a mighty good reason, 'cause from what I know about Barry Lapelle he allus knows which way he's goin' to leap long before he leaps. He's sorter like a painter in that way."

Kenneth, knowing that he meant panther when he said painter, was properly impressed.

"It is very strange," he said, frowning. It was suddenly revealed to him that if Lapelle had tricked him it was because the messenger had brought word from Viola, at the farmhouse, and that the baffled lovers might even now be laying fresh plans to outwit the girl's mother. This fear was instantly dissipated by the next remark of Isaac Stain.

"Nope. It wuzn't him that told me about you, pardner. It wuz Violy Gwyn. She went by here with her ma, jes' as I wuz startin' off to look at my traps, —'long about seven o'clock, I reckon,—headed for town. She sez to me, sez she: 'Ike, there'll be a young man an' a darkey boy come ridin' this way some time this forenoon an' I want you to give him a message for me.' 'With pleasure,' sez I; 'anything you ask,' sez I. 'Well,' sez she, 'it's this. Fust you ask him ef his name is Kenneth Gwynne, an 'ef he sez it is, then you look an' see ef he is a tall feller an' very good-lookin', without a beard, an' wearin' a blue cape, an' when you see that he answers that description, why, you tell him to come an' see me as soon as he gits to town. Tell him it's very important.' 'All right,' sez I, 'I'll tell him.' "

"Where was her mother all this time?"

"Settin' right there in the buggy beside her, holdin' the reins. Where else would she be?"

"Did she say anything about my coming to see her daughter?"

"Nope. She never said anythin' 'cept 'Good mornin', Ike,' an' I sez 'Good mornin', Mrs. Gwyn.' She don't talk much, she don't. You see, she's in mournin' fer her husband. I guess he wuz your pa, wuzn't he?"

"Yes," said Kenneth briefly. "Was there anything else?"

"Nothin' to amount to anything. Violy sez, 'When did you get the linx skins, Ike?' an' I sez, 'Last Friday, Miss Violy,' an' she sez, 'Ain't they beautiful?' an' I sez—"

"She wants me to come to her house?" broke in Kenneth, his brow darkening.

"I reckon so."

"Well, I thank you, Mr. Stain. You are very kind to have waited so long for me to arrive. I—"

"Oh, I'd do a whole lot more'n that fer her," said the hunter quickly. "You see, I've knowed her ever since she wuz knee-high to a duck. She wuzn't more'n five or six when I brung her an' her folks up the Wabash in my perogue, all the way from Vincennes, an' it wuz me that took her down to St. Louis when she went off to school—her an' some friends of her pa's. Skinny, gangling sort of a young 'un she wuz, but let me tell you, as purty as a picter. I allus said she'd be the purtiest woman in all creation when she got her growth an' filled out, an', by hokey, I wuz right. Yes, sir, I used to run a boat on the river down below, but I give it up quite awhile ago an' come up here to live like a gentleman." He waved his hand proudly over his acre and a half estate. "I wuz talkin' to Bill Digby not long ago an' he sez this is a wonderful location for a town, right here at the fork of two o' the best fishin' cricks in the state. An' Bill he'd ort to know, 'cause he's laid out more towns than anybody I know of. The only trouble with Bill is that as soon as he lays 'em out somebody comes along an' offers him a hundred dollars er so fer 'em, er a team of hosses, er a good coon dog, an' he up an' sells. Now, with me, I— Got to be movin' along, have you? Well, good-bye, an' be a little keerful when you come to Durkee's Run bridge. It's kinder wobbly."

They were fording a creek some distance beyond Stain's cabin when Kenneth broke the silence that had followed the conversation with the hunter by exploding violently:

"Under no circumstances,—and that's all there is to it."

Zachariah, ever ready to seize an opportunity to raise his voice, either in expostulation or agreement, took this as a generous opening. He exclaimed with commendable feeling:

"Yas, suh! Undeh no suckemstances! No, suh!"

"It is not even to be thought of," declared his master, frowning heavily.

"No, suh! We can't even think about it, Marse Kenneth," said Zachariah, a trifle less decisively.

"So that is the end of it,—absolutely the end."

"Dat's what Ah say,—yas, suh, dat's what Ah say all along, suh!"

His master suddenly turned upon him. "I cannot go to that woman's house. It is unthinkable, Zachariah."

Zachariah began to see light. "Yo' all got to be mighty car'ful 'bout dese yere strange women, Marse Kenneth. Don' you forget what done happen in 'at ole Garden of Eden. Dis yere old Eve, she—"

"Still I am greatly relieved to know that she is in town and not out on the farm. It *is* a relief, isn't it, Zachariah?"

"Yas, suh,—hit sho'ly am."

They progressed slowly up a long hill and came to an extensive clearing, over which perhaps half a dozen farmhouses were scattered. Beyond this open space

they entered a narrow strip of wood and, upon emerging, had their first glimpse of the Wabash River.

Stopping at the brow of the hill, they looked long
and curiously over the valley into which they were
about to descend. The panorama was magnificent.
To the left flowed the swollen, turgid river, high among
the willows and sycamores that guarded the low-lying
bank. Far to the north it could be seen, a clayish,
ugly monster, crawling down through the heart of the
bowl-like depression. Mile after mile of sparsely
wooded country lay revealed to the gaze of the travellers, sunken between densely covered ridges, one on
either side of the river. Half a mile beyond where
they stood feathery blue plumes of smoke rose out of
the tree tops and, dispersing, floated away on the
breeze,—and there lay the town of Lafayette, completely hidden from view.

The road wound down the hill and across a clumsily
constructed bridge spanning the Run and thence along
the flat shelf that rimmed the bottom-land, through
a maze of wild plum and hazel brush squatting, as it
were, at the feet of the towering forest giants that
covered the hills.

Presently the travellers came upon widely separated
cabins and gardens, and then, after passing through
a lofty grove, found themselves entering the town
itself. Signs of life and enterprise greeted them from
all sides. Here, there and everywhere houses were in
process of erection,—log-cabins, frame structures, and
even an occasional brick dwelling-place. Turning into
what appeared to be a well-travelled road,—(he afterwards found it to be Wabash Street), Kenneth came
in the course of a few minutes to the centre of the
town. Here was the little brick courthouse and the

jail, standing in the middle of a square which still contained the stumps of many of the trees that originally had flourished there. At the southwest corner of the square was the tavern, a long story and a half log house,—and it was a welcome sight to Gwynne and his servant, both of whom were ravenously hungry by this time.

The former observed, with considerable satisfaction, that there were quite a number of substantial looking buildings about the square, mostly stores, all of them with hitching-racks along the edge of the dirt sidewalks. As far as the eye could reach, in every direction, the muddy streets were lined with trees.

Half a dozen men were standing in front of the tavern when the newcomers rode up. Kenneth dismounted and threw the reins to his servant. Landlord Johnson hurried out to greet him.

CHAPTER VII

THE END OF THE LONG ROAD

"WE'VE been expecting you, Mr. Gwynne," he said in his most genial manner. "Step right in. Dinner'll soon be ready, and I reckon you must be hungry. Take the hosses around to the stable, nigger, and put 'em up. I allowed you'd be delayed some by the bad roads, but I guess you must have got a late start this mornin' from Phin Striker's. Mrs.—er—ahem! I mean your step-mother sent word that you were on the way and to have accommodations ready for you. Say, I'd like to make you acquainted with—"

"My step-mother sent word to you?" demanded Kenneth, incredulously.

"She did. What would you expect her to do, long as she knew you were headed this way? I admit she isn't specially given to worryin' about other people's comforts, but, when you get right down to it, I guess she considers you a sort of connection of hers, spite of everything, and so she lays herself out a little. But I want to tell you one thing, Mr. Gwynne, you're not going to find her particularly cordial, as the sayin' is. She's about as stand-offish and unneighbourly as a Kickapoo Indian. But, as I was sayin', I'd like to make you acquainted with some of our leadin' citizens. This is Daniel Bugher, the recorder, and Doctor Davis, Matt Scudder, Tom Benbridge and John McCormick. It was moved and seconded, soon as you heaved in sight, that we repair at once to Sol Hamer's grocery for a little——"

"Excuse me," broke in Kenneth, laughing; "I have heard of that grocery, and I think it would be wise for me to become a little better acquainted with my surroundings before I begin trading there."

The landlord rubbed his chin and the other gentlemen laughed uproariously.

"Well," said the former, "I can see one thing mighty plain. You're going to be popular with my wife and all the other women in town. They'll point to you and say to practically nine-tenths of the married men in Lafayette: 'There's a man that don't drink, and goodness knows *he* isn't a preacher!'"

"I am hardly what you would call a teetotaler, gentlemen," said Gwynne, still smiling.

"Wait till you get down with a spell of the Wabash shakes," said Mr. McCormick. "That'll make a new man of him, won't it, Doc?"

"Depends somewhat on his constitution and the way he was brought up," said the doctor, with a professional frown which slowly relaxed into an unprofessional smile.

"I was brought up by my grandmother," explained Kenneth, vastly amused.

"That settles it," groaned Mr. Johnson. "You're not long for this world. Before we go in I wish you'd take a look at the new courthouse. We're mighty proud of that building. There isn't a finer courthouse in the state of Indiana,—or maybe I'd better say there won't be if it's ever finished."

"I noticed it as I came by," said the newcomer, dismissing the structure with a glance. "If you will conduct me to my room, Mr. Johnson, I——"

"Just a second," broke in the landlord, his gaze fixed on a horseman who had turned into the street some distance below. "Here comes Barry Lapelle,—down there by that clump of sugar trees. He's the most elegant fellow we've got in town, and you'll want to know him. Makes Lafayette his headquarters most of the—"

"I have met Mr. Lapelle," interrupted Kenneth. "This morning, out in the country."

"You don't say so!" exclaimed Johnson. The citizens exchanged a general look of surprise.

"Thought you said he went down the river on yesterday's boat," said Scudder.

"That's just what he did," said Johnson, puzzled. "Packed some of his things and said he'd be gone a week or so. He must have got off at Attica,—but, no, he couldn't have got here this soon by road. By glory, I hope the boat didn't strike a snag or a rock, or run ashore somewhere. Looks kind of serious, boys."

"Couldn't he have landed almost anywhere in a skiff?" inquired Gwynne, his eyes on the approaching horseman.

"Certainly he could,—but why? He had business down at Covington, he said."

"He told me this morning he had very important business here. That is why he could not ride in with me," said Kenneth, affecting indifference. "By the way, is he riding his own horse?"

"Yes," said Benbridge. "That's his mare Fancy,— thoroughbred filly by King Philip out of Shawnee Belle. He sent her down to Joe Fell's to stud yesterday and— Say, that accounts for him being on her now. You made a good guess, Mr. Gwynne. He must have landed at La Grange, rowed across the river, and hoofed it up to Fell's farm. But what do you suppose made him change his mind so suddenly?"

"He'll probably tell you to go to thunder if you ask him," said the landlord.

"I'm not going to ask him anything," retorted Benbridge.

"He's working tooth and nail against the Wabash and Erie Canal that's projected to run from Lake Erie to the mouth of the Tippecanoe, Mr. Gwynne," said one of the citizens. "But it's coming through in spite of him and all the rest of the river hogs."

"I see," said the young man, a grim smile playing about his lips.

He knew that the mare Fancy had been in waiting for her master when he clambered ashore on the river bank opposite La Grange, and he also suspected that the little steamboat had remained tied up at the landing all night long and well into the morning, expecting two passengers who failed to come aboard. He could not suppress a chuckle of satisfaction.

Lapelle rode up at this instant and, throwing the bridle rein to a boy who had come running up from the stable, dismounted quickly. He came straight to Gwynne, smiling cordially.

"I see you beat me in. After we parted I decided to cut through the woods to have a look at Jack Moxley's keel boat, stuck in the mud on this side of the river. You'd think the blame fool would have sense enough to keep well out in mid stream at a time like this. Happy to have you here with us, and I hope you will like us well enough to stay."

"Thank you. I shall like you all better after I have had something to eat," said Kenneth.

"And drink," added Lapelle. It was then that Kenneth noticed that his eyes were slightly blurred and his voice a trifle thick. He had been drinking.

"What turned you back, Barry?" inquired McCormick. "Thought you were to be gone a week or—"

"Changed my mind," said Lapelle curtly, and then, apparently on second thought, added: "I got off the boat at La Grange and crossed over to spend the night at Martin Hawk's, the man you saw with me this morning, Mr. Gwynne. He is a hunter down Middleton way. I fish and hunt with him a good deal. Well, I reckon I'd better go in and get out of these muddy boots and pants."

Without another word, he strode up the steps, across the porch and into the tavern, his head high, his gait noticeably unsteady.

"Martin Hawk!" growled the landlord. "The orneriest cuss this side of hell. Plain no-good scalawag. Barry'll find it out some day, and then maybe he'll wish he had paid some attention to what I've been tellin' him."

"Wouldn't surprise me a bit if Mart knows a whole lot more about what became of some mighty good yearlin' colts that used to belong to honest men down on the Wea," said one of the group, darkly.

"I wouldn't trust Mart Hawk as far as I could throw a thousand pound rock," observed Mr. Johnson, compressing his lips. "Well, come on in, Mr. Gwynne, and slick up a bit. The dinner bell will be ringin' in a few minutes, and I want you to meet the cook before you risk eatin' any of her victuals. My wife's the cook, so you needn't look scared. Governor Noble almost died of over-feedin' the last time he was here,—but that wasn't her fault. And my daughters, big and little, seem anxious to get acquainted with the celebrated

Kenneth Gwynne. People have been talkin' so much about you for the last six months that nearly everybody calls you by your first name, and Jim Crouch's wife is so taken with it that she has made up her mind to call her baby Kenneth,—that is, providing nature does the right thing. Next week some time, ain't it, Doc?"

"That's what most everybody in town says, Bob," replied the doctor solemnly, "so I guess it must be true."

"We begin counting the inhabitants of the town as far as a month ahead sometimes," explained Mr. McCormick drily. "I don't know as we've been out of the way more than a day or a day-and-a-half on any baby that's been born here in the last two years. Hope to see you in my store down there, Mr. Gwynne—any time you're passing that way. You can't miss it. It's just across the street from that white frame building with the green stripes running criss-cross on the front door, —Joe Hanna's store."

"Robert Gwyn's son is always welcome at my store and my home," said another cordially. "We didn't know till last fall that he had a son, and—well, I hope you don't mind my saying we couldn't believe it at first."

"You spell the name different from the way he spelled it," answered Bugher, the recorder. "I noticed it in your letters, and it struck me as queer."

"My father appears to have reverted to the original way of spelling the name," said Kenneth, from the upper step. "My forebears were Welsh, you see. The manner of spelling it was changed when they came to America, over a hundred years ago."

His bedroom was in the small wing off the dining-

room. Its one window looked out upon the courthouse,
the view being somewhat restricted by the presence of
a pair of low-branched oak trees in the side-yard,
almost within arm's length of the wall,—they were so
close, in fact, that their limbs stretched out over the
rough shingle roof, producing in the wind an everlasting sound of scratching and scraping. There was a
huge four-poster feather bed of mountainous proportions, leaving the occupant scant space in which to
move about the room.

"Last people to occupy this room," said Mr. Johnson, standing in the doorway, "were George Ripley
and Edna Cole, three weeks ago last night. They
came in from the Grand Prairie and only stayed the
one night. Had to get back to the farm next day on
account of it bein' wash-day. I guess I forgot to say
they were on their weddin'-trip. Generally speaking,
it takes about three years for people to get over callin'
a girl by her maiden name,—so you needn't think there
was anything wrong about George and Edna stayin'
here. I wish you could have been here to drive out to
the infare at her pa's house two nights after the weddin'. It was the biggest ever held on that side of the
river,—and as for the shiveree,—my Lord, it *was* something to talk about. Tin cans, cowbells, shot-guns,
tenor-drums,—but I'm keeping you, Mr. Gwynne.
You'll find water in that jug over there, and a towel
by the lookin' glass. Come out when you're ready."

When Kenneth returned to the dining-room, he found
Johnson waiting there with his wife and two of his
comely daughters. They were presented to the new
guest with due informality, and then the landlord went
out upon the front porch to ring the dinner-bell.

"I guess you won't be stayin' here long, Mr. Gwynne,"

said Mrs. Johnson. "Your mother,—I should say, your step-mother,—has got your house all ready for you to move right in. Job Turner moved out last week, and she took some of the furniture and things over so's you could be sort of at home right away." Observing his start, and the sudden tightening of his lips, she went on complacently: " 'Twasn't much trouble for her. Your house isn't more than fifty yards from hers,—just across lots, you might say. She—"

Kenneth, forgetting himself in his agitation, interrupted her with the startling question:

"Where does Rachel Carter live?"

"Rachel who?"

He collected his wits, stammering:

"I believe that was her name before she—before she married my father."

"Oh, I see. Her name is Rachel, of course. Well, her house is up Columbia street,—that's the one on the other side of the square,—almost to the hill where Isaac Edwards has his brickyard, just this side of the swamp."

After dinner, which was eaten at a long table in company with eight or ten "customers," to whom he was introduced by the genial host, he repaired to the office of Recorder Bugher.

"Everything's in good shape," announced Bugher. "There ain't a claim against the property, now that Mrs. Gwyn has given up her idea of contesting the will. The property is in your name now, Mr. Gwynne, —and that reminds me that your father, in his will, spells your name with a double n and an e, while he spells hers with only one n. He took into consideration the fact that you spelled your name in the new-fangled way, as you say he used to spell it in Kentucky. And that also accounts for his signing the will 'Robert Gwyn, formerly known as Robert Gwynne.' It's legal, all right, properly witnessed and attested by two reliable men of this county."

"I have seen a copy of the will."

"Another queer thing about it is that he bequeathed certain property to you as 'my son, Kenneth Gwynne,' —while he fails to mention his daughter Viola at all, except to say that he bequeaths so-and-so to 'Rachel Gwyn, to give, bequeath and devise as she sees fit.' Of course, Viola, by law, is entitled to a share of the estate and it should have been so designated. Judge Wylie says she can contest the will if she so desires, on the ground that she is entitled to as much as you, Mr. Gwynne. But she has decided to let it stand as it is, and I guess she's sensible. All that her mother now has will go to her when said Rachel dies, and as it will be a full half of the estate instead of what might have been only a third, I guess she's had pretty good advice from some one."

"The fact that my half-sister was not mentioned in the will naturally led me to conclude that no such person existed. I did not know till this morning, Mr. Bugher, that I had a half-sister."

"Well," began the recorder, pursing his lips, "for that matter she didn't know she had a half-brother till the will was read, so she was almost as ignorant as you."

"It's all very strange,—exceedingly strange."

"When did your own mother die, if it's a fair question?"

"In the year 1812. My father was away when she died."

"Off to the war, I suppose."

"Yes," said the young man steadily. "Off to the war," he lied, still staring out of the window. "I was left with my grandparents when he went off to make his fortune in this new country. It was not until I was fairly well grown that we heard that he was married to a woman named Rachel Carter."

"Well, I guess it's something you don't like to talk about," said Mr. Bugher, and turned his attention to the records they were consulting.

Later the young man called at the office of Mr. Cornell, the lawyer who had charge of his affairs. He had come to Lafayette prepared to denounce Rachel Carter, to drive her in shame and disgrace from the town, if necessary. Now he found himself confronted by a condition that distressed and perplexed him; his bitter resolve was rudely shaken and he was in a dire state of uncertainty. He was faced by a most unexpected and staggering situation.

To denounce Rachel Carter would be to deliberately strike a cruel, devastating blow at the happiness and peace of an innocent person,—Viola Gwyn, his own half-sister. A word from him, and that lovely girl, serene in her beliefs, would be crushed for life. The whole scheme of life had been changed for him in the twinkling of an eye, as it were. He could not wreak vengeance upon Rachel Carter without destroying Viola Gwyn,—and the mere thought of that caused him to turn cold with repugnance. How could he publish Rachel Carter's infamy to the world with that innocent girl standing beside her to receive and sustain the worst of the shock? Impossible! Viola must be spared,—and so with her, Rachel Carter!

Then there was the strange message he had received from Viola, through the hunter, Stain. What was

back of the earnest request for him to come and see
her at her mother's house? Was she in trouble? Was
she in need of his help? Was she depending upon him,
her blood relation, for counsel in an hour of duress?
He was sadly beset by conflicting emotions.

In the course of his interview with the lawyer, from
whom he had decided to withhold much that he had
meant to divulge, he took occasion to inquire into the
present attitude of Rachel Carter,—or ·Gwyn, as he
reluctantly spoke of her,—toward him, an open and
admitted antagonist.

"Well," said Cornell, shaking his head, "I don't believe you will catch her asking any favours of you.
She has laid down her arms, so to speak, but that
doesn't mean she intends to be friendly. As a matter
of fact, she simply accepts the situation,—with very
bad grace, of course,—but she'll never be able to alter
her nature or her feelings. She considers herself
cheated, and that's all there is to it. I doubt very
much whether she will even speak to you, Mr. Gwynne.
She is a strange woman, and a hard one to understand. She fought desperately against your coming
here at all. One of her propositions was that she
should be allowed to buy your share of the estate, if
such a transaction could be arranged, you will remember. You declined to consider it. This was after she
withdrew her proposed contest of the will. Then she
got certain Crawfordsville men interested in the purchase of your land, and they made you a bona fide offer,
—I think they offered more than the property is worth,
by the way. I think, back of everything, she could
not bear the thought of you, the son of a former wife,
living next door to her. Jealousy, I suppose,—but
not unnatural, after all, in a second wife, is it?

They're usually pretty cantankerous when it comes to the first wife's children. As regards her present attitude, I think she'll let you alone if you let her alone."

"My sister has asked me to come up to the house to see her this afternoon," said Kenneth.

The lawyer looked surprised. "Is that so? Well," with a puzzled frown, "I don't quite understand how she came to do that. I was under the impression that she felt about as bitterly toward you as her mother does. In fact, she has said some rather nasty things about you. Boasted to more than one of her friends that she would slap your face if you ever tried to speak to her."

Kenneth smiled, a reminiscent light in his eyes. "She has done so, figuratively speaking, Mr. Cornell. I am confident she hates me,—but if that's the case, why should she leave word for me to come and see her?"

"Experience has taught me that women have a very definite object in view when they let on as if they had changed their minds," was the judicial opinion of Mr. Cornell. "Maybe they don't realize it, but they are as wily as the devil when they think, and you think, and everybody else thinks, they're behaving like an angel. It's not for me to say whether you should go to see her or not, but I believe I would if I were in your place. Maybe she has made up her mind to be friendly, on the surface at least, and as you are bound to meet each other at people's houses, parties, and all such, perhaps it would be better to bury the hatchet. I think you will be quite safe in going up there to-day, so far as Mrs. Gwyn is concerned. She will not appear on the scene, I am confident. You will not come in contact with her. You say that she has put some of her furniture at your disposal, but she doubtless did so on the advice of her lawyer. You must not forget that your father, in his will, left half of his personal effects to you. She is just smart enough to select in advance the part that she is willing for you to have, feeling that you will not be captious about it."

"I have no desire to exact anything of—"

"Quite so, quite so," broke in the lawyer. "But she could not be expected to know that. She is a long-headed woman, Mr. Gwynne. I suspect she is considerably worried about Viola. Your half-sister is being rather assiduously courted by a young man named Lapelle. Mrs. Gwyn does not approve of him. She is strait-laced and—er—puritanical."

"Puritanical, eh?" said Kenneth, with a short laugh that Mr. Cornell totally misinterpreted.

"Barry isn't exactly what you would call sanctimonious," admitted the lawyer, with a dry smile. "The worst of it is, I'm afraid Viola is in love with him."

His client was silent for a moment, reflecting. Then he arose abruptly and announced:

"I agree with you, Mr. Cornell. I will go up to see her this afternoon. I bear her no grudge,—and after all, she is my sister. Good day, sir. I shall give myself the pleasure of calling in to see you to-morrow."

CHAPTER VIII

KENNETH strolled about the town for awhile before returning to the tavern to shave, change his boots, and "smarten" himself up a bit in preparation for the ceremonious call he had dreaded to make. On all sides he encountered the friendliest interest and civility from the townspeople. The news of his arrival had spread over the place with incredible swiftness. Scores of absolute strangers turned to him and tendered to him the welcome to be found in a broad and friendly smile.

Shortly after three o'clock he set forth upon his new adventure. Assailed by a strange and unaccustomed timidity,—he would have called it bashfulness had Viola been other than his sister—he approached the young lady's home by the longest and most round-about way, a course which caused him to make the complete circuit of the three-acre pond situated a short distance above the public square—a shallow body of water dignified during the wet season of the year by the high-sounding title of "Lake Stansbury," but spoken of scornfully as the "slough" after the summer's sun had reduced its surface to a few scattered wallows, foul and green with scum. It was now full of water and presented quite an imposing appearance to the new citizen as he skirted its brush-covered banks; in his ignorance he was counting the probability of one day building a handsome home on the edge of this tiny lake.

118

A man working in a garden pointed out to him Mrs. Gwyn's house half-hidden among the trees at the foot of a small slope.

"That other house, a couple of hundred foot further on,—you can just see it from here,—well, that belonged to Robert Gwyn. I understand his long-lost son is comin' to live in it one of these days. They say this boy when he was a baby was stolen by the Injins and never heard of ag'in until a few months ago. Lived with the Injins right up to the time he was found and couldn't speak a word of English. I have heard that he—what are ye laughin' at, mister?"

"I was laughing at the thought of how surprised you are going to be some day, my friend. Thank you. The house with the green window blinds, you say?"

He proceeded first to the house that was to be his home. It was a good stone's throw from the pretentious two-story frame structure in which Rachel Carter and her daughter lived, but nearer the centre of the town when approached by a more direct route than he had followed. This smaller house, an insignificant, weather-beaten story and a half frame, snuggling among the underbrush, was where his father had lived when he first came to Lafayette. Later on he had erected the larger house and moved into it with his family, renting the older place to a man named Turner.

It was faced by a crudely constructed picket fence, once white but now mottled with scales of dirty sunblistered paint, and inside the fence rank weeds, burdocks and wild grass flourished without hindrance. He strode up the narrow path to the low front door. Finding it unlocked, he opened it and stepped into the low, roughly plastered sitting-room. The window blinds

were open, permitting light and air to enter, and while
the room was comparatively bare, there was ample evidence that it had been made ready for occupancy by
a hand which, though niggardly, was well trained in
the art of making a little go a long way. The bedroom and the kitchen were in order. There were rag
carpets on the floors, and the place was immaculately
clean. A narrow, enclosed stairway ran from the end
of the sitting-room to the attic, where he discovered a
bed for his servant. Out at the back was the stable
and a wagonshed. These he did not inspect. A high
rail fence stretched between the two yards.

As he walked up the path to the front door of the
new house, he was wondering how Viola Gwyn would
look in her garb of black,—the hated black she had
cast aside for one night only. He was oppressed by
a dull, cold fear, assuaged to some extent by the thrill
of excitement which attended the adventure. What
was he to do or say if the door was opened by Rachel
Carter? His jaw was set, the palms of his hands were
moist, and there was a strange, tight feeling about
his chest, as if his lungs were full and could not be
emptied. After a moment's hesitation, he rapped firmly
on the door with his bare knuckles.

The door was opened by a young coloured woman
who wore a blue sunbonnet and carried a red shawl
over her arm.

"Is Miss Viola at home?" he inquired.

"Is dis Mistah Gwynne, suh?"

"Yes."

"Come right in, suh, an' set down."

He entered a small box of a hallway, opening upon
a steep set of stairs.

"Right in heah, suh," said the girl, throwing open
a door at his left.

As he walked into this room, he heard the servant
shuffling up the staircase. He deposited his hat and
gloves on a small marble-top table in the centre of the
room and then sent a swift look of investigation about
him. Logs were smouldering in the deep, wide fireplace
at the far end of the room, giving out little spurts of
flame occasionally from their charred, ash-grey skeletons. The floor was covered with a bright, new rag
carpet, and there was a horse-hair sofa in the corner,
and two or three stiff, round-backed little chairs, the
seats also covered with black horse-hair. A thick, gilt-
decorated Holy Bible lay in the centre of the marble-
top table, shamed now by contact with the crown of his
unsaintly hat. On the mantel stood a large, flat ma-
hogany clock with floral decorations and a broad, white
face with vivid black numerals and long black hands.
The walls were covered with a gaudy but expensive
paper, in which huge, indescribable red flowers mingled regularly with glaring green leaves. Two
"mottoes," worked in red and blue worsted and framed
with narrow cross-pieces of oak, hung suspended in
the corners beside the fireplace. One of them read
"God Bless Our Home," the other a sombre line done
in black: "Faith, Hope and Charity."

Three black oval oak frames, laden with stiff leaves
that glistened under a coat of varnish, contained
faded, unlovely portraits,—one of a bewhiskered man
wearing a tall beaver hat and a stiff black stock: another of a sloping-shouldered woman with a bonnet,
from which a face, vague and indistinct, sought vainly
to emerge. The third contained a mass of dry, brown

leaves, some wisps of straw, and a few colourless pressed blossoms.   On a table in front of one of the two windows stood a spindling Dutch lamp of white and delft blue, with a long, narrow chimney.   There were two candlesticks on the mantel.

All these features of the room he took in while he stood beside the centre table, awaiting the entrance of Viola Gwyn.   He heard a door open softly and close upstairs, and then some one descending the steps; a few words spoken in the subdued voice of a woman and the less gentle response of the darky servant, who mumbled "Yas'm," and an instant later went out by the front door.   Through the window he saw her go down the walk, the red shawl drawn tightly about her shoulders.

He smiled.   The clever Viola getting rid of the servant so that she could be alone with him, he thought, as he turned toward the door.

A tall woman in black appeared in the doorway, paused there for a second or two, and then advanced slowly into the room.   He felt the blood rush to his head, almost blinding him.   His hand went out for the support of the table, his body stiffened and suddenly turned cold.   The smile with which he intended to greet Viola froze on his lips.

"God Al—" started to ooze from his stiff lips, but the words broke off sharply as the woman stopped a few steps away and regarded him steadily, silently, unsmilingly.   He stood there like a statue staring into the dark, brilliant eyes, sunken deep under the straight black eyebrows.   Even in the uncertain light from the curtained windows he could see that her face was absolutely colourless,—the pallor of death seemed to have been laid upon it.   Swiftly she lifted a hand to her throat, her eyes closed for a second and then flew wide open again, now filled with an expression of utter bewilderment.

"Is it—is it you, Robert? Is it really you, or am I—" she murmured, scarcely above a whisper. Once more she closed her eyes, tightly; as if to shut out the vision of a ghost,—an unreal thing that would not be there when she looked again.

The sound of her voice released him from the brief spell of stupefaction.

"I know you. I remember you. You are Rachel Carter," he said hoarsely.

She was staring at him as if fascinated. Her lips moved, but no sound issued from them.

He hesitated for an instant and then turned to pick up his hat and gloves. "I came to see your daughter, madame,—as well you know. Permit me to take my departure."

"You are so like your—" she began with an effort, her voice deep and low with emotion. "So like him I— I was frightened. I thought he had—" She broke off abruptly, lowered her head in an attempt to hide from him the trembling lips and chin, and to regain, if possible, the composure that had been so desperately shaken. "Wait!" she cried, stridently. "Wait! Do not go away. Give me time to—to—"

"There is no need for us to prolong—" he began in a harsh voice.

"I will not keep you long," she interrupted, every trace of emotion vanishing like a shadow that has passed. She was facing him now, her head erect, her voice steady. Her dark, cavernous eyes were upon him; he experienced an odd, indescribable sensation,— as of shrinking,—and without being fully aware of what he was doing, replaced his hat upon the table, an act which signified involuntary surrender on his part.

"Where is Viola?" he demanded sternly. "She left word for me to come here. Where is she?"

"She is not here," said the woman.

He started. "You don't mean she has—has gone away with—"

"No. She has gone over to spend the afternoon with Effie Wardlow. I will be frank with you. This is not the time for misunderstanding. She asked Isaac Stain to give you that message at my request,—or command, if you want the truth. I sent her away because what I have to say to you must be said in private. There is no one in the house besides ourselves. Will you do me the favour to be seated? Very well; we will stand."

She turned away to close the hall door. Then she walked to one of the windows and, drawing the curtain aside, swept the yard and adjacent roadway with a long, searching look.

The strong light fell full upon her face; its warmth seemed suddenly to paint the glow of life upon her pallid skin. He gazed at her intently. Out of the past there came to him with startling vividness the face of the Rachel Carter he had known. Despite the fact that she was now an old woman,—he knew that she must be at least forty-six or -seven,—she was still remarkably handsome. She was very tall, deep-chested, and as straight as an arrow. Her smoothly brushed hair was as black as the raven's wing. Time and the toil of long, hard hours had brought deep furrows to her cheeks, like lines chiselled in a face of marble, but they had not broken the magnificent body of the Rachel Carter who used to toss him joyously into the air with her strong young arms and sure hands. But there was left no sign of the broad, rollicking smile that always attended those gay rompings. Her lips were firm-set, straight and unyielding,—a hard mouth flanked by what seemed to be absolutely immovable lines. Her chin was square; her nose firm and noticeably "hawk-like" in shape; her eyes clear, brilliant and keenly penetrating.

She faced him, standing with her back to the light.

"Sooner or later we would have had to meet," she said. "It is best for both of us to have it over with at the very start."

"I suppose you are right," said he stiffly. "You know how I feel toward you, Rachel Carter. There is nothing either of us can say that will make the situation easier or harder, for that matter."

"Yes,—I understand," said she calmly. "You hate me. You have been brought up to hate me. I do not question the verdict of those who condemned me, but you may as well understand at once that I do not regret what I did twenty years ago. I have not repented. I shall never repent. We need not discuss that side of the question any farther. You know my history, Kenneth Gwynne. You are the only person in this part of the world who does know it. When the controversy first came up over the settlement of your father's estate, I feared that you would reveal the story of my—"

He held up his hand, interrupting her. "Permit me to observe, Rachel Carter, that for many months after being notified of my father's death and the fact that he had left me a portion of his estate, I was without positive proof as to the identity of the woman mentioned in the correspondence as his widow. It was not until a copy of the will was forwarded to me that I was sure. By that time I had made up my mind to keep my own counsel. I can say to you now, Rachel Carter, that I do not intend to rake up that ugly story. I do not make war on helpless women."

Her lips writhed slightly, and her eyes narrowed as if with pain. It was but a fleeting exposition of vulnerability, however, for in another instant she had recovered.

"You could not have struck harder than that if you had been warring against a strong man," she said gently.

A hot flush stained his cheek. "It is the way I feel, nevertheless, Rachel Carter," he said deliberately.

"You can think of me only as Rachel Carter," she said. "My name is Rachel Gwyn. Still it doesn't matter. I am past the point where I can be hurt. You may tell the story if it suits your purpose. I shall deny nothing. It may even give you some satisfaction to see me wrap my soiled robes about me and steal away, leaving the field to you. I can sell my lands tomorrow and disappear. It will matter little whether I am forgotten or not. The world is large and I am not without fortitude. I wanted you to come here today, to see me alone, to hear what I have to say,— not about myself,—but about another. I am a woman of quick decisions. When I learned early this morning that you would be in Lafayette to-day, I made up my mind to take a certain step,—and I have not changed it."

"If you are referring to your daughter—to my half-sister, if you will—I have only to remind you that my mind is already made up. You need have no fear that I shall do or say anything to hurt that innocent girl. I am assuming, of course, that she knows nothing of—well, of what happened back there in Kentucky."

"She knows nothing," said the woman, in a voice strangely low and tense. "If she ever knew, she has forgotten."

"Forgotten?" he cried. "Good God, how could she have forgotten a thing so—"

She moved a step nearer, her burning eyes fixed on his.

"You remember Rachel Carter well enough. Have you no recollection of the little girl you used to play with? Minda? The babe who could scarcely toddle when you—"

"Of course I remember her," he cried impatiently. "I remember everything. You took her away with you and—why did you not leave her behind as my father left me? Why could you not have been as fair to your child as he was to his?"

She was silent for a moment, pondering her answer. "I do not suppose it has ever occurred to you that I might have loved my child too deeply to abandon her," she said, a strange softness in her voice.

"My father loved me," he cried out, "and yet he left me behind."

"He loved you,—yes,—but he would not take you. He left you with some one who also loved you. Don't ever forget that, Kenneth Gwynne. I would not go without Minda. No more would your mother have gone without you. Stop! I did not mean to offend. So you *do* remember little Minda?"

"Yes, I remember her. But she is dead. Why do you mention her—"

"Minda is not dead," said she slowly.

"Not—why, she was drowned in the—"

"No. Minda is alive. You saw her last night,—at Phineas Striker's house."

He started violently. "The girl I saw last night was —Minda?" he cried. "Why, Striker told me she was—"

"I know,—I know," she interrupted impatiently. "Striker told you what he believed to be true. He told you she was Robert Gwyn's daughter and your half-sister. But I tell you now that she is Minda Carter. There is not a drop of Gwyn blood in her body."

"Then, she is not my half-sister?" he exclaimed, utterly dazed, but aware of the exquisite sensation of relief that was taking hold of him.

"She is no blood relation of yours."

"But she is,—yes, now I understand,—she is my step-sister," he said, with a swift fall of spirits.

"I suppose that is what you might call her," said Rachel Gwyn, indifferently. "I have not given it much thought."

"Does she know that she is not my father's daughter?"

"No. She believes herself to be his own flesh and blood,—his own daughter," said she with the deliberateness of one weighing her words, that they might fall with full force upon her listener.

"Why are you telling me all this?" he demanded abruptly. "What is your object? If she does not know the truth, why should I? Good God, woman, you—you do not expect *me* to tell her, do you? Was that your purpose in getting me here? You want me to tell her that—"

"No!" she cried out sharply. "I do not want you

or any one else to do that. Listen to me. I sha'n't beat about the bush,—I will not waste words. So far as Viola and the world are concerned, she is Robert Gwyn's daughter. That is clear to you, is it not? She was less than two years old when we came away,—too young to remember anything. We were in the wilderness for two or three years, and she saw but one or two small children, so that it was a very simple matter to deceive her about her age. She is nearly twenty-two now, although she believes she is but nineteen. She does not remember any other father than Robert Gwyn. She has no recollection of her own father, nor does she remember you. She—"

"Last night she described her father to me," he interrupted. "Her supposed father, I mean. She made it quite plain that he did not love her as a father should love his own child."

"It was not that," she said. "He was afraid of her,—mortally afraid of her. He lived in dread of the day when she would learn the truth and turn upon him. He always meant to tell her himself, and yet he could not find the courage. Toward the end he could not bear to have her near him. It would not be honest in me to say that he loved her. I do not believe he would have loved a child if one had come to him and me,—no child of mine could take the place you had in his heart." She spoke with calm bitterness. "You say she told you about him last night. I am not surprised that she should have spoken of him as she did. It was not possible for her to love him as a father. Nature took good care of that. There was a barrier between them. She was not his child. The tie of blood was lacking. Nature cannot be deceived. She has never told me what her true feelings toward him were, but I have sensed them. I could understand. I think she is and always has been bewildered. It is possible that away back in her brain there is something too tiny to ever become a thought, and yet it binds her to a man she does not even remember. But we are wasting time. You are wondering why I have told you the truth about Viola. The secret was safe, so why should I reveal it to you,— my enemy,—isn't that what you are thinking?"

"Yes. I don't quite grasp your motive in telling me, especially as I am still to look upon Viola as my half-sister. I have already stated that under no circumstances will I hurt her by raking up that old, infamous story. I find myself in a most difficult position. She believes herself to be my sister while I know that she is not. It must strike even you, Rachel Carter, as the ghastliest joke that fate ever played on a man,—or a woman, either."

"I have told you the truth, because I am as certain as I am that I stand here now that you would have found it all out some day,—some day soon, perhaps. In the first place your father did not mention her in his will. That alone is enough to cause you to wonder. You are not the only one who is puzzled by his failure to provide for her as well as for you. Before long you would have begun to doubt, then to speculate, and finally you would have made it your business to find out why she was ignored. In time you could have unearthed the truth. The truth will always out, as the saying goes. I preferred to tell it to you at once. You understand I cannot exact any promises from you. You will do as you see fit in the matter. There is one thing that you must realize, however. Viola has not robbed you of any-

thing,—not even a father's love. She does not profit
by his death. He did not leave her a farthing, not
even a spadeful of land. I am entitled to my share
by law. The law would have given it to me if he
had left no will. I am safe. That is clear to you, of
course. I earned my share,—I worked as hard as he
did to build up a fortune. When I die my lands and
my money will go to my daughter. You need not
hope to have any part of them. I do not ask you to
keep silent on my account. I only ask you to spare
her. If I have sinned,—and in the sight of man, I
suppose I have,—I alone should be punished. But she
has not sinned. I have thought it all out carefully.
I have lain awake till all hours of the night, debating
what was the best thing to do. To tell you or not
to tell you, that was the question I had to settle. This
morning I decided and this is the result. You know
everything. There is no need for you to speculate.
There is nothing for you to unravel. You know who
Viola is, you know why she was left out of your
father's will. The point is this, when all is said,—
she must never know. She must always,—do you hear
me?—she must always look upon you as her brother.
She must never know the truth about me. I put her
happiness, her pride, her faith, in your hands, Kenneth
Gwynne."

He had listened with rigid attention, marvelling at
the calm, dispassionate, unflinching manner in which
she stated her case and Viola's,—indeed, she had stated
his own case for him. Apparently she had not even
speculated on the outcome of her revelations; she was
sure of her ground before she took the first step.

"There is no other course open to me," he said, taking up his hat. He was very pale. "There is nothing

more to say,—now or hereafter. We have had, I trust, our last conversation. I hate you. I could wish you all the unhappiness that life can give, but I am not such a beast as to tell your daughter what kind of a woman you are. So there's the end. Good-day, Rachel Carter."

He turned away, his hand was on the door-latch, before she spoke again.

"There is something more," she said, without moving from the spot where she had stood throughout the recital. The same calm, cold voice,—the same compelling manner. "It was my pleading, back in those other days, that finally persuaded Robert Gwyn to let me bring Minda up as his daughter. He was bitterly opposed to it at first. He never quite reconciled himself to the deception. He did not consider it being honest with her. He was as firm as a rock on one point, however. He would bring her up as his daughter, but he would not give her his name. It was after he agreed to my plan that he changed the spelling of his own name. She was not to have his name,— the name he had given his own child. That was his real reason for changing his name, and not, as you may suspect, to avoid being traced to this strange land."

"A belated attempt to be fair to me, I suppose," he said, ironically.

"As you like," she said, without resentment. "In the beginning, as I have told you, he believed it to be his duty to tell her the truth about herself. He was sincere in that. But he did not have the heart to tell her after years had passed. Now let me tell you what he did a few weeks before he passed away,—and you will know what a strange man he was. He came

home one day and said to me: 'I have put Viola's case
in the hands of Providence. You may call it luck or
chance, if you like, but I call it Providence. I cannot
go to her face to face and tell her the truth by word
of mouth, but I have told her the whole story in writing.' I was shocked, and cried out to know if he
had written to her in St. Louis. He smiled and shook
his head. 'No, I have not done that. I have written
it all out and I have hidden the paper in a place where
she is not likely to ever find it,—where I am sure she
will never look. I will not even tell you where it is
hidden,—for I do not trust you,—no, not even you.
You would seek it out and destroy it.' How well he
knew me! Then he went on to say, and I shall never
forget the solemn way in which he spoke: 'I leave it all
with Providence. It is out of my hands. If she ever
comes across the paper it will be a miracle,—and
miracles are not the work of man. So it will be
God Himself who reveals the truth to her.' Now you
can see, Kenneth, that the secret is not entirely in
our keeping. There is always the chance that she
may stumble upon that paper. I live in great dread.
My hope now is that you will find it some day and
destroy it. I have searched in every place that I
can think of. I confess to that. It is hidden on
land that some day will belong to Viola,—that much
he confided to me. It is not on the land belonging
to you,—nor in your house over there."

"You are right," he said, deeply impressed. "There
is always the chance that it will come to light. There
is no telling how many times a day she may be within
arm's length of that paper,—perhaps within inches
of it. It is uncanny."

He cast a swift, searching look about the room, as

if in the hope that his eyes might unexpectedly alight upon the secret hiding place.

"He could not have hidden it in this house without my knowing it," she said, divining his thought.

He was silent for a moment, frowning reflectively. "Are you sure that no one else knows that she is not his daughter?"

"I am sure .of it," she replied with decision.

"And there is nothing more you have to tell me?"

"Nothing. You may go now."

Without another word he left her. He was not surprised by her failure to mention the early morning episode at Striker's cabin. His concluding question had opened the way; it was clear that she had no intention of discussing with him the personal affairs of her daughter. Nevertheless he was decidedly irritated. What right had she to ask him to accept Viola as a sister unless she was also willing to grant him the privileges and interests of a brother? Certainly if Viola was to be his sister he ought to have something to say about the way she conducted herself,—for the honour of the family if for no other reason.

As he walked rapidly away from the house in the direction of Main Street, he experienced a sudden sense of exaltation. Viola was not his sister! As suddenly came the reaction, and with it stark realization. Viola could never be anything to him except a sister.

CHAPTER IX

A S he turned into Main Street he espied the figure of a woman coming toward him from the direction of the public Square. She was perhaps a hundred yards farther down the street and was picking her way gingerly, mincingly, along the narrow path at the roadside. His mind was so fully occupied with thoughts of a most disturbing character that he paid no attention to her, except to note that she was dressed in black and that in holding her voluminous skirt well off the ground to avoid the mud-puddles, she revealed the bottom of a white, beruffled petticoat.

His meditations were interrupted and his interest suddenly aroused when he observed that she had stopped stock-still in the path. After a moment, she turned and walked rapidly, with scant regard for the puddles, in the direction from which she had come. Fifteen or twenty paces down the road, she came to what was undoubtedly a path or "short cut" through the wood. Into this she turned hastily and was lost to view among the trees and hazel-brush.

He had recognized her,—or rather he had divined who she was. He quickened his pace, bent upon overtaking her. Then, with the thrill of the hunter, he abruptly whirled and retraced his steps. With the backwoodsman's cunning he hastened over the ground he had already traversed, chuckling in anticipation of

135

her surprise when she found him waiting for her at
the other end of the "short cut."

He had noticed a path opening into the woods at a
point almost opposite his own house, and naturally
assumed that it was the one she was now pursuing
in order to avoid an encounter with him. His long
legs carried him speedily to the outlet and there he
posted himself. He could hear her coming through
the brush, although her figure was still obscured by
the tangle of wildwood; the snapping of dead twigs
under her feet; the scuffling of last year's leaves on
the path, now wet and plastered with mud and the
slime of winter; the swish of branches as she thrust
them aside.

She emerged, breathless, into a little open spot, not
twenty feet away, and stopped to listen, looking back
through the trees and underbrush to see if she was
being followed. Her skirts were drawn up almost to
the knees and pinched closely about her grey-stock-
inged legs. He gallantly turned away and pretended to
be studying the house across the road. Presently he
felt his ears burning; he turned to meet the onslaught
of her scornful, convicting eyes.

She had not moved. Her hands, having released
the petticoat, were clenched at her sides. Her cheeks
were crimson, and her dark eyes, peering out from the
shade of the close-fitting hood of her black bonnet,
smouldered with wrath,—and, if he could have read
them better, a very decided trace of maidenly dismay.

"Ah, there you are," he cried, lifting his hat. "I
was wondering whether you would come out at this—"

"Can't you see I am trying to avoid you?" she demanded with extreme frigidity.

"I rather fancied you were," said he easily. "So I

hurried back here to head you off. I trust you will not turn around and run the other way, now that I have almost trapped you. Because if you do, I shall catch up with you in ten jumps."

"I wish you would go away," she cried. "I don't want to see you,—or talk to you."

"Then why did you leave word for me to come to your house to see you?" he challenged.

"I suspect you know by this time," she replied, significantly.

He hesitated, regarding her with some uneasiness. "What do you mean?" he fenced.

"Well, you surely know that it was my mother who wanted to see you, and not I," she said, almost insolently. "Are you going to keep me standing here in the mud and slush all day?"

"No, indeed," he said. "Please come out."

"Not until you go away."

"Why don't you want to talk to me? What have I done?"

"You know very well what you have done," she cried, hotly. "In the first place, I don't like you. You have made it very unpleasant for my mother,—who certainly has never done you any harm. In the second place, I resent your interference in my affairs. Wait! Do not interrupt me, please. Maybe you have not exactly interfered as yet, but you are determined to do so,—for the honour of the family, I suppose." She spoke scathingly. "I defy you,—and mother, too. I am not a child to be—"

"I must interrupt you," he exclaimed. "I haven't the slightest idea what you are talking about."

"Don't lie," she cried, stamping her foot. "Give me credit for a little intelligence. Don't you suppose

I know what mother wanted to see you about? There!
I can see the guilty look in your eyes. You two
have been putting your heads together, in spite of
all the ill-will you bear each other, and there is no
use in denying it. I am a naughty little girl and my
big brother has been called in to put a stop to my
foolishness. If you— What are you laughing at, Mr.
Gwynne?" she broke off to demand furiously.

"I am laughing at you," he replied, succinctly. "You
are like a little girl in a tantrum,—all over nothing
at all. Little girls in tantrums are always amusing,
but not always naughty. Permit me to assure you
that your mother and I have not discussed your interesting affair with Mr. Lapelle. We talked of business mat—"

"Then," she cried, "how do you happen to know
anything about Mr. Lapelle and me? Aha! You're not
as clever as you think you are. That slipped out,
didn't it? Now I know you were discussing my affairs
and nothing else. Well, what is the verdict? What are
you going to do to me? Lock me in my room, or tie
me hand and foot, or— Please stay where you are.
It is not necessary to come any nearer, Mr. Gwynne."

He continued his advance through the thicket, unde-
terred by the ominous light in her eyes. She stood
her ground.

"I think we had better talk the matter over quietly,
—Viola," he said, affecting sternness. "We can't stand
here shouting at each other. It is possible we may
never have another chance to converse freely. As a
matter of fact, I do not intend to thrust myself upon
you or your mother. That is understood, I hope. We
have nothing in common and I daresay we can go
our own ways without seriously inconveniencing

one another. I want you to know, however, that I
went to that house over there this afternoon because
I thought you wanted to consult with me about something. I was prepared to help you, or to advise you,
or to do anything you wanted me to do. You were
not there. I felt at first that you had played me a
rather shabby trick. Your mother,—my step-mother,
—got me there under false pretences, solely for the
purpose of straightening out a certain matter in connection with the—well, the future. She doubtless realized that I would not have come on her invitation, so
she used you as a decoy. In any event, I am now
glad that I saw her and talked matters over. It does
not mean that we shall ever be friendly, but we at
least understand each other. For your information I
will state that your mother did not refer to the affair
at Striker's, nor did I. I know all about it, however.
I know that you went out there to meet Lapelle. You
planned to run away with him and get married. I
may add that it is a matter in which I have not the
slightest interest. If you want to marry him, all well
and good. Do so. I shall not offer any objection as
a brother or as a counsellor. If you were to ask for
my honest opinion, however, I should—"

"I am not asking for it," she cried, cuttingly.

"—I should advise you to get married in a more
or less regular sort of way in your mother's home."

"Thank you for the advice," she said, curtly. "I
shall get married when and where I please,—and to
whom I please, Mr. Gwynne."

"In view of the fact that I am your brother, Viola,
I would suggest that you call me Kenneth."

"I have no desire to claim you as a brother, or to
recognize you as one," said she.

He smiled. "With all my heart I deplore the evil
fate that makes you a sister of mine."

She was startled. "That—that doesn't sound very
—pretty," she said, a trifle dashed.

"The God's truth, nevertheless. At any rate, so
long as you have to be my sister, I rejoice in the fact
that you are an extremely pretty one. It is a great
relief. You might have turned out to be a scarecrow.
I don't mind confessing that last night I said to myself, 'There is the most beautiful girl in all the world,'
and I can't begin to tell you how shocked I was this
morning when Striker informed me that you were my
half-sister. He knocked a romantic dream into a
cocked hat,—and— But even so, sister or no sister,
Viola, you still remain beyond compare the loveliest
girl I have ever seen."

There was something in his eyes that caused her
own to waver,—something that by no account could
be described as brotherly. She looked away, suddenly
timid and confused. It was something she had seen
in Barry Lapelle's eyes, and in the eyes of other ardent
men. She was flustered and a little distressed.

"I—I—if you mean that," she said, nervously, "I
suppose I—ought to feel flattered."

"Of course, I mean it,—but you need not feel flattered. Truth is no form of flattery."

She had recovered herself. "Who told you about
Barry Lapelle and me?" she demanded.

"You mean about last night's adventure?" he coun-
tered, a trifle maliciously.

She coloured. "I suppose some one has— Oh, well,
it doesn't matter. I sha'n't ask you to betray the
sneak who—"

"Tut, tut, my dear Viola! You must not—"

"Don't call me your dear Viola!"

"Well, then, my dear sister,—surely you cannot expect me to address you as Miss Gwyn?" in mild surprise.

"Just plain Viola, if you must have a name for me."

"That's better," said he, approvingly.

"Whoever told you was a sneak," she said, wrathfully. She turned her face away, but not quickly enough to prevent his seeing her chin quiver slightly.

"At any rate, it was not your mother," he said. "I have Striker's permission to expose what you call his treachery. He thought it was his duty to tell me under the circumstances. And while I am about it, I may as well say that I think you conspired to take a pretty mean advantage of those good and faithful friends. You deceived them in a most outrageous manner. It wasn't very thoughtful or generous of you, Viola. You might have got them into very serious trouble with your mother,—who, I understand, holds the mortgage on their little farm and could make it extremely unpleasant for them if she felt so inclined."

She was staring at him in wide-eyed astonishment, her red lips slightly parted. She could not believe her ears. Why, he was actually scolding her! She was being reprimanded! He was calmly, deliberately reproving her, as if she were a mischievous child! Amazement deprived her momentarily of the power of speech.

"To be sure," he went on reflectively, "I can appreciate the extremities to which you were driven. The course of true love was not running very smoothly. No doubt your mother was behaving abominably. Mothers frequently do behave that way. This young man of yours may be,—and I devoutly hope he is,— a very worthy fellow, one to whom your mother ought to be proud and happy to see you married. In view of her stand in the matter, I will go so far as to say that you were probably doing the right thing in running away from home to be married. I think I mentioned to you last night that I am of a very romantic nature. Lord bless you, I have lain awake many a night envying the dauntless gentlemen of feudal days who bore their sweethearts away in gallant fashion pursued by ferocious fathers and a score or more of blood-thirsty henchmen. Ah, that was the way for me! With my lady fair seated in front of me upon the speeding palfrey, my body between her and the bullets and lances and bludgeons of countless pursuers! Zounds! Oddsblood! Gadzooks! and so forth! Not any of this stealing away in the night for me! Ah, me! How different we are in these prosaic days! But, even so, if I were you, the next time I undertake to run away with the valiant Mr. Lapelle I should see to it that he does his part in the good old-fashioned way. And I should not drag such loyal, honest folk as Striker and his wife into the business and then ride merrily off, leaving them to pay the Piper."

His heart smote him as he saw her eyes fill with tears. He did not mistake them for tears of shame or contrition,—far from it, he knew they were born of speechless anger. He had hurt her sorely, even deliberately, and he was overcome by a sudden charge of compassion—and regret. He wanted to comfort her, he wanted to say something,—anything,—to take away the sting of chastisement.

He was not surprised when she swept by him, her head high, her cheeks white with anger, her stormy eyes denying him even so much as a look of scorn. He stood aside, allowing her to pass, and remained

motionless, gazing after her until she turned in at her
own gate and was lost to view. He shook his head
dubiously and sighed.

"Little Minda," he mused, under his breath. "You
were my playmate once upon a time,—and now! Now
what are you? A rascal's sweetheart, if all they say
is true. Gad, how beautiful you are!" He was walking slowly through the path, his head bent, his eyes
clouded with trouble. "And how you are hating me
at this moment. What a devil's mess it all is!"

His eye fell upon something white lying at the edge
of the path a few feet ahead. It was a neatly folded
sheet of note paper. He stood looking down at it for
a moment. She must have dropped it as she came
through. It was clean and unsoiled. A message, perhaps, from Barry Lapelle, smuggled to her through the
connivance of a friendly go-between,—the girl she had
gone to visit, what was her name? He stooped to pick
it up, but before his fingers touched it he straightened
up and deliberately moved it with the toe of his boot
to a less exposed place among the bushes, where he
would have failed to see it in passing. Then he strode
resolutely away without so much as a glance over his
shoulder, and, coming to the open road, stepped briskly
off in the direction of the public Square. His conscience
would have rejoiced had he betrayed it by secreting
himself among the bushes for a matter of five minutes,—
quaint paradox, indeed!—for he would have seen her
steal warily, anxiously into the thicket in search of
the lost missive,—and he would have been further ex-
alted by the little cry of relief that fell from her lips
as she snatched it up and sped incontinently homeward,
as if pursued by all the eyes in Christendom.

As a matter of fact, it was not a letter from Barry

to Viola. It was the other way round. She had written him a long letter absolving herself from blame in the *contretemps* of the night before, at the same time confessing that she was absolutely in the dark as to how her mother had found out about their plans. Suffice to say, she *had* found out early in the evening and, to employ her own words, "You know the result." Then she went on to say that, all things considered, she was now quite sure she could never, never consent to make another attempt.

"I am positive," she wrote, ingenuously, "that mother will relent in time, and then we can be married without going to so much trouble about it." Farther on she admitted that, "Mother is very firm about it now, but when she realizes that I am absolutely determined to marry you, I am sure she will give in and all will be well." At the end she said: "For the present, Barry dear, I think you had better not come to the house. She feels very bitter toward you after last night. We can see each other at Effie's and other places. After all, she has had a great sorrow and she is so very unhappy that I ought not to hurt her in any way if I can help it. I love you, but I also love her. Please be kind and reasonable, dear, and do not think I am losing heart. I am just as determined as ever. Nothing can change me. You believe that, don't you, Barry dear? I know how impulsive you are and how set in your ways. Sometimes you really frighten me but I know it is because you love me so much. You must not do anything rash. It would spoil everything. I do wish you would stay away from that awful place down by the river. Mother would feel differently toward you, I know, if you were not there so much. She knows the men play cards there for money and drink and swear. I believe you will keep your promise never to touch a drop of whiskey after we are married, but when I told her that she only laughed at me. By this time you must know that my brother has come to Lafayette. He arrived this morning. He knows nothing about what happened last night but I am afraid mother will tell him when she sees him to-day. It would not surprise me if they bury the hatchet and join hands and try to make a good little girl out of me. I think he is quite a prim young man. He spent the night at Striker's and I saw him there. I must say he is good-looking. He is so good-looking that nobody would ever suspect that he is related to me." She signed herself, "Your loving and devoted and loyal Viola."

She had been unable to get the letter to him that day, and for a very good reason. Her messenger, Effie Wardlow's young brother, reached the tavern just in time to see Barry emerge, quite tipsy and in a vile temper, arguing loudly with Jack Trentman and Syd Budd, the town's most notorious gamblers.

The three men went off toward the ferry. The lad very sensibly decided this was no time to deliver a love letter to Mr. Lapelle, so forthwith returned it to the sender, who, after listening bleakly to a somewhat harrowing description of her lover's unsteady legs and the direction in which they carried him, departed for home fully convinced that something dreadful was going to happen to Barry and that she would be to blame for it.

Halfway home she decided that her mother was equally if not more to blame than she, and, upon catching sight of her lordly, self-satisfied brother, acquitted herself of *all* responsibility and charged everything to her meddling relatives. Her encounter with the exasperating Kenneth, however, served to throw a new and most unwelcome light upon the situation. It *was* a shabby trick to play upon the Strikers. She had not thought of it before. And how she hated him for making her think of it!

The first thing she did upon returning to the house with the recovered letter was to proceed to the kitchen, where, after reading it over again, she consigned it to the flames. She was very glad it had not been delivered to Barry. The part of it referring to the "place down by the river" would have to be treated with a great deal more firmness and decision. That was something she would have to speak very plainly about.

By this time she had reached the conclusion that Barry was to blame for *that*, and that nothing more terrible could happen to him than a severe headache,— an ailment to which he was accustomed and which he treated very lightly in excusing himself when she took him to task for his jolly lapses. "All red-blooded fellows take a little too much once in a while," he had said, more than once.

CHAPTER X

RACHEL GWYN was seated at the parlor window when Viola entered the house. She was there ten or fifteen minutes later when her daughter came downstairs.

"May I have a word with you, mother?" said the girl, from the doorway, after waiting a moment for her mother to take some notice of her presence.

She spoke in a very stiff and formal manner, for there had been no attempt on the part of either to make peace since the trying experiences of early morning. Viola had sulked all day, while her mother preserved a stony silence that remained unbroken up to the time she expressed a desire to be alone with Kenneth when he called.

Apparently Mrs. Gwyn did not hear Viola's question. The girl advanced a few steps into the room and stopped again to regard the motionless, unresponsive figure at the window. Mrs. Gwyn's elbow was on the sill, her chin resting in the hand. Apparently she was deaf to all sound inside the room.

A wave of pity swept over Viola. All in an instant her rancour took flight and in its place came a longing to steal over and throw her arms about those bent shoulders and whisper words of remorse. Desolation hung over that silent, thinking figure. Viola's heart swelled with renewed anger toward Kenneth Gwynne.

147

What had he said or done to wound this stony, indomitable mother of hers?

The room was cold. The fire had died down; only the huge backlog showed splotches of red against the charred black; in front of it were the faintly smoking ashes of a once sprightly blaze. She shivered, and then, moved by a sudden impulse, strode softly over and took down from its peg beside the fireplace the huge turkey wing used in blowing the embers to life. She was vigorously fanning the backlog when a sound from behind indicated that her mother had risen from the chair. She smiled as she glanced over her shoulder.

Her mother was standing with one of her hands pressed tightly to her eyes. Her lips were moving.

"He is Robert—Robert himself," she was murmuring. "As like as two peas. I was afraid he might be— would be—" The words trailed off into a mumble, for she had lowered her hand and was staring in dull surprise at Viola.

"What is it, mother?" cried the girl, alarmed by the other's expression. "What were you saying?"

After a moment her mother said, quite calmly: "Oh, it's you, is it? When did you get home?"

"A few minutes ago. How cold it is! The fire is almost out. Shall I get some kindling and start it up?"

"Yes. I don't know how I came to let it go down."

When Viola returned from the kitchen with the fagots and a bunch of shavings, the older woman was standing in front of the fireplace staring moodily down at the ashes. She moved to one side while her daughter laid the kindling and placed three or four sticks of firewood upon the heap. Not a word was spoken until after Viola had fanned a tiny flame out of the embers and lighted the shavings with a spill.

"I met my brother out there in the grove," said she, arising and brushing the wood dust from her hands.

"Yes?"

"I thought maybe you and he had been discussing Barry Lapelle and me and what happened last night, so I started to give him a piece of my mind," said Viola, crimsoning.

A faint smile played about the corners of Mrs. Gwyn's lips. "I can well imagine his astonishment," she said, drily.

"He knew all about it, even if he did not get it from you, mother," said the girl, darkly. "Phin Striker told him everything."

"Everybody in town will know about it before the week is out," said the mother, a touch of bitterness in her voice. "I would have given all I possess if it could have been kept from Kenneth Gwynne. Salt in an open sore, that's what it is, Viola. It smarts, oh, how it smarts."

Viola, ignorant of the true cause of her mother's pain, snapped her fingers disdainfully.

"That's how much I care for his opinion, one way or the other. I wouldn't let him worry me if I were you, mother. Let him think what he pleases. It's nothing to us. I guess we can get along very well without his good opinion or his good will or anything else. And I will not allow him to interfere in my affairs. I told him so in plain words out there awhile ago. He comes here and the very first thing he does is to—"

"He will think what he pleases, my child," broke in her mother; "so do not flatter yourself that he will be affected by your opinion of him. We will not discuss him, if you please. We have come to an understanding on certain matters, and that is all that is necessary to tell you about our interview. He will go his own way and we will go ours. There need be no conflict between us."

Viola frowned dubiously. "It is all very well for you to take that attitude, mother. But I am not in the same position. He is my half-brother. It is going to be very awkward. He is nothing to you,—and people will understand if you ignore him,—but it—it isn't quite the same with me. Can't you see?"

"Certainly," admitted Mrs. Gwyn without hesitation. "You and he have a perfect right to be friendly. It would not be right for me to stand between you if you decide to—"

"But I do not want to be friendly with him," cried the girl, adding, with a toss of her head,—"and I guess he realizes it by this time. But people know that we had the same father. They will think it strange if—if we have nothing to do with each other. Oh, it's terribly upsetting, isn't it?"

"What did he say to you out there?"

"He was abominable! Officious, sarcastic, insolent,—"

"In plain words, he gave you a good talking to," interrupted Mrs. Gwyn, rather grimly.

"He said some things I can never forgive."

"About you and Barry?"

"Well,—not so much about me and Barry as about the way I— Oh, you needn't smile, mother. He isn't going to make any fuss about Barry. He told me in plain words that he did not care whether I married him or not,—or ran away with him, for that matter. You will not get much support from him, let me tell you. And now I have something I want to say to you. We may as well have it out now as any other time. I

am going to marry Barry Lapelle." There was a ring
of defiance in her voice.

Rachel Gwyn looked at her steadily for a moment
before responding to this out-and-out challenge.

"I think it would be only fair of you," she began,
levelly, "to tell Mr. Lapelle just what he may expect
in case he marries you. Tell him for me that you will
never receive a penny or an inch of land when I die. I
shall cut you off completely. Tell him that. It may
make some difference in his calculations."

Viola flared. "You have no right to insinuate that
he wants to marry me for your money or your lands.
He wants me for myself,—he wants me because he loves
me."

"I grant you that," said Mrs. Gwyn, nodding her
head slowly. "He would be a fool not to want you—
now. You are young and you are very pretty. But
after he has been married a few years and you have
become an old song to him, he will feel differently about
money and lands. I know Mr. Lapelle and his stripe.
He wants you now for yourself, but when you are thirty
years old he will want you for something entirely different. At any rate, you should make it plain to him
that he will get nothing but you,—absolutely nothing
but you. Men of his kind do not love long. They love
violently—but not long. Idle, improvident men, such
as he is, are able to crowd a whole lot of love into a
very short space of time. That is because they have
nothing much else to do. They run through with love
as they run through with money,—quickly. The man
who wastes money will also waste love. And when he
has wasted all his love, Barry Lapelle will still want
money to waste. Be good enough to make him understand that he will never have a dollar of my money to

waste,—never, my child, even though his wife were
starving to death."

Viola stared at her mother incredulously, her face
paling. "You mean—you mean you would let me
starve,—your own daughter? I—why, mother, I can't
believe you would be so—"

"I mean it," said Rachel Gwyn, compressing her lips.

"Then," cried Viola, hotly, "you are the most unnatural, cruel mother that ever—"

"Stop! You will not find me a cruel and inhuman
mother when you come creeping back to my door after
Barry Lapelle has cast you off. I am only asking you
to tell him what he may expect from me. And I am
trying hard to convince you of what you may expect
from him. There's the end of it. I have nothing more
to say."

"But I have something more to say," cried the girl.
"I shall tell him all you have said, and I shall marry
him in spite of everything. I am not afraid of starving.
I don't want a penny of father's money. He did not
choose to give it to me; he gave half of all he possessed
to his son by another woman, he ignored me, he cut me
off as if I were a—"

"Be careful, my child," warned Rachel Gwyn, her
eyes narrowing. "I cannot permit you to question his
acts or his motives. He did what he thought was best,
—and we—I mean you and I—must abide by his decision."

"I am not questioning your husband's act," said
Viola, stubbornly. "I am questioning my *father's* act."

Mrs. Gwyn started. For a second or two her eyes
wavered and then fell. One corner of her mouth
worked curiously. Then, without a word, she turned
away from the girl and left the room.

Viola, greatly offended, heard her ascend the stairs and close a door; then her slow, heavy tread on the boards above. Suddenly the girl's anger melted. The tears rushed to her eyes.

"Oh, what a beast I was to hurt her like that," she murmured, forgetting the harsh, unfeeling words that had aroused her ire, thinking only of the wonder and pain that had lurked in her mother's eyes,—the wonder and pain of a whipped dog. "The only person in all the world who has ever really loved me,—poor, poor old mother." She stared through her tears at the flames, a little pucker of uncertainty clouding her brow. "I am sure Barry never, never can love me as she does, or be as kind and good to me," she mused. "I wonder—I wonder if what she says is true about men. I wish he had not gone to drinking to-day. But I suppose the poor boy really couldn't help it. He hates so to be disappointed."

Later on, at supper, she abruptly asked:

"Mother, how old is Kenneth?"

They had spoken not more than a dozen words to each other since sitting down to table, which was set, as usual, in the kitchen. Both were thoughtful;—one of them was contrite.

Rachel Gwyn, started out of a profound reverie, gave her daughter a sharp, inquiring look before answering.

"I do not know. Twenty-five or six, I suppose."

"Did you know his mother?"

"Yes," after a perceptible pause.

"How long after she died were you and father married?"

"Your father had been a widower nearly two years when we were married," said Rachel, steadily.

"Why doesn't Kenneth spell his name as we do?"

"Gwyn is the way it was spelled a great many years ago, and it is the correct way, according to your father. It was his father, I believe, who added the last two letters,—I do not know why, unless it was supposed to be more elegant."

"It seems strange that he should spell it one way and his own son another," ventured the girl, unsatisfied.

"Kenneth was brought up to spell it in the new-fangled way, I guess," was Rachel Gwyn's reply. "You need not ask me questions about the family, Viola. Your father never spoke of them. I am afraid he was not on good terms with them. He was a strange man. He kept things to himself. I do not recollect ever hearing him mention his first wife or his son or any other member of his family in,—well, in twenty years or more."

"I should think you would have been a little bit curious. I know I should."

"I knew all that was necessary for me to know," said Rachel, somewhat brusquely.

"Can't you tell me something more about father's people?" persisted the girl.

"I only know that they lived in Baltimore. They never came west. Your father was about twenty years old when he left home and came to Kentucky. That is all I know, so do not ask any more questions."

"He never acted like a backwoodsman," said Viola. "He did not talk like one or—"

"He was an educated man. He came of a good family."

"And you are different from the women we used to see down the river. Goodness, I was proud of you and father. There isn't a woman in this town who—"

"I was born in Salem, Massachusetts, and lived there till I was nearly twenty," interrupted Mrs. Gwyn, calmly. "I taught school for two years after my father died. My mother did not long survive him. After her death I came west with my brother and his wife and a dozen other men and women. We lived in a settlement on the Ohio River for several years. My brother was killed by the Indians. His widow took their two small children and went back to Salem to live. I have never heard from her. We did not like each other. I was glad to have her go."

"Where did you first meet father?"

She regretted the question the instant the words were out of her mouth. The look of pain,—almost of pleading,—in her mother's eyes caused her to reproach herself.

"Forgive me, mother," she cried. "I did not stop to think. I know how it hurts you to talk about him, and I should have—"

"Be good enough to remember in the future," said Rachel Gwyn, sternly, her eyes now cold and forbidding. She arose and stalked to the kitchen window, where she stood for a long time looking out into the gathering darkness.

"Clear the table, Hattie," said Viola, presently. "We are through."

Then she walked over to her mother and timidly laid an arm across her shoulder.

"I am sorry, mother," she said.

To this Mrs. Gwyn did not reply. She merely observed: "We have had very little sleep in the last six and thirty hours. Come to bed, child."

As was her custom, Rachel Gwyn herself saw to the locking and bolting of the doors and window shutters at the front of the house. To-night Viola, instead of Hattie, followed the tall black figure from door to window, carrying the lighted candle. They stood together, side by side, in the open front door for a few moments, peering at the fence of trees across the road.

Off in the distance some one was whistling a doleful tune. The spring wind blowing in their faces was fresh and moist, a soft wind laden with the smell of earth. A clumsy hound came slouching around the corner of the little porch and, wagging his tail, stopped below them; the light shone down into his big, glistening eyes. Viola spoke to him softly. He wagged his tail more briskly.

Rachel had turned her head and was looking toward the house that was to be Kenneth's home. Its outlines could be made out among the trees to the right, squat and lonely in a setting less black than itself.

"Before long there will be lights in the windows again," she was saying, more to herself than to Viola. "A haunted house. Haunted by a living, mortal ghost. Eh?" she cried out, sharply, turning to Viola.

"I did not speak, mother."

A look of awe came to Rachel's eyes.

"I was sure I heard—" she began, and then, after a short pause, laughed throatily. "I guess it was the wind. Come in. I want to lock the door."

Viola was a long time in going to sleep. It seemed to her as she lay there, staring wide awake, that everything in the world was unsettled and topsy-turvy. Nothing could ever be right again. What with the fiasco of the night just gone, the appearance of the mysterious brother, the counterbalancing of resolve and remorse within her troubled self, the report of

Barry's lapse from rectitude, her mother's astounding sophistry, her tired brain was in such a whirl as never was.

There was a new pain in her breast that was not of thwarted desires nor of rancour toward this smug, insolent brother who had come upon the scene. It hurt her to think that up to this night she had known so little, ay, almost nothing, about her own mother's life. For the first time, she heard of Salem, of her mother's people and her occupation, of the journey westward, of the uncle who was killed by the Indians and the wife who turned back; of unknown cousins to whom she was also unknown. There was pain in the discovery that her mother was almost a stranger to her.

CHAPTER XI

A ROADSIDE MEETING

KENNETH remained at the tavern for a month. He did not go near the 'house of his stepmother. He saw her once walking along the main street, and followed her with his eyes until she disappeared into a store. A friendly citizen took occasion to inform him that it was the "fust time" he had seen her on the street in a coon's age.

"She ain't like most women," he vouchsafed. "Never comes down town unless she's got some reason to. Most of 'em never stay to home unless they've got a derned good reason to, setch as sickness, or the washin' and ironin', or it's rainin' pitchforks. She's a mighty queer woman, Rachel Gwyn is. How air you an' her makin' out these days, Kenneth?"

"Oh, fair to middlin'," replied the young man, dropping into the vernacular.

"I didn't know but what ye'd patched things up sorter," said the citizen, invitingly.

"There is nothing to patch up," said Kenneth.

"Well, I guess it ain't any of my business, anyhow," remarked the other, cheerfully.

The business of taking over the property, signing the necessary papers, renewing an agreement with the man who farmed his land on the Wea, taking account of all live-stock and other chattels, occupied his time for the better part of a fortnight. He spent two days

158

and a night at the little farmhouse, listening with ever increasing satisfaction to the enthusiastic prophecies of the farmer, a stout individual named Jones whose faith in the new land was surpassed only by his ability to till it. Even out here on his own farm Kenneth was unable to escape the unwelcome influence of Rachel Carter. Mr. Jones magnanimously admitted that she was responsible for all of the latest conveniences about the place and characterized her as a "woman with a head on her shoulders, you bet."

He confessed: "Why, dodgast it, she stopped by here a couple o' weeks ago an' jest naturally raised hell with me because my wife's goin' to have another baby. She sez, sorter sharp-like, 'The only way to make a farm pay is to stock it with somethin' besides children.' That made me a leetle mad, so I up an' sez back to her: 'I wouldn't swap my seven children fer all the hogs an' cattle in the state o' Indianny.' So she sez, kind o' grinnin', 'Well, I'll bet your wife would jump at the chance to trade your *next* seven children, sight onseen, fer a new pair o' shoes er that bonnet she's been wantin' ever sence she got married.' That sorter mixed me up. I couldn't make out jest what she was drivin' at. Must ha' been nine o'clock that night when it come to me all of a sudden. So I woke Sue up an' told her what Rachel Gwyn said to me, an', by gosh, Sue saw through it quicker'n a flash. 'You bet I would,' sez she. 'I'd swap the next *hundred*.' Then she kinder groaned an' said, 'I guess maybe I'd better make it the next ninety-nine.' Well, sir, that sot me to thinkin', an' the more I thought, the more I realized what a lot o' common sense that mother-in-law o' your'n has got. She—"

"You mean my step-mother, Jones."

"They say it amounts to the same thing in most

families," said the ready Mr. Jones, and continued to
expatiate upon the remarkable qualities of Rachel
Gwyn.

Kenneth found it difficult to think of the woman as
Rachel Gwyn. To him, she was unalterably Rachel
Carter. Time and again he caught himself up barely in
time to avoid using the unknown name in the presence
of others. The possibility that he might some day
inadvertently blurt it out in conversation with Viola
caused him a great deal of uneasiness and concern. He
realized that he would have to be on his guard all of
the time.

There seemed to be no immediate prospect of such a
calamity, however. Since the memorable encounter in
the thicket he had not had an opportunity to speak to
the girl. For reasons of her own she purposely
avoided him, there could be no doubt about that. On
more than one occasion she deliberately had crossed
a street to escape meeting him face to face, and there
was the one especially irritating instance when, finding
herself hard put, she had been obliged to turn squarely
in her tracks and hurry back in the direction from
which she came. This would have been laughable to
Kenneth but for the distressing fact that it was even
more laughable to others. Several men and women, wit-
nessing the manœuvre, had sniggered gleefully,—one of
the men going so far as to slap his leg and roar:
"Well, by gosh, did you ever see anything like that?"
His ejaculation, like that of a town-crier, being audible
for a hundred feet or more, had one gratifying result.
It caused Viola to turn and transfix the offender with
a stare so haughty that he abruptly diverted his attention to the upper north-east corner of the court-house,
where, fortunately for him, a pair of pigeons had just

alighted and were engaged in the interesting pastime of bowing to each other.

A week or so after his return from the farm Kenneth saw her riding off on horseback with two other young women and a youth named Hayes. She passed within ten feet of him but did not deign to notice him, although her companions bowed somewhat eagerly. This was an occasion when he felt justified in swearing softly under his breath—and also to make a resolve—to write her a very polite and formal letter in which he would ask her pardon for presuming to suggest, as a brother, that she was making a perfect fool of herself, and that people were laughing "fit to kill" over her actions. It goes without saying that he thought better of it and never wrote the letter.

She was a graceful and accomplished horsewoman. He watched her out of the corner of his eye as she cantered down the street, sitting the spirited sorrel mare with all the ease and confidence of a practised rider. Her habit was of very dark blue, with huge puffed sleeves and a high lace collar. She wore a top-hat of black, a long blue veil trailing down her back. He heartily agreed with the laconic bystander who remarked that she was "purtier than most pictures."

Later on, urged by a spirit of restlessness, he ordered Zachariah to saddle his horse and bring him around to the front of the tavern, where he mounted and set out for a ride up the Wild Cat road. Two or three miles above town he met Hayes and the two young women returning. The look of consternation that passed among them did not escape him. He smiled a trifle maliciously as he rode on, for now he knew what had become of the missing member of the party.

Half a mile farther on he came upon Viola and Barry

Lapelle, riding slowly side by side through the narrow lane. He drew off to one side to allow them to pass, doffing his beaver ceremoniously.

Lapelle's friendly greeting did not surprise him, for the two had seen a great deal of each other, and at no time had there been anything in the lover's manner to indicate that Viola had confided to him the story of the meeting in the thicket. But he was profoundly astonished when the girl favoured him with a warm, gay smile and cried out a cheery "How do you do, Kenneth!"

More than that, she drew rein and added to his amazement by shaking her finger reproachfully at him, saying:

"Where on earth have you been keeping yourself? I have not laid eyes on you for more than a week."

Utterly confounded by this unexpected attack, Kenneth stammered: "Why, I—er—I have been very busy." Not laid eyes on him, indeed! What was her game? "Now that I come to think of it," he went on, recovering himself, "it is fully a week since I've seen you. Don't you ever come down town, Viola?"

"Every day," she said, coolly. "We just happen never to see each other, that's all. I am glad to have had this little glimpse of you, Kenneth, even though it is away out here in the woods."

There was no mistaking the underlying significance of these words. They contained the thinly veiled implication that he had followed for the purpose of spying upon her.

"Better turn around and ride back with us, Kenny," said Barry, politely but not graciously.

"I am on my way up to the Wild Cat to see a man on business," said Kenneth, lamely.

"Kenny?" repeated Viola, puckering her brow.

"Where have I heard that name before? I seem to remember—oh, as if it were a thousand years ago. Do they call you Kenny for short?"

"It grew up with me," he replied. "Ever since I can remember, my folks—"

He broke off in the middle of the sentence, confronted by a disconcerting thought. Could it be possible that somewhere in Viola's brain,—or rather in Minda's baby brain,—that familiar name had stamped itself? Why not? If it had been impressed upon his own baby brain, why not in a less degree upon hers? He made a pretence of stooping far over to adjust a corner of his saddle blanket. Straightening up, he went on:

"Any name is better than what the boys used to call me at school. I was known by the elegant name of Piggy, due to an appetite over which I seemed to have no control. Well, I must be getting along. Good day to you."

He lifted his hat and rode off. He had gone not more than twenty rods when he heard a masculine shout from behind: turning, he discovered that the couple were still standing where he had left them. Lapelle called out:

"Your sister wants to have a word with you."

She rode swiftly up to where he was waiting.

"I just want to let you know that I intend to tell mother about meeting Barry out here to-day," she said, unsmilingly. "I shall not tell her that we planned it in advance, however. We *did* plan it, so if you want to run and tell her yourself, you may do so. It will make no—"

"Is that all you wanted to say to me, Viola?" he interrupted.

For a moment she faced him rebelliously, hot words on her lips. Then a surprising change came over her. Her eyes quailed under the justifiable scorn in his. She hung her head.

"No," she said, miserably. "I thought it was all, but it isn't. I want to say that I am sorry I said what I did."

He watched the scarlet flood sweep over her cheeks and then as swiftly fade. It was abject surrender, and yet he had no thrill of triumph.

"It's—it's all right, Viola," he stammered, awkwardly. "Don't think anything more about it. We will consider it unsaid."

"No, we'll not," she said, looking up. "We will just let it stand as another black mark against me. I am getting a lot of them lately. But I *am* sorry, Kenneth. Will you try to forget it?"

He shook his head. "Never! Forgetting the bitter would mean that I would also have to give up the sweet," said he, gallantly. "And you have given me something very sweet to remember."

She received this with a wondering, hesitating little smile.

"I never dreamed that brothers could say such nice things to their sisters," she said, and he was aware of a deep, questioning look in her eyes. "They usually say them to other men's sisters."

"Ah, but no other fellow happens to have you as a sister," he returned, fatuously. She laughed aloud at this, perhaps a little uncertainly.

"Bless me!" he exclaimed. "It sounds good to hear you laugh like that,—such a jolly, friendly sort of laugh."

"I must be going now," she said, biting her lip.

"Good-bye,—Kenny." A faint frown clouded her brow after she had uttered the name. "I must ask mother if she remembers hearing father speak of you as Kenny."

"Say, Viola," came an impatient shout from Barry Lapelle, "are you going to take all day?"

It was plain to be seen that the young man was out of temper. There was a sharp, domineering note of command in his voice. Viola straightened up in her saddle and sent a surprised, resentful look at the speaker. Kenneth could not repress a chuckle.

"Better hurry along," he said, grimly, "or he'll take your head off. Lord, we are going to have a storm. I see a thundercloud gathering just below the rim of Barry's hat. If you—"

"Please keep your precious wit to yourself," she flamed, but with all her show of righteous indignation she could not hide from him the chagrin and mortification that lurked in her tell-tale eyes.

She rode off in high dudgeon, and he was left to curse his ill-timed jest. What a blundering fool he had been! Her first, timid little advance,—and he had met it with boorish, clownish wit! A scurvy jest, indeed! She was justified in despising him.

If Viola had turned her proud head a few moments later, she would have beheld an amazing spectacle: her supposedly smug and impeccable brother riding away at break-neck speed down the soggy lane, regardless of overhanging branches and flying mud, fleeing in wrath from the scene of his discontent.

Dusk was falling when he rode slowly into the town again. He had reached a decision during that lonely ride. He would not remain in Lafayette. He foresaw misery and unhappiness for himself if he stayed there,

—for, be it here declared, he was in love with Viola
Gwyn. No, worse than that, he was in love with Minda
Carter,—and therein lay all the bitterness that filled his
soul. He could never have her. Even though she cast
off the ardent Lapelle, still he could not have her for
his own. The bars were up, and it was now beyond his
power to lower them. And so, with this resolve firmly
fixed in his mind, he gave himself up to a strange sort
of despair.

After supper at the tavern, he set out for a solitary
stroll about the town before going to bed. He took
stock of himself. No later than that morning he had
come to a decision to open an office and engage in the
practice of Law in Lafayette. He had made many
friends during his brief stay in the place, and from
all sides he had been encouraged to "hang out his
shingle" and "grow up with the town." He liked the
people, he had faith in the town, he possessed all the
confidence and courage of youth. The local members
of the bar, including the judge and justices, seriously
urged him to establish himself there—there was room
for him,—the town needed such men as he,—indeed, one
of the leading lawyers had offered to take him into
partnership, an opportunity not to be despised, in view
of this man's state-wide reputation as a lawyer and
orator, and who was already being spoken of for high
honours in the councils of state and nation.

All this was very gratifying to the young stranger.
He was flattered by the unmistakable sincerity of these
new friends. And he was in a position to weather the
customary paucity of clients for an indefinite period,
a condition resulting to but few young men starting
out for themselves in the practice of law. He was com-
fortably well-off in the matter of worldly goods, not

only through his recently acquired possessions, but as the result of a substantial legacy that had come to him on the death of his grandmother. He had received his mother's full share of the Blythe estate, a no inconsiderable fortune in lands and money.

And now everything was changed. He would have to give up his plan to settle in Lafayette, and so, as he strolled gloomily about the illy-lighted town, he was casting about for the next best place to locate. The incomprehensible and incredible had come to pass. He had fallen in love with Viola Gwyn at first sight, that stormy night at Striker's. The discovery that she was his own half-sister had, of course, deluded his senses— temporarily, but now he realized that the strange, primitive instincts of man had not been deceived and would not be denied.

His blood had known the truth from the instant he first laid eyes upon the lovely stranger. Since that first night there had been revelations. First of all, Viola was the flesh and blood of an evil woman, and that woman his mortal foe. Notwithstanding her own innocence and purity, it was inconceivable that he should ever think of taking her to himself as wife. Secondly, he was charged with a double secret that must forever stand between him and her: the truth about her mother and the truth about herself.

There was but one thing left for him to do,—go away. He loved her. He would grow to love her a thousand-fold more if he remained near her, if he saw her day by day. These past few days had brought despair and jealousy to him, but what would the future bring? Misery! No, he would have to go. He would wind up his affairs at once and put longing and temptation as far behind him as possible. There was the town of Louisville. From all reports it was a prosperous, growing town, advantageously situated on the River Ohio. Crawfordsville was too near. He would have to go farther, much farther away than that,— perhaps back to the old home town.

"What cruel foul luck!" he groaned, aloud.

His wanderings had carried him through dark, winding cow-paths and lanes to within a stone's throw of Jack Trentman's shanty, standing alone like the pariah it was, on the steep bank of the river near the ferry. Back in a clump of sugar trees it seemed to hide, as if shrinking from the accusing eye of every good and honest man. Kenneth had stopped at the edge of the little grove and was gazing fiercely at the two lighted windows of the "shanty." He was thinking of Barry Lapelle as he muttered the words, thinking of the foul luck that seemed almost certain to deliver Viola into his soiled and lawless hands. The fierceness of his gaze was due to the knowledge that Lapelle was now inside Trentman's notorious shanty and perhaps gambling.

This evening, as on two or three earlier occasions, he had been urged by Barry to come down to the shanty and try his luck at poker. He had steadfastly declined these invitations. Trentman's place was known far and wide as a haven into which "cleaned out" river gamblers sailed in the hope of recovering at least enough of their fortunes to enable them to return to more productive fields down the reaches of the big river. These whilom, undaunted rascals, like birds of passage, stayed but a short time in the new town of Lafayette. They came up the river with sadly depleted purses, confident of "easy pickings" among the vainglorious amateurs, and be it said in behalf of their

astuteness, they seldom if ever boarded the south-
bound boats as poor as when they came.

In due time they invariably returned again to what
they called among themselves "the happy hunting-
ground." The stories of big "winnings" and big "losings" were rife among the people of the town. More
than one adventurous citizen or farmer had been
"wiped out," with no possible chance of ever recovering
from his losses. It was common talk that Barry Lapelle was "fresh fish" for these birds of prey. He possessed the gambling instinct but lacked the gambler's
wiles. He was reckless where they were cool. They
"stripped" him far oftener than he won from them,
but it was these infrequent winnings that encouraged
him. He believed that some day he would make a big
"killing"; the thought of that was ever before him,
beckoning him on like the dancing will-o'-the-wisp. He
took no note of the fact that these bland gentlemen
could pocket their losings as well as their winnings.
It was part of their trade to suffer loss. They had
everything to gain and nothing to lose, so they throve
on uncertainty.

Not so with Barry, or others of his kind. They could
only afford to win. It was no uncommon experience for
the skilled river gambler to be penniless; it was all in
the day's work. It did not hurt him to lose, for the
morrow was ahead. But it was different with his vic-
tims. The morrow was not and never could be the
same; when they were "cleaned out" it meant desolation. They went down under the weight and never
came up, while the real gambler, in similar case, scraped
his sparse resources together and blithely began all over
again,—a smiling loser and a smiling winner. Full
purse or empty, he was always the same. Rich to-day,

poor to-morrow,—all the same to him.   Philosopher,
rascal, soldier, knave,—but never the craven,—and you
have the Mississippi gambler.

Barry, after coming in from his ride with Viola, had
"tipped the jug" rather liberally.   He kept a demi-
john of whiskey in his room at the tavern, and to its
contents all the "afflicted" were welcome.   It could not
be said of him that he was the principal consumer, for,
except under unusual circumstances, he was a fairly
abstemious man.   As he himself declared, he drank
sparingly except when his "soul was tried."   The fact
that he had taken several copious draughts of the fiery
Mononga-Durkee immediately upon his return was an
indication that his soul was tried, and what so reasonable as to assume that it had been tried by Viola.

In a different frame of mine, Kenneth might have
accepted this as a most gratifying augury.   But, being
without hope himself, he took no comfort in Barry's
gloom.   What would he not give to be in the roisterer's
boots instead of his own?

The spoken lament had barely passed his lips when
the wheel of fate took a new and unexpected turn,
bringing his dolorous meditations to a sudden halt and
subsequently upsetting all his plans.

He thought he was alone in the gloom until he was
startled by the sound of a man's voice almost at his
elbow.

"Evenin', Mr. Gwynne."

CHAPTER XII

WHIRLING, he made out the lank shadow of a man leaning against a tree close by.

"Good evening," he muttered in some confusion, conscious of a sense of guilt in being caught in the act of spying.

"I've been follerin' you fer quite a ways," observed the unknown. "Guess you don't remember me. My name is Stain, Isaac Stain."

"I remember you quite well," said Kenneth, stiffly. "May I inquire why you have been following me, Mr. Stain?"

"Well, I jest didn't know of anybody else I could come to about a certain matter. It has to do with that feller, Lapelle, up yander in Trentman's place. Fust, I went up to Mrs. Gwyn's house, but it was all dark, an' nobody to home 'cept that dog o' her'n. He knowed me er else he'd have jumped me. I guess we'd better mosey away from this place. A good many trees have ears, you know."

They walked off together in the direction of town. Stain was silent until they had put a hundred paces or more between them and the grove.

"Seems that Violy is right smart taken with this Lapelle feller," he observed. "Well, I thought I'd oughter tell her ma what I heerd about him to-day. Course, everybody's heerd queer things about him, but this beats anything I've come acrosst yet. Martin

Hawk's daughter, Moll, come hoofin' it up to my cabin this mornin' an' told me the derndest story you've ever heerd. She came to me, she sez, on account of me bein' an old friend of Rachel's, an' she claims to be a decent, honest girl in spite of what her dodgasted father is. Everybody believes Mart is a hoss thief an' sheep-stealer an' all that, but he hain't ever been caught at it. He's purty thick with Barry Lapelle. Moll Hawk sez her dad'll kill her if he ever finds out she come to me with this story. Seems that Barry an' Violy are calculatin' on gettin' married an' the old woman objects. Some time this past week, Violy told Barry she wouldn't marry him anywheres 'cept in her own mother's house. Well, from what Moll sez, Barry has got other idees about it."

He paused to bite off a fresh chew of tobacco.

"Go on, Stain. What did the girl tell you?"

" 'Pears that Barry ain't willin' to take chances on gettin' married jest that way, an' besides he's sort of got used to havin' anything he wants without waitin' very long fer it. Now, I don't know whuther Violy's a party to the scheme or not,—maybe she is an' maybe she ain't. But from what Moll Hawk sez there's a scheme on foot to get the best of Rachel Gwyn by grabbin' Violy some night an' rushin' her to a hidin' place down the river where Barry figgers he c'n persuade her to marry him an' live happy ever afterwards, as the sayin' is. Seems that Barry figgers that you, bein' a sort o' brother to her, will put your foot down on them gettin' married, so he's goin' to get her away from here before it's too late. Moll sez it's all fixed up, 'cept the time fer doin' it. Martin Hawk an' a half dozen fellers from some'eres down the river is to do the job. All she knows is it's to be in the dark o'

the moon, an' that's not fer off. Moll sez she believes
Violy knows about the plan an' sort of agrees to—"

"I don't believe it, Stain," broke in Kenneth. "She
would not lend herself to a low-down trick like that."

Stain shook his head. "They say she's terrible in
love with Barry, an' gosh only knows what a woman'll
stoop to in order to git the man she's set her heart on.
Why, I could tell you somethin' about a woman that
was after me some years back,—a widder down below
Vincennes,—her husband used to run a flatboat,—an',
by cracky, Mr. Gwynne, you wouldn't believe the things
she done. Chased me clean down to Saint Louis an'
back ag'in, an' then trailed me nearly fifty miles
through the woods to an Injin village on the White
River. I don't know what I'd have done if it hadn't
been fer an Injin I'd befriended a little while back.
He shot her in the leg an' she was laid up fer nearly
six weeks, givin' me that much of a start. That was
four years ago an' to this day I never go to sleep at
night without fust lookin' under the bed. Some day I'll
tell you all about that woman, but not now. I'm jest
tellin' this to show you what a woman'll do when she
once makes up her mind, an' maybe Violy ain't any different from the rest of 'em."

"Nevertheless, Viola is not that kind," asserted
Kenneth, stubbornly. "She may be in love with Lapelle, but if she has made up her mind to be married at
her mother's house, that's the end of it. See here,
Stain, I've been thinking while you were talking. If
there is really anything in this story, I doubt the wisdom of going to Mrs. Gwyn with it, and certainly it
would be a bad plan to speak to Viola. We've got to
handle this matter ourselves. I want to catch Barry
Lapelle red-handed. That is the surest way to con-

vince Viola that he is an unworthy scoundrel. It is my duty to protect my—my sister—and I shall find a way to do so, whether she likes it or not. You know, perhaps, that we are not on the friendliest of terms."

"Yep, I know," said Stain. "You might as well know that I am on their side, Mr. Gwynne. Whatever the trouble is between you an' them two women, I am for them an' ag'in you. That's understood, ain't it?"

"It is," replied Kenneth, impressed by the hunter's frankness. "But all the more reason why in a case like this you and I should work hand in hand. I am glad you came to me with the Hawk girl's story. Hawk and his crew will find me waiting for them when they come. They will not find their job a simple one."

"I guess you'll need a little help, Mr. Gwynne," said Stain, drily. "What are you goin' to do? Call in a lot o' these dodgasted canary birds to fight the hawks? If you do, you'll get licked. What you want is a man er two that knows how to shoot an' is in the habit o' huntin' varmints. You c'n count on me, Mr. Gwynne, if you need me. If you feel that you don't need me, jest say so, an' I'll go it alone. I don't like Martin Hawk; we got a grudge to settle, him an' me. So make your choice. You an' me will work in cahoots with each other, or we'll go at it single-hand."

"We will work together, Stain," said Kenneth, promptly. "You know your man, you know the lay of the land, and you are smarter than I am when it comes to handling an affair of this kind. I will be guided by you. Shake hands."

The two men shook hands. Then the lawyer in Gwynne spoke.

"You should see this Hawk girl again and keep in

touch with their plans. We must not let them catch us napping."

"She's comin' to see me in a day er so. Mart Hawk went down to Attica to-day, him an' a feller named Suggs who's been soberin' up at Mart's fer the past few days. The chances are he's gone down there on this very business."

"Will you keep in touch with me?"

"Yes, sir. If you ain't got anything to do to-morrow, you might ride out to my place, where we c'n talk a little more free-like."

"A good idea, Stain. You are sure nothing is likely to happen to-night?"

"Not till the dark o' the moon, she sez."

"By the way, why is she turning against her father like this?"

"Well, you remember what I was jest sayin' about women,—how sot they are in their ways concarnin' a man? Well, Moll is after Barry Lapelle,—no question about that. She's an uncommon good-lookin' girl, I might say, an' I guess Barry ain't blind. Course, she's an unedicated girl an' purty poor trash,—you couldn't expect much else of a daughter of Martin Hawk, I guess,—but that don't seem to make much difference when it comes to fallin' in love. You don't need to have much book learnin' fer that. I could tell ye about a girl I used to know,—but we'll save it fer some other time."

"I see," mused Kenneth, reflectively. "She wants Lapelle for herself. But doesn't she realize that if they attempt this outrage her own father stands a pretty good chance of being shot?"

"Lord love ye, that don't worry her none," explained

the hunter. "She don't keer much what happens to
him. Why, up to this day he licks the daylights out
o' her, big as she is. You c'n hear her yell fer half a
mile. That's how she comes to be a friend o' mine. I
happened to be huntin' down nigh Mart's place last fall
an' heerd her screamin',—you could hear the blows
landin' on her back, too,—so I jest stepped sort o' spry
to'ards his cabin an' ketched him layin' it on with a
willer branch as thick as your thumb, an' her a
screechin' like a wild-cat in a trap. Well, what happened inside the next minute made a friend o' her fer
life,—an' an enemy o' him. You'd have thought any
dootiful an' loyal offspring would o' tried to pull me
off'n him, but all she done was to stand back an' egg
me on, 'specially when I took to tannin' him with the
same stick he'd been usin' on her. Seems like Mart's
never felt very friendly to'ards me sence that day."

"I shouldn't think he would."

"When I got kind o' wore out with wollopin' him, I
sot down to rest on the edge o' the waterin' trough, an'
she comes over to me an' sez she wished I'd stay an'
help her bury the old man. She said if I'd wait there
she'd go an' get a couple o' spades out'n the barn,—
well, to make a long story short, soon as Mart begin
to realize he was dead an' wasn't goin' to have a regular funeral, with mourners an' all that, he sot up an'
begin to whine all over ag'in. So I up an' told him
if I ever heerd of him lickin' his gal ag'in, I'd come
down an' take off what little hide there was left on him.
He said he'd never lick her ag'in as long as he lived. So
I sez to Moll, sez I, 'If you ever got anything to com-
plain of about this here white-livered weasel, you jest
come straight to me, an' I'll make him sorry he didn't
get into hell sooner.' Well, sir, after that he never

licked her without fust tyin' somethin' over her mouth
so's she couldn't yell, an' it wasn't till this afternoon
that I found out he'd been at it all along, same as ever,
'cept when Barry Lapelle was there. Seems that Barry
stopped him from lickin' her once, an' that made Moll
foller him around like a dog tryin' to lick his hand.
No, sir, she won't be heartbroke if somebody puts a
rifle ball between Mart's eyes an' loses it some'eres
back inside his skull. She'd do it herself if she wasn't
so doggoned sure somebody else is goin' to do it, sooner
or later."

"You say there was no one at home up at Mrs.
Gwyn's?" observed Kenneth, apprehensively. "That's
queer. Where do you suppose they are?"

"That's what I'm wonderin' about. Mrs. Gwyn
never goes nowhere, 'cept out to the farm, an' I'm
purty sure she didn't— Say, do you hear somebody
comin' up the road behind us?"

He laid a hand on Kenneth's arm and they both
stopped to listen.

"I hear no one," said the young man.

"Well, you ain't got a hunter's ears," said the other.
"Some one's follerin' us,—a good ways back. I've got
so's I c'n hear an acorn drop forty mile away."

They drew off into the shadows at the roadside and
waited. Twenty yards or more ahead gleamed the
lights in the windows of the nearest store. A few
seconds elapsed, and then Kenneth's ears caught the
sound of footsteps in the soft dirt road, and presently
the subdued murmur of voices.

"Women," observed Stain, laconically, lowering his
voice. "Let 'em pass. If we show ourselves now,
they'll think we're highwaymen or something, an' begin
screechin' fer dear life."

Two vague, almost indistinguishable figures took shape in the darkness down the road and rapidly drew nearer. They passed within ten feet of the two men,— black voiceless shadows. Stain's hand still gripped his companion's arm. The women had almost reached the patches of light cast upon the road from the store windows, before the hunter spoke.

"Recognize 'em?" he whispered.

"No."

"Well, I guess I know now why there wasn't nobody to home up yander. That was Violy an' her ma."

Kenneth started. "You—you don't mean it!"

"Yep. An' if you was to ask me what they air doin' down here by the river I'd tell you. Mrs. Gwyn jest simply took Violy down there to Trentman's shanty an' *showed* her Barry Lapelle playin' cards."

"Impossible! I would have seen them."

"Not from where you stood. The winders on the river side air open, an' you c'n see into the house. On the side facin' this way, Jack's got curtains hangin'. Well, Mrs. Gwyn took Violy 'round on t'other side where she could look inside. Maybe you didn't hear what they was sayin' when we fust heared 'em talkin'. Well, I did. I heared Violy say, plain as day, 'I don't keer what you say, mother, he swore to me he never plays except fer fun.' An' Rachel Gwyn, she sez, 'There ain't no setch thing as playin' fer fun in that place, so don't talk foolish.' That's all I heared 'em say,—an' they ain't spoke a word sence."

"Come along, Stain," said Kenneth, starting forward. "We must follow along behind, to see that they reach home safely."

The hunter gave vent to a deprecating grunt. "They won't thank us if they happen to turn around

an' ketch us at it. 'Sides, I got to be startin' to'ards
home. That ole hoss o' mine ain't used to bein' out
nights. Like as not, he's sound asleep this minute,
standin' over yander in front o' Curt Cole's blacksmith
shop, an' whenever that hoss makes up his mind he's
asleep there ain't nothin' that'll convince him he ain't.
There they go, turnin' off Main street, so's they won't
run across any curious-minded saints. Guess maybe
we'd better trail along behind, after all."

Fifteen minutes later the two men, standing back
among the trees, saw lights appear in the windows of
Mrs. Gwyn's house. Then they turned and wended
their way toward the public square. They had spoken
but few words to each other while engaged in the
stealthy enterprise, and then only in whispers. No
one may know what was in the mind of the hunter, but
in Kenneth's there was a readjustment of plans. A
certain determined enthusiasm had taken the place of
his previous depression. The excitement of possible
conflict, the thrill of adventure had wrought a complete change in him. His romantic soul was aflame.

"See here, Stain," he began, when they were down
the slope; "I've been thinking this matter over and I
have come to the conclusion that the best thing for me
to do is to go straight to Lapelle and tell him I am
aware of his—"

"Say, you're supposed to be a lawyer, ain't you?"
drawled his companion, sarcastically.

"Yes, I am," retorted Kenneth.

"Well, all I got to say is you'd make a better woodchopper. Barry'd jest tell you to go to hell, an' that'd
be the end of it as fer as you're concarned. Course,
he'd give up the plan, but he'd make it his business to
find out how you got wind of it. Next thing we'd

know, Moll Hawk would have her throat slit er somethin',—an' I reckon that wouldn't be jest what most people would call fair, Mr. Gwynne. I guess we'd better let things slide along as they air an' ketch Mart an' his crowd in the act. You don't reckon that Barry is goin' to take a active part in this here kidnappin' job, do you? Not much! He won't be anywheres near when it happens. He's too cute fer that. You won't be able to fasten anything on him till it's too late to do anything."

Kenneth was properly humbled. "You are right, Stain. If you hear of anybody who wants to have some wood chopped, free of charge, I wish you'd let me know."

"Well," began the laconic Mr. Stain, "it takes considerable practice to get to be even a fair to middlin' woodchopper."

CHAPTER XIII

BRIGHT and early the next morning Kenneth gave orders to have his new home put in order for immediate occupancy. Having made up his mind to remain in Lafayette and face the consequences that had seemed insurmountable the night before, he lost no time in committing himself to the final resolve. Zachariah was despatched with instructions to lay in the necessary supplies, while two women were engaged to sweep, scrub and furbish up the long uninhabited house. He had decided to move in that very afternoon.

Meanwhile he rented an "office" on the north side of the public square, a small room at the back of a furniture store, pending the completion of the two story brick block on the south side. With commendable enterprise he lost no time in outfitting the temporary office from the furniture dealer's stock. His scanty library of law books,—a half dozen volumes in all,—Coke, Kent and Chitty, among them,—had been packed with other things in the cumbersome saddle bags, coming all the way from Kentucky with him.

Of necessity he had travelled light, but he had come well provided with the means to purchase all that was required in the event that he decided to make Lafayette his abiding place.

As he was hurrying away from the tavern shortly after breakfast, he encountered Lapelle coming up

from the stable-yard. The young Louisianian appeared to be none the worse for his night's dissipa-
tion. In fact, he was in a singularly amiable frame of
mind.

"Hello," he called out. Kenneth stopped and
waited for him to come up. "I'm off pretty soon for
my place below town. Would you care to come along?
It's only about eight miles. I want to arrange with
Martin Hawk for a duck shooting trip the end of the
week. He looks after my lean-to down there, and he
is the keenest duck hunter in these parts. Better come
along."

"Sorry I can't make it," returned Kenneth. "I am
moving into my house to-day and that's going to keep
me pretty busy."

"Well, how would you like to go out with us a little
later on for ducks?"

"I'd like to, very much. That is, after I've got thoroughly settled in my new office, shingles painted, and
so forth. Mighty good of you to ask me."

Barry was regarding him somewhat narrowly.

"So you are moving up to your house to-day, are
you? That will be news to Viola. She's got the whim
that you don't intend to live there."

"I was rather undecided about it myself,—at least
for the present. I am quite comfortable here at Mr.
Johnson's."

"It isn't bad here,—and he certainly sets a good
table. Say, I guess I owe you a sort of apology,
Kenny. I hope you will overlook the way I spoke last
night when you said you couldn't go to Jack Trentman's. I guess I was a—well, a little sarcastic, wasn't
I?"

There was nothing apologetic in his voice or bearing. On the contrary, he spoke in a lofty, casual manner, quite as if this perfunctory concession to the civilities were a matter of form, and was to be so regarded by Gwynne.

"I make it a rule to overlook, if possible, anything a man may say when he is drinking," said Kenneth, smiling.

Barry's pallid cheeks took on a faint red tinge; his hard eyes seemed suddenly to become even harder than before.

"Meaning, I suppose, that you considered me a trifle tipsy, eh?" he said, the corner of his mouth going up in mirthless simulation of a grin.

"Well, you had taken something aboard, hadn't you?"

"A drink or two, that was all," said the other, shrugging his shoulders. "Anyhow, I have apologized for jeering at you, Gwynne, so I've done all that a sober man should be expected to do," he went on carelessly. "You missed it by not going down there with me last night. I cleaned 'em out."

"You did, eh?"

"A cool two thousand," said the other, with a satisfaction that bordered on exultation. "By the way, changing the subject, I'd like to ask you a question. Has a mother the legal right to disinherit a son in case said son marries contrary to her wishes?"

Kenneth looked at him sharply. Could it be possible that Lapelle's mother objected to his marriage with Viola, and was prepared to take drastic action in case he did so?

"Different states have different laws," he answered. "I should have to look it up in the statutes, Barry."

"Well, what is your own opinion?" insisted the

other, impatiently. "You fellows always have to look things up in a book before you can say one thing or another."

"Well, it would depend largely on circumstances," said Kenneth, judicially. "A parent can disinherit a child if he so desires, provided there is satisfactory cause for doing so. I doubt whether a will would stand in case a parent attempted to deprive a child of his or her share of an estate descending from another parent who was deceased. For example, if your father left his estate to his widow in its entirety, I don't believe she would have the right to dispose of it in her will without leaving you your full and legal share under the statutes of this or any other state. Of course, you understand, there is nothing to prevent her making such a will. But you could contest it and break it, I am sure."

"That's all I want to know," said the other, drawing a deep breath as of relief. "A close friend of mine is likely to be mixed up in just that sort of unpleasantness, and I was a little curious to find out whether such a will would stand the test."

"Your friend should consult his own lawyer, if he has one, Lapelle. That is to say, he should go to some one who knows all the circumstances. If you want my advice, there it is. Don't take my word for it. It is too serious a matter to be settled off-hand,—and my opinion in the premises may be absolutely worthless."

"I was only asking for my own satisfaction, Gwynne. No doubt my friend has already consulted a lawyer and has been advised. I must be off. Sorry you can't come with me."

Kenneth would have been surprised and disturbed if

he could have known all that lay behind these casual
questions. But it was not for him to know that Viola
had repeated Mrs. Gwyn's threat to her impatient, arrogant lover, nor was it for him to connect a simple
question of law with the ugly plot that had been revealed to Isaac Stain by Moll Hawk.

After two nights of troubled thought, Barry Lapelle had hit upon an extraordinary means to circum-
vent Rachel Gwyn. With Machiavellian cunning he
had devised a way to make Viola his wife without
jeopardizing her or his own prospects for the future.
No mother, he argued, could be so unreasonable as to
disinherit a daughter who had been carried away by
force and was compelled to wed her captor rather than
submit to a more sinister alternative.

Shortly after the noon meal, Kenneth rode up to the
old Gwyn house. He found Zachariah beaming on the
front door step.

"Yas, suh,—yas, suh!" was the servant's greeting.
"Right aroun' dis way, Marse Kenny. Watch out,
suh, ailse yo' scrape yo' hat off on dem branches."

He grasped the bit, after his master had dismounted
in the weed-covered little roadway at the side of the
house, and ceremoniously waved his hand toward the
open door.

"Step right in, suh,—yas, suh,—an' make yo'self to
home, suh. Sit right down front of de fiah, Marse
Kenny. Ah won't be more'n two shakes, suh, stablin'—
yas, suh! Come on hyar, yo' Brandy Boy! Ise gwine
show yo' whar yo's gwine to be de happies' hoss in—
yas, suh,—yas, suh!"

The young man looked long and searchingly through
the trees before entering the house, but saw no sign of
his neighbours. He thought he detected a slight move-

ment of a curtain in one of the windows,—the parlor window, if his memory served him right.

It was late in the afternoon before he saw either of his relatives. He had had occasional glimpses of the negro servant-girl and also of a gaunt stable-man, both of whom favoured his partially obscured abode with frank interest and curiosity. A clumsy, silent hound came up to the intervening fence several times during the afternoon and inspected the newcomers with seeming indifference, an attitude which misled Zachariah into making advances that were received with alarming ill-temper.

Kenneth was on his front doorstep, contemplating with secret despair the jungle of weeds and shrubbery that lay before him, completely obliterating the ancient path down to the gate. The whole place was overgrown with long, broken weeds, battered into tangled masses by the blasts of winter; at his feet were heaps of smitten burdocks and the dead, smothered stems of hollyhocks, geraniums and other garden plants set out and nurtured with tender care by Rachel Gwyn during her years of occupancy. The house needed painting, the roof required attention, the front gate was half open and immovably imbedded in the earth.

He was not aware of Viola's presence on the other side of the fence dividing the two yards until her voice fell upon his ears. It was clear and sweet and bantering.

"I suppose you are wondering why we haven't weeded the yard for you, brother Kenny."

As he made his way through the weeds to the fence, upon which she rested her elbows while she gazed upon him with a mocking smile in the eyes that lay far back in the shovel-like hood of her black quaker bonnet, he

experienced a sudden riotous tumult in the region of his
heart. Shaded by the dark, extended wings of the
bonnet, her face was like a dusky rose possessed of the
human power to smile. The ribbon, drawn close under
her chin, was tied in a huge bow-knot, while at the back
of her head the soft, loose cap of the bonnet fitted
snugly over hair that he knew would gleam with tints
of bronze if exposed to the rays of the sinking sun.

"Not at all," he rejoined. "I am wondering just
where I'd better begin."

"Did you find the house all right?"

"Yes. You have saved me a lot of trouble, Viola."

"Don't give me credit for it. Mother did everything. I suppose you know that the furniture and
other things belong to you by rights. She didn't give
them to you out of charity."

"The last thing in the world I should expect would
be charity from your mother," he said, stung by the
obvious jibe.

She smiled tolerantly. "She is more charitable than
you imagine. It was only last night that she said she
wished Barry Lapelle was half as good and upright as
you are."

"That was very kind of her. But if such were the
case, I dare say it never would have occurred to you
to fall in love with him."

He had come up to the fence and was standing with
his hand on the top rail. She met his ironic gaze for
a moment and then lowered her eyes.

"I wish it were possible for us to be friends, Kenny,"
she surprised him by saying. "It doesn't seem right
for us to hate each other," she went on, looking up at
him again. "It's not our fault that we are who and
what we are. I can understand mother's attitude to-

ward you. You are the son of another woman, and I suppose it is only natural for her to be jealous. But you and I had the same father. It—it ought to be different with us, oughtn't it?"

"It ought to be,—and it shall be, Viola, if you are willing. It rests entirely with you."

"It is so hard to think of you as a brother. Somehow I wish you were not."

"It is pretty hard luck, isn't it? You may be sure of one thing. If I were not your brother I would be Barry Lapelle's most determined rival."

She did not laugh at this. On the contrary, her eyes clouded.

"The funny part of it is, Kenny, I have been wondering what would have happened if you had come here as a total stranger and not as my relation." Then she smiled whimsically. "Goodness knows poor Barry is having a hard enough time of it as it is, but what a time he would be having if you were some one else. You see, you are very good-looking, Kenny, and I am a very silly, frivolous, susceptible little goose."

"You are nothing of the kind," he exclaimed warmly, adding in some embarrassment, "except when you say that I am good-looking."

"And I have also been wondering how many girls have been in love with you," she went on archly; "and whether you have a sweetheart now,—some one you are engaged to. You needn't be afraid to tell me. I can keep a secret. Is there some one back in Kentucky or in the east who—"

"No such luck," whispered simple, honest Kenneth. "No one will have me."

"Have you ever asked anybody?" she persisted.

"No,—I haven't."

"Then, how do you know that no one will have you?"

"Well, of course, I—I mean to say I can't imagine any one caring for me in that way."

"Don't you expect ever to get married?"

"Why,—er,—naturally I—" he stammered, bewildered at this astonishing attack.

"Because if you want to remain a bachelor, I would advise you not to ask any one of half a dozen girls in this town that I could mention. They would take you so quick your head would swim."

By this time he had recovered himself. Affecting grave solicitude, he inquired:

"Is there any one here that you would particularly desire as a sister-in-law?"

She shook her head, almost pensively. "I don't want you to bring any more trouble into the family than you've already brought, and goodness knows *that* would be doing it. But I shouldn't have said that, Kenny. There are lots of fine, lovely girls here. I wouldn't know which one to pick out for you if you were to ask me to do your choosing."

"I will leave it entirely in your hands," said he, grinning boyishly. "Pick me out a nice, amiable, rather docile young lady,—some one who will come the nearest to being a perfect sister-in-law, and I will begin sparking her at once. By the way, I hope matters are going more smoothly for you and Barry."

Her face clouded. She shot a suspicious, questioning look at him.

"I—I want to talk to you about Barry some day," she said seriously.

"You seemed to resent it most bitterly the last time I attempted to talk to you about him," said he, somewhat pointedly.

"You were horrid that day," said she. "I have a good deal to forgive. You said some very mean, nasty things to me that day over there," indicating the thicket with a jerk of her head.

"I am glad to see that you took them to heart and have profited," he ventured boldly.

She hesitated, and then spoke with a frankness that shamed him. "Yes, I did take them to heart, Kenny. I will not say that I have profited, but I'll never make the same kind of a fool of myself again. I hated you with all my soul that day,—and for a long time afterward,—but I guess you took the right way with me, after all. If I was fair and square, I would say that I am grateful to you. But, you see, I am not fair and square. I am as stubborn as a mule."

"The best thing about a mule is that he takes his whalings without complaining."

She sighed. "I often wonder what a mule thinks about when he stands there without budging while some angry, infuriated man beats him until his arm gets tired."

"That's very simple. He just goes on thinking what a fool the man is for licking a mule."

"Good! I hope you will remember that the next time you try to reason with me."

"What is it you want to say to me about Barry?" he asked, abruptly.

"Oh, there is plenty of time for that," she replied, frowning. "It will keep. How are you getting along with the house?"

"Splendidly. It was in very good order. I will be settled in a day or two and as comfortable as anything. To-night Zachariah and I are going to make a list of everything we need and to-morrow I shall start out on a purchasing tour. I intend to buy quite a lot of new furniture, things for the kitchen, carpets and—"

Viola interrupted him with an exclamation. Her eyes were shining, sparkling with eagerness.

"Oh, won't you take me along with you? Mr. Hanna has just received a wonderful lot of things from down the river, and at Benbridge & Foster's they have a new stock of—"

"Hurrah!" he broke in jubilantly. "It's just what I wanted, Viola. Now you are being a real sister to me. We will start early in the morning and—and buy out the town. Bless your heart, you've taken a great load off my mind. I haven't the intelligence of a snipe when it comes to fitting up a—why, say, I tell you what I'll do. I will let you choose everything I need, just as if you were setting up housekeeping for yourself. Curtains, table cloths, carpets, counterpanes, china, Queensware, chairs, chests—"

"Brooms, clothes-pins, rolling-pins, skillets, dough-bowls, cutlery—"

"Bureaus, looking-glasses, wardrobe, antimacassar tidies, bedspreads, towels—"

"Oh, Kenny, what fun we'll have," she cried. "And, first of all, you must let me come over right now and help you with your list. I know much better than you do what you really need,—and what you don't need. We must not spend too much money, you see."

" 'Gad," he gulped, "you—you talk just as if you and I were a poor, struggling young couple planning to get married."

"No, it only proves how mean and selfish I am. I am depriving your future bride of the pleasure of furnishing her own house, and that's what all brides like better than anything. But I promise to pick out

things that I know she will like. In the meantime, you
will be happy in knowing that you have something
handsome to tempt her with when the time comes. As
soon as you are all fixed up, you must give a party.
That will settle everything. They'll all want to marry
you,—and they'll have something to remember me by
when I'm gone. Come on, Kenny, let's go in and start
making the list."

She started off toward her own gate, but stopped as
he called out to her.

"Wait! Are you sure your mother will approve of
your—"

"Of course she will!" she flung back at him. "She
doesn't mind our being friendly. Only,"—and she came
back a few steps, "I am afraid she will never be friends
with you, Kenny. I am sorry."

He was silent. She waited for a moment before
turning away, shaking her head slightly as if attempting to dismiss something that perplexed her sorely.
There was a yearning in his eyes as they followed her
down to the gate; then he shot a quick, accusing glance
at the house in which his enemy lived. He saw the white
curtains in the north parlor window drop into place,
flutter for a second or two, and then hang perfectly
still. Rachel Gwyn had been watching them. He made
no effort to hide the scowl that darkened his brow as he
continued to stare resentfully at the window.

He met Viola at his own disabled gate, which cracked
and shivered precariously on its rusty hinges as he
jerked it open.

"I lived for nearly three years in this house, Kenny,"
she said as she picked her way through the weeds. "I
slept on a very hard straw tick up in the attic. It
was dreadfully cold in the winter time. I used to shiver

all night long curled up with my knees up to my chin.
And in the summer time it was so hot I slept with absolutely nothing,—" She broke off in sudden confusion.
"Our new house is only about a year old," she went
on after a moment. Pointing, she added: "That is
my bedroom window up there. You can get a glimpse
of it through the trees but when the leaves are out
you can't see it at all from here."

"I shall keep an eye on that window," said he, with
mock severity, "and if ever I catch you climbing down
on a ladder to run away with—well, I'll wake the dead
for miles around with my yells. See to it, my dear
sister, that you attempt nothing rash at the dead hour
of night."

She laughed. "Have you seen our dog? I pity the
valiant knight who tries to put a ladder up to my
window."

They spent the better part of an hour going over
the house. She was in an adorable mood. Once she
paused in the middle of a sentence to ask why he was
so solemn.

"Goodness me, Kenny, you look as if you had lost
your very best friend. Aren't you interested? Shall
we stop?"

A feeling of utter desolation had stricken him. He
was sick at heart. Every drop of blood in his body
was crying out for her. Small wonder that despair
filled his soul and lurked in his gloomy, disconsolate
eyes. She had removed her bonnet. If he had thought
her beautiful on that memorable night at Striker's he
now realized that his first impression was hopelessly
inadequate. Her eyes, dancing with eagerness, no
longer reflected the disdain and suspicion with which
she had regarded him on that former occasion. Her

smile was frank and warm and joyous. He saw her now as she really was, incomparably sweet and charming—and so his heart was sick.

"I wouldn't stop for the world," he exclaimed, making a determined effort to banish the tell-tale misery from his eyes.

"I know!" she cried, after a searching look into his eyes. "You are in love with some one, Kenny, and you are wishing that she were here in my place, helping you to plan the—"

"Nonsense," he broke in gruffly. "Put that out of your head, Viola. I tell you there is no—er—no such girl."

"Then," she said darkly, "it must be the dreadful extravagance I am leading you into. Goodness, when I look at this list, I realize what a lot of money it is going to take to—"

"We're not half through," he said, "and I am not thinking of the expense. I am delighted with everything you have suggested. I shudder when I think how helpless I should have been without you. Didn't I tell you in the beginning that I wanted you to fix this house up just as if you were planning to live in it yourself? Put down all the things you would most like to have, Viola, and—and—well, confound the expense. Come along! We're losing time. Did you jot down that last thing we were talking about? That— er—that—" He paused, wrinkling his forehead.

"I don't believe you have been paying any attention to what— Now, tell me, what *was* the last thing we were talking about?"

He squinted hard at the little blank book in her hand. She closed it with a snap.

"Have you got it down?" he demanded severely.

"I have."

"Then, there's no use worrying about it," he said, with great satisfaction. "Now, let me see: don't you think I ought to have a clock for the mantelpiece?"

"I put that down half an hour ago," she said. "The big gold French clock I was telling you about."

"That's so. The one you like so well down at Currie's."

They proceeded. He had followed about, carrying the ink pot into which she frequently dipped the big quill pen. She overlooked nothing in the scantily furnished house. She even went so far as to timidly suggest that certain articles of furniture might well be replaced by more attractive ones, and he had promptly agreed. At last she announced that she must go home.

"If you buy all the things we have put down here, Kenny, you will have the loveliest house in Lafayette. My, how I shall envy you!"

"I have a feeling I shall be very lonely—amidst all this splendour," he said.

"Oh, no, you won't. I shall run in to see you every whipstitch. You will get awfully sick of having me around."

"I am thinking of the time when you are married, Viola, and,—and have gone away from Lafayette."

"Well," she began, her brow clouding, "you seem to have got along without me for a good many years, —so I guess you won't miss me as much as you think. Besides, we are supposed to be enemies, aren't we?"

"It doesn't look much like it now, does it?"

"No," she said dubiously, "but I—I must not do anything that will make mother feel unhappy or—"

He broke in a little harshly. "Are you forgetting

how unhappy it will make her if you marry Barry Lapelle?"

"Oh, that may be a long way off," she replied calmly. "You see, Barry and I quarrelled yesterday. We both have vile tempers,—perfectly detestable tempers. Of course, we will make up again—we always do—but there may come a time when he will say, 'Oh, what's the use trying to put up with you any longer?' and then it will all be over."

She was tying her bonnet strings as she made this astonishing statement. Her chin being tilted upward, she looked straight up into his eyes the while her long, shapely fingers busied themselves with the ribbons.

"I guess you have found out what kind of a temper I have, haven't you?" she added genially. As he said nothing (being unable to trust his voice): "I know I shall lead poor Barry a dog's life. If he knew what was good for him he would avoid me as he would the plague."

He swallowed hard. "You—you will not fail to come with me to-morrow morning on the purchasing tour," he said, rather gruffly. "I'll be helpless without you."

"I wouldn't miss it for anything," she cried.

As they walked down to the gate she turned to him and abruptly said:

"Barry is going down the river next week. He expects to be away for nearly a fortnight. Has he said anything to you about it?"

Kenneth started. Next week? The dark of the moon.

"Not a word," he replied grimly.

CHAPTER XIV

KENNETH'S first night in the old Gwyn house was an uneasy, restless one, filled with tormenting doubts as to his strength or even his willingness to continue the battle against the forces of nature.

Viola's night was also disturbed. Some strange, mysterious instinct was at work within her, although she was far from being aware of its significance. She lay awake for a long time thinking of him. She was puzzled. Over and over again she asked herself why she had blushed when he looked down at her as she was tying her bonnet-strings, and why had she felt that queer little thrill of alarm? And why did he look at her like that? She answered this question by attributing its curious intensity to a brotherly interest—which was quite natural—and the awakening of a dutiful affection—but that did not in any sense account for the blood rushing to her face, so that she must have reminded him of a "turkey gobbler." She announced to her mother at breakfast:

"I don't believe I can ever think of Kenny as a brother."

Rachel Gwyn looked up, startled. "What was that you called him?" she asked.

"Kenny. He has always been called that for short. And somehow, mother, it sounds familiar to me. Have I ever heard father speak of him by that name?"

"I—I am sure I do not know," replied her mother uneasily. "I doubt it. It must be a fancy, Viola."

"I can't get over feeling shy and embarrassed when he looks at me," mused the girl. "Don't you think it odd? It doesn't seem natural for a girl to feel that way about a brother."

"It is because you are not used to each other," interrupted Rachel. "You will get over it in time."

"I suppose so. You are sure you don't mind my going to the stores with him, mother?"

Her mother arose from the table. There was a suggestion of fatalism in her reply. "I think I can understand your desire to be with him." She went to the kitchen window and looked over at the house next door. "He is out in his back yard now, Viola," she said, after a long pause, "all dressed and waiting for you. You had better get ready."

"It will not hurt him to wait awhile," said Viola perversely. "In fact, it will do him good. He thinks he is a very high and mighty person, mother." She glanced at the clock on the kitchen wall. "I shall keep him waiting for just an hour."

Rachel's strong, firm shoulders drooped a little as she passed into the sitting-room. She sat down abruptly in one of the stiff rocking-chairs, and one with sharp ears might have heard her whisper to herself:

"We cannot blindfold the eyes of nature. They see through everything."

It was nine o'clock when Viola stepped out into her front yard, reticule in hand, and sauntered slowly down the walk, stopping now and then to inspect some Maytime shoot. He was waiting for her outside his own gate.

"What a sleepy-head you are," was her greeting as she came up to him.

"I've been up since six o'clock," he said.

"Then, for goodness' sake, why have you kept me waiting all this time?"

"My dear Viola, I was not born yesterday, nor yet the day before," he announced, with aggravating calmness. "Long before you were out of short frocks and pantalettes I was a wise old gentleman."

"I don't know just what you mean by that."

"I learned a great many years ago that it is always best to admit you are in fault when a charming young lady says you are. If you had kept me waiting till noon I should still consider it my duty to apologize. Which I now do."

She laughed merrily. "Come along with you. We have much to do on this fine May day. First, we will go to the hardware store, saving the queensware store till the last,—like float at the end of a Sunday dinner.

And so they advanced upon the town, as fine a pair as you would find in a twelvemonth's search. First she conducted him to Jimmy Munn's feed and wagon-yard, where he contracted to spend the first half-dollar of the expedition by engaging Jimmy to haul his purchases up to the house.

"Put the sideboards on your biggest wagon, Jimmy," was Viola's order, "and meet us at Hinkle's."

She proved to be a very sweet and delightful autocrat. For three short and joyous hours she led him from store to store, graciously leaving to him the privilege of selection but in nine cases out of ten demonstrating that he was entirely wrong in his choice, always with the naïve remark after the purchase was completed and the money paid in hand: "Of course,

Kenny, if you would rather have the other, don't for the world let me influence you."

"You know more about it than I do," he would invariably declare. "What do I know about carpets?"— or whatever they happened to be considering at the time.

She was greatly dismayed, even appalled, as they wended their way homeward, followed by the first wagonload of possessions, to find that he had spent the stupendous, unparalleled sum of two hundred and forty-two dollars and fifty cents.

"Oh, dear!" she sighed. "We must take a lot of it back, Kenny. Why didn't you keep track of what you were spending? Why, that's nearly a fourth of one thousand dollars."

He grinned cheerfully. "And we haven't begun to paint the house yet, or paper the walls, or set out the flower beds, or—"

"Goodness me!" she cried, aghast. "You are not going to do all that now, are you?"

"Every bit of it," he affirmed. "I am going to rebuild the barn, put in a new well, dig a cistern, build a smokehouse, lay a brick walk down to the front gate and put up a brand new picket fence—"

"You must be made of money," she cried, eyeing him with wonder in her big, violet eyes.

"I am richer now than when we started out this morning," said he, magnificently.

"When you say things like that, you almost make me wish you were not my brother," said she, after a moment, and to her annoyance she felt the blood mount to her face.

"And what would you do if I were not your brother?" he inquired, looking straight ahead.

Whereupon she laughed unrestrainedly. "You would be dreadfully shocked if I were to tell you,—but I can't help saying that Barry would be so jealous he wouldn't know what to do."

"You might find yourself playing with fire."

"Well," she said, flippantly, "I've got over wanting to play with dolls. Now don't scold me! I can see by your face that you'd like to shake me good and hard. My, what a frown! I am glad it isn't January. If your face was to freeze— There! That's better. I shouldn't mind at all if it froze now. You look much nicer when you smile, Kenny." Her voice dropped a little and a serious expression came into her eyes. "I don't believe I ever saw father smile. But I've seen him when he looked exactly as you did just then. I— I hope you don't mind my talking that way about your father, Kenny. I wouldn't if he were not mine as well."

"You knew him far better than I," he reminded her. Then he added brightly: "I shall try to do better from now on. I'll smile—if it kills me."

"Don't do that," she protested, with a pretty grimace. "I've been in mourning for ages, it seems, and I'm sure I should hate you if you kept me in black for another year or two."

As they parted at Kenneth's gate,—it seemed to be mutely understood that he was to go no farther,— they observed a tall, black figure cross the little front porch of the house beyond and disappear through the door. Kenneth's eyes hardened. The girl, looking up into those eyes, shook her head and smiled wistfully.

"Will you come over and help me put all these things where they belong?" he asked, after a moment.

"This afternoon, Kenny?"

"If you haven't anything else you would rather—" he began.

"I can't wait to see how the house will look when we get everything in place. I will be over right after dinner,—unless mother needs me for something."

.   .   .   .

That evening Zachariah was noticeably perturbed. He had prepared a fine supper, and to his distress it was scarcely touched by his preoccupied master. Now, Zachariah was proud of his cooking. He was pleased to call himself, without fear of contradiction, "a natteral bo'n cook, from de bottom up." Moreover, his master was a gentleman whose appetite was known to be absolutely reliable; it could be depended upon at almost any hour of the day or night. Small wonder then that Zachariah was not only mystified but grieved as well. He eyed the solemn looking young man with anxiety.

"Ain't yo' all feelin' well, Marse Kenneth?" he inquired, with a justifiable trace of exasperation in his voice.

"What's that, Zachariah?" asked Kenneth, startled out of a profound reverie.

"Is dey anything wrong wid dat ham er—"

"It is wonderful, Zachariah. I don't believe I have ever tasted better ham,—and certainly none so well broiled."

"Ain't—ain't de co'n-bread fitten to eat, suh?"

"Delicious, Zachariah, delicious. You have performed wonders with the—er—new baking pan and—"

"What's de matteh wid dem b'iled pertaters, suh?"

"Matter with them? Nothing! They are fine."

"Well, den, suh, if dere ain't nothin' de matteh wid

de vittels, dere suttinly mus' be somefin de matteh wid you, Marse Kenneth. Yo' all ain't etten enough fo' to fill a grasshoppeh."

"I am not hungry," apologized his master, quite humbly.

" 'Cause why? Yas, suh,—'cause why?" retorted Zachariah, exercising a privilege derived from long and faithful service. " 'Cause Miss Viola she done got yo' all bewitched. Can't fool dis yere nigger. Wha' fo' is yo' all feelin' dis yere way 'bout yo' own sister? Yas, suh,—Ah done had my eyes open all de time, suh. Yo' all was goin' 'round lookin' like a hongry dog, 'spectin'— Yas, suh! Yas, *suh!* Take plenty, suh. Marse Johnson he say to me, he say, 'Dis yere sap come right outen de finest maple tree in de State ob Indianny, day befo' yesterday,' he say. A leetle mo' coffee, suh? Yas, suh! Das right! Yo' suttinly gwine like dat ham soon as ever yo' get a piece in yo' mouth,—yas, *suh!*"

Kenneth's abstraction was due to the never-vanishing picture of Viola, the sleeves of her work-dress rolled up to the elbows, her eyes aglow with enthusiasm, her bonny brown hair done up in careless coils, her throat bare, her spirits as gay as the song of a roistering gale. She had come over prepared for toil, an ample apron of blue gingham shielding her frock, her skirts caught up at the sides, revealing the bottom of her white petticoat and a glimpse of trim, shapely ankles.

She directed the placing of all the furniture carried in by the grunting Jimmy Munn and Zachariah; she put the china safe and pantry in order; she superintended the erection of the big four poster bed, measured the windows for the new curtains, issued irrevocable commands concerning the hanging of several gay English hunting prints (the actual hanging to be done by Kenneth and his servant in a less crowded hour,—after supper, she suggested); ordered Zachariah to remove to the attic such of the discarded articles of furniture as could be carried up the pole ladder, the remainder to go to the barn; left instructions not to touch the rolls of carpet until she could measure and cut them into sections, and then went away with the promise to return early in the morning not only with shears and needle but with Hattie as well, to sew and lay the carpets,—a "Brussels" of bewildering design and an "ingrain" for the bedroom.

"When you come home from the office at noon, Kenny, don't fail to bring tacks and a hammer with you," she instructed, as she fanned her flushed face with her apron.

"But I am not going to the office," he expostulated. "I have too much to see to here."

"It isn't customary for the man of the house to be anywhere around at a time like this," she informed him, firmly. "Besides you ought to be down town looking for customers. How do you know that some one may not be in a great hurry for a lawyer and you not there to—"

"There are plenty of other lawyers if one is needed in a hurry," he protested. "And what's more, I can't begin to practise law in this State without going through certain formalities. You don't understand all these things, Viola."

"Perhaps not," she admitted calmly; "but I do understand moving and house-cleaning, and I know that a man is generally in the way at such times. Oh, don't look so hurt. You have been fine this afternoon. I

don't know how I should have got along without you.
But to-morrow it will be different.   Hattie and I will
be busy sewing carpets and—and—well, you really will
not be of any use at all, Kenny.   So please stay away."

He was sorely disgruntled at the time and so disconsolate later on that it required Zachariah's startling
comment to lift him out of the slough of despond.
Spurred by the desire to convince his servant that his
speculations were groundless, he made a great to-do
over the imposed task of hanging the pictures, jesting
merrily about the possibility of their heads being
snapped off by Mistress Viola if she popped in the next
morning to find that they had bungled the job.

Four or five days passed, each with its measure of
bitter and sweet.   By the end of the week the carpets
were down and the house in perfect order.   He invited
her over for Sunday dinner.   A pained, embarrassed
look came into her eyes.

"I was afraid you would ask me to come," she said
gently.   "I don't think it would be right or fair for me
to accept your hospitality.   Wait!   I know what you
are going to say.   But it isn't quite the same, you see.
Mother has been very kind and generous about letting
me come over to help you with the house,—and I suppose she would not object if I were to come as your
guest at dinner,—but I have a feeling in here somewhere that it would hurt her if I came here as your
guest.   So I sha'n't come.   You understand, don't
you?"

"Yes," he said gravely,—and reluctantly.   "I understand, Viola."

Earlier in the week he had ridden out to Isaac
Stain's.   The hunter had no additional news to give
him, except that Barry, after spending a day with

Martin Hawk, had gone down to Attica by flat-boat and was expected to return to Lafayette on the packet *Paul Revere*, due on Monday or Tuesday.

Lapelle's extended absence from the town was full of meaning. Stain advanced the opinion that he had gone down the river for the purpose of seeing a Williamsport justice of the peace whose record was none too good and who could be depended upon to perform the contemplated marriage ceremony without compunction if his "palm was satisfactorily greased."

"If we could only obtain some clear and definite idea as to their manner of carrying out this plan," said Kenneth, " I would be the happiest man on earth. But we will be compelled to work in the dark,—simply waiting for them to act."

"Well, Moll Hawk hain't been able to find out just yet when er how they're goin' to do it," said Stain. "All she knows is that two or three men air comin' up from Attica on the *Paul Revere* and air goin' to get off the boat when it reaches her pa's place. Like as not this scalawag of a justice will be one of 'em, but that's guesswork. That reminds me to ask, did you ever run acrosst a feller in the town you come from named Jasper Suggs?"

"Jasper Suggs? I don't recall the name."

"Well, she says this feller Suggs that's been stayin' at Martin's cabin fer a week er two claims to have lived there some twenty odd years ago. Guess you must ha' been too small to recollect him. She says he sort of brags about bein' a renegade durin' the war an' fightin' on the side of the Injins up along the Lakes. He's a nasty customer, she says. Claims to be a relation of old Simon Girty's,—nephew er something like that."

"Does he claim to have known any of my family down there?" inquired Kenneth, apprehensively.

"From what Moll says he must have knowed your pa. Leastwise, he says the name's familiar. He was sayin' only a day or two ago that he'd like to see a picter of your pa. He'd know if it was the same feller he used to know soon as he laid eyes on it."

Kenneth pondered a moment and then said: "Do you suppose you could get a letter to Moll Hawk if I were to write it, Stain?"

"I could," said the other, "but it wouldn't do any good. She cain't read er write. Besides, if I was you, I wouldn't risk anything like that. It might fall into Hawk's hands, and the fust thing he would do would be to turn it over to Lapelle,—'cause Martin cain't read himself."

"I was only wondering if she could find out a little more about this man Suggs,—just when he lived there and—and all that."

"He's purty close-mouthed, she says. Got to be, I reckon. He fell in with Martin ten er twelve years ago, an' there was a price on his head then. Martin hid him for awhile an' helped him to git safe away. Like as not Suggs ain't his real name anyhow."

Kenneth was a long time in deciding to speak to Rachel Gwyn about the man Suggs. He found an opportunity to accost her on the day that the *Paul Revere* came puffing up to the little log-built landing near the ferry. Viola had left the house upon learning that the boat had turned the bend in the river two or three miles below town, and had made no secret of her intention to greet Lapelle when he came ashore. This was Gwynne's first intimation that she was aware of her lover's plan to return by the *Paul Revere*. He was distinctly annoyed by the discovery.

Rachel was in her back yard, feeding the chickens, when he came up to the fence and waited for her to look in his direction. All week,—in fact, ever since he had come up there to live,—he had been uncomfortably conscious of peering eyes behind the curtains in the parlor window. Time and again he had observed a slight flutter when he chanced to glance that way, as of a sudden release of the curtains held slightly apart by one who furtively watched from within. On the other hand, she never so much as looked toward his house when she was out in her own yard or while passing by on the road. Always she was the straight, stern, unfriendly figure in black, wrapped in her own thoughts, apparently ignorant of all that went on about her.

She turned at last and saw him standing there.

"May I have a word with you?" he said.

She did not move nor did she speak for many seconds, but stood staring hard at him from the shade of her deep black bonnet.

"What is it you want, Kenneth Gwynne?"

"No favour, you may be sure, Rachel Carter."

She seemed to wince a little. After a moment's hesitation, she walked slowly over to the fence and faced him.

"Well?" she said curtly.

"Do you remember a man at home named Jasper Suggs?"

"Are you speaking of my old home in Salem or of—of another place?"

"The place where I was born," he said, succinctly.

"I have never heard the name before," she said. "Why do you ask?"

"There is a man in this neighbourhood,—a rascal, I am told,—who says he lived there twenty years ago."

She eyed him narrowly. "Well,—go on! What has he to say about me?"

"Nothing, so far as I know. I have not talked with him. It came to me in a roundabout way. He is staying with a man named Hawk, down near the Wea."

"He keeps pretty company," was all she said in response to this.

"I have been told that he would like to see a daguerreotype of my father some time, just to make sure whether he was the Gwynne he used to know."

"Has he ever seen you, Kenneth Gwynne?" She appeared to be absolutely unconcerned.

"No."

"One look at you would be sufficient," she said. "If you are both so curious, why not arrange a meeting?"

"I am in no way concerned," he retorted. "On the other hand, I should think you would be vitally interested, Rachel Carter. If he knew my father, he certainly must have known you."

"Very likely. What would you have me do?" she went on ironically. "Go to him and beg him to be merciful? Or, if it comes to the worst, hire some one to assassinate him?"

"I am not thinking of your peace of mind. I am thinking of Viola's. We have agreed, you and I, to spare her the knowledge of—"

"Quite true," she interrupted. "You and I have agreed upon that, but there it ends. We cannot include the rest of the world. Chance sends this man,

whoever he may be, to this country. I must likewise
depend upon Chance to escape the harm he may be in a
position to do me. Is it not possible that he may have
left before I came there to live? That chance remains,
doesn't it?"

"Yes," he admitted. "It is possible. I can tell you
something about him. He is related to Simon Girty,
and he was a renegade who fought with the Indians up
north during the war. Does that throw any light upon
his identity?"

"He says his name is Suggs?" she inquired.

He was rewarded by a sharp catch in her breath and
a passing flicker of her eyes.

"Jasper Suggs."

She was silent for a moment. "I know him," she said
calmly. "His name is Simon Braley. At any rate,
there was a connection of Girty's who went by that
name and who lived down there on the river for a year
or two. He killed the man he was working for and
escaped. That was before I—before I left the place.
I don't believe he ever dared to go back. So, you see,
Chance favours us again, Kenneth Gwynne."

"You forget that he will no doubt remember you as
Rachel Carter. He will also remember that you had a
little girl."

"Let me remind you that I remember the cold-blooded
murder of John Hendricks and that nobody has been
hung for it yet," she said. "My memory is as good as
his if it should come to pass that we are forced to
exchange compliments. Thank you for the information. The sheriff of this county is a friend of mine.
He will be pleased to know that Simon Braley, murderer and renegade, is in his bailiwick. From what I

know of Simon Girty's nephew, he is not the kind of man who will be taken alive."

He started. "You mean,—that you will send the sheriff out to arrest him?"

She shook her head. "Not exactly," she replied. "Did you not hear me say that Simon Braley would never be taken alive?"

With that, she turned and walked away, leaving him to stare after her until she entered the kitchen door. He was conscious of a sense of horror that began to send a chill through his veins.

CHAPTER XV

THE *Paul Revere* tied up at the landing shortly after two o'clock. The usual crowd of onlookers thronged the bank, attention being temporarily diverted from an important game of "horseshoes" that was taking place in the sugar grove below Trentman's shanty.

Pitching horseshoes was the daily fair-weather pastime of the male population of the town. At one time or another during the course of the day, practically every man in the place came down to the grove to shy horseshoes at the stationary but amazingly elusive pegs. It was not an uncommon thing for a merchant to close his place of business for an hour or so in order to keep an engagement to pitch horseshoes with some time-honoured adversary.

On this occasion a very notable match was in progress between "Judge" Billings and Mr. Pennington Sawyer, the real estate agent. They were the recognized champions. Both were accredited with the astonishing feat of ringing eight out of ten casts at twenty paces; if either was more than six inches away from the stake on any try the crowd mutely attributed the miss to inhibitions of the night before. Not only was the betting lively when these two experts met but all other matches were abandoned during the classic clash.

The "Judge" did not owe his title to service on the

bench nor even at the bar of justice. It had been bestowed upon him by a liberal-minded community because of his proficiency as a judge of horse races, foot races, shooting matches, dog or rooster fights, and other activities of a similar character. He was, above all things, a good judge of whiskey. When not engaged in judging one thing or another, he managed to eke out a comfortable though sometimes perilous living by trading horses,—a profession which made him an almost infallible judge of men, notwithstanding two or three instances where he had erred with painful results to his person. Notably, the prodigious thrashing Jake Miller had given him two days after a certain trade, and an almost identical experience with Bud Shanks who had given a perfectly sound mare and seventeen dollars to boot for a racehorse that almost blew up with the heaves before Bud was half-way home.

But, whatever his reputation may have been as a horse-trader, "Judge" Billings was unaffectedly noble when it came to judging a contest of any description. Far and wide he was known to be "as honest as the day is long," proof of which may be obtained from his publicly uttered contention that "nobody but a derned fool would do anything crooked while a crowd was lookin' on, with more'n half of 'em carryin' guns or some other weapon that can't be expected to listen to argument."

He was Kenneth Gwynne's first client. In employing the young man to defend a suit brought by Silas Kenwright, he ingenuously announced that the plaintiff had a perfectly good case and that his only object in fighting the claim was to see how near Silas could come to telling the truth under oath. Mr. Kenwright was demanding twenty-five dollars damages for slander. In the complaint Mr. Billings was charged with having held Mr. Kenwright up to ridicule and contumely by asseverating that said plaintiff was "a knock-kneed, cross-eyed, red-headed, white-livered liar."

"The only chance we've got," he explained to Gwynne, "is on the question of his liver. We can prove he's a liar,—in fact, he admits that,—but, dog-gone it, he's as bow-legged as a barrel hoop, he's wall-eyed, and what little hair he's got is as black as the ace o' spades. I don't suppose the Court would listen to a request to have him opened up to see what colour his liver is,—and that's where he's got us. It ain't so much being called a liar that riles him; he's used to that. It's being called knock-kneed and cross-eyed. He don't mind the white-livered part so much, or the way I spoke about his hair, 'cause one of 'em you can't see an' the other could be dyed or sheared right down to the skin if the worst came to the worst. If I'd only called him a lousy, ornery, low-lived, sheep-steal-ing liar, this here suit never would have been brought. But what did I do but up and hurt his feelings by callin' him knock-kneed and cross-eyed. That comes of not stickin' to the truth, Mr. Gwynne,—and it's a derned good lesson for me. Honesty is the best policy, as the feller says. It'll probably cost me forty or fifty dollars for being so slack with my veracity."

Kenneth's suggestion that an effort be made to set-tle the controversy out of court had met with instant opposition.

"It ain't to be thought of," declared Mr. Billings firmly. "Why, dodgast it, you don't suppose I'm going to pay that feller any money, do you? Not much! I'm willing enough to let him get a judgment against me for any amount he wants, just fer the fun of it, but,

by gosh, when you begin to talk about me giving him
money, why, that's serious. I'm willing to pay you
your ten dollars fee and the court costs, but the only
way Si Kenwright can ever collect a penny from me
will be after I'm dead and he sneaks in when nobody's
around and steals the coppers off my eyes."

This digression serves a simple purpose. It intro-
duces a sporty gentleman of unique integrity whose
friendship for Kenneth Gwynne flowered as time went
on and ultimately bore such fruits as only the most
favoured of men may taste. In passing he may be described as a pudgy, middle-aged individual, with mild
blue eyes, an engaging smile, cherubic cheeks, sandy
hair, and a highly pitched, far-reaching voice. He
also had a bulbous nose resembling a large, ripe straw-
berry.

Before coming to rest alongside the wharf, the *Paul
Revere* indulged in a vast amount of noise. She whistled and coughed and sputtered and gasped with all the
spasmodic energy of a choking monster; her bells kept
up an incessant clangour; her wheel creaked and grov-
elled on the bed of the river, churning the water into a
yellowish, foaming mass; her captain bellowed and
barked, her crew yelped, her passengers shouted; the
flat boats and perogues moored along the bank, aroused
from their lassitude, began to romp gaily in the swirl
of her crazy backwash; ropes whined and rasped and
groaned, the deck rattled hollowly with the tread of
heavy feet and the shifting of boxes and barrels and
crates; the gangplank came down with a crash,—and
so the mighty hundred and fifty ton leviathan of the
Wabash came to the end of her voyage!

There were a score of passengers on board, among
them Barry Lapelle. He kept well in the rear of the

motley throng of voyagers, an elegant, lordly figure, approached only in sartorial distinction by the far-famed gambler, Sylvester Hornaday, who likewise held himself sardonically aloof from the common horde, occupying a position well forward where, it might aptly be said, he could count his sheep as they straggled ashore.

From afar Barry had recognized Viola standing among the people at the top of the bank, and his eager, hungry gaze had not left her. She, too, had caught sight of him long before the boat was near the landing. She waved her kerchief.

He lifted his hat and blew a kiss to her. A thrill of exultation ran through him. He had not expected her to meet him at the landing. Her mere presence there was evidence of a determination to defy not only her mother but also to brave the storm of gossip that was bound to attend this public demonstration of loyalty on her part, for none knew so well as he how the towns-people looked upon their attachment. A most satisfying promise for the future, he gloated; here was the proof that she loved him, that her tantalizing outbursts of temper were not to be taken seriously, that his power over her was irresistible. There were times when he felt uncomfortably dubious as to his hold upon her affections. She was whimsical, perverse, maddening in her sudden transitions of mood. And she had threatened more than once to have nothing more to do with him unless he mended his ways! Now he smiled triumphantly as he gazed upon her. All that pother about nothing! Henceforth he would pay no attention to her whims; let her rail and fume and lecture as much as she liked, there was nothing for him to be worried about. She would always come round like a lamb,—

and when she was his for keeps he would take a lot of the nonsense out of her!

With few exceptions the passengers on board the *Revere* were strangers,—fortune-seekers, rovers, land-buyers and prospectors from the east and south come to this well-heralded region of promise, perhaps to stay, perhaps to pass on. Three or four Lafayette men, home after a trip down the river, crowded their way ashore, to be greeted by anxious wives. The strangers were more leisurely in their movements. They straggled ashore with their nondescript possessions and ambled off between two batteries of frank, appraising eyes.

Judge Billings, shrewd calculator of human values, quite audibly disclosed his belief that at least three of the newcomers would have to be run out of town before they were a day older, possibly astraddle of a rail.

One of these marked individuals was a tall, swart, bearded fellow with black, shifty eyes and a scowling brow. His baggage consisted of a buckskin sack slung across his shoulder and a small bundle which he carried under his arm. He appeared to have no acquaintances among the voyagers.

"You don't know how happy this makes me, Viola," exclaimed Lapelle as he clasped the girl's hand in his. He was devouring her with a bold, consuming gaze.

She reddened. "I told mother I was coming down to meet you," she explained, visibly embarrassed by the stares of those nearby. "I—I wanted to see you the instant you arrived, Barry. Shall we walk along slowly behind the rest?"

"What's happened?" he demanded suspiciously, his brow darkening.

"Don't be impatient. Wait till they are a little ahead."

" 'Gad, it sounds ominous. I thought you came down to meet me because you love me and were—well, glad to see me."

"I am glad to see you. You didn't expect me to make an exhibition of myself before all those people, did you?"

His face brightened. "Well, *that* sounds better." His mouth went up at the corner in its habitual curl. "I'd give all I possess if it was dark now, so that I could grab you and squeeze the—"

"Sh! They will hear you," she whispered, drawing away from him in confusion.

They held back until the throng had moved on a short distance. Then she turned upon him with a dangerous light in her eyes.

"And what's more," she said in a low voice, "I don't like to hear you say such things. They sound so cheap and low—and vulgar, Barry. I—"

"Oh, you're always jumping on me for saying the things I really feel," he broke in. "You're my girl, aren't you? Why shouldn't I tell you how I feel? What's vulgar about my telling you I want to hold you in my arms and kiss you? Why, I don't think of anything else, day or night. And what do I get? You put me off,—yes, you do!—bringing up some silly notion about—about—what is it?—propriety! Good Lord, Viola, that's going back to the days of the Puritans,—whoever they were. They just sat around and held hands,—and that's about all I've been allowed to do with you. It's not right,—it's not natural, Viola. People who are really in love with each other just simply can't help kissing and—"

"I guess you were right when you said you were not expecting me down to meet the boat, Barry," she interrupted, looking straight before her.

"Well, didn't I tell you how happy it made me?"

"If you had thought there was any chance of me coming down to meet you, you wouldn't have taken so much to drink," she went on, a little catch in her voice.

Whereupon he protested vigorously that he had not tasted a drop,—except one small dram the captain had given him early that morning when he complained of a chill.

"Why, you're drunk right now," she said miserably. "Oh, Barry, won't you ever—"

"Drunk? I'm as sober as the day I was born," he retorted, squaring his shoulders. "Look at me,—look me in the eye, Viola. Oh, well, if you *won't* look you won't, that's all. And if I'm as drunk as you imagine I am I should think you'd be ashamed to be seen in my company." She did not respond to this, so, with a sneering laugh, he continued: "Suppose I have had a little too much,—who's the cause of it? You! You drive me to it, you do. The last couple of weeks you've been throwing up all my faults to me, tormenting me till I'm nearly crazy with uncertainty. First you say you'll have me, that you'll do anything I wish, and then, just as I begin to feel that everything's all right, you up and say you're not sure whether you care for me or not and you're going to obey your mother in every— And, say, that reminds me. Unless I am very much mistaken, I think I'll soon have a way to bring your mother to time. She won't—"

He brought himself up with a jerk, realizing that his loose tongue was running away with his wits. She was looking at him with startled, inquiring eyes.

"What do you mean by that, Barry Lapelle?" she asked, and he was quick to detect the uneasiness in her manner.

He affected a grin of derision. "I'm going to put my case in the hands of Kenny Gwynne, the rising young barrister. With him on our side, my dear, I guess we'll bring her to time. All he has to do is to stand up to her and say he isn't going to put up with any more nonsense, and she'll see the light of wisdom. If he thinks it's all right for you to marry me, I guess that will end the matter. He's the head of the family, isn't he?"

This hastily conceived explanation of his luckless remark succeeded in deceiving her. She stared at him in distress.

"Oh, Barry, you—you surely can't be thinking of asking Kenneth to intercede—"

"Why not? He doesn't see any reason why we shouldn't be married, my dear. In fact, he told me so a few days ago. He—"

"I don't believe it," she cried.

"You don't?" he exclaimed sharply.

"No, I don't," she repeated.

"Has he been talking to you about me?" he demanded, an ugly gleam flashing into his eyes.

"He has never said a word against you,—not one. But I don't believe you when you say he told you that we ought to get married." She felt her cheeks grow hot. She had turned her face away from him.

"I'm a liar, am I?" he snarled.

"I—I don't believe he ever said it," she said stubbornly.

"Well,—you're right," he admitted, after a moment's

hesitation. "Not in so many words. But he did say to me that he had told you he saw no reason why you shouldn't marry me if you wanted to. Did he ever tell you that?"

She remembered only too well the aggravating encounter in the thicket path.

"Yes, he did," she replied, lifting her head defiantly. "And," she added, "I hated him for it. I hate him more and more every time I think of it. He—he was perfectly abominable."

"Well, you're—you're damned complimentary," he grated, his face expressing the utmost bewilderment.

She walked on for eight or ten paces before speaking again. Her head was lowered. She knew that he was glaring at the wing of the bonnet which shielded her whitening cheek. Suddenly she turned to him.

"Barry, let's sit down on that log over there for a few minutes. There is something I've got to say to you,—and I'm sorry. You must not be angry with me. Won't you come over there with me,—and listen to what I have to tell you?"

He hung back for a moment, his intuition grasping at something vague and yet strangely definite.

"You—you are going to tell me it's all over between us, Viola?" he ventured, going white to the lips. He was as sober now as though he had never touched liquor in his life.

"Come and sit down," she said gently, even compassionately.

He followed her in silence to the log she had indicated, a few rods back from the roadside at the edge of the clearing. He sat down beside her and waited for her to speak, and as she remained speechless, evidently in distress, his lips curled in a smile of reviving confidence. He watched the quick rise and fall of her bosom, exulting in her difficulty.

Birds were piping among the fresh green twigs overhead. The air was redolent of the soft fragrance of May: the smell of the soil, the subtle perfume of unborn flowers, the tang of the journeying breeze, the spice of sap-sweating trees. The radiance of a warm, gracious sun lay soft upon the land.

At last she spoke, not tremulously as he had expected but with a firmness that boded ill for his composure.

"Barry," she began, still staring straight ahead, "I don't know just how to begin. It is awfully hard to—to say what I feel I must say. Perhaps I should have waited till—well, till you were home for a little while,—before doing what I have made up my mind to do. But I thought it right to have it over with as soon as possible."

She paused for a moment and then resolutely faced him. He saw the pain in her dark, troubled eyes, and the shadow of an appealing smile on her lips. His face hardened.

"So," she went on unflinchingly, "I came down to the landing to meet you in case you were on the *Paul Revere*. I cannot marry you, Barry. I—I don't love you as I should. I thought I did but—but—well, that's all. I don't know what has happened to make me see things so differently, but whatever it is I know now that I was mistaken,—oh, so terribly mistaken. I know I am hurting you, Barry,—and you have a right to despise me. I—I somehow hope you will,—because I deserve it."

He smiled indulgently. "I hope you don't think I

am taking this seriously. This isn't the first time I've
heard you take on like—"

"But I mean it this time, Barry,—I do truly and
honestly," she cried. "I know I've played hot and cold
with you,—and that's just the point. It proves that
I never really cared for you in—in that way—down
in my soul, I mean. I am sure of it now. I have been
dreadfully unhappy about it,—because, Barry dear, I
can't bear to hurt you. We are not suited to each
other. We think differently about a great many things.
We—"

"Look here," he exclaimed roughly, no longer able to
disguise his anger; "you've got to stop this everlasting—"

"Let go of my arm, Barry Lapelle!" she cried.
"Don't you dare lay your hand on me like that!"

He loosened his grip on her arm and drew back
sulkily. "Ah,—I didn't mean to hurt you and you
know it. I wouldn't hurt you for anything in the
world. I'm sorry if I was rough with—"

"I don't blame you," she broke in, contritely. "I
guess it would serve me right if you beat me black and
blue."

"What I was going to say," he growled, controlling
himself with difficulty, "is this: if you think I'm going
to take this as final, you're very much mistaken.
You'll get over this, just as you've gotten over your
peevishness before. I've spoiled you, that's the truth of
the matter. I always give in to you—"

"I tell you I am in earnest," she cried hotly. "This
is for good and all,—and you make me furious when
you talk like that. I am doing my best to be kind and
considerate, so you'd better be careful, Barry Lapelle,
not to say too much."

He looked into her flaming eyes for a moment and then muttered slowly, wonderingly: "By heaven, Viola, I believe you *do* mean it. You—you are actually throwing me over,—giving me the mitten?"

"I can't help it, Barry," she insisted. "Something, —I don't know what,—has come over me. Nothing seems to be the same as it used to be. I only know that I cannot bear the thought of—why, Barry dear, for the past three or four nights I've lain awake for hours thinking of the awful consequences if we had succeeded in making our escape that night, and had been married as we planned. How terrible it would have been if I had found out too late that I did not love you,—and we were tied to each other for life. For your sake as well as my own, Barry. Can you imagine anything more horrible than to be married to a woman who— who didn't love you?"

"Yes," he snapped, "I can. It's worse a thousand times over not to be married to the girl you love,—and to see her married to some one else. That would be hell,—hell, do you understand?"

She drew a little away from him. "But not the hell it would be for me when I found out—too late. Won't you understand, Barry? Can't you see how terrible it would be?"

"Say, when did you get this idea into your head?" he demanded harshly. "What put it there? You were loving me hard enough a while ago,—couldn't get along without me, you claimed. Now you're singing another tune. Look here! Is—is there some one else?"

"You know there isn't," she cried indignantly. "Who else could there be? Don't be foolish, Barry."

"By God, if some one else has cut me out, I'll— I'll—"

"There is no one else, I tell you! I don't love anybody,—I swear it."

He eyed her narrowly. "Has Kenny Gwynne anything to do with all this?"

She started. "Kenny? Why,—no,—of course not. What on earth could he have to do with my loving or not loving you?"

"It would be just like him to turn you against me because he thinks I'm not fit to— Say, if I find out that he's been sticking his nose into my affairs, I'll make it so hot for him,—brother or no brother,—that he'll wish he'd never been born. Wait a minute! I'll tell you what I think of him while I'm about it—and you can run and tell him as quick as you please. He's a G— d—— snake in the grass, that's what he is. He's a conceited, sanctimonious, white-livered—"

"Stop that!" she cried, springing to her feet, white with fury, her eyes blazing. "You are forgetting yourself, Barry Lapelle. Not another word! How dare you speak like that about my brother?"

He sat staring up at her in a sort of stupefaction.

"How dare you?" she repeated furiously.

He found his voice. "You weren't sticking up for him this time last week," he sneered. "You were hating him like poison. Has the old woman had a change of heart, too? Is she letting him sit in her lap so's she can feed him with a spoon when he's hungry and—"

"I wouldn't marry you if you were the only man in the world, Barry Lapelle," said she, her voice low with passion.

She whirled and walked rapidly away from him, her head in the air, her hands clenched. Leaping to his feet, he started after her, calling:

"Wait a minute, Viola! Can't you see I'm almost

out of my head over what you've— Oh, well, go it! I'm not going to *crawl* after you! But let me tell you one thing, my girl. You'll be talking out of the other side of your mouth before you're much older. You'll be down on your knees—"

"Don't you follow me another step!" she cried over her shoulder.

He was not more than two yards behind her when she uttered this withering command. He stopped short in his tracks.

"Well, this is a hell of a way to treat a gentleman!" he shouted, hoarse with fury.

CHAPTER XVI

CONCERNING TEMPESTS AND INDIANS

SHORTLY after dark that evening, the tall, swarthy man who had come up on the *Paul Revere* sauntered slowly up and down that part of Main Street facing the Court House. Ostensibly he was inspecting store windows along the way, but in reality he was on the lookout for a man he had agreed to meet at a point just above the tavern,—a casual meeting, it was to appear, and between two strangers.

Barry Lapelle came out of the tavern at the stroke of eight and walked eastward a few paces, halting at the dark open lot between Johnson's place and Smith's store beyond. The swarthy man approached slowly, unconcernedly. He accosted Lapelle, inquiring:

"Is that the tavern, Mister?"

"Yes," replied Barry, needlessly pointing down the street. "Well?"

"It's her," said the stranger. "I had a good look at her 'long about five o'clock from the woods across from her house. She's a heap sight older but I knowed her all right."

"You are sure?"

"Sure as my name is—"

"Sh!"

"Course I'm sure. She was Owen Carter's widder. He was killt by a tree fallin' on him. Oh, I got a good memory. I can't afford to have a bad one. I remem-

ber her as plain as if it wuz yestiday." He pointed
off in a westerly direction for the benefit of a passerby.
"Thank ye, mister. You say it's not more'n six mile
out yan way?" Lowering his voice, he went on: "A
feller wouldn't be likely to fergit a woman like her.
Gosh, I used to wish—but wishin' don't count fer much
in this world."

"Get on with it. We can't stand here talking all
night."

"Well, she's the woman that run off with Bob
Gwynne. There ain't no doubt about it. Everybody
knowed it. I wuz there at the time, workin' fer Ed
Peters. He left his wife an' a little boy. His wife was
a daughter of ole Squire Blythe,—damn his heart!
He had me hoss-whipped in public fer—well, fer some
triflin' thing I done. Seems to me Mrs. Carter had a
little baby girl. Maybe not. I ain't much of a hand
fer noticin' babies."

"You are sure,—absolutely positive about all this?"
whispered Lapelle intensely.

"You bet yer boots I am."

"She ran off with a married man?"

"She did. A feller by the name o' Gwynne, as I
said afore,—Bob Gwynne. An' I want to tell you, he
got out o' that town jest in time or I'd have slit his
gizzard fer him. He had me arrested fer stealin' a
saddle an' bridle. He never *would* have got away ef
I hadn't been locked up in Jim Hatcher's smokehouse
with two men settin' outside with guns fer a solid
month, keepin' watch on me day an' night. I wuz—"

"That's all for to-night," snapped Barry impatiently. "You get out of town at once. Mart will be
waiting for you down below Granny Neff's cabin,—
this side of the tanyard,—as arranged."

"What about that other business? Mart'll want to know when we're to—"

"He knows. The *Paul Revere* goes south day after to-morrow morning. If the plans are changed before that time, I'll get word to him. It may not be necessary to do anything at all. You've given me information that may bring the old woman to her senses."

"Them two fellers that come up on the boat to-day. Air you sure you c'n—"

"That's all for to-night," interrupted Barry, and strode off up the street, leaving Jasper Suggs, sometime Simon Braley of the loathsome Girty stock, to wend his lonely way out into a silence as black as the depths of his own benighted soul.

The night was sultry. Up in the marshy fastnesses of Lake Stansbury all the frogs in the universe seemed to have congregated for a grand festival of song. The treble of baby frogs, the diapason of ancient frogs, the lusty alto of frogs in the prime of life, were united in an unbroken, penetrating chant to the starless sky. The melancholy hoot of the owl, the blithesome chirp of the cricket, even the hideous yawp of the roaming loon, were lost in the din and clatter of Lake Stansbury's mighty chorus.

There was promise of storm in the lifeless air. Zachariah, resting his elbows on the fence, confided this prognostication to an almost invisible Hattie on the opposite side of the barrier between two back yards.

"Ah allus covers my haid up wid de blanket—an' de bolster—an' de piller when hit's astormin'," said Hattie, in an awed undertone. "An' Ah squeals lak a pig ev' time hit claps."

"Shucks, gal!" scoffed Zachariah. "What yo' all so skeert o' lightnin' fo'? Why, good lan' o' Goshen,

Ah hain't no mo' askeert o' storms dan Ah is ob—ob *you!*" He chuckled rather timorously after blurting out this inspired and (to him) audacious remark. To his relief and astonishment, Hattie was not offended.

"Ah bet yo' all hain't see no setch thunderstorms as we has 'round dis yere neck o' de woods," said she, with conviction. "Ah bet yo' be skeert ef you—"

"Don' yo' talk to me, gal," boasted Zachariah. "Wuzzin Ah in de wustest storm dis yere valley has seed sence dat ole Noah he climb up in dat ole ark an' sez, 'Lan' sakes, Ah wonder ef Ah done gone an' fergit anyt'ing.' Yes, *ma'am,*—dat evenin' out to Marse Striker's—dat wuz a storm, gal. Wuz Ah skeert? No, *suh!* Ah stup right out in de middle of it, lightnin' strikin' all 'round an' de thunder so turrible Marse Kenneth an' ever'body ailse wuz awonderin' ef de good Lord could hear 'em prayin' fo' mercy. Yas, suh— yas, *suh!* Dat's de gospel trufe. An' me right out dere in dat ole barnyard doin' de chores fo' ole Mis' Striker. Marse Kenneth he stick his haid out'n de winder an' yell, 'Zachariah, yo' come right in heah dis minnit! Yo' heah me? Wha' yo' all doin' out dere in dat hell-fire an' brimstone? Ah knows yo' is de bravest nigger in all dis world, but fo' mah sake, Zachariah, won't yo' *please* come in?' Well, suh, jes' den Ah happens to look up from what Ah wuz doin' an' sees a streak o' lightnin' comin' straight to'ards de cabin. So Ah yells fo' him to pull his haid in mighty quick, an' shore 'nuff he got it in jes' in de nick o' time. Dat streak o' lightnin' went right pass de winder an' hit de groun'. Den hit sort o' bounce up in de air an' lep right over mah haid an' hitten a tree—"

"Wuz hit rainin' all dis time?"

"Rainin'?   Mah lan', gal, course hit wuz rainin'," replied Zachariah, somewhat testily.   "Hitten a tree not more'n ten foot from where Ah wuz—"

"Hain't yo' all got no sense at all, nigger?" demanded Hattie, witheringly.   "Don' yo' know 'nough to go in out'n de rain?"

Zachariah was flabbergasted. Here was a bolt from a supposedly clear and tranquil sky; it flattened him out as no stroke of lightning could ever have done. For once in his life he was rendered speechless.

Hattie, who had got religion on several unforgettable occasions and was at this very time on the point of returning to the spiritual fold which she had more or less secretly abandoned at the behest of the flesh, regarded this as an excellent opportunity to re-establish herself as a disciple of salvation.

"An' what's more, nigger," she went on severely, "ef de good Lord ever cotch setch a monst'ous liar as yo' is out in a hurricane lak what yo' all sez it wuz, dere wouldn't be no use buryin' what wuz lef' of yo'. 'Cause why, 'cause yo' jes' gwine to be a lil black cinder no bigger'n a chinkapin. I knows all about how brave yo' wuz out to Marse Striker's. Miss Violy she done tell how yo' all snuck under de table an' prayed an' carried on somefin' scan'lous."

Zachariah, though crushed, made a noble effort to extricate himself from the ruins. "Ah lak to know what Miss Violy knows about me on dat yere occasion. Yas, suh,—dat's what Ah lak to know. She never lay eyes on me dat night. 'Ca'se why? 'Ca'se I wuz out in de barnlot all de time. She done got me contwisted wid dat other fool nigger, dat's what she done."

"What other fool nigger?"

"Didden she tell yo' all about dat nigger we fotch along up from Craffordsville to—"

"Yas, suh, she done tole all about dat Craffordsville nigger, ef dat's de one yo' means."

Zachariah was staggered. "She—she tole yo' about —about dat Craffordsville nigger?"

"Yas, suh,—she did. Miss Violy she say he wuz de han'-somest boy she ever did see,—great big strappin' boy wid de grandest eyes an'—"

"Dat's enough,—dat'll do," exclaimed Zachariah in considerable heat. "Marse Kenneth he got to change his tune, dat's all I got to say. He say Ah am de biggest liar in dis yere land,—but, by golly, he ain' ever heared about dis yere gal Hattie. No, *suh!* When Ah lies, Ah lies about *somefin'*, but when yo' lies, yo' jes' lies about *nuffin'*,—'ca'se why? 'Ca'se dat Craffords-ville nigger he ain' nuffin'. Yo' ought to be 'shamed o' yo'self, nigger, makin' out Miss Violy to be a liar lak dat,—an' her bein' de fines' lady in—"

"Go on 'way wid yo', nigger," retorted Hattie airily. "Don' yo' come aroun' heah no mo' makin' out how brave yo' is,—'ca'se Ah knows a brave nigger when Ah sees one, lemme tell yo' dat, Mistah Zachariah What-ever-yo'-name is."

Silence followed this Parthian shot. Zachariah, being a true philosopher, rested his case without further argument. He appeared to have given himself up to reflection. Presently Hattie, tempering her voice with honey, remarked:

"Ah suttinly is mighty glad yo' is come up yere to live, Zachariah."

"Look here, gal,—don' yo' go countin' on me too much," said he, suspiciously. "Ah got all Ah c'n do 'tendin' to mah own wo'k 'thout comin' over yander an' hulpin' yo'—"

"Lan's sakes, man, 'tain't mah look-out ef yo' come over yere an' tote mah clo'se-basket an' ev'thing 'round fo' me,—no, suh! Ah ain' nev' ast yo', has Ah? All Ah does is to hole Cato so he won't chaw yo' laig off when yo' come botherin' me to please 'low yo' to hulp me,—das all Ah do. An' lemme tell yo', nigger, dat ain' no easy job. 'Ca'se ef dere's one t'ing Cato do enjoy hit's dark meat,—yas, suh, hit's come so he won't even look at light meat no mo', he so sick o' feedin' off'n dese yere white shin-bones."

"Well, den, why is yo' glad Ah come up yere to live?" demanded Zachariah defensively.

" 'Ca'se o' dis yere ole Black Hawk."

"Ah don' know nuffin' 'bout no ole Black Hawk."

"Yo' all gwine to know 'bout him mighty quick," said she solemnly. "He's on de rampage. Scalpin' an' burnin' white folks at de stake an' des wallerin' in blood. Yas, suh,—Ah suttinly ain't gwine feel so skeert o' dat ole Black Hawk 'long as yo' is livin' right nex' do', Zachariah."

"Wha' yo' all talkin' about?"

"Marse Joe,—he de sheriff dis yere county,—he done tole ole Mis' Gwyn dis evenin' all de news 'bout dat ole Black Hawk. Yas, suh,—ole Black Hawk he on de warpath. All de Injuns in dis yere—"

"Injuns?" gulped Zachariah.

"Dey all got dere warpaint on an' dere tommy-hawks—"

"How come Marse Kenneth he don' know nuffin' 'bout all dis?" demanded Zachariah, taking a step or two backward and glancing anxiously over one shoulder, then the other. "He a lawyer. How come he don' know nuffin' 'bout— Say, how close dat ole sheriff say dem Injuns is?"

"Dat's what I can't make out, Zachariah. He talk so kind o' low an' me lettin' de dishpan drop right in de middle—"

"Ah guess Ah better go right straight in de house an' tell Marse Kenneth 'bout dis," hastily announced Zachariah. Then he bethought himself to add: " 'Ca'se me an' him got a lot to do ef dese here Injuns come 'roun' us lookin' fo' trouble. Yas, suh! Ah got to git de guns an' pistols an' huntin' knives all ready fo'—"

The words froze on his lips. A low, blood-curdling moan that seemed to end in a gasp,—or even a death-rattle,—fell upon the ears of the two negroes. It was close at hand,—not more than twenty feet away. This was succeeded, after a few seconds of intense stillness —(notwithstanding the uproarious frogs!)—by a hair-raising screech from Hattie. An instant later she was scuttling for her own kitchen door, emitting inarticulate cries of terror.

As for Zachariah? His course was a true one so far as direction was concerned. Blind instinct located the back door for him and he made a bee-line toward it regardless of all that lay between. First he encountered a tree-stump. This he succeeded in passing without the slightest deviation from the chosen route. Scrambling frantically to his feet after landing with a mighty grunt some two yards beyond the obstacle, he dashed onward, tearing his way through a patch of gooseberry bushes, coming almost immediately into contact with the wood-pile. Here he was momentarily retarded in his flight. There was a great scattering of stove-wood and chips, accompanied by suppressed

howls, and then he was on his feet again. Almost
simultaneously the heavy oak door received and with-
stood the impact of his flying body; a desperate clawing
at the latch, the spasmodic squeak of rusty hinges, a
resounding slam, the jar of a bolt being shot into place,
—and Zachariah vociferously at prayer in a sanctuary
behind the kitchen stove.

CHAPTER XVII

REVELATIONS

THAT sepulchral groan had issued not from a mortal in the agony of impending death but from the smiling red lips of Viola Gwyn. The grewsome "death-rattle" was the result of the means she took to suppress a shriek of laughter by frantically clapping both hands to her convulsed mouth.

For some time she had been standing at the fence, her elbows on the top rail, gazing pensively at the light in Kenny's window. A clump of honeysuckle bushes was between her and the unsuspecting servants. At first she had paid little or no attention to the gabble of the darkies, her thoughts being centred on her own serious affairs. She had been considerably shaken and distressed by the unpleasant experience of the early afternoon. Somehow she longed to take her troubles to Kenneth, to rid herself of them in the comfort of his approbation, to be reassured by his brotherly counsel. She knew he was sitting beside the table in the cosy sitting-room, poring over one of his incomprehensible law books. How jolly, how consoling to her own agitated mind, if she could only be there in the same room with him, quiet as a mouse so as not to disturb his profound studies, and reposing in that comfortable new rocker on the opposite side of the table where she could watch the studious frown on his brow while she waited patiently for him to lay aside the book.

Indeed, she had come out of the house animated by

a sudden impulse to pay him a brief, surreptitious visit; then to run back home before she was missed by her mother. This impulse was attended by a singularly delightful sensation of guilt. She had never been over to see him at night. In fact, it had never occurred to her to do such a thing before. But even as she started forth from the house, a strange timidity assailed her. It halted her impetuous footsteps, turned them irresolutely aside, and led her not to the gate but to the barrier fence. She could not explain, even to herself, the queer, half-frightened thumping of her heart, nor the amazing shyness, nor the ridiculous feeling that it would be improper for her to be alone with him at night.

But why, she argued,—why should it be improper? What could be wrong in going to see her own brother? What difference did it make whether it was night or day? Still the doubt persisted,—a nagging yet agreeable doubt that made her all the more eager to defy its feeble authority. First she sought to justify her inclination by reminding herself that her mother had never by word or look signified the slightest opposition to her intimacy with Kenneth. This attitude of resignation on her mother's part, however, was a constant thorn in her side, a prick to her conscience. It caused her many a pang.

Then she called to mind certain of her girl friends who had brothers,—one in particular who declared that she had slept in the same bed with her brother up to the time she was fourteen years old. She felt herself turn scarlet. That was really quite dreadful, even though the cabin in which her friend dwelt was very tiny and there were six children in the family. She had bitterly envied certain others, those who told of the jolly good times they had had with their brothers, the fun they had in quarrelling and the way they teased the boys when they first began "going out" with the girls.

What fun to have had a brother when she was little, —a brother to play with! Kenny was so unreal. He was not like a brother at all. He was no different from other men,—she did not believe she could ever get used to thinking of him as a brother,—even a half-brother. This very thought was in her mind,—perhaps it was an ever-present thought,—as she stood gazing shyly at his window.

She wanted to tell him about her break with Barry. Somehow,—although she was not quite conscious of it,—she longed to have him pat her on the shoulder, or clasp her hands in his, and tell her she had done the right thing and he was glad. The corners of her mouth were drooping a little.

But the pensive droop slowly disappeared as she harkened to the valiant words of Zachariah. It was not until Kenny's servant lifted his voice in praise of his own deeds at Phineas Striker's that she became acutely aware of the close proximity of the speakers. Gradually she surrendered to the spirits of mirth and mischief. The result of her awesome moan,—even though it narrowly escaped ending in a shriek of laughter,—has already been revealed. The manner of Zachariah's flight sobered her instantly. Too late she regretted the experiment.

"Oh, goodness!" she murmured, blanching. "The poor fellow has hurt himself—"

The slamming of the door behind Zachariah was reassuring. At any rate he was alive and far too sprightly to have suffered a broken leg or a cracked skull. A few seconds later she saw Kenny's shadow flit hurriedly past the window as he dashed toward the kitchen. For some time she stood perfectly still, listening to the confused jumble of voices in the house across the way, debating whether she should hurry over to explain,—and perhaps to assist in dressing poor Zachariah's cuts and bruises. Suddenly she decided; and, without thought of her garments, she scrambled hastily over the fence. Just as her feet touched the ground, the front door of Kenneth's house flew open and a figure, briefly revealed by the light from within, rushed out into the yard and was swallowed up by the darkness. She whirled and started to climb back over into her own yard, giggling hysterically. She heard the rush of feet through the weeds and shrubbery. They halted abruptly, and then:

"Stop where you are, damn you! I've got you covered and, so help me God, I'll put a bullet through—"

"Kenny! Kenny!" she cried out. "It's I—Viola!"

There was a moment's silence.

"My God! You? Viola?" came in suppressed, horrified tones from the darkness. "Drop down,—drop to the ground! They may begin firing at me. You—"

"Firing at you?" she cried, shakily. "What on earth are you talking about? There's—there's no one here. I am all alone. I did it. I'm the ghost. It was all in fun. I didn't dream—"

"Do as I tell you!" he called out sharply. "There is a pack of ruffians—"

"Pack your granny!" she cried, with a shrill laugh. "I tell you I am all alone. My goodness, what on earth did Zachariah think was after him? A regiment of soldiers?"

As he came quickly toward her she shrank back,

seized by a strange, inexplicable panic. He loomed
above her in the darkness as she half-crouched against
the fence. For a few seconds he stood looking down
at her, breathing sharply. She heard something drop
at his feet, and then both his hands gripped her shoulders, drawing her roughly up to him.

"Oh-h! Wh-what are you doing?" she gasped as
his arm went around her. That arm of steel drew her
so close and held her so tightly to his breast that she
could feel the tremendous thumping of his heart. She
felt herself trembling—trembling all over; the light in
the window up beyond seemed to draw nearer, swelling
to vast proportions as it bore down upon her. She
closed her eyes. What was happening to her,—what
was causing this strange languor, this queer sensation
as of falling?

As abruptly as he had clasped her to him, he released her, springing back with a muttered execration.
She tottered dizzily, and involuntarily reached out to
clutch his arm for support. He shook her hand off.

"What is the matter, Kenny?" she murmured, hazily.

He did not answer. He leaned heavily against the
fence, his head on his arm. She did not move for many
seconds. Then he heard her gasp,—a gasp of actual
terror.

"Who are you?" she whispered tensely. "You are
not my brother. You are not the real Kenneth Gwynne!
Who are you?" She waited for the answer that did
not come. Then as she drew farther away from him:
"You are an impostor. You have deceived us. You
have come here representing yourself to be—to be my
brother,—and you are not—you are not! I know it—
oh, I know it now. You are—"

This aroused him. "What is that you are saying?"

he cried out, fighting to pull his disordered wits together. "Not your brother? Impostor? What are
you saying, Viola?"

"I want the truth," she cried. "Are you what you
claim to be?"

"Of course I am," he answered, stridently. "I am
Kenneth Gwynne. Your brother. Have you lost your
senses?"

"Then, why—" she began huskily. "Why did you—
Oh, Kenny, I don't know what I am saying," she murmured piteously. "I—I don't know what has come
over me. Something—something— Oh, I don't know
what made me feel—I mean, what made me say that
to you. You are Kenneth Gwynne. You are my half-
brother. You are not—"

"There, there!" he interrupted, his voice shaking a
little. "You were frightened. I came so near to shooting— Yes, that is it! And I was so happy, so relieved that I—I almost ate you alive,—my little sister.
God, what a horrible thing it would have been if I had
—fired and the bullet had—"

She interrupted him, speaking rapidly, breathlessly
in her effort to regain command of herself. "But you
didn't—you didn't, you see,—so what is the use of
worrying about it now?" She laughed jerkily. "But,
my goodness, it is a good lesson for me! I'll never
try to scare anybody else again as I did poor
Zachariah."

He stooped and, feeling among the weeds, recovered
not one but both of the long duelling pistols.

"I was after bigger game than you," he muttered.
"Here are my pistols,—all primed and ready for business."

She stretched out her hand and touched one of the

weapons. "Ready for what business?" she inquired. "What did you mean by a pack of ruffians?" As he did not answer at once, she went on to explain what had actually occurred, ending with, "I suppose Zachariah ran in and told you that old Black Hawk and his warriors were attacking the town."

"I couldn't get much out of him, he was so excited. But I was mortally afraid they had stolen a march on us, and you were already in their hands. You see, Isaac Stain was to have kept me informed and we were to have laid a trap for them. Oh, Lord!" he exclaimed in sudden consternation. "I am letting the cat out of the bag."

"Will you please tell me what you are talking about, Kenneth Gwynne?" she said impatiently.

He came to a quick decision. "Yes, I will tell you everything. I guess I was a fool not to have told you before,—you and your mother. There is a plot afoot, Viola, to abduct you. Stain got wind of it, through— well, he got wind of it. He came to me with the story. I don't suppose you will believe me,—and you will probably despise me for what I am about to say,—but the man you love and expect to marry is behind the scheme. I mean Barry Lapelle. He—"

"When did you hear of this?" she interrupted quickly. "After the *Revere* came in?"

"More than a week ago. He came home on the *Revere* to-day. His plan is to—"

"I know. I saw him. We quarrelled. It is all over between us, Kenny. He was furious. I thought he nay have—but you say you knew of this a week ago? I don't—I can't understand it. A week ago there was no heed of—of carrying me off against my will."

"It is all over between you?" he cried, and he could

not disguise the joy in his voice. "You have ended it, Viola?"

"Yes,—it is all over," she said stiffly. "I am not going to marry him. I was coming over to tell you. But—go on. What is this cock-and-bull story about abducting me? Goodness, I am beginning to feel like a girl in a story-book."

"It is no laughing matter," he said, a little gruffly. "Does it look like it when I come rushing out here with two loaded pistols and come near to shooting you? Come up to the house. We will talk it all over, and then,—" he hesitated for a moment,—"then I'll go over and see your mother."

He took her arm and led her up to the house. As they entered the front door, Zachariah's groans fell upon their ears. She looked at Kenny in alarm, and for the first time realized that he was without coat or waistcoat. His hair was tousled in evidence of his studious application to the open law books that lay on the floor.

"He must be quite badly hurt," she cried miserably. "Oh, I'm *so* sorry."

Kenny went to the kitchen door. "Zachariah! Stop that groaning. You're not hurt. Here! What are you doing with that rifle?"

"Ah was jes' co-comin' out, Marse Kenny, fo' to he'p yo' kill—yas, suh! Ah was—" The remainder was lost as Kenneth deliberately closed the door behind him and walked over to the negro, who was squatting in a corner with a rifle in his hands. Viola, left alone, crossed to the window and looked out. She was pale and anxious. Her wide, alarmed eyes tried to pierce the darkness outside. Suddenly she started back, pressing her hands to her cheeks.

"Oh, my soul!" she murmured. "They could have shot him dead. He could not have seen them." She felt herself turn faint. Then a thrill of exaltation swept over her and she turned quickly toward the kitchen door, her eyes glowing. "And he was not afraid! He ran out to face them alone. He thought they were out there,—he risked being shot to save me from—"

The door opened and Kenneth came swiftly into the room. He stopped short, staring at her radiant face.

"Oh, Kenny, you—you really believed they were out there,—a crowd of them,—trying to carry me off? Why,—why, that was the bravest thing a man—"

"Shucks!" he scoffed. "My tragedy turns out to be the most uproarious farce. I've never seen a funnier one in the theatre. But there is a serious side to it, Viola. Sit down for a minute or two, and I'll tell you. Zachariah is all right. Barked his shins a little, that's all."

At the conclusion of his short, unembellished recital, he said:

"There is nothing for you to be worried about. They cannot carry out the plot. We are all forewarned now. I should have told you all this before, but I was afraid you would think I was trying to blacken La-pelle. I wanted to catch him red-handed, as the saying is. Isaac Stain is coming in to sleep here to-morrow night, and Zachariah, for all his fear of ghosts and lightning, is, not afraid of men. We will be ready for them if they come,—so don't you worry."

There was a puzzled frown in her eyes. "I don't see why he should have planned this a week ago, Kenny. I had told him I would marry him. There must be something back of all this."

"Do you know anything about a friend of his who is going to be married soon? He spoke to me about it the other day, and asked if a parent could legally deprive a daughter of a share in her deceased father's—"

"Why,—that's me, Kenny," she cried excitedly. "I told him that mother would disinherit me entirely if I married him without her consent."

A light broke over him. "By jingo!" he cried. "I am beginning to see. Why, it's as plain as day to me now. The beastly scoundrel!"

"What do you mean?"

"Could your mother very well carry out her threat if he made off with you by force and compelled you to marry him, whether or no?"

She stiffened. "I would never,—never consent, Kenny. I would die first."

"I suppose you imagine there could be no worse fate than that?" he said, pity in his eyes.

She looked puzzled for a moment and then grasped his meaning. Her face blanched.

"I said I would die first," she repeated in a low, steady voice.

"Well," he cried, starting up briskly from his chair, "I guess we'd better hurry if we want to catch your mother before she goes to bed. And that reminds me, Viola,—I would like to speak with her alone. You see," he went on lamely, "you see, we're not friends and I don't know how she will receive me."

She nodded her head without speaking and together they left the house.

CHAPTER XVIII

RACHEL was standing on her porch as they came up the walk. The light through the open door at her back revealed her tall, motionless figure but not her face which was in shadow.

"Kenneth wants to talk to you about something very important," said Viola unevenly, as they drew near.

The woman on the porch did not speak until they paused at the bottom of the steps.

"Have you been over at his house, Viola?" she asked levelly.

"Yes, mother."

After a moment's hesitation: "Come in, Kenneth." She stood aside to let Viola pass. Kenneth, who had hastily donned his coat, followed the two women into the house. There was a light in the parlor. "Will you sit down, or do you prefer to remain standing in my house, Kenneth Gwynne?"

He bowed stiffly, indicating a chair with a gesture. "Will you be seated first, madam?"

His sophomoric dignity drew a faint, ironic smile to her lips. "Thank you," she said calmly, and seated herself on the little horsehair sofa. If there was any uneasiness in the look she sent from one to the other of the young people it was not noticeable. "Hattie came in a little while ago," she said, "scared out of her wits. I suspected that you were up to one of your

246

pranks, Viola. I do wish you would stop frightening
the girl."

"Kenneth will tell you what happened," said the girl,
hurriedly. "He wants to see you alone. I am going
upstairs."

She left the room, closing the door behind her.
Neither spoke until they heard her footsteps on the
floor overhead.

"Well, what have you been telling her?" asked
Rachel, leaning forward, her eyes narrowing.

He drew a chair up close to the sofa and sat down.
"Nothing that she should not know," he answered. "I
will first tell you what happened a little while ago, and
then—the rest of it. There is evil afoot. I have
been wrong, I realize, in not warning you and Viola."

She listened intently to the end; not once did she
interrupt him, but as he proceeded to unfold the
meagre details of the plot as presented to him by Isaac
Stain, her brow darkened and her fingers began to work
nervously, restlessly in her lap. His account of the
frightening of Zachariah and its immediate results took
up but little time. He was careful to avoid any mention of that stirring scene at the fence, its effect upon
the startled girl, or how near he was to betraying the
great secret.

Rachel Gwyn's eyes never left his face during the
whole of the unbroken recital. Toward the end he
had the disconcerting impression that she was reading
his turbulent thoughts, that she was successfully searching his soul.

"That's the story as it came to me," he concluded.
"I deserve your condemnation for not preparing Viola
against a trick that might have resulted disastrously
while we were marking time."

"Why did Isaac Stain go to you instead of coming to me?" was her first question.

"Because he believes I am her brother, and this happens to be a man's job," he said, lowering his voice. "It is only fair, however, to state that he wanted to come to you and I, in my folly, advised him not to do so."

She was silent for a moment. Then: "And why did you think it not advisable to tell me?"

"I will be frank with you," he replied, colouring under her steady gaze. "I wanted her to find out for herself just what kind of man Lapelle really is. I was prepared to let the plot go almost to the point of consummation. I—I wanted to be the one to save her." He lowered his eyes, afraid that she would discover the truth in them.

Again she hesitated, apparently weighing her words. "You are in love with her, Kenneth."

He looked up, startled, almost aghast. Involuntarily he started to rise to his feet, his eyes still fixed on hers, vehement denial on his parted lips, only to sink back into the chair again, convicted. There was no use attempting to deceive this cold, clear-headed woman. She knew. No lie, no evasion could meet that direct statement. For a long time they looked straight into each other's eyes, and at length his fell in mute confession.

"God help me,—I am," he groaned.

"Oh, the pity of it!" she cried out. He looked up and saw that she was trembling, her ashen face working as in pain.

"No! The curse of it, Rachel Carter!"

She appeared not to have heard his words. " 'God

works in a mysterious way,'" she muttered, almost inaudibly. "The call of the blood is unfailing. The brain may be deceived, the heart never." With an effort, she regained control of herself. "She has broken off with Barry Lapelle. Do you know the reason why? Because, all unbeknownst to her, she has fallen in love with you. Yes! It is true. I know. I have seen it coming."

She arose and crossed to the door, which she cautiously opened. For a moment she remained there listening, then closing it gently, she came over and stood before him.

"Love is a wonderful thing, Kenneth," she said slowly. "It is the most powerful force in all the world. It overcomes reason, it crushes the conscience, it makes strong men weak and weak men strong. For love a woman will give her honour, for love a man will barter his chance for eternal salvation. It overlooks faults, it condones crime, it rises above every obstacle that the human mind can put before it. It knows no fear, it has no religion, it serves no God. You love my girl, Kenneth. She is the daughter of the woman you despise, the daughter of one you call evil. Is your love for her great enough,—or will it ever be great enough,—to overcome these obstacles? In plain words, would you take her unto yourself as your wife, to love and cherish and honour,—mind you, *honour*,—to the end of your days on earth?"

He stood up, facing her, his face white.

"She has done nothing dishonourable," he said levelly.

"'The sins of the mother,'" she paraphrased, without taking her eyes from his.

"Was her mother any worse than my father? Has the sin been visited upon one of us and not upon the other?"

"Then, you *would* be willing to take Viola as your wife?"

He seemed to wrench his gaze away. "Oh, what is the use of talking about the impossible?" he exclaimed. "I have confessed that I love her,—yes, in spite of everything,—and you—"

"You have not answered my question."

"No, I have not," he said deliberately,—"and I do not intend to answer it. You know as well as I that I cannot ask her to marry me, so why speak of it? Good God, could I ask my own sister to be my wife?"

"She is not your sister. She has not one drop of Gwynne blood in her veins."

He gave a short, bitter laugh. "But who is going to tell her that, may I ask, Rachel Carter?"

She turned away, took two or three turns up and down the room, her head bent, a heavy frown between her eyes, and then sank wearily into a chair.

"I will put it this way, Kenneth," she said. "Would you ask her to be your wife if the time should ever come when she knows the truth?"

He hesitated a long time. "Will you be kind enough to tell me what your object is in asking me these questions?"

"I want to know whether you are truly in love with her," she replied steadily.

"And if I say that I could not ask her to marry me, would that prove anything to you?"

"Yes. It would prove two things. It would prove that you do not love her with all your heart and soul, and it would prove that you are the same kind of man that your father was before you."

He started. It was the second reason that caused him to look at her curiously. "What do you mean?"

"When you have answered my question, I will answer yours, Kenneth."

"Well," he began, setting his jaw, "I *do* love her enough to ask her to be my wife. But I would ask her as Owen Carter's daughter. And," he added, half closing his eyes as with pain, "she would refuse to have me. She could not look at the matter as I do. Her love,—if she should ever come to have such a feeling for me,—her love would revolt against— Oh, you know what I mean! Do you suppose it would survive the shock of realization? No! She has a clean heart. She would never marry the son of the man who—who—" He found himself unable to finish the sentence. A strange, sudden reluctance to hurt his enemy checked the words even as they were being framed on his lips,—reluctance due not to compassion nor to consideration but to a certain innate respect for an adversary whose back is to the wall and yet faces unequal odds without a sign of shrinking.

"Shall I say it for you?" she asked in a cold, level voice. But she had winced, despite her iron control.

"It is not necessary," said he, embarrassed.

"In any case," she said, with a sigh, "you have answered my question. If you could do this for my girl I am sure of your love for her. There could be no greater test. I shall take a little more time before answering your question. There are one or two more things I must say to you before I come to that,—and then, if you like, we will take up this story of Isaac

Stain's. Kenneth, the time may come,—I feel that it is sure to come, when—"

She stopped. A sound from above caught her ear, —a regular, rhythmic thumping on the floor. After a few seconds she remarked:

"It is all right. That is a rocking-chair. She is getting impatient." Nevertheless she lowered her voice and leaned forward in her chair. "The time is sure to come when Viola will learn the truth about herself and me,—and you, as well. I feel it in my bones. It may not come till after I am dead. But no matter when it comes, I want to feel sure now,—to-night, Kenneth,—that you will never undertake to deprive her of the lands and money I shall leave to her."

He stared at her in astonishment. "What is this you are saying?" She slowly repeated the words. "Why, how could I dispossess her? It is yours to bequeath as you see fit, madam. Do you think I am a mercenary scoundrel,—that I would try to take it away from her? I know she is not my father's daughter, but—why, good heaven, I would never dream of fighting for what you—"

"Your love for her,—though unrequited,—aye, even though she became embittered toward you because of what happened years ago,—you love her enough to stand aside and allow her to hold what I shall leave to her?"

"You are talking in riddles. What on earth are you driving at?"

"You will not fight her right, her claim to my estate?" she insisted, leaning still closer.

"Why, of course not!" he exclaimed, angrily.

"Even though the law might say she is not entitled to it?"

"The law can take no action unless I invoke its aid," said he. "And that is something I shall never do," he added, with finality.

"I wish I could be sure of that," she murmured, wistfully.

He came to his feet. "You may be sure of it," he said, with dignity. "Possess your soul in peace, if that is all that is troubling it."

"Sit down," she said, a strange huskiness in her voice. He obeyed her. "Your father left a certain part of his fortune to me. There was no provision made for Viola. You understand that, don't you?"

"Yes. I know all about that," said he, plainly bewildered. "On the other hand, he did not impose any restrictions upon you. You are at liberty to dispose of your share by will, as you see fit, madam. I am not likely to deny my step-sister what is rightfully hers. And that reminds me. She is not my blood relation, it's true. But she is my step-sister. That settles another point. I could not ask my step-sister to be my wife. The law would—"

"Now we have come to the point where I shall answer the question you asked a while ago," she interrupted, straightening up in her chair and regarding him with a fixed, steady light in her eyes that somehow seemed to forewarn him of what was about to be revealed. "I said it would prove two things to me. One of them was that you are the same kind of man that your father was before you. I mean if you had said you could not ask Viola to be your wife." She paused, and then went on slowly, deliberately. "I lived with your father for nearly twenty years. In all that time he never asked me to be his wife."

At first he stared blankly at her, uncomprehending.

Then a slow, dark flush spread over his face. He half-started up from his chair.

"You—you mean—" he stammered.

"He never asked me to be his wife," she repeated without emotion.

He sank back, incredulous, dumbfounded. "My God! Am I to understand that you—that you were never married to my father?"

"Yes. I waited twenty years for him to ask me to marry him,—but he never did."

He was still somewhat stupefied. The disclosure was so unexpected, so utterly at odds with all his understanding that he could not wholly grasp its significance. Somewhat footlessly he burst out:

"But surely you must have demanded—I mean, did you never ask him to—to marry you?"

Her eyebrows went up slightly.

"How could I?" she inquired, as if surprised by the question. "I had not sunk so low in my own estimation as that, Kenneth Gwynne. My bed was made the day I went away with him. Some day you may realize that even such as I may possess the thing called pride. No! I would have died rather than ask him to marry me. I chose my course with my eyes open. It was not for me to demand more than I gave. He was not a free man when I went to him. He made no promises, nor did I exact any."

She spoke in the most matter-of-fact way. He regarded her in sheer wonder.

"But he *should* have made you his wife," he exclaimed, his sense of fairness rising above the bitter antipathy he felt toward her.

"That was for him to decide," said she, calmly. "I respected his feelings in the matter,—and still do. He had no right to marry me when we went away together. He did not take me as a wife, Kenneth Gwynne. He took me as a woman. He had a wife. Up to the day he died he looked upon her as his wife. I was his woman. I could never take her place. Not even after she had been in her grave for twenty years. He never forgot her. I see the scorn in your eyes. He does not quite deserve it, Kenneth. After all is said and done, he was fair to me. Not one man in a thousand would have done his part so well as he.

"I don't suppose you know what men do with their mistresses when they begin to feel that they are through with them and there is no legal bond to hold them. They desert them. They cast them off. And then they turn to some honest woman and marry her. That is the way with men. But he was not like that. I can tell what you are about to say. It is on your lips to say that he deserted an honest woman. Well, so he did. And therein lies the secret of his constancy to me,—even after he had ceased to love me and the passion that was in him died. He would never desert another woman who trusted him. He paid too dearly in his conscience for the first offence to be guilty of a second.

"You see I am laying bare my innermost soul to you. It hurts me to say that through all these years he loved and honoured and revered his wife,—and the memory of her. He was never unkind to me,—he never spoke of her. But I knew, and he knew that I knew. He loved you, his little boy. I, too, loved you once, Kenneth. When you were a little shaver I adored you. But I came to hate you as the years went by. It is needless to tell you the reason why. When it came time for him to die he left you half of his fortune.

The other half,—and a little over,—he gave to me."
Her voice faltered a little as she added: "For good
and faithful service, I suppose."

During this long speech Kenneth had succeeded in
collecting his thoughts. He had been shocked by her
confession, and now he was mentally examining the
possibilities that might arise from the aspect it bared.

First of all, Viola was not even his step-sister. He
experienced a thrill of joy over that,—notwithstanding the ugly truth that gave her the new standing;
to his simple, straightforward mind, Viola's mother
was nothing more than a prostitute. (In his thoughts
he employed another word, for he lived in a day when
prostitutes were called by another name.) Still,
Viola was not to blame for that. That could never
be held against her.

"Why have you told me all this?" he asked bluntly.
"I had no means of learning that you were never
married to my father. There was never a question
about it in my mind, nor in anybody else's, so far as I
know. You have put a very dangerous weapon in my
hand in case I should choose to use it against you."

She was silent for a long time, struggling with herself. He could almost feel the battle that was going
on within her. Somehow it appalled him.

The wind outside was rising. It moaned softly,
plaintively through the trees. A shutter creaked somewhere at the back of the house and at intervals banged
against the casement. The frogs down in the hollow
had ceased their clamour and no doubt took to themselves credit for the storm that was on the way in
answer to their exhortations. The even, steady thump
of the rocking-chair in the room overhead stopped
suddenly, and Viola's quick tread was heard crossing

the floor. She closed a window. Then, after a moment, the sound of the rocking-chair again.

Rachel left her chair and walked over to the window to peer out into the night.

"It is coming from the west," she said, as if to test the steadiness of her voice.

A far-off flicker of lightning cast a faint, phosphorescent glow into the dimly lighted room, quivering for a second or two on the face of the woman at the window, then dying away with what seemed to be a weird suggestion of reluctance.

She stood before him, looking down. "I have at last obeyed a command imposed by Robert Gwynne when he was on his death-bed. Almost his last words to me were in the nature of a threat. He told me that if I failed to carry out his request,—he did not call it a command,—he would haunt me to my dying day. You may laugh at me if you will, but he *has* been haunting me, Kenneth Gwynne. If I ever cherished the notion that I could ignore his command and go on living in the security of my own secret, I must have known from the beginning that it would be impossible. Day and night, ever since you came, some force that was not my own has been driving at my resistance. You will call it compunction, or conscience or an honest sense of duty. I do not call it by any of those names. Your father commanded me to tell you with my own lips,—not in writing or through the mouth of an agent,—he commanded me to say to you that your mother was the only wife he ever had. I have done this to-night. I have humbled myself,—but it was after a long, cruel fight."

She sat down, and it seemed to him that her very soul went out in the deep, long sigh that caused her bosom to flatten and her shoulders to droop forward.

"He was either an ingrate or a coward," said he harshly, after a short silence.

"It is not for you to pass judgment on my master," said she, simply. "May I beg you to refrain from putting your own judgment of him into words? Will you not spare me that?"

He stared at her in astonishment. He saw that she was in earnest, desperately in earnest. Choking back the words that had rushed to his lips, he got up from his chair and bent his head gravely.

"Yes, if it is any comfort to you, Rachel Carter," he said, acute pity in his eyes. "I cannot resist saying, however, that you have not spared yourself. It cost you a great deal to pay one of the debts he left for you to settle. I shall not forget it."

She arose and all the humility fell away from her. Once more she was the strong, indomitable,—even formidable,—figure he had come to know so well. Her bosom swelled, her shoulders straightened, and into her deepset, sombre eyes came the unflinching light of determination.

"Then we are done with that," she said quietly. "I have asked no favours save this last one for myself,— but it is a greater one than you may think. You know everything now, Kenneth. You have called me Rachel Carter. Was it divination or was it stubborn memory? I wonder. So far as I know, you are the only person left in the world who knows that I was not his wife, the only one who knows that I am still Rachel Carter. No matter what this man Braley may know, or what he may tell, he— But we are wasting time. Viola must be wondering. Now as to this plan of Barry Lapelle's. I think I can safely assure you that nothing will come of it."

"Then, you knew about it before I told you?" he exclaimed.

"No. You brought me word of Jasper Suggs this morning. You said he was staying at Martin Hawk's cabin. You may have forgotten what I said to you at the time. Now you bring me word that Barry Lapelle's plot was hatched at Martin Hawk's. Well, this afternoon I went to the Court House and swore out a warrant charging Martin Hawk with stealing some of my yearling calves and sheep. That warrant is now in the hands of the sheriff. It will be served before another day is gone."

"That's pretty sharp work," he said, but still a little puzzled. "Naturally it will upset Barry's plans, but Suggs is still to be accounted for. You mentioned something about charging him with a murder back in—"

"I guess that can wait till another day," said she, with a smile that he did not quite understand. "It would be rather stupid of me, don't you think, to have him arrested?"

"You said he was not the kind of a man to be taken alive," he remarked, knitting his brows.

"I think I said something of the kind. The name of Simon Braley is known from one end of this State to the other. It is a name to conjure fear with. Every Indian uprising in the past ten years has had Braley's name connected with it. It was he who led the band of Chippewas twelve years ago when they massacred some fifteen or eighteen women and children in a settlement on White River while their men were off in

the fields at work. Isn't it rather significant that
the renegade Simon Braley should turn up in these
parts at a time when Black Hawk is— But that is
neither here nor there. My warrant calls for the
arrest of Martin Hawk. For more than two years
Hawk has been suspected of stealing livestock down
on the Wea, but no one has ever been willing to make
a specific charge against him. He is very cunning and
he has always covered his tracks."

"Do you think he will resist the sheriff? I mean,
is there likely to be fighting?"

"It all depends on whether Martin is caught napping," she replied in a most casual manner. "By the
way, has Isaac Stain told you much about himself?"

Kenneth could not repress a smile. "He has mentioned one or two affairs of the heart."

"His sister was one of the women massacred by
the Chippewas down on White River that time. She
was the young wife of a settler. Isaac will be over-
joyed when he finds out that Jasper Suggs and Simon
Braley are one and the same person."

He was speechless for a moment, comprehension coming slowly to him. "By all that's holy!" he exclaimed,
something like awe in his voice. "I am beginning to
understand. Stain will be one of the sheriff's party?"

"We will stop at his cabin on the way to Hawk's,"
she replied. "If he chooses to join us after I have
told him who I think this man Suggs really is, no one
will object."

"You say 'we.' Do you mean to tell me that you
are going along with the posse? Good God, woman,
there will be shooting! You must not think of—"

She checked him with an imperious gesture. "I cannot send these men to face a peril that I am not willing

to face myself. That would be dastardly. I will take my chances with the rest of them. You seem to forget that I spent a good many years of my life in the wilderness. This will not be my first experience with renegades and outlaws. When I first came to this State, the women had to know how to shoot. Not only to shoot birds and beasts, but men as well. Those were hard days. I was not like the men who cut notches in their rifle stocks for every Indian they slew, and yet there is a gun in my room upstairs that could have two notches on it if I had cared to put them there."

"What time do you start?" he said, the fire of excitement in his eyes. "I insist on being one of the—"

"You will not be needed," she said succinctly. "I think you had better go now. The storm will soon be upon us. Thank you for coming here to-night, Kenneth."

CHAPTER XIX

LAPELLE SHOWS HIS TEETH

KENNETH went to bed that night firmly resolved to accompany the sheriff when he set out to arrest Martin Hawk. Zachariah had instructions to call him at daybreak and to have breakfast ready on the dot.

No doubt the posse would start about sunrise,—in any case, he would be up and prepared to take to his saddle the instant he saw his neighbour leaving her house.

The thunderstorm came rollicking down the valley, crashed and rolled and roared for half an hour or so, and then stole mumbling away in the night, leaving in its wake a sighing wind and the drip of forsaken raindrops.

He was astir at cockcrow. The first faint glow of red in the greying east found him at breakfast, with Zachariah sleepily serving him with hot corn-cakes, lean side-meat and coffee.

"Take plenty dis yere hot coffee, Marse Kenneth," urged Zachariah, at the end of a prodigious yawn. "Yo' all gwine need sumpin to keep yo' 'wake, suh, so's yo' won't fall out'n de saddle. Dis yere—"

"Speaking of saddles, have you fed Brandy Boy?"

"Yas, suh. Ah dunno as Ah evah see a hoss mo' took by 'stonishment dan he wuz when Ah step brisk-like into his stall an' sez 'Doggone yo', Brandy Boy, don't yo' know de sun's gwine to be up in less'n two hours? Wha' fo' is yo' keepin' me an' Marse Kenneth waitin' lak dis? Git ep dar, yo' lazy, good-fer-nuffin,—' "

"And what did Brandy Boy say in response to that?" broke in his master, airily.

"How dat, suh?"

"Did he reply in courteous terms or was he testy and out of sorts? Now, just what *did* he say?"

Zachariah stared at the speaker in some uneasiness. "Ah reckon yo' all better go on back to bed, suh, an' lemme call yo' when yo' is wide awake. Ain' no sense in yo' startin' off on dis yere hossback ride when yo' is still enjoyin' setch a good night's sleep. No, *suh!*"

"I will take another cup of your excellent coffee, Zachariah. That will make three, won't it?"

Zachariah shuffled over to the stove, muttering as he lifted the coffee pot: "Fust Ah is seein' things in de evenin' an' den Ah hears all dis yere talk 'bout a hoss *sayin'* things in de mornin',— Yas, suh,—yas, *suh!* Comin' right along, suh. Little mo' side-meat, suh?"

"Take a peep out of the window and see if any one is stirring over at Mrs. Gwyn's."

" 'Pears lak Ah c'n see a lady out in de front yard, suh," said Zachariah, at the window.

"You don't say so! Is it Mrs. Gwyn?" cried Kenneth, hastily gulping his coffee as he pushed his chair back from the table.

"Hit ain' light enough fo' to see—"

"Run out and saddle Brandy Boy at once, and be quick about it."

"No, suh, hit ain' Mrs. Gwyn. Hit's Miss Violy. 'Pears lak she comin' over here, suh. Leastwise she come out'n de gate kind o' fast-like,—gotten a shawl wrap aroun'—"

Kenneth waited for no more. He dashed from the house and down to the fence,—where stood Viola, pulling at the swollen, water-soaked gate peg. She was bareheaded, her brown hair hanging down her back in long, thick braids. It was apparent at a glance that she had dressed hastily and but partially at that. With one hand she pinched close about her throat the voluminous scarlet shawl of embroidered crêpe in which the upper part of her body was wrapped.

Later he was to observe that her heavy shoes were unlaced and had been drawn on over her bare feet. Her eyes were filled with alarm.

"I don't know where mother is," she said, without other greeting. "She is not in the house, Kenny. I am worried almost sick."

He stared at her in dismay. "Oh, blast the luck! She must have— Say, are you sure she's gone?"

"I can't find her anywhere," cried she, in distress. "I've been out to the barn and— Why, what ails you, Kenneth?"

"She got away without my knowing it. But maybe it's not too late. I can catch up with them if I hurry. Hey, Zachariah!"

"Then, you know where she is?" cried the girl, grasping his arm as he turned to rush away. "For goodness' sake, tell me! Where has she gone?"

"Why, don't you— But of course you don't!" he exclaimed. "You poor girl! You must be almost beside yourself,—and here I go making matters worse by—"

"Where is she?" she broke in, all the colour going from her face as she shook his arm impatiently.

"Come in the house," he said gently, consolingly. "I'll tell you all I know. There's nothing to be worried about. She will be home, safe and sound, almost before you know it. I will explain while Zachariah is saddling Brandy Boy." He laid his hand upon her shoulder. "Come along,—dear."

She held back. "If anything happens to her and you could have—" she began, a threat in her dark, harassed eyes.

"I had no idea she would start at such an unearthly hour. I had made up my mind to go with her, whether or not. Didn't she tell you she had made an affidavit against Martin Hawk?"

"No. The sheriff was up here last night, just after supper, but,— Oh, Kenny, what is it all about?"

His arm stole about her shoulders. She leaned heavily, wearily against him as they walked up the drenched path.

"Have you any idea at all what time she left the house?" he asked.

"I heard her go down the stairs. It was pitch dark, but the clock struck one quite a long time afterward. I did not think anything about it then, because she often gets up in the middle of the night and goes down to sit in the kitchen. Ever since father died. I must have gone to sleep again because I did not hear her come back upstairs. I awoke just at daybreak and got up to see if she needed me. She—she had not gone to bed at all, Kenny,—and I couldn't find her anywhere. Then I thought that Martin Hawk and the others had come and taken her away by mistake, thinking it was me in the darkness."

"Sit down, Viola. I'll light the fire. It's quite chilly and you are shaking like a—"

"I want to know where she has gone," she insisted.

Then he told her briefly as much as he thought she ought to know. She was vastly relieved. She even smiled.

"There's no use of your trying to catch up with her. Thank you for lighting the fire, Kenny. If you don't mind, I will sit here awhile, and I may go to sleep in this comfortable chair of yours. Goodness, I must look awful. My hair—"

"Don't touch it! It is beautiful as it is. I wish girls would always wear their hair in braids like that."

She yawned, stretched her legs out to the fire, and then suddenly realizing that her ankles were bare, drew them back again to the shelter of her petticoat with a quick, shy glance to see if he had observed.

"I wish I could cut it off,—like a boy's. It is miles too long. You might as well head Zachariah off. She has been gone since one o'clock. I am sure I heard the front door close before I dropped off to sleep. Don't fidget, Kenny. They've probably got old Martin in the calaboose by this time. Mother never fails when she sets out to do a thing. That good-for-nothing sleepy-head, Hattie, never heard a sound last night. What a conscience she must have!"

He frowned at his big silver watch. "It's after five. See here, Viola, suppose you just curl up on the sofa there and get some sleep. You look tired. I'll put a quilt over you and—"

She half-started up from the chair, flushing in embarrassment.

"Oh, I ought not to stay here, Kenny. Suppose somebody were to come along and catch me here in your—"

"Shucks! You're my sister, aren't you?"

"I suppose it's all right," she said dubiously, sinking back into the chair again. "But somehow, Kenny, I don't believe I will ever be able to think of you as a brother; not if I live a thousand years. I'm sorry to hurt your feelings, but—well, I just can't help being a little bit afraid of you. I suppose it's silly of me, but I'm so ashamed to have you see me with my hair down like this, and no stockings on, and only half-dressed. I—I feel hot all over. I didn't think of it at first, I was so worried, but now I—"

"It is very silly of you," he said, rather thickly. "You did right in coming over, and I'm going to make you comfortable now that you are here. Lie down here and get some sleep, like a good little girl, and when you wake up Zachariah will have a nice hot breakfast for you."

"I'd rather not lie down," she stammered. "Let me just sit here awhile,—and don't bother about breakfast for me. Hattie will—"

"But he has to get breakfast anyhow," he argued.

She looked at him suspiciously. "Haven't you had your breakfast?"

"No," he lied. Then he hurried off to give guilty instructions to Zachariah.

"Fo' de lan's sake," the latter blurted out as he listened to his master's orders; "is yo' all gwine to eat another breakfast?"

"Yes, I am," snapped Kenneth. "I'll take care of Brandy Boy. You go in and clear the table,—and see to it that you don't make any noise. If you do, I'll skin you alive."

An hour later, Kenneth arose from his seat on the front doorstep and stole over to the sitting-room window.

She was asleep in the big rocking-chair, her head twisted limply toward her left shoulder, presenting a three-quarters view of her face to him as he gazed long and ardently upon her. He could see the deep rise and fall of her bosom. The shawl, unclasped at the throat, had fallen away, revealing the white flannel nightgown over which she had hastily drawn a petticoat before sallying forth.

He went to the kitchen door and found Zachariah sitting grumpily on the step.

"She's still sound asleep," he announced.

"So's dat lazy Hattie over yander," lamented Zachariah, with a jerk of his head. "Ain' no smoke comin' out'n her chimbley, lemme tell yo'."

"Fill that wash-pan and get me a clean towel," ordered his master. He looked at his watch. "I'm going to awaken her,—in half an hour."

It was nearly seven o'clock when he stamped noisily into the sitting-room with towel and basin. He had thrice repeated his visit to the window, and with each succeeding visit had remained a little longer than before, notwithstanding the no uncertain sense of guilt that accused him of spying upon the lovely sleeper.

She awoke with a start, looked blankly about as if bewildered by her strange surroundings, and then fixed her wide, questioning eyes upon him, watching him in silence as he placed the basin of spring-water on a chair and draped the coarse towel over the back.

"Breakfast will be ready in ten minutes, Miss," he announced, bowing deeply. "If you desire to freshen yourself a bit after your profound slumbers, you will find here some of the finest water in the universe and a towel warranted to produce a blush upon the cheek of a graven image."

"Has mother come home?" she inquired anxiously, as she drew the shawl close about her throat again.

"No sign of her. Hurry along, and as soon as we've had a bite to eat I'll ride down to the Court House and see if she's there."

He left her, and presently she came out into the kitchen, her skin glowing warmly, her braids loosely coiled on the crown of her head, her eyes like violet stars.

Zachariah marvelled at his master's appetite. Recollection of an already devoured meal of no small proportions caused him to doubt his senses. From time to time he shook his head in wonder and finally took to chuckling. The next time Marse Kenneth complained about having no appetite he would know what to say to him.

"I must run home now," said Viola at the close of the meal. "It's been awfully nice,—and so exciting, Kenny. I feel as if I had been doing something I ought not to do. Isn't it queer? Having breakfast with a man I never saw until six weeks ago!"

"It does my heart good to see you blush so prettily," said he warmly. Then his face darkened. "And it turns my blood cold to think that if you had succeeded in doing something you ought not to have done six weeks ago, you might now be having breakfast with somebody else instead of with me."

"I wish you would not speak of that, Kenneth," she said severely. "You will make me hate you if you bring it up again." Then she added with a plaintive little smile: "The Bible says, 'Love thy neighbour as thyself.' I am doing my best to live up to that, but sometimes you make it awfully hard for me."

He went to the door with her. She paused for a

moment on the step to look searchingly up the road and through the trees. There was no sign of her mother. The anxious, worried expression deepened in her eyes.

"Don't come any farther with me," she said. "Go down to the Court House as fast as you can."

He watched her till she passed through the gate. As he was on the point of re-entering the house he saw her come to an abrupt stop and stare straight ahead. He shot a swift, apprehensive glance over his shoulder.

Barry Lapelle had just emerged from Rachel's yard, his gaze fixed on the girl who stood motionless in front of Gwynne's gate, a hundred feet away. Without taking his eyes from her, he slowly closed the gate and leaned against it, folding his arms as he did so.

Viola, after a moment's indecision and without a glance at Kenneth, lifted her chin and went forward to the encounter. Kenneth looked in all directions for Lapelle's rascals. He was relieved to find that the discarded suitor apparently had ventured alone upon this early morning mission. What did it portend?

Filled with sharp misgivings, he left his doorstep and walked slowly down to the gate, where he halted. It occurred to him that Barry, after a sleepless night, had come to make peace with his tempestuous sweetheart. If such was the case, his own sense of fairness and dignity would permit no interference on his part unless it was solicited by the girl herself. He was ready, however, to take instant action if she made the slightest sign of distress or alarm. While he had no intention of spying or eavesdropping, their voices reached him distinctly and he could not help hearing what passed between them.

"Have you been up to the house, Barry?" were

Viola's first words as she stopped in front of the man who barred the way.

Lapelle did not change his position. His chin was lowered and he was looking at her through narrowed, unsmiling eyes.

"Yes, I have."

"Where was the dog?" she inquired cuttingly.

"He came and licked my hand. He's the only friend I've got up here, I reckon."

"I will have him shot to-day. What do you want?"

"I came to see your mother. Where is she?"

"She's away."

"Over night?"

"It will do you no good to see her, Barry. You might as well realize it first as last."

Lapelle glanced past her at the man beyond and lowered his voice. Kenneth could not hear what he said.

"Well, I'm going to see her, and she will be down on her knees before I'm through with her, let me tell you. Oh, I'm sober, Viola! I had my lesson yesterday. I'm through with whiskey forever. So she was away all night, eh? Out to the farm, eh? That nigger girl of yours says she must have gone out to the farm last night, because her bed wasn't slept in. And you weren't expecting visitors as early as this or you would have got home a little sooner yourself, huh?"

"What are you talking about?"

"Soon as she is out of the house you scoot over to big brother Kenny's, eh? Afraid to sleep alone, I suppose. Well, all I've got to say is you ought to have taken a little more time to dress."

"Oh! Oh,—you—you low-lived dog!" she gasped, going white to the roots of her hair. "How dare you say—"

"That's right! Call me all the pretty names you can think of. And say, I didn't come up here to beg anything from you or your mother. I'm not in a begging humour. I'm through licking your boots, Viola. What time will the old woman be back?"

"Stand away from that gate!" she said in a voice low and hoarse with fury. "Don't you dare speak to me again. And if you follow me to the house I'll— I'll—"

"What'll you do?" he jeered. "Call brother Kenny? Well, go ahead and call him. There he is. I'll kick him from here to the pond,—and that won't be half so pleasant as rocking little sister to sleep in her cradle while mamma is out for the night."

"And I used to think I was in love with you!" she cried in sheer disgust. "I could spit in your face, Barry Lapelle. Will you let me pass?"

"Certainly. But I'm going into the house with you, understand that. I'd just as soon wait there for your mother as anywhere else."

"When my mother hears about this she will have you horsewhipped within an inch of your life," cried the girl furiously.

These words, rising on a wave of anger, came distinctly to Kenneth's ears. He left his place at the gate and walked swiftly along inside his fence until he came to the corner of the yard, where the bushes grew thickly. Here he stopped to await further developments. He heard Barry say, with a harsh laugh:

"Oh, she will, will she?"

"Yes, she will. She knows more about you than you think she does,—and so do I. Let me by! Do you hear me, Bar—"

"That's funny," he interrupted, lowering his voice to

a half-whisper. "That's just what I came up to see her about. I want to tell her that I know more about her than she thinks I do. And when I get through telling her what I know she'll change her mind about letting us get married. And you'll marry me, too, my girl, without so much as a whimper. Oh, you needn't look around for big brother,—God, I bet you'd be happy if he wasn't your brother, wouldn't you? Well, he has sneaked into the house, just as I knew he would if it looked like a squall. He's a white-livered coward. How do you like that?"

He was not only astonished but distinctly confounded by the swift, incomprehensible smile that played about her disdainful lips.

"What the hellfire are you laughing at?" he exploded.

"Nothing much. I was only thinking about last night."

"Christ!" he exclaimed, the blood rushing to his face. "Why,—why, you—" The words failed him. He could only stare at her as if stunned by the most shocking confession.

"Please remember that you are speaking to—"

He broke in with a snarling laugh. "By thunder, I'm beginning to believe you're no better than she was. She wasn't anything but a common ———, and I'm blessed if I think it's sensible to marry into the family, after all."

"Oh!" she gasped, closing her eyes as she shrank away from him. The word he had used stood for the foulest thing on earth to her. It had never passed her clean, pure lips. For the moment she was petrified, speechless.

"It's about time you learned the truth about that

damned old hypocrite,—if you don't know it already,"
he continued, raising his voice at the urge of the now
reckless fury that consumed him. He stood over her
shrinking figure, glaring mercilessly down into her
horror-struck eyes. "You don't need to take my word
for it. Ask Gwynne. He knows. He knows what
happened back there in Kentucky. He knows she ran
off with his father twenty years ago, taking him away
from the woman he was married to. That's why he
hates her. That's why he never had anything to do
with his dog of a father. And, by God, he probably
knows you were born out of wedlock,—that you're a
love-child, a bas—"

CHAPTER XX

HE never finished the word. A whirlwind was upon him. Before he could raise a hand to defend himself, Kenneth Gwynne's brawny fist smote him squarely between the eyes. He went down as though struck by a sledge-hammer, crashing to the ground full six feet from where he stood. Behind that clumsy blow was the weight of a thirteen stone body, hurled as from a mighty catapult.

He never knew how long afterward it was that he heard a voice speaking to him. The words, jumbled and unintelligible, seemed to come from a great distance. He attempted to rise, gave it up, and fell back dizzily. His vision was slow in clearing. What he finally saw, through blurred, uncertain eyes, was the face of Kenneth Gwynne, far above him,—and it was a long time before it stopped whirling and became fixed in one place. Then he realized that it was the voice of Gwynne that was speaking to him, and he made out the words. Something warm and wet crept along the sides of his mouth, over his chin, down his neck. His throat was full of a hot nauseous fluid. He raised himself on one elbow and spat.

"Get up! Get up, you filthy whelp! I'm not going to hit you again. Get up, I say!"

He struggled to his knees and then to his feet, sagging limply against the fence, to which he clung for support. He felt for his nose, filled with a horrid, sickening dread that it was no longer on his face.

"I ought to kill you," he heard Gwynne saying. "You black-hearted, lying scoundrel. Get out of my sight!"

He succeeded in straightening up and looked about him through a mist of tears. He tried to speak, but could only wheeze and sputter. He cleared his throat raucously and spat again.

"Where—where is she?" he managed to say at last.

"Shut up! You've dealt her the foulest—"

He broke off abruptly, struck by the other's expression: Lapelle was staring past him in the direction of the house and there was the look of a frightened, trapped animal in his glassy eyes.

"My God!" fell from his lips, and then suddenly he sprang forward, placing Kenneth's body between him and the object of his terror. "Stop her! For God's sake, Gwynne,—stop her!"

For the first time since Barry went crashing to earth and lay as one dead, Gwynne raised his eyes from the blood-smeared face. Vaguely he remembered the swift rush of Viola's feet as she sped past him,—but that was long ago and he had not looked to see whither she fled.

She was now coming down the steps of the porch, a half-raised rifle in her hands. He was never to forget her white, set face, nor the menacing look in her eyes as she advanced to the killing of Barry Lapelle,—for there was no mistaking her purpose.

"Drop down!" he shouted to Lapelle. As Barry sank cowering behind him, he cried out sharply to the girl: "Viola! Drop that gun! Do you hear me? Good God, have you lost your senses?"

She came on slowly, her head a little to one side the

better to see the partially obscured figure of the crouch-
ing man.

"It won't do you any good to hide, Barry," she said,
in a voice that neither of the men recognized.

"Don't be a fool, Viola!" cried Kenneth. "Leave
him to me. Go back to the house. I will attend to
him."

She stopped and lifted her eyes to stare at the
speaker in sheer wonder and astonishment.

"Why,—you heard what he said. You heard what
he called my mother. Stand away from him, Kenneth."

"I can't allow you to shoot him, Viola. You will
have to shoot me first. My God, child,—do you want
to have a man's life-blood on your hands?"

"He said she ran away with your father," she cried,
a spasm of pain crossing her face. "He said I was
born before they were married. I have a right to kill
him. Do you hear? I have a right to—"

"Don't you know it would be murder? Cold-blooded
murder? No! You will have to kill me first. Do you
understand? I shall not move an inch. I am not
going to let you do something you will regret to the
end of your life. Put it down! Drop that gun, I say!
If there is to be any killing, I will do it,—not you!"

She closed her eyes. Her tense body relaxed. The
two men, watching her with bated breath and vastly
different emotions, could almost visualize the struggle
that was going on within her. At last the long rifle
barrel was lowered; as the muzzle touched the ground
she opened her eyes. Slowly they went from Kenneth
to the man who crouched behind him. She gazed at
the bloody face as if seeing it for the first time.

The woman in her revolted at the spectacle. After
a moment of indecision, she turned with a shudder and

walked toward the house, dragging the rifle by the stock. As she was about to mount the steps she paused to send a swift glance over her shoulder and then, obeying the appeal in Kenneth's eyes, reluctantly, even carefully, leaned the gun against a post and disappeared through the door.

"Stand up!" ordered Gwynne, turning to Lapelle. "I ought to kill you myself. It's in my heart to do so. Do you know what you've done to her?"

Barry drew himself up, his fast swelling, bloodshot eyes filled with a deadly hatred. His voice was thick and unsteady.

"You'd better kill me while you have the chance," he said. "Because, so help me God, I'm going to kill you for this."

"Go!" thundered the other, his hands twitching. "If you don't, I'll strangle the life out of you."

Lapelle drew back, quailing before the look in Kenneth's eyes. He saw murder in them.

"You didn't give me a chance, damn you," he snarled. "You hit me before I had a chance to—"

"I wish to God I had hit you sooner,—and that I had killed you," grated Kenneth.

"You will wish that with all your soul before I am through with you," snarled Barry. "Oh, I'm not afraid of you! I know the whole beastly story about your father and that—"

"Stop!" cried Kenneth, taking a step forward, his arm drawn back. "Not another word, Lapelle! You've said enough! I know where you got your information, —and I can tell you, here and now, that the man lied to you. I'm going to give you twenty-four hours to get out of this town for good. And if I hear that you have repeated a word of what you said to her I'll see

to it that you are strung up by the neck and your
miserable carcass filled with bullets. Oh, you needn't
sputter! It will be your word against mine. I guess
you know which of us the men of this town will believe. And you needn't expect to be supported by
your friend Jasper Suggs or the gentle Mr. Hawk,—
Aha, *that* got under your pelt, didn't it? If either of
them is still alive at this minute, it's because he surrendered without a fight and not because God took
care of him. Your beautiful game is spoiled, Lapelle,
—and you'll be lucky to get off with a whole skin. I'm
giving you a chance. Get out of this town,—and stay
out!"

Barry, recovering quickly from the shock, made a
fair show of bravado.

"What are you talking about? What the devil have
I got to do with—"

"That's enough! You know what I'm talking about.
Take my advice. Get out of town before you are a
day older. You will save yourself a ride on a rail and
a rawhiding that you'll not forget to your dying day."

"I will leave this town when I feel like it, Gwynne,"
said Lapelle, drawing himself up. "I don't take orders
from you. You will hear from me later. You've got
the upper hand now,—with that nigger of yours standing over there holding an axe in his hands, ready to
kill me if I make a move. We'll settle this in the regular way, Gwynne,—with pistols. You may expect a
friend of mine to call on you shortly."

"As you like," retorted the other, bowing stiffly.
"You may name the time and place."

Lapelle bowed and then cast an eye about in quest
of his hat. It was lying in the road some distance
away. He strode over and picked it up. Quite nat-

urally, perhaps unconsciously, he resorted to the habit of years: he cocked it slightly at just the right angle over his eye. Then, without a glance behind, he crossed the road and plunged into the thicket.

Kenneth watched him till he disappeared from view. Suddenly aware of a pain in his hand, he held it out before him and was astonished to find that the knuckles were already beginning to puff. He winced when he tried to clench his fist. A rueful smile twitched at the corners of his mouth.

"Mighty slim chance I'll have," he said to himself. "Won't be able to pull a trigger to save my life."

He hurried up the path and, without knocking, opened the door and entered the house. Hattie was coming down the stairs, her eyes as round as saucers.

"Where is Miss Viola?"

"She done gone up stairs, suh. Lan' sakes, Mistah Gwynne, what fo' yo' do dat to Mistah Barry? He her beau. Didn't yo'all know dat? Ah close mah eyes when she tooken dat gun out dar. Sez Ah, she gwine to shoot Mistah Gwynne——"

"Tell her I'm here, Hattie. I must see her at once. It's all right. She isn't angry with me."

The girl hesitated. "She look mighty white an' sick, suh. She never say a word. Jes' go right up stairs, she did. Ah follers, 'ca'se Ah was skeert about de way she look. She shutten de do' an' drop de bolt,—yas, suh, dat's what she do. Lordy, Ah wonder why her ma don't come home an' look after——"

"See here," he broke in, "don't disturb her now. I will come back in a little while. If she wants me for anything you will find me out at the gate. Do you understand? Don't fail to call me. I am going out there to wait for her mother."

It suddenly had occurred to him that he ought to intercept Rachel Carter before she reached the house, not only to prepare her for the shock that awaited her but to devise between them some means of undoing the harm that already had been done. They would have to stand together in denouncing Barry, they would have to swear to Viola that the story was false. He realized what this would mean to him: an almost profane espousal of his enemy's cause, involving not only the betrayal of his own conscience, but the deliberate repudiation of the debt he owed his mother and her people. He would have to go before Viola and proclaim the innocence of the woman who had robbed and murdered his own mother. The unthinkable, the unbelievable confronted him.

A cold sweat broke out all over him as he stood down by the gate, torn between hatred for one woman and love for another: Rachel and Minda Carter. He could not spare one without sparing the other; lying to one of them meant lying for the other. But there was no alternative. The memory of the look in Viola's eyes as she shrank away from Lapelle, the thought of the cruel shock she must have suffered, the picture of her as she came down the path to kill—no, there could be no alternative!

And so, as he leaned rigidly against the gate, sick at heart but clear of head, waiting for Rachel Carter, he came to think that, after all, a duel with Barry Lapelle might prove to be the easiest and noblest way out of his difficulties.

CHAPTER XXI

IT wanted half an hour of daybreak when a slow-riding, silent group of men came to a halt and dismounted in the narrow lane some distance from the ramshackle abode of Martin Hawk, squatting unseen among the trees that lined the steep bank of the Wabash. A three hours' ride through dark, muddy roads lay behind them. There were a dozen men in all, —and one woman, at whose side rode the hunter, Stain. They had stopped at the latter's cabin on the way down, and she had conversed apart with him through a window. Then they rode off, leaving him to follow.

There were no lights, and no man spoke above a whisper. The work of tethering the horses progressed swiftly but with infinite caution. Eyes made sharp by long hours of darkness served their owners well in this stealthy enterprise.

The half-hour passed and the night began to lift. Vague unusual objects slowly took shape, like gloomy spectres emerging from impenetrable fastnesses. Blackness gave way to a faint drab pall; then the cold, unearthly grey of the still remote dawn came stealing across the fields.

At last it was light enough to see, and the advance upon the cabin began. Silently through the dense, shadowy wood crept the sheriff and his men,—followed by the tall woman in black and a lank, bearded man

282

whose rifle-stock bore seven tiny but significant notches, —sinister epitaphs for as many by-gone men.

A dog barked,—the first alarm. Then another, and still a third joined in a fierce outcry against the invaders. Suddenly the door of the hut was thrown open and a half-dressed man stooped in the low aperture, peering out across the dawn-shrouded clearing. The three coon-dogs, slinking out of the shadows, crowded up to the door, their snarling muzzles pointed toward the encircling trees.

Two men stepped out of the underbrush and advanced. Even in the dim, uncertain light, Martin Hawk could see that they carried rifles. His eyes were like those of the bird whose name he bore. They swept the clearing in a flash. As if by magic, men appeared to right of him, to left of him, in front of him. He counted them. Seven,—no, there was another,—eight. And he knew there were more of them, back of the house, cutting off retreat to the river.

"Don't move, Martin," called out a voice.

"What do you want?" demanded Hawk, in a sharp, querulous voice.

"I am the sheriff. Got a warrant for your arrest. No use makin' a fight for it, Hawk. You are completely surrounded. You can't get away."

"I ain't done nothin' to be arrested fer," cried the man in the doorway. "I'm an honest man,—I hain't ever done—"

"Well, that's not for me to decide," interrupted the sheriff, now not more than a dozen feet away. "I've got a warrant charging you with sheep-stealing and so on, and that's all there is to it. I'm not the judge and jury. You come along quiet now and no foolishness."

"Who says I stole sheep?"

"Step outside here and I'll read the affidavit to you. And say, if you don't want your dogs massacreed, you'd better call 'em off."

Martin Hawk looked over his shoulder into the dark interior of the hut, spoke to some one under his breath, and then began cursing his dogs.

"I might have knowed you'd git me into trouble, you lop-eared, sheep-killin' whelps!" he whined. "I'd ought to shot the hull pack of ye when you was pups. Git out'n my sight! There's yer sheep-stealers, sheriff,—them ornery, white-livered, blood-suckin'—"

"I don't know anything about that, Martin," snapped the sheriff. "All I know is, you got to come along with me,—peaceable or otherwise,—and I guess if you're half as smart as I think you are, you won't come otherwise. Here! Don't go back in that house, Hawk."

"Well, I got to tell my daughter—"

"We'll tell her. There's another man or two in there. Just tell 'em to step outside,—and leave their weapons behind 'em."

"There ain't a livin' soul in thar, 'cept my daughter,—so he'p me God, sheriff," cried Hawk, his teeth beginning to chatter. The sheriff was close enough to see the look of terror and desperation in his eyes.

"No use lyin', Hawk. You've got a man named Suggs stayin' with you. He ain't accused of anything, so he needn't be afraid to come out. Same applies to your daughter Moll. But I don't want anybody in there to take a shot at us the minute we turn our backs. Shake 'em out, Hawk."

"I tell ye there ain't nobody here but me an' Moll,— an' she's sick. She can't come out. An'—an' you,

can't go in,—not unless you got a warrant to search
my house. That's what the law sez,—an' you know it.
I'll go along with you peaceable,—an' stand my trial
fer sheep-stealin' like a man. Lemme get my hat an'
coat, an' I'll come—"

"I guess there's something queer about all this,"
interrupted the sheriff. The man beside him had just
whispered something in his ear. "We'll take a look
inside that cabin, law or no law, Hawk. Move up,
boys!" he called out to the scattered men. "Keep your
eyes skinned. If you ketch sight of a rifle ball comin'
to'ards you,—dodge. And you, Martin, step outside
here, where you won't be in the way. I'm going in
there."

Martin Hawk looked wildly about him. On all sides
were men with rifles. There was no escape. His craven
heart failed him, his knees gave way beneath him and an
instant later he was grovelling in the mud at the
sheriff's feet.

"I didn't do it! I didn't do it! I swear to God I
didn't. It was her. She done it,—Moll done it!" he
squealed in abject terror.

He was grabbed by strong hands and jerked to his
feet. While others held him, the sheriff and several of
the men rushed into the cabin.

Off at the edge of the clearing stood Rachel Carter
and Isaac Stain, watching the scene at the door.

"One look will be enough," the woman had said
tersely. "Twenty years will not have changed Simon
Braley much. I will know him at sight."

"You got to be sure, Mrs. Gwyn," muttered the
hunter. "Ef you got the slightest doubt, say so."

"I will, Isaac."

"And ef you say it's him, fer sure an' no mistake,

I'll foller him to the end of the world but what I git him."

"If it is Simon Braley he will make a break for cover. He is not like that whimpering coward over yonder. And the sheriff will make no attempt to bring him down. There is no complaint against him. No one knows that he is Simon Braley."

"Well, I'll be on his heels," was the grim promise of Isaac Stain, thinking of the sister who had been slain by Braley's Indians down on the River White.

One of the men rushed out of the cabin. He was vastly excited.

"Don't let go of him," he shouted to the men who were holding Martin. "There's hell to pay in there. Where is Mrs. Gwyn?"

"I never done it!" wailed Martin, livid with terror. "I swear to God—"

"Shut up!"

"She's over there, Sam,—with Ike Stain."

Ignoring the question that followed him, the man called Sam hurried up to the couple at the edge of the bush.

"Better clear out, Mrs. Gwyn," he said soberly. "I mean, don't stay around. Something in there you oughtn't to see."

"What is it?" she inquired sharply.

"Well, you see,—there's a dead man in there,— knifed. Blood all over everything and—"

"The man called Suggs?"

"I reckon so. Leastwise it must be him. 'Pears to be a stranger to all of us. Deader'n a door nail. He's—"

"I am not chicken-hearted, Mr. Corbin," she announced. "I have seen a good many dead men in my time. The sight of blood does not affect me. I will go in and see him. No! Please do not stay me."

Despite his protestations, she strode resolutely across the lot. As she passed Martin Hawk that cowering rascal stared at her, first without comprehension, then with a suddenly awakened, acute understanding.

It was she who had brought the authorities down upon him. She had made "affidavy" against him,—she had got him into this horrible mess by swearing that he stole her sheep and calves. True, he had stolen from her,—there was no doubt about that,—but he had covered his tracks perfectly. Any one of a half-dozen men along the river might have stolen her stock,—they were stealing right and left. How then did she come to fix upon him as the one to accuse? In a flash he leaped to a startling conclusion. Barry Lapelle! The man who knew all about his thievish transactions and who for months had profited by them. Hides, wool, fresh meats from the secret lairs and slaughter pens back in the trackless wilds, all these had gone down the river on Barry's boats, products of a far-reaching system of outlawry, with Barry and his captains sharing in the proceeds.

Now he understood. Lapelle had gone back on him, had betrayed him to his future mother-in-law. The fine gentleman had no further use for him; Mrs. Gwyn had given her consent to the marriage and in return for that he had betrayed a loyal friend! And now look at the position he was in, all through Barry Lapelle. Sheep stealing was nothing to what he might have to face. Even though Moll had done the killing, he would have a devil of a time convincing a jury of the fact. More than likely, Moll would up and deny

that she had anything to do with it,—and then what?
It would be like the ornery slut to lie out of it and let
'em hang her own father, just to pay him back for the
lickin's he had given her.

All this raced through the fast-steadying brain of
Martin Hawk as he watched his accuser pass him by
without a look and stop irresolutely on his threshold
to stare aghast at what lay beyond. It became a conviction, rather than a conjecture. Barry had set the
dogs upon him! Snake! Well,—just let him get loose
from these plagued hounds for half an hour or so and,
by glory, they'd have something to hang him for or
his name wasn't Martin Hawk.

Isaac Stain did not move from the spot where she
had left him, over at the edge of the clearing. His
rifle was ready, his keen eyes alert. Rachel Carter
entered the hut. Many minutes passed. Then she
came to the door and beckoned to him.

"It is Simon Braley," she said quietly. "He is dead.
The girl killed him, Isaac. Will you ride over to my
farm and have Allen come over here with a wagon?
They're going to take the body up to town,—and the
girl, too."

Stain stood his rifle against the wall of the hut.
"I guess I won't need this," was all he said as he turned
and strode away.

The man called Jasper Suggs lay in front of the
tumble-down fireplace, his long body twisted gro-
tesquely by the final spasm of pain that carried him
off. The lower part of his body was covered by a
filthy strip of rag carpet which some one had hastily
thrown over him as Rachel Carter was on the point
of entering the house. His coarse linsey shirt was
soaked with blood, now dry and almost black. The

harsh light from the open door struck full upon his bearded face and its staring eyes.

In a corner, at the foot of a straw pallet, ordinarily screened from the rest of the cabin by a couple of suspended quilts, stood Moll Hawk, leaning against the wall, her dark sullen eyes following the men as they moved about the room. The quilts, ruthlessly torn from their fastenings on the pole, lay scattered and trampled on the floor, sinister evidence of the struggle that had taken place between woman and beast. At the other end of the room were two similar pallets, unscreened, and beside one of these lay Jasper Suggs' rawhide boots.

From her place in the shadows Moll Hawk watched the other woman stoop over and gaze intently at the face of the slain man. She was a tall, well-developed girl of twenty or thereabouts. Her long, straight hair, the colour of the raven's wing, swung loose about her shoulders, an occasional strand trailing across her face, giving her a singularly witchlike appearance. Her body from the waist up was stripped almost bare; there were several long streaks of blood across her breast, where the fingers of a gory hand had slid in relaxing their grip on her shoulder. With one hand she clutched what was left of a tattered garment, vainly seeking to hide her naked breasts. The stout, coarse dress had been almost torn from her body.

Mrs. Gwyn left the hut but soon returned. After a few earnest words with the sheriff, she came slowly over to the girl. Moll shrank back against the wall, a strange glitter leaping into her sullen, lifeless eyes.

"I don't want nobody prayin' over me," she said huskily. "I jest want to be let alone."

"I am not going to pray over you, my girl. I want you to come out in the back yard with me, where I can wash the blood off of you and put something around you."

"What's the use'n that? They're goin' to take me to jail, ain't they?"

"Have you another frock to put on, Moll?"

The girl looked down at her torn, disordered dress, a sneering smile on her lips.

"This is all I got,—an' now look at it. I ain't had a new dress in God knows how long. Pap ain't much on dressin' me up. Mr. Lapelle he promised me a new dress but—say, who air you?"

"I am Mrs. Gwyn, Moll."

"I might ha' knowed it. You're her ma, huh? Well, I guess you'd better go on away an' let me alone. I ain't axin' no favours off'n—"

"I am not trying to do you a favour. I am only trying to make you a little more presentable. You are going up to town, Moll."

"Yes,—I guess that's so. Can't they hang me here an' have it over?" A look of terror gleamed in her eyes, but there was no flinching of the body, no tremor in her voice.

The sheriff came over. "Better let Mrs. Gwyn fix you up a little, Moll. She's a good, kind lady and she'll—"

"I don't want to go to town," whimpered the girl, covering her face with her hands. "I don't want to be hung. I jest had to do it,—I jest had to. There wuz no other way,—'cept to—'cept to—an' I jest couldn't do that. Now I wish I had,—oh, Lordy, how I wish I had! That wuz bad enough, but hangin's wuss. He wuz goin' away in a day or two, anyhow, so—"

"You're not going to be hung, Moll," broke in the sheriff. "Don't you worry about that. We don't hang women for killing men like that feller over there. Like as not you'll be set free in no time at all. All you've got to do is to tell the truth about how it happened and that'll be all there is to it."

"You're lyin' to me, jest to git me to go along quiet," she quavered, but there was a new light in her eyes.

"I'm not lying. You will have to stand trial, of course,—you understand that, don't you?—but there isn't a jury on earth that would hang you. We don't do that kind of thing to women. Now you go along with Mrs. Gwyn and do what she says,—and you can tell me all about this after a while."

"I'll wash, but I hain't got no more clothes," muttered the girl.

"We will manage somehow," said Mrs. Gwyn. "One of the men will give you a coat,—or you may have my cape to wear, Moll."

Moll looked at her in surprise. Again she said the unexpected thing. "Why, ever'body says you air a mighty onfeelin' woman, Mis' Gwyn. I can't believe you'd let me take your cape."

"You will see, my girl. Come! Show me where to find water and a comb and—"

"Wait a minute," said Moll abruptly. "Somehow I ain't as skeert as I wuz. You're shore they won't hang me? 'Ca'se I'd hate to be hung,—I'd hate to die that-away, Mister."

"They won't hang you, Moll,—take my word for it."

"Well, then," said she, bringing forward the hand she had been holding behind her back all the time;

"here's the knife I done it with. It's his'n. He was braggin' last night about how many gullets he had slit with it,—I mean men's gullets. I wuz jest sort o' hangin' onto it in case I—but I don't believe I ever could a' done it. 'Tain't 'ca'se I'm afeared to die but they say a person that takes his own life is shore to go to hell—'ca'se he don't git no chance fer to repent. Take it, Mister."

She handed the big sheath-knife to the sheriff. Then she followed Rachel Carter out of the hut, apparently unconscious of the curious eyes that followed her. She passed close by the corpse. She looked down at the ghastly face and twisted body without the slightest trace of emotion,—neither dread nor repugnance nor interest beyond a curious narrowing of the eyes as of one searching for some sign of trickery on the part of a wily adversary. On the way out she stopped to pick up a wretched, almost toothless comb and some dish-rags.

"I guess we better go down to the river," she said as they stepped out into the open. " 'Tain't very fer, Mrs. Gwyn,—an' the water's cleaner. Hain't no danger of me tryin' to git away," she went on, with a feeble grin as her eyes swept the little clearing, revealing armed men in all directions. Her gaze rested for a moment on Martin Hawk, who was staring at her from his seat on a stump hard by.

"There's my pap over yonder," she said, with a scowl. "He's the one that ort to be strung up fer all this. He didn't do it,—but he's to blame, just the same. They ain't got him 'rested fer doin' it, have they? 'Ca'se he didn't. He'll tell you he's as innocent as a unborn child,—he allus does,—an' he is as fer as the killin' goes. But ef he'd done what wuz right hit never would 'a' happened. Thet's whut I got ag'inst him."

Rachel Carter was looking at the strange creature with an interest not far removed from pity. Despite the sullen, hang-dog expression she was a rather handsome girl; wild, untutored, almost untamed she was, and yet not without a certain diffidence that bespoke better qualities than appeared on the surface. She was tall and strongly built, with the long, swinging stride of the unhampered woodswoman. Her young shoulders and back were bent with the toil and drudgery of the life she led. Her eyes, in which lurked a never-absent gleam of pain, were dark, smouldering, deep set and so restless that one could not think of them as ever being closed in sleep.

The girl led the way down a narrow path to a little sand-bar.

"I go in swimmin' here every day, 'cept when it's froze over," she volunteered dully. "Hain't you skeert at the sight o' blood, ma'am? Some people air. We wuz figgerin' on whuther we'd dig a grave fer him or jest pull out yonder into the current an' drop him over. Pap said we had to git rid of him 'fore anybody come around. 'Nen the dogs begin to bark an' he thought mebby it wuz Mr. Lapelle, so he—say, you mustn't get Mr. Lapelle mixed up in this. He—"

"I know all about Mr. Lapelle, Moll," interrupted the older woman.

The girl gave her a sharp, almost hostile look. "Then you hain't goin' to let him have your girl, air you?"

Mrs. Gwyn shook her head. "No, Moll,—I am not," she said.

"You set here on this log," ordered the girl as they

came down to the water's edge. "I'll do my own washin'. I'm kind o' 'shamed to have any one see me as naked as this. There ain't much left of my dress, is they? We fit fer I don't know how long, like a couple o' dogs. You c'n see the black an' blue places on my arms out here in the daylight,—an' I guess his finger marks must be on my neck, where he wuz chokin' me. I wuz tryin' to wrassle around till I could git nigh to the table, where his knife wuz stickin'. My eyes wuz poppin' right out'n my head when I—"

"For heaven's sake, girl!" cried Rachel Carter. "Don't! Don't tell me any more! I can't bear to hear you talk about it."

Moll stared at her for a moment as if bewildered, and then suddenly turned away, her chin quivering with mortification. She had been reprimanded!

For several minutes Rachel stood in silence, watching her as she washed the blood from her naked breast and shoulders. Presently the girl turned toward her, as if for inspection.

"I'm sorry, ma'am, if I talked too much," she mumbled awkwardly. "I'd ort to have knowed better. Is—is it all off?"

"I think so," said Rachel, pulling herself together with an effort. "Let me—"

"No, I'll finish it," said the girl stubbornly. She dried her brown, muscular arms, rubbed her body vigorously with one of the rags and then began to comb out her long, tangled hair,—not gently but with a sort of relentless energy. Swiftly, deftly she plaited it into two long braids, which she left hanging down in front of her shoulders, squaw fashion.

"How long had you known this man Suggs, Moll?" suddenly inquired the other woman.

"Off an' on ever sence I kin remember," replied the girl. "Pap knowed him down south. We hain't seed much of him fer quite a spell. Four—five year, I guess mebby. He come here last week one day."

The eyes of the two women met. Moll broke the short silence that ensued. She glanced over her shoulder. The nearest man was well out of earshot. Still she lowered her voice.

"He claims he use ter know you a long time ago," she said.

"Yes?"

"Mebby you'd recollect him ef I tole you his right name."

"His name was Simon Braley," said Rachel Carter calmly.

Moll's eyes narrowed. "Then what he sez wuz true?"

"I don't know what he said to you, Moll."

"He sez you run off with some other woman's husband," replied Moll bluntly.

"Did he tell this to any one except you and your father?"

"He didn't tell no one but me, fer as I know. He didn't tell Pap."

"When did he tell you?"

"Las' night," said Moll, suddenly dropping her eyes. "He wuz drinkin',—an' I thought mebby he wuz lyin'."

"You are sure he did not tell your father?"

"I'm purty shore he didn't."

"Why did he tell you?"

The girl raised her eyes. There was a deeper look of pain in them now. "I'd ruther not tell," she muttered.

"You need not be afraid."

"Well, he wuz arguin' with me. He said there wuzn't

any good women in the world. 'Why,' sez he, 'I seen a woman this very day that everybody thinks is as good as the angels up in heaven, but when I tell you whut I know about her you'll—' "

"You need not go on," interrupted Rachel Carter, drawing her brows together. "Would you believe me if I told you the man lied, Moll Hawk?"

"Yes, ma'am,—I would," said the girl promptly. "Fer as that goes, I *tole* him he lied."

Rachel started to say something, then closed her lips tightly and fell to staring out over the river. The girl eyed her for a moment and then went on:

"You needn't be skeert of me ever tellin' anybody whut he said to me. Hit wouldn't be right to spread a lie like thet, Mis' Gwyn. You—"

"I think they are waiting for us, Moll," interrupted Rachel, suddenly holding out her hand to the girl. "Thank you. Come, give me your hand. We will go back to them, hand in hand, my girl."

Moll stared at her in sheer astonishment.

"You—you don't want to hold my hand in yours, do you?" she murmured slowly, incredulously.

"I do. You will find me a good friend,—and you will need good friends, Moll."

Dumbly the girl held out her hand. It was clasped firmly by Rachel Carter. They were half-way up the bank when Moll held back and tried to withdraw her hand.

"I—I can't let you,—why, ma'am, that's the hand I —I held the knife in," she cried, agitatedly.

Rachel gripped the hand more firmly. "I know it is, Moll," she said calmly.

CHAPTER XXII

T HE grewsome cavalcade wended its way town-
ward. Moll Hawk sat between the sheriff and
Cyrus Allen on the springless board that served
as a seat atop the lofty sideboards of the wagon. The
crude wooden wheels rumbled and creaked and jarred
along the deep-rutted road, jouncing the occupants of
the vehicle from side to side with unseemly playfulness.
Back in the bed of the wagon, under a gaily coloured
Indian blanket, lay the outstretched body of Jasper
Suggs, seemingly alive and responsive to the jolts and
twists and turns of the road. The rear end gate had
been removed and three men sat with their heels dan-
gling outside, their backs to the sinister, unnoticed
traveller who shared accommodations with them. The
central figure was Martin Hawk, grim, saturnine, silent,
his feet and hands secured with leather thongs. Trot-
ting along under his heels, so to speak, were his three
dogs,—their tongues hanging out, their tails drooping,
their eyes turning neither to right nor left. They
were his only friends.

Some distance behind rode three horsemen, leading
as many riderless steeds. On ahead was another group
of riders. Rachel Carter rode alongside the wagon.

Moll had firmly refused to wear the older woman's
cape. She had on a coat belonging to one of the men
and wore a flimsy, deep-hooded bonnet that once had

been azure blue. Her shoulders sagged wearily, her back was bent, her arms lay limply upon her knees. She was staring bleakly before her over the horses' ears, at the road ahead. The reaction had come. She had told the story of the night, haltingly but with a graphic integrity that left nothing to be desired.

Martin Hawk had spent a black and unhappy hour. He was obliged to listen to his daughter's story and, much to his discontent, was not permitted to contradict her in any particular. Two or three mournful attempts to reproach her for lying about her own,—and, he always added, her *only*—father, met with increasingly violent adjurations to "shut up," the last one being so emphatic that he gave vent to a sharp howl of pain and began feeling with his tongue to see if all his teeth were there.

Luckily for him, he was impervious to the scorn of his fellow-man, else he would have shrivelled under the looks he received from time to time. Especially distressing to him was that part of her recital touching upon his unholy greed; he could not help feeling, with deep parental bitterness, that no man alive ever had a more heartless, undutiful daughter than he,—a conviction that for the time being at least caused him to lament the countless opportunities he had had to beat her to death instead of merely raising a few perishable welts on her back. If he had done that, say a month ago, how different everything would be now!

This part of her story may suffice:

"Pap never wanted anything so bad in all his life as that powder horn an' shot flask. They wuz all fixed up with gold an' silver trimmin's an' I guess there wuz rubies an' di'monds too. Fer three days Pap dickered with him, tryin' to make some kind of a

swap. Jasper he wouldn't trade 'em er sell 'em nuther.
He said they wuz wuth more'n a thousand dollars.
Some big Injun Chief made him a present of 'em, years
ago,—fer savin' his life, he said. First Pap tried to
swap his hounds fer 'em, 'nen said he'd throw in one
of the hosses. Jasper he jest laughed at him. Yesterday I heerd Pap tell him he would swap him both
hosses, seven hogs, the wagon an' two boats, but Jasper
he jest laughed. They wuz still talkin' about it when
they got home from town last night, jest ahead of the
storm. I could hear 'em arguin' out in the room. They
wuz drinkin' an' talkin' so loud I couldn't sleep.

"Purty soon Pap said he'd trade him our cabin an'
ever'thing else fer that pouch an' flask. It wuz rainin'
so hard by this time I couldn't hear all they said but
when it slacked up a little I cotch my own name. They
wuz talkin' about me. I heerd Jasper tell Pap he'd
give him the things ef he'd promise to go away an'
leave him an' me alone in the cabin. That kind o' surprised me. But all Pap sez wuz that he hated to
go out in the rain. So Jasper he said fer him to wait
till hit stopped rainin'. Pap said all right, he would,
an' fer Jasper to hand over the pouch and flask.
Jasper cussed an' said he'd give 'em to him three hours
after sunrise the nex' morning' an' not a minute sooner,
an' he wuz to stay away from the house all that time
or he wouldn't give 'em to him at all. Well, they
argued fer some time about that an' finally Pap said
he'd go out to the hoss shed an' sleep if Jasper would
hand over the shot pouch then an' there an' hold back
the powder flask till mornin'. Jasper he said all right,
he would. I never guess what wuz back of all this. So
when Pap went out an' shut the door behind him, I
wuz kind o' thankful, ca'se all the arguin' an' jawin'

would stop an' I could go to sleep ag'in. Jasper he let down the bolt inside the door."

.   .   .   .

It was after eight o'clock when the wagon and its escort entered the outskirts of the town. Grim, imperturbable old dames sitting on their porches smoking their clay or corncob pipes regarded the strange procession with mild curiosity; toilers in gardens and barnyards merely remarked to themselves that "some'pin must'a happened some'eres" and called out to housewife or offspring not to let them forget to "mosey up to the square" later in the day for particulars, if any. The presence of the sheriff was more or less informing; it was obvious even to the least sprightly intelligence that somebody had been arrested. But the appearance of Mrs. Gwyn on horseback, riding slowly beside the wagon, was not so easily accounted for. That circumstance alone made it absolutely worth while to "mosey up to the square" a little later on.

Martin Hawk was lodged in the recently completed brick jail adjoining the courthouse. He complained bitterly of the injustice that permitted his daughter, a confessed murderess, to enjoy the hospitality of the sheriff's home whilst he, accused of nothing more heinous than sheep-stealing, was flung into jail and subjected to the further indignity of being audibly described as a fit subject for the whipping post, an institution that still prevailed despite a general movement to abolish it throughout the state.

It galled him to hear the fuss that was being made over Moll. Everybody seemed to be taking her part. Why, that Gwyn woman not only went so far as to say she would be responsible for Moll's appearance in court, but actually arranged to buy her a lot of new

clothes. And the sheriff patted her on the shoulder
and loudly declared that the only thing any judge
or jury could possibly find her guilty of was criminal
negligence in only half-doing the job. This was sup-
plemented by a look that left no doubt in Martin's
mind as to just what he considered to be the neglected
part of the job.

He bethought himself of the one powerful friend
he had in town,—Barry Lapelle. So he sent this message by word of mouth to the suspected dandy:

"I'm in jail. I want you to come and see me right
off. I mean business."

Needless to say, this message,—conveying a far
from subtle threat,—was a long time in reaching Mr.
Lapelle, who had gone into temporary retirement at
Jack Trentman's shanty, having arrived at that unsa-
voury retreat by a roundabout, circuitous route which
allowed him to spend some time on the bank of a se-
questered brook.

Meanwhile Rachel Carter approached her own home,
afoot and weary. As she turned the bend she was
surprised and not a little disturbed by the sight of
Kenneth Gwynne standing at her front gate. He
hurried up the road to meet her.

"The worst has come to pass," he announced, stopping in front of her. "Before you go in I must tell
you just what happened here this morning. Come in
here among the trees where we can't be seen from
the house."

She listened impassively to his story. Only the
expression in her steady, unswerving eyes betrayed
her inward concern and agitation. Not once did she
interrupt him. Her shoulders, he observed, drooped
a little and her arms hung limply at her side, mute

evidence of a sinking heart and the resignation that comes with defeat.

"I am ready and willing," he assured her at the end, "to do anything, to say anything you wish. It is possible for us to convince her that there is no truth in what he said. We can lie—"

She held up her hand, shaking her head almost angrily. "No! Not that, Kenneth. I cannot permit you to lie for *me*. That would be unspeakable. I am not wholly without honour. There is nothing you can do for her,—for either of us at present. Thank you for preparing me,—and for your offer, Kenneth. Stay away from us until you have had time to think it all over. Then you will realize that this generous impulse of yours would do more harm than good. Let her think what she will of me, she must not lose her faith in you, my boy."

"But—what of her?" he expostulated. "What are you going to say to her when she asks you—"

"I don't know," she interrupted, lifelessly. "I am not a good liar, Kenneth Gwynne. Whatever else you may say or think of me, I—I have never wilfully lied."

She started away, but after a few steps turned back to him. "Jasper Suggs is dead. Moll Hawk killed him last night. She has been arrested. There is nothing you can do for Viola at present, but you may be able to help that poor, unfortunate girl. Suggs told her about me. She will keep the secret. Go and see the sheriff at once. He will tell you all that has happened."

Then she strode off without another word. He watched the tall, black figure until it turned in at the gate and was lost to view, a sort of stupefaction gripping him. Presently he aroused himself and walked slowly homeward. As he passed through his own gate he looked over at the window of the room in which Viola had sought seclusion. The curtains hung limp and motionless. He wondered what was taking place inside the four walls of that room.

Out of the maze into which his thoughts had been plunged by the swift procession of events groped the new and disturbing turn in the affairs of Rachel Carter. What was back of the untold story of the slaying of Jasper Suggs? What were the circumstances? Why had Moll Hawk killed the man? Had Rachel Carter figured directly or indirectly in the tragedy? He recalled her significant allusion to Isaac Stain the night before and his own rather startling inference,—and now she was asking him to help Moll Hawk in her hour of tribulation. A cold perspiration started out all over him. The question persisted: What was back of the slaying of Jasper Suggs?

He gave explicit and peremptory directions to Zachariah in case Mrs. Gwyn asked for him, and then set out briskly for the courthouse.

By this time the news of the murder had spread over the town. A crowd had gathered in front of Scudder's undertaking establishment. Knots of men and women, disregarding traffic, stood in the streets adjoining the public square, listening to some qualified narrator's account of the night's expedition and the tragedy at Martin Hawk's.

Kenneth hurried past these crowds and made his way straight to the office of the sheriff. Farther down the street a group of people stood in front of the sheriff's house, while in the vicinity of the little jail an ever-increasing mob was collecting.

"Judge" Billings espied him. Disengaging himself

from a group of men at the corner of the square, the defendant in the case of Kenwright vs. Billings made a bee-line for his young attorney.

"I've been over to your office twice, young man," he announced as he came up. "Where the devil have you been keepin' yourself? Mrs. Gwyn left word for you to come right up to her house. She wants you to take charge of the Hawk girl's case. Maybe you don't know it, but you've been engaged to defend her. You better make tracks up to Mrs. Gwyn's and—"

"I have seen Mrs. Gwyn," interrupted Kenneth. "She sent me to the sheriff. Where is he?"

"Over yonder talkin' to that crowd in front of the tavern. He's sort o' pickin' out a jury in advance, —makin' sure that the right men get on it. He got me for one. He don't make any bones about it. Just tells you how it all happened an' then asks you whether you'd be such a skunk as to even think of convictin' the girl for what she did. Then you up an' blaspheme considerable about what you'd like to do to her dodgasted father, an' before you git anywhere's near through, he holds up his hand an' says, 'Now, I've only got to git three more (or whatever it is), an' then the jury's complete!' We're figgerin' on havin' the trial to-morrow mornin' between nine an' ten o'clock. The judge says it's all right, far as he's concerned. We'd have it to-day, only Moll's got to have a new dress an' bonnet an' such-like before she can appear in court. All you'll have to do, Kenny, is jest to set back,—look wise an' let her tell her story. 'Cordin' to law, she's got to stand trial fer murder an' she's got to have counsel. Nobody's goin' to object to you makin' a speech to the jury,—bringin' tears to our eyes, as the sayin' is,—only don't make it too long.

I've got to meet a man at half-past ten in regards
to a hoss trade, an' I happen to know that Tom Rank's
clerk is sick an' he don't want to keep his store locked
up fer more than an hour. I'm jest tellin' you this so's
you won't have to waste time to-morrow askin' the
jurymen whether they have formed an opinion or not,
or whether they feel they can give the prisoner a fair
an' impartial trial or not. The sheriff's already asked
us that an' we've all said yes,—so don't delay matters
by askin' ridiculous questions."

The "Judge" interrupted himself to look at his
watch.

"Well, I've got to be movin' along. I'm on the coro-
ner's jury too, and we're goin' up to Matt's right
away to view the remains. The verdict will probable
be: 'Come to his death on account of Moll Hawk's self-
defense,' or somethin' like that. 'Never put off till to-
morrow what you can do to-day,' as the sayin' goes.
Wouldn't surprise me a bit if he was buried before
three o'clock to-day. Then we won't have him on our
minds to-morrow. Well, see you later—if not sooner."

An hour later Kenneth accompanied the sheriff to
the latter's home for an interview with his client. He
had promptly consented to act as her counsel after
hearing the story of the crime from the sheriff.

"Mrs. Gwyn told my wife to go out and get some
new clothes for the girl," said the sheriff as they strode
down the street, "and she'd step into the store some
time to-day and settle for them. By thunder, you
could have knocked me over with a feather, Kenneth.
If your stepmother was a man we'd describe her as a
skinflint. She's as stingy and unfeeling as they make
'em. Hard as nails and about as kind-hearted as a
tombstone. What other woman on this here earth

would have gone out to Martin Hawk's last night just for the satisfaction of seein' him arrested? We didn't want her,—not by a long shot,—but she made up her mind to go, and, by gosh, she went. I guess maybe she thought we'd make a botch of it, and so she took that long ride just to make sure she'd git her money's worth. 'Cause, you see, I had to pay each of the men a dollar and a half and mileage before they'd run the risk of bein' shot by Hawk and his crowd. Hard as nails, I said, but doggone it, the minute she saw that girl out there she turned as soft as butter and there is nothin' she won't do for her. It beats me, by gosh,—it certainly beats me."

"Women are very strange creatures," observed Kenneth.

"Yep," agreed the other. "You can most always tell what a man's goin' to do, but I'm derned if you can even *guess* what a woman's up to. Take my wife, for instance. Why, I've been livin' with that woman for seventeen years and I swear to Guinea she's still got me puzzled. Course I know what she's talking about most of the time, but, by gosh, I never know what she's thinkin' about. Women are like cats. A cat is the thoughtfulest animal there is. It's always thinkin'. It thinks when it's asleep,—and most of the time when you think it's asleep it ain't asleep at all. Well, here we are. I guess Moll's out in the kitchen with my wife. I told Ma to roll that old dress of Moll's up and save it for the jury to see. It's the best bit of evidence she's got. All you'll have to do is to hold it up in front of the jury and start your speech somethin' like this: 'Gentlemen of the jury, I ask you to gaze upon this here dress, all tattered and

torn,—' and that's as far as you'll get, 'cause this jury
is goin' to be composed of gentlemen and they'll probably stand up right then and there and say 'Not guilty.'
Come right in, Mr. Gwynne."

After considerable persuasion on the part of the
sheriff and his kindly wife, Moll repeated her story to
Gwynne. She was abashed before this elegant young
man. A shyness and confusion that had been totally
lacking in her manner toward the other and older
men took possession of her now, and it was with difficulty that she was induced to give him the complete
details of all that took place in her father's cabin.

When he shook hands with her as he was about to
take his departure, she suddenly found courage to
say:

"Kin I see you alone fer a couple of minutes, Mr.
Gwynne?"

"Certainly, Miss Hawk," he replied, gravely courteous. "I am sure Mr. and Mrs.—"

"Come right in the sitting-room, Mr. Gwynne," interrupted the housewife, bustling over to open the door.

Moll stared blankly at her counsel. No one had ever
called her Miss Hawk before. She was not quite sure
that she had heard aright. Could it be possible that
this grand young gentleman had called her Miss Hawk?
Still wondering, she followed him out of the kitchen,
sublimely unconscious of the ridiculous figure she cut
in the garments of the older woman.

"Shut the door," she said, as her keen, wood-wary
eyes swept the room. She crossed swiftly to the window and looked out. Her lips curled a little. "Most
of them people has been standin' out yonder sence nine
o'clock, tryin' to see what sort of lookin' animile I am,

Mr. Gwynne. Hain't nobody got any work to do?"

"Vulgar curiosity, nothing more," said he, joining her at the window.

" 'Tain't ever' day they get a chance to see a murderer, is it?" she said, lowering her head suddenly and putting a hand to her quivering chin. For the first time she seemed on the point of breaking down.

He made haste to exclaim, "You are not a murderer. You must not think or say such things, Miss Hawk."

She kept her head down. A scarlet wave crept over her face. "I—I wish you wouldn't call me that, Mr. Gwynne. Hit—hit makes me feel kind o'—kind o' lonesome-like. Jest as—ef I didn't have no friends. Call me Moll. That's all I am."

He studied for a moment the half-averted face of this girl of the forest. He could not help contrasting it with the clear-cut, delicate, beautifully modelled face of another girl of the dark frontier,—Viola Gwyn. And out of this swift estimate grew a new pity for poor Moll Hawk, the pity one feels for the vanquished.

"You will be surprised to find how many friends you have, Moll," he said gently.

There was no indication that she was impressed one way or the other by this remark. She drew back from the window and faced him, her eyes keen and searching.

"Do you reckon anybody is listenin'?" she asked.

"I think not,—in fact, I am sure we are quite alone."

"Well, this is somethin' I don't keer to have the shurreff know, or anybody else, Mr. Gwynne. Hit's about Mr. Lapelle."

"Yes?" he said, as she paused warily.

"Mrs. Gwyn she tole me this mornin' that whatever I said to my lawyer would be sacred an' wouldn't ever be let out to anybody, no matter whut it wuz. She said it wuz ag'inst the code er somethin'. Wuz she right?"

"In a sense, yes. Of course, you must understand, Moll, that no honest lawyer will obligate himself to shield a criminal or a fugitive from justice, or—I may as well say to you now that if you expect that of me I must warn you not to tell me anything. You would force me to withdraw as your counsel. For, you see, Moll, I am an honest lawyer."

She looked at him in a sort of mute wonder for a moment, and then muttered: "Why, Pap,—Pap he sez there ain't no setch thing as a honest lawyer." An embarrassed little smile twisted her lips. "I guess that must ha' been one of Pap's lies."

"It is possible he may never have come in contact with one," he observed drily.

"Well, I guess ef you're a honest lawyer," she said, knitting her brows, "I'd better keep my mouth shut. I wuz only thinkin' mebby you could see your way to do somethin' I wuz goin' to ask. I jest wanted to git some word to Mr. Lapelle."

"Mr. Lapelle and I are not friends, Moll."

"Is it beca'se of whut I asked Ike Stain to tell ye?"

"Partly."

"I mean about stealin' Miss Violy Gwyn an' takin' her away with him?"

"I want to thank you, Moll, for sending me the warning. It was splendid of you."

"Oh, I didn't do it beca'se—" she began, somewhat defiantly, and then closed her lips tightly. The sullen look came back into her eyes.

"I understand. You—you like him yourself."

"Well,—whut ef I do?" she burst out. "Hit's my look-out, ain't it?"

"Certainly. I am not blaming you."

"I guess there ain't no use talkin' any more," she said flatly. "You wouldn't do whut I want ye to do anyhow, so what's the sense of askin' you. We better go back to the kitchen."

"It may console you to hear that I have already told Mr. Lapelle that he must get out of this town before to-morrow morning," said he deliberately. "And stay out!"

She leaned forward, her face brightening. "You tole him to git away to-night?" she half-whispered, eagerly. "I thought you said you wuzn't a friend o' his'n."

"That is what I said."

"Then, whut did you warn him to git away fer?"

He was thinking rapidly. "I did it on account of Miss Gwyn, Moll," he replied, evasively.

"Do you think he'll go?" she asked, a fierce note of anxiety in her voice.

"That remains to be seen." Then he hazarded: "I think he will when he finds out that your father has been arrested."

"He's been a good friend to me, Mr. Gwynne, Mr. Lapelle has," said she, a little huskily. She waited a moment and then went on earnestly and with a garrulousness that amazed him: "I don't keer whut he's done that ain't right, er whut people is goin' to say about him, he's allus been nice to me. I guess mebby you air a-wonderin' why I tole Ike Stain about him figgerin' on carryin' Miss Gwyn away. That don't look very friendly, I guess. Hit wuzn't beca'se I thought I might git him fer myself some time,—no, hit wuzn't that, Mr. Gwynne. I ain't setch a fool as to think he could ever want to be sparkin' me. I reckon

Ike Stain tole ye I wuz jealous. Well, I wuzn't, I declare to goodness I wuzn't. Hit wuz beca'se I jest couldn't 'low her to git married to him, knowin' whut I do. I wuz tryin' to make up my mind to go an' see her some time an' tell her not to marry him, but I jest couldn't seem to git the spunk to do it. She used to come to see me when I wuz sick last winter an' she wuz mighty nice to me.

"First thing I know, him an' Pap begin to fix up this plan to carry her off. So I started up to town to tell her. I got as fer as Ike's when I figgered I better let him do it, him bein' a man, so I drapped in at his cabin an' tole him. I didn't know whut else to do. I had to stop 'em from doin' it somehow. Hit wouldn't do no good fer me to beg Pap to drap it, er to rare up on my hind-legs an' make threats ag'inst 'em,—ca'se they'd soon put a stop to that. Course I had it all figgered out whut I wuz goin' to do when thet pack o' rascals got caught tryin' to steal her,— some of 'em shot, like as not,—and I didn't much keer whuther my Pap wuz one of 'em er not.

"I knowed where Mr. Lapelle wuz to meet 'em down the river accrosst from Le Grange, so I was figgerin' on findin' him there an' tellin' him whut had happened an' fer him to make his escape down the river while he had setch a good start. I wuzn't goin' to let him be ketched an' at the same time I wuzn't goin' to let anything happen to Miss Violy Gwyn ef I could help it. I—I sort of figgered it out as a good way to help both o' my friends, Mr. Gwynne, an'—an' then this here thing happened. I want Mr. Lapelle to git away safe,—ca'se I know whut Pap's goin' to do. He's goin' to blat out a lot o' things. He says he's sure Mr. Lapelle put Mrs. Gwyn up to havin' him arrested."

"I think you may rest easy, Moll," said he, a trifle grimly. "Mr. Lapelle had an engagement with me for to-morrow morning, but I'll stake my life he will not be here to keep it."

"All right," she said, satisfied. "Ef you say so, Mr. Gwynne, I'll believe it. Whut do you think they'll do to Pap?"

"He will probably get a dose of the whipping-post, for one thing."

She grinned. "Gosh, I wish I could be some'eres about so's I could see it," she cried.

CHAPTER XXIII

K ENNETH could hardly contain himself until the time came for him to go home for his noon-day meal. Try as he would, he could not divorce his thoughts from the trouble that had come to Viola. The sinister tragedy in Martin Hawk's cabin was as nothing compared to the calamity that had befallen the girl he loved, for Moll Hawk's troubles would pass like a whiff of the wind while Viola's would endure to the end of time,—always a shadow hanging over her brightest day, a cloud that would not vanish. Out of the silence had come a murmur more desolating than the thunderbolt with all its bombastic fury; out of the silence had come a voice that would go on forever whispering into her ear an unlovely story.

A crowd still hung about the jail and small, ever-shifting groups held sober discourse in front of business places. He hurried by them and struck off up the road, his mind so intent upon what lay ahead of him that he failed to notice that Jack Trentman had detached himself from the group in front of the undertaker's and was following swiftly after him. He was nearly half-way home when he turned, in response to a call from behind, and beheld the gambler.

"I'd like a word with you, Mr. Gwynne," drawled Jack.

"I am in somewhat of a hurry, Mr.—"

"I'll walk along with you, if you don't mind," said

the other, coming up beside him. "I'm not in the habit of beating about the bush. When I've got anything to do, I do it without much fiddling. Barry Lapelle is down at my place. He has asked me to represent him in a little controversy that seems to call for physical adjudication. How will day after to-morrow at five in the morning suit you?"

"Perfectly," replied Kenneth stiffly. "Convey my compliments to Mr. Lapelle and say to him that I overlook the irregularity and will be glad to meet him at any time and any place."

"I know it's irregular," admitted Mr. Trentman, with an apologetic wave of the hand, "but he was in some doubt as to who might have the honour to act for you, Mr. Gwynne, so he suggested that I come to you direct. If you will oblige me with the name of the friend who is to act as your second, I will make a point of apologizing for having accosted you in this manner, and also perfect the details with him."

"I haven't given the matter a moment's thought," said Kenneth, frowning. "Day after to-morrow morning, you say?"

"Yes, sir."

"Can't you arrange it for to-morrow morning?"

Mr. Trentman spread out his hands in a deprecatory manner. "In view of the fact that you are expected to appear in court at nine to-morrow morning to defend an unfortunate girl, Mr. Lapelle feels that he would be doing your client a very grave injustice if he killed her lawyer—er—a trifle prematurely, you might say. He has confided to me that he is the young woman's friend and can't bear the thought of having her chances jeopardized by—"

"Pardon me, Mr. Trentman," interrupted Kenneth

shortly. "Both of you are uncommonly thoughtful and considerate. Now that I am reminded of my pleasant little encounter with Mr. Lapelle this morning, I am constrained to remark that I have had all the satisfaction I desire. You may say to him that I am a gentleman and not in the habit of fighting duels with horse-thieves."

Mr. Trentman started. His vaunted aplomb sustained a sharp spasm that left him with a slightly fallen jaw.

"Am I to understand, sir, that you are referring to my friend as a horse-thief?" he demanded, bridling.

"I merely asked you to take that message to him," said Kenneth coolly. "I might add cattle-thief, sheep-stealer, hog-thief or—"

"Why, good God, sir," gasped Mr. Trentman, "he'd shoot you down like a dog if I—"

"You may also tell Mr. Lapelle that his bosom friend Martin Hawk is in jail."

"Well, what of it?"

"Does Lapelle know that Martin is in jail?"

"Certainly,—and he says he ought to be hung. That's what he thinks of Hawk. A man that would sell his own—"

"Hawk is in jail for stock-stealing, Mr. Trentman."

"What's that got to do with the case? What's that got to do with your calling my friend a horse-thief?"

"A whole lot, sir. You will probably find out before the day is over that you are harbouring and concealing a thief down there in your shanty, and you may thank Martin Hawk for the information in case you prefer not to accept the word of a gentleman. If you were to come to me as a client seeking counsel, I should not hesitate to advise you,—as your lawyer,—that there is a law against harbouring criminals and that you are laying yourself open to prosecution."

Trentman dubiously felt of his chin.

"Being well versed in the law," he said, "I suppose you realize that Mr. Lapelle can recover heavy damages against you in case what you have said to me isn't true."

"Perfectly. Therefore, I repeat to you that I cannot engage in an affair of honour with a thief. I knocked him down this morning, but that was in the heat of righteous anger. For fear that your report to him may lead Mr. Lapelle to construe my refusal to meet him day after to-morrow morning as cowardice on my part, permit me to make this request of you. Please say to him that I shall arm myself with a pistol as soon as I have reached my house, and that I expect to be going about the streets of Lafayette as usual."

"I see," said Mr. Trentman, after a moment. "You mean you'll be ready for him in case he hunts you up."

"Exactly."

"By the way, Mr. Gwynne, have you ever fought a duel?"

"No."

"Would it interest you to know that Mr. Lapelle has engaged in several, with disastrous results to his adversaries?"

"I think he has already mentioned something of the kind to me."

"I'd sooner be your friend than your enemy, Mr. Gwynne," said the gambler earnestly. "I am a permanent citizen of this town and I have no quarrel with you. As your friend, I am obliged to inform you that Barry Lapelle is a dead shot and as quick as lightning with a pistol. I hope you will take this in the same spirit that it is given."

"I thank you, sir," said Kenneth, courteously. "By the way, do you happen to have a pistol with you at present, Mr. Trentman?"

The other looked at him keenly for a few seconds before answering. "I have. I seldom go without one."

"If you will do me the kindness to walk with me up to the woods beyond the lake and will grant me the loan of your weapon for half a minute, I think I may be able to demonstrate to you that Mr. Lapelle is not the only dead shot in the world. I was brought up with a pistol in my hand, so to speak. Have you ever tried to shoot a ground squirrel at twenty paces? You have to be pretty quick to do that, you know."

Trentman shook his head. "There's a lot of difference between shooting a ground squirrel and blazing away at a man who is blazing away at you at the same time. I'll take your word for the ground squirrel business, Mr. Gwynne, and bid you good day."

"My regrets to your principal and my apologies to you, Mr. Trentman," said Kenneth, lifting his hat.

The gambler raised his own hat. A close observer would have noticed a troubled, anxious gleam in his eye as he turned to retrace his steps in the direction of the square. It was his custom to saunter slowly when traversing the streets of the town, as one who produces his own importance and enjoys it leisurely. He never hurried. He loitered rather more gracefully when walking than when standing still. But now he strode along briskly,—in fact, with such lively decision that for once in his life he appeared actually to be going somewhere. As he rounded the corner and came in sight of the jail, he directed a fixed, consuming glare upon the barred windows; a quite noticeable scowl settled upon his ordinarily unruffled brow,—the scowl of one searching intently, even apprehensively.

He was troubled. His composure was sadly disturbed. Kenneth Gwynne had given him something to think about,—and the more he thought about it the faster he walked. He was perspiring quite freely and he was a little short of breath when he flung open the door and entered his "den of iniquity" down by the river. He took in at a glance the three men seated at a table in a corner of the somewhat commodious "card-room." One of them was dealing "cold hands" to his companions. A fourth man, his dealer, was leaning against the window frame, gazing pensively down upon the slow-moving river. Two of the men at the table were newcomers in town. They had come up on the *Revere* and they had already established themselves in his estimation as "skeletons"; that is, they had been picked pretty clean by "buzzards" in other climes before gravitating to his "boneyard." He considered himself a good judge of men, and he did not like the looks of this ill-favoured pair. He had made up his mind that he did not want them hanging around the "shanty"; men of that stripe were just the sort to give the place a bad name! One of them had recalled himself to Barry Lapelle the night before; said he used to work for a trader down south or somewhere.

Without the ceremony of a knock on the door, Mr. Trentman entered a room at the end of the shanty, and there he found Lapelle reclining on a cot. Two narrow slits in a puffed expanse of purple grading off to a greenish yellow indicated the position of Barry's eyes. The once resplendent dandy was now a sorry sight.

"Say," began Trentman, after he had closed the door, "I want to know just how things stand with you and Martin Hawk. No beating about the bush, Barry. I want the truth and nothing else."

Barry raised himself on one elbow and peered at his host. "What are you driving at, Jack?" he demanded, throatily.

"Are you mixed up with him in this stock-running business?"

"Well, that's a hell of a question to ask a—"

"It's easy to answer. Are you?"

"Certainly not,—and I ought to put a bullet through you for asking such an insulting question."

"He's in jail, charged with stealing sheep and calves, and he's started to talk. Now, look here, Lapelle, I'm your friend, but if you are mixed up in this business the sooner you get out of here the better it will suit me. Wait a minute! I've got more to say. I know you're planning to go down on the boat to-morrow, but I don't believe it's soon enough. I've seen Gwynne. He says in plain English that he won't fight a duel with a horse-thief. He must have some reason for saying that. He has been employed as Moll Hawk's lawyer. She's probably been talking, too. I've been thinking pretty hard the last ten minutes or so, and I'm beginning to understand why you wanted me to arrange the duel for day after to-morrow when you knew you were leaving town on the *Revere* in the morning. You were trying to throw Gwynne off the track. I thought at first it was because you were afraid to fight him, but now I see things differently. I'll be obliged to you if you'll come straight out and tell me what's in the air. I'm a square man and I like to know whether I'm dealing with square men or not."

Lapelle sat up suddenly on the edge of the bed. Somehow, it seemed to Trentman, the greenish yellow had spread lightly over the rest of his face.

"You say Martin's in jail for stealing?" he asked, gripping the corn-husk bedtick with tense, nervous fingers, "and not in connection with the killing of Suggs?"

"Yep. And I sort of guess you'll be with him before you're much older, if Gwynne knows what he's—"

"I've got to get out of this town to-night, Jack," cried the younger man, starting to his feet. "Understand, I'm not saying I am mixed up in any way with Hawk and his crowd, but—but I've got important business in Attica early to-morrow morning. That's all you can get me to say. I'll sneak up the back road to the tavern and pack my saddle-bags this afternoon, and I'll leave money with you to settle with Johnson. I may have to ask you to fetch my horse down here—"

"Just a minute," broke in Trentman, who had been regarding him with hard, calculating eyes. "If it's as bad as all this, I guess you'd better not wait till to-night. It may be too late,—and besides I don't want the sheriff coming down here and jerking you out of my place. You don't need to tell me anything more about your relations with Hawk. I'm no fool, Barry. I know now that you are mixed up in this stock-stealing business that's been going on for months. It don't take a very smart brain to grasp the situation. You've probably been making a pretty good thing out of moving this stuff down the river on your boats, and— Now, don't get up on your ear, my friend! No use trying to bamboozle me. You're scared stiff,—

and that's enough for me. And you've got a right
to be. This will put an end to your company's boats
coming up here for traffic,—it will kill you deader'n a
doornail so far as business is concerned. So you'd
better get out at once. I never liked you very much
anyhow and now I've got no use for you at all. Just
to save my own skin and my own reputation as a
law-abiding citizen, I'll help you to get away. Now,
here's what I'll do. I'll send up and get your horse
and have him down here inside of fifteen minutes.
There's so darned much excitement up in town about
this murder that nobody's going to notice you for the
time being. And besides a lot of farmers from over
west are coming in, scared half to death about Black
Hawk's Indians. They'll be out looking for you before
long, your lordship, and it won't be for the purpose of
inviting you to have a drink. They'll probably bring
a rail along with 'em, so's you'll at least have the
consolation of riding up to the calaboose. You'll—"

"Oh, for God's sake!" grated Barry, furiously.
"Don't try to be comical, Trentman. This is no time
to joke,—or preach either. Give me a swig of—"

"Nope! No whiskey, my friend," said the gambler
firmly. "Whiskey always puts false courage into a
man, and I don't want you to be doing anything foolish.
I'll have your mare Fancy down here in fifteen minutes,
saddled and everything, and you will hop on her and
ride up the street, right past the court house, just
as if you're out for an hour's canter for your health.
You will not have any saddle-bags or traps. You'll
ride light, my friend. That will throw 'em off the
track. But what I want you to do as soon as you get
out the other side of the tanyard is to turn in your

saddle and wave a last farewell to the Star City. You might throw a kiss at it, too, while you're about it. Because you've got a long journey ahead of you and you're not coming back,—that is, unless they overtake you. There's some pretty fast horses in this town, as you may happen to remember. So I'd advise you to get a good long start,—and keep it."

If Lapelle heard all of this he gave no sign, for he had sidled over to the little window and was peering obliquely through the trees toward the road that led from the "shanty" toward the town. Suddenly he turned upon the gambler, a savage oath on his lips.

"You bet I'll come back! And when I do, I'll give this town something to talk about. I'll make tracks now. It's the only thing to do. But I'm not licked— not by a long shot, Jack Trentman. I'll be back inside of—"

"I'll make you a present of a couple of pistols a fellow left with me for a debt a month or so ago. You may need 'em," said Trentman blandly. "Better get ready to start. I'll have the horse here in no time."

"You're damned cold-blooded," growled Barry, pettishly.

"Yep," agreed the other. "But I'm kind-hearted."

He went out, slamming the door behind him. Twenty minutes later, Barry emerged from the "shanty" and mounted his sleek, restless thoroughbred. Having recovered, for purposes of deception, his lordly, cock-o'-the-walk attitude toward the world, he rode off jauntily in the direction of the town, according Trentman the scant courtesy of a careless wave of the hand at parting. He had counted his money, examined the borrowed pistols, and at the last moment had hurriedly dashed off a brief letter to Kenneth Gwynne, to be posted the following day by the avid though obliging Mr. Trentman.

Stifling his rancour and coercing his vanity at the same time, he cantered boldly past the Tavern, bitterly aware of the protracted look of amazement that interrupted the conversation of some of the most influential citizens of the place as at least a score of eyes fell upon his battered visage. Pride and rage got the better of him. He whirled Fancy about with a savage jerk and rode back to the group.

"Take a good look, gentlemen," he snapped out, his eyes gleaming for all the world like two thin little slivers of red-hot iron. "The coward who hit me before I had a chance to defend myself has just denied me the satisfaction of a duel. I sent him a challenge to fight it out with pistols day after to-morrow morning. He is afraid to meet me. The challenge still stands. If you should see Mr. Gwynne, gentlemen, between now and Friday morning, do me the favour to say to him that I will be the happiest man on earth if he can muster up sufficient courage to change his mind. Good day, gentlemen."

With this vainglorious though vicarious challenge to an absent enemy, he touched the gad to Fancy's flank and rode away, his head erect, his back as stiff as a ramrod, leaving behind him a staring group whose astonishment did not give way to levity until he was nearing the corner of the square. He cursed softly under his breath at the sound of the first guffaw; he subdued with difficulty a wild, reckless impulse to turn in the saddle and send a shot or two at them. But this was no time for folly,—no time to lose his head.

Out of the corner of his eye he took in the jail and
the group of citizens on the court house steps. Something seemed to tell him that these men were saying,
"There he goes,—stop him! He's getting away!"
They were looking at him; of that he was subtly conscious, although he managed to keep his eyes set
straight ahead. Only the most determined effort of
the will kept him from suddenly putting spur to the
mare. Afterwards he complimented himself on his
remarkable self-control, and laughed as he likened his
present alarm to that of a boy passing a graveyard
at night. Nevertheless, he was now filled with an
acute, very real sense of anxiety and apprehension;
every nerve was on edge.

It was all very well for Jack Trentman to say that
this was the safest, most sensible way to go about it,
but had Jack ever been through it himself? At any
moment Martin Hawk might catch a glimpse of him
through the barred window of the jail and let out a
shout of warning; at any moment the sheriff himself
might dash out of the court house with a warrant in
his hand,—and then what? He had the chill, uneasy
feeling that they would be piling out after him before
he could reach the corner of the friendly thickets at
the lower end of the street.

A pressing weight seemed to slide off his shoulders
and neck as Fancy swung smartly around the bend
into the narrow wagon-road that stretched its aimless
way through the scrubby bottom-lands and over the
ridge to the open sweep of the plains beyond. Presently
he urged the mare to a rhythmic lope, and all the while
his ears were alert for the thud of galloping horses
behind. It was not until he reached the table-land to
the south that he drove the rowels into the flanks of

the swift four-year-old and leaned forward in the saddle
to meet the rush of the wind.   Full well he knew that
given the start of an hour no horse in the county could
catch his darling Fancy!

And so it was that Barry Lapelle rode out of the
town of Lafayette, never to return again.

CHAPTER XXIV

IT was characteristic of Rachel Carter that she should draw the window curtains aside in Viola's bedroom, allowing the pitiless light of day to fall upon her face as she seated herself to make confession. She had come to the hour when nothing was to be hidden from her daughter, least of all the cheek that was to be smitten.

The girl sat on the edge of the bed, her elbow on the footboard, her cheek resting upon her hand. Not once did she take her eyes from the grey, emotionless face of the woman who sat in the light.

In course of time, Rachel Carter came to the end of her story. She had made no attempt to justify herself, had uttered no word of regret, no signal of repentance, no plea for forgiveness. The cold, unfaltering truth, without a single mitigating alloy in the shape of sentiment, had issued from her tired but unconquered soul. She went through to the end without being interrupted by the girl, whose silence was eloquent of a strength and courage unsurpassed even by this woman from whom she had, after all, inherited both. She did not flinch, she did not cringe as the twenty-year-old truth was laid bare before her. She was made of the same staunch fibre as her mother, she possessed the indomitable spirit that stiffens and remains unyielding in the face of calamity.

"Now you know everything," said Rachel Carter

326

wearily. "I have tried to keep it from you. But the truth will out. It is God's law. I would have spared you if I could. You are of my flesh and blood, you are a part of me. There has never been an instant in all these hard, trying years when I have not loved and cherished you as the gift that no woman, honest or dishonest, can despise. You will know what that means when you have a child of your own, and you will never know it until that has come to pass. You may cast me out of your heart, Viola, but you cannot tear yourself out of mine. So! I have spoken. There is no more."

She turned her head to look out of the window. Viola did not move. Presently the older woman spoke again.

"Your name is Minda Carter. You will be twenty-two years old next September. You have no right to the name of Gwynne. The boy who lives in that house over yonder is the only one who has a right to it. But his birthright is no cleaner than yours. You can look him in the face without shame to yourself, because your father was an honest man and your mother was his loyal, faithful wife,—and Kenneth Gwynne can say no more than that."

"Nor as much," burst from the girl's lips with a fervour that startled her mother. "His father was not a loyal, faithful husband, nor was he an honest man or he would have married you."

She was on her feet now, her body bent slightly forward, her smouldering eyes fixed intently upon her mother's face.

Rachel Carter stared incredulously. Something in Viola's eyes, in the ring of her voice caused her heart to leap.

"I was his wife in the eyes of God," she began, but something rushed up into her throat and seemed to choke her.

"And you have told Kenneth all this?" cried Viola, a light as of understanding flooding her eyes. "He knows? How long has he known?"

"I—I can't remember. Some of it for weeks, some of it only since last night."

"Ah!" There was a world of meaning in the cry. Even as she uttered it she seemed to feel his arms about her and the strange thrill that had charged through her body from head to foot. She sat down again on the edge of the bed; a dark wave of colour surging to her cheek and brow.

"I am waiting," said her mother, after a moment. Her voice was steady. "It is your turn to speak, my child."

Viola came to her side.

"Mother," she began, a deep, full note in her voice, "I want you to let me sit in your lap, with your arms around me. Like when I was a little girl."

Rachel lifted her eyes; and as the girl looked down into them the hardness of years melted away and they grew wondrous soft and gentle.

"Is this your verdict?" she asked solemnly.

"Yes," was the simple response.

"You do not cast me out of your heart? Remember, in the sight of man, I am an evil woman."

"You are my mother. You did not desert me. You would not leave me behind. You have loved me since the day I was born. You will never be an evil woman in my eyes. Hold me in your lap, mother dear. I shall always feel safe then."

Rachel's lips and chin quivered. . . . A long time

afterward the girl gently disengaged herself from the strong, tense embrace and rose to her feet.

"You say that Kenneth hates you," she said, "and you say that you do not blame him. Is it right and fair that he should hate you any more than I should hate his father?"

"Yes," replied Rachel Carter, "it is right and fair. I was his mother's best friend. His father did not betray his best friend as I did, for my husband was dead. There is a difference, my child."

Viola shook her head stubbornly. "I don't see why the woman must always be crucified and the man allowed to go his way—"

"It is no use, Viola," interrupted Rachel, rising. Her face had hardened again. "We cannot change the ways of the world." She crossed the room, but stopped with her hand on the door-latch. Turning to her daughter, she said: "Whatever Kenneth may think of me, he has the greatest respect and admiration for you. He bears no grudge against Minda Carter. On the contrary, he has shown that he would lay down his life for you. You must bear no grudge against him. You and he are children who have walked in darkness for twenty years, but now you have come to a place where there is light. See to it, Viola, that you are as fair to him as you would have him be to you. You stand on common ground with the light of understanding all about you. Do not turn your backs upon each other. Face one another. It is the only way."

Viola's eyes flashed. She lifted her chin.

"I am not ashamed to look Kenneth Gwynne in the face," said she, a certain crispness in her voice. Then, with a quick change to tenderness, "You are so tired, mother. Won't you lie down and sleep awhile?"

"After I have eaten something. Come downstairs. I want to hear what happened here this morning. Kenneth told me very little and you have done nothing but ask questions of me."

"Did he tell you that he struck Barry Lapelle?"

"No."

"Or how near I came to shooting him?"

"Merciful heaven!"

"Well, I guess Barry won't rest till he has told the whole town what we are,—and then we'll have to face something cruel, mother. But we will face it together."

She put her arm about her mother's shoulders and they went down the narrow staircase together.

"It will not cost me a single friend, Viola," remarked Rachel grimly. "I have none to lose. But with you it will be different."

"We don't have to stay in the old town," said Viola bravely. "The world is large. We can move on. Just as we used to before we came here to live. Always moving on, we were."

Rachel shook her head. They were at the bottom of the stairs.

"I will not move on. This is where I intend to live and die. The man I lived for is up yonder in the graveyard. I will not go away and leave him now,—not after all these years. But you, my child, you must move on. You have something else to live for. I have nothing. But I can hold my head up, even here. You will not find it so easy. You will—"

"It will be as easy for me as it will for Kenneth Gwynne," broke in the girl. "Wait and see which one of us runs away first. It won't be me."

"He will not go away and leave you," said Rachel Carter.

Viola gave her a quick, startled look. They were in the kitchen, however, before she spoke. Then it was to say:

"Now I understand why I have never been able to think of him as my brother." That, and nothing more; there was an odd, almost frightened expression in her eyes.

She got breakfast for her mother, Hattie having been sent down into the town by her mistress immediately upon her return home, ostensibly to make a few purchases but actually for the purpose of getting rid of her. Viola, in relating the story of the morning's events, was careful to avoid using the harshest of Barry's terms, but earnestly embellished the account of Kenny's interference with some rather formidable expressions of her own, putting them glibly into the mouth of her champion. Once her mother interrupted her to inquire:

"Did Kenneth actually use those words, Viola? 'Pusillanimous varlet,'—and 'mendacious scalawag'? It does not sound like Kenneth."

Viola had the grace to blush guiltily. "No, he didn't. He swore harder than anybody I've ever—"

"That's better," said Rachel, somewhat sternly.

Later on they sat on the little front porch, where the older woman, with scant recourse to the graphic, narrated the story of Moll Hawk. Pain and horror dwelt in Viola's wide, lovely eyes.

"Oh, poor, poor Moll," she murmured at the end of the wretched tale. "She has never known a mother's love, or a mother's care. She has never had a chance."

Then Rachel Carter said a strange thing. "When all this is over and she is free, I intend to offer her a home here with me."

The girl stared, open-mouthed. "With you? Here with us?"

"You will not always be here with me," said her mother.

"How can you say such a thing?" with honest indignation. Then quickly: "I know I planned to run off and leave you a little while ago, but that was before I came to know how much you need me."

Rachel experienced one of her rare smiles. "And before you came to know Kenneth Gwynne," she said. "No, my dear, the time is not far off when you will not need a mother. Moll Hawk needs one now. I shall try to be a mother to that hapless girl."

Viola looked at her, the little line of perplexity deepening between her eyes.

"Somehow it seems to me that I am just beginning to know my own mother," she said.

A bluejay, sweeping gracefully out over the tree-tops, came to rest upon a lofty bough in the grove across the road. They sat for a long time without speaking, these two women, watching him preen and prink, a bit of lively blue against the newborn green. Then he flew away. He "moved on,"—a passing symbol.

How simple, how easy it was for this bright, gay vagabond to return to the silence from which he had come.

CHAPTER XXV

VIOLA was alone on the porch when Kenneth came into view at the bend in the road. He had chuckled more than once after parting from the gambler; a mental vision of the inwardly agitated though outwardly bland Mr. Trentman making tracks as fast as his legs would carry him to warn Lapelle of his peril afforded him no small amount of satisfaction. If he knew his man,—and he thought he did,—Barry would lose no time in shaking the dust of Lafayette from his feet. The thought of that had sent his spirits up. He went even farther in his reflections and found himself hoping that Barry's flight might be so precipitous that he would not have the opportunity to disclose his newfound information concerning Rachel Carter.

He was nearing his own gate before he saw Viola, seated on the porch. Involuntarily he slackened his pace. A sort of panic seized him. Was she waiting there to question him? He experienced a sudden overwhelming dismay. What was he to say to her? How was he to face the unhappy, stricken,—but even as he contemplated a cowardly retreat, she arose and came swiftly down the path. He groaned inwardly. There was no escape.

Now, as he hesitated uncertainly at his own gate, his heart in his boots, she serenely beckoned to him. "I want to see you, Kenny," she called out.

This was no stricken, unhappy creature who approached him. Her figure was proudly erect; she walked briskly; there was no trace of shame or humiliation in her face; if anything, she was far more at ease than he.

"I want to thank you," she said calmly, "for what you did this morning. Not only for what you did to him but for keeping me from shooting him." She held out her hand, but lowered it instantly when she saw that his own was rather significantly hidden inside the breast of his coat. A look of pain fluttered across her eyes.

"Where is your mother?" he asked lamely.

She seemed to read his thoughts. "Mother and I have talked it all over, Kenneth. She has told me everything."

"Oh, you poor darling!" he cried.

"Don't waste any sympathy on me," she retorted, coldly. "I don't want it. Not from Robert Gwynne's son at any rate."

He was now looking at her steadily. "I see. You don't care for the breed, is that it?"

"Kenny," she began, a solemn note in her voice, "there is no reason why you and I should hurt each other. If I hurt you just now I am sorry. But I meant what I said. I do not want the pity of Robert Gwynne's son any more than you want to be pitied by the daughter of Rachel Carter. We stand on even terms. I just want you to know that my heart is as stout as yours and that my pride is as strong."

He bowed his head. "All my life I have thought of my father as a Samson who was betrayed by a Delilah. I have never allowed myself to think of him as anything but great and strong and good. I grew to man's estate still believing him to be the victim of an evil woman. I am not in the ordinary sense a fool and yet I have been utterly without the power to reason. My eyes have been opened, Viola. I am seeing with a new vision. I have more to overlook, more to forgive in my father than you have in your mother. I speak plainly, because I hope this is to be the last time we ever touch upon the subject. You, at least, have grown up to know the enduring love of a mother. She did not leave you behind. She was not altogether heartless. That is all I can say, all I shall ever say, even to you, about my father."

He spoke with such deep feeling and yet so simply that her heart was touched. A wistful look came into her eyes.

"I am still bewildered by it all, Kenny," she said. "In the wink of an eye, everything is altered. I am not Viola Gwyn. I am Minda Carter. I am not your half-sister. You seem suddenly to have gone very far away from me. It hurts me to feel that we can never be the same toward each other that we were even this morning. I had come to care for you as a brother. Now you are a stranger. I—I loved being your sister and—and treating you as if you were my brother. Now all that is over." She sighed deeply.

"Yes," he said gently, "all that is over for you, Viola. But I have known for many weeks that you are not my sister."

"I bear no grudge against you," she said, meeting his gaze steadily. "My heart is bitter toward the man I have always looked upon as my father. But it does not contain one drop of bitterness toward you. What matters if I have walked in darkness and you in the light? We were treading the same path all the time.

Now we meet and know each other for what we really are. The path is not wide enough for us to walk beside each other without our garments touching. Are we to turn back and walk the other way so that our unclean garments may not touch?"

"For heaven's sake, Viola," he cried in pain, "what can have put such a thought into your head? Have I ever said or done anything to cause you to think I—"

"You must not forget that you can walk by yourself, Kenny. Your father is dead. The world is kind enough to let the dead rest in peace. But it gives no quarter to the living. My mother walks with me, Kenneth Gwynne. The world, when it knows, will throw stones at her. That means it will have to throw stones at me. She did not abandon me. I shall not abandon her. She sinned,"—here her lip trembled,— "and she has been left to pay the penalty alone. It may sound strange to you, but my mother was also deserted by your father. God let him die, but I can't help feeling that it wasn't fair, it wasn't right for him to die and leave her to face this all alone."

"And you want to know where I stand in the matter?"

"It makes no difference, Kenny. I only want you to understand. I don't want to lose you as a friend,— I would like to have you stand up and take your share of the—"

"And that is just what I intend to do," he broke in. "We occupy strange positions, Viola. We are,—shall I say birds of a feather? This had to come. Now that it has come and you know all that I know, are we to turn against each other because of what happened when we were babies? We have done no wrong. I love you, Viola,—I began loving you before I found

out you were not my half-sister. I will love you all
my life. Now you know where I stand."

She looked straight into his eyes for a long time; in
her own there was something that seemed to search
his soul, something of wonder, something groping and
intense as if her own soul was asking a grave, perplex-
ing question. A faint, slow surge of colour stole into
her face. "I must go in the house now," she said, a
queer little flutter in her voice. "After dinner I am
going down with mother to see Moll Hawk. If—if
you mean all that you have just said, Kenny, why did
you refuse to shake hands with me?"

He withdrew his bruised right hand from its hiding-
place. "It is an ugly thing to look at but I am proud
of it," he said. "I would give it for you a thousand
times over."

"Oh, I'm—I'm sorry I misjudged you—" she cried
out. Then both of her hands closed on the unsightly
member and pressed it gently, tenderly. There was
that in the touch of her firm, strong fingers that sent
an ecstatic shock racing into every fibre in his body.
"I will never question that hand again, Kenny," she
said, and then, releasing it, she turned and walked
rapidly away.

He stood watching her until she ran nimbly up the
porch steps and disappeared inside the house. Whereupon he lifted the swollen but now blessed knuckles
to his lips and sighed profoundly.

"Something tells me she still loves Barry, in spite
of everything," he muttered, suddenly immersed in
gloom. "Women stick through thick and thin. If
they once love a man they never—"

"Dinner's ready, Marse Kenneth," announced Zachariah from the door-step.

CHAPTER XXVI

THE FLIGHT OF MARTIN HAWK

NOW, Martin Hawk was not a patient man. He waited till mid-afternoon for some word from Barry Lapelle in response to his message, and, receiving none,—(for the very good reason that it was never delivered),—fell to blaspheming mightily, and before he was through with it revealed enough to bring about an ultimate though fruitless search for the departed "go-between."

He was, however, careful to omit any mention of the *Paul Revere's* captain, remembering just in time that hardy riverman's promise to blow his brains out if he even so much as breathed his name in connection with certain nefarious transactions,—and something told him that Cephas Redberry would put a short, sharp stop to any breathing at all on his part the instant he laid eyes on him. He was not afraid of Barry Lapelle but he was in deadly terror of Redberry. The more he thought of Ceph being landed in the same jail with him, the longer the goose feathers grew on his shrinking spine. So he left the Captain out of it altogether, —indeed, he gave him a perfectly clean bill of health.

Along about dusk that evening a crowd began to collect in the neighbourhood of the jail. Martin, peering from behind a barred window, was not long in grasping the significance of this ominous gathering. He was the only inmate of the "calaboose"; therefore, he was in no doubt as to the identity of the person to whom so many different terms of opprobrium were being applied by certain loud-voiced citizens in the crowd. He also gathered from remarks coming up to the window that the person referred to stood in grave danger of being "skinned alive," "swung to a limb," "horsewhipped till he can't stand," "rode on a rail," "ham-strung," "drownded," "hung up by the thumbs," "dogged out o' town," "peppered with bird-shot," "filled with buckshot," and numerous other unpleasant alternatives, no one of which was conducive to the peace of mind.

As the evening wore on, Martin became more and more convinced that his life wasn't worth a pinch of salt, and so began to pray loudly and lustily. The crowd had increased to alarming proportions. In the light of torches and bonfires he recognized men from far-off Grand Prairie, up to the northwest of town. Wagons rumbled past the jail and court house and were lost in the darkness of the streets beyond. He was astonished to see that most of these vehicles contained women and children, and many of them were loaded high with household goods. This, thought Martin, was the apex of attention. People were coming from the four corners of the world to witness his execution! Evidently it was to be an affair that every householder thought his women-folk and the children ought to see. Some men might have been gratified by all this interest, but not Martin. He began to increase the fervor of his prayers by inserting, here and there, hair-raising oaths,—not bravely or with the courage of the defiant, but because all other words failed him in his extremity.

He had no means of knowing, of course, that he was dividing the honours, so to speak, with another and far more imposing rascal,—the terrible Black Hawk. How was he to know, locked up in jail, that all evening long panic-stricken people from the distant and thinly-settled prairies were piling into town because of the report that bands of Black Hawk's warriors had been seen by reputable settlers along the upper edge of the Prairie?

Like reports had been filtering into town for several days, but not much credence had been given them. Indian scares were not uncommon, and for the most part people had scoffed at them. But now there was an actual threat from the powerful Black Hawk, whose headquarters were up along the Rock River, in the northern part of Illinois. The chieftain had at last thrown down the gauntlet; he had refused to recognize the transfer of lands and rights as laid down by the Government, and had openly announced his intention to fight. Already troops from the forts were on the move, and there was talk of the State militia being called out. Some of the leading spirits in Lafayette had been moved to organize a local company.

Naturally, Martin Hawk knew nothing of all this. He knew, through Simon Braley, that Indian troubles were bound to come, but how was he to know that redskins in warpaint had been seen on the Grand Prairie, or that he was not the only subject of conversation? All he knew was that if the Lord didn't take a hand pretty soon he would be— Well, it was useless to fix his mind on any particular form of destruction, so many and so varied were the kinds being disputatiously considered by the people in the street.

Suddenly the sound of fife and drum smote upon his ear, coming from somewhere up the street. He huddled down in a corner and began to moan. He

knew the meaning of that signal-call. They were organizing for a rush upon the jail,—an irresistible,
overwhelming charge that would sweep all opposition
before it. Then he heard the shuffling of many feet,
loud exclamations and an occasional cheer. Finally
he screwed up the courage for another cautious peep
through the bars. The crowd was moving off up the
street. A small group remained undecided near a bonfire in the court house yard. One of these men held a
long rope in his hand, and seemed argumentative.

Martin listened with all ears, trying to catch what
was being said. What an infernal noise that fife and
drum were making! At last the little knot of men
moved away from the fire, coming toward the window.
Martin, being a wary rascal, promptly ducked his
head, but kept his ears open.

"It's a trick, that's what it is," he heard some one
growl. "A trick to get us away from the jail. They
know we'll get him, sure as God made little apples, so
they've fixed this up to—"

"Well, what if it is a trick?" broke in another. "It
ain't going to work. The crowd'll be back here again
inside of ten minutes an' all the sheriffs an' constables
in the State can't stop us from taking him out an'
stringin' him up."

"We might as well go and see what's up," said another. "I guess he's where he'll keep. He'll be here
when we come back, Bill. He can't get out till we
open the door, so what's the use cussin' about ten or
fifteen minutes' delay? Come on! I don't take any
stock in this talk about Indians, but, great snakes, if
they want to get up a company to go out and—"

The rest of the remark was lost to Martin when the
group turned the corner of the jail.

"Ten or fifteen minutes," he groaned.   In ten or
fifteen minutes the whole town would be out there,
breaking down the door—the work of a few seconds.
He remembered hearing people laugh and joke about
the new jail.   No less a person than Cap' Redberry
had said, after a casual inspection of the calaboose,
that if *that* was what they called a jail he'd hate to
be inside of it if a woodpecker started to peckin' at it,
'cause if such a thing happened the whole blamed she-
bang would cave in and like as not hurt him considerable.   And Cap' was not the only one who spoke de-
risively of the new jail.   Ed Bloker declared he had
quit walkin' past it on his way home from the grocery
because he was in mortal terror of staggerin' up against
it and knockin' it all to smash.   Of course, Martin
knew that it was not as bad as all that, but, even so, it
could not hold out for more than a minute if some one
began pounding at the door with a sledge-hammer.

There were two rooms, or compartments, to the jail:
a little ante-room and the twelve-by-sixteen foot
"cage," of which he was the sole occupant.   A single
cornhusk mattress had been put in for him that afternoon.   He never seemed quite able to fix its position
in his mind, a circumstance that caused him to stumble
over it time and again as he tramped restlessly about
the place in the darkness.

Suddenly he stopped as if shot.   A tremendous idea
struck him, and for a moment his head spun dizzily.
If it was so blamed easy to break *into* the jail, why
should it be so all-fired difficult to break out of it?
Why, he hadn't even tried the door, or the bars in the
window; now that he thought of it, the grate in the
south window had appeared to be a little shaky.   Inspired by a wild, alluring hope, he sprang over to the

window and gripped the thin iron bars; with all his might and main he jerked, bracing his feet against the wall. No use! It would come just so far and no farther. He tried the other window, with even less encouraging results. In eight or ten minutes now, the crowd would be,—he leaped to the barred door. It, too, resisted his crazy strength. The huge padlock on the other side clattered tauntingly against the grating, but that was all. All the while he was grunting and whining: "If I ever get out of this, it'll take a streak o' greased lightnin' to ketch me. Oh, Lordy! That drum's gettin' closer! They're comin'! If I ever get out of this, nobody'll ever see me closer'n a hundred mile o' this here town,—never as long as I live. Gimme a half hour's start an'— Jehosophat!"

He had shoved a trembling hand between the bars and was fumbling with the padlock. His ejaculation was due to a most incredible discovery. Some one had forgotten to take the key out of the padlock! He laughed shrilly, witlessly. Twenty seconds later he was out in the little anteroom or vestibule, panting and still chortling. The outer door opened readily to the lifting of the latch. He peeped out cautiously, warily. The square was deserted save for a few men hurrying along the street toward the drill ground up beyond Horton's tanyard,—where the drum and fife were playing and men were shouting loudly.

Thereupon Martin Hawk did the incomprehensible thing. He squared his brawny shoulders, set his hat rakishly over one ear, and sauntered out of the jail, calmly stopping to latch the door—and even to rattle it to make sure that it had caught!

He was far too cunning to dart around the corner and bolt for safety. That would have been the worst kind of folly. Instead, he strode briskly off in the direction from whence came the strains of martial music! So much for the benefit of watchful, suspicious eyes. But as he turned the corner of Baker's store his whole demeanour changed. He was off like a frightened rabbit, and as soft-footedly. He ran as the huntsman or the Indian runs,—almost soundlessly, like the wind breezing over dead leaves or through the tops of reeds. Three men stepped out from behind a wagon on the far side of the square. The flare of a bonfire reached dimly to the corner around which the fugitive had scurried. One of the men gave vent to a subdued snort and then spat hurriedly and copiously.

"We'll never see hide nor hair of him again," quoth he. "He won't stop running till daybreak. I guess you'd better wait about ten minutes, Jake, and then fire a few shots. That'll put new life into him. Course, a lot of blamed fools will cuss the daylights out of me for letting him get away right under my nose, and all that, but let 'em talk. He's gone for good, you can bet on that,—and the county's lucky to get rid of him so cheaply."

"I guess you're right, Sheriff," agreed one of his companions. "From all I hear, Mrs. Gwyn would have a hard time provin' it was him as stole her—"

"Supposin' she did prove it, what then?" broke in the high sheriff of the bailiwick. "The county would have to feed him for a couple of months or so and then turn him loose again to go right back to stealing, same as before. The best way to punish a thief, accordin' to my notion, is to keep him everlastingly on the jump, scared to death to show his face anywheres and always hatin' to go to sleep for fear he'll wake up and find somebody pointin' a pistol at him and sayin,'

'Well, I got you at last, dang ye.' Besides, lockin' Mart up isn't going to bring back Mrs. Gwyn's sheep, is it?"

"When that gal of his tells her story in court tomorrow," advanced the third member of the group, "there'll be plenty of people in this town that won't be put off a second time by any fife and drum shinanigan."

"Anyhow," said the sheriff, "I didn't want to have the blamed skunk on my mind while we're organizin' the company. It's bad enough havin' to go out and fight Indians without worryin' all the time I'm away about whether anybody back here has had sense enough to keep Martin from starvin' to death. I guess we'd better mosey along up to the drill ground, boys. Martin's got into the bushes by this time, and if I'm any kind of a guesser he ain't dawdlin' along smellin' every spring flower he comes across."

"Don't you think you'd better go over an' take a look around the jail first?"

"What for? There ain't anybody in it."

"No, but like as not the dog-gasted whelp run off with that padlock, an' we'd ought to know it before he gets too big a start. Padlocks cost money," explained the other, with a dry chuckle and a dig in the sheriff's ribs.

"So do prisoners," was the rejoinder of this remarkable sheriff.

And thus it came to pass that between the sheriff and Kenneth Gwynne and Moll Hawk, the county got rid of three iniquitous individuals. One rode forth in broad daylight on a matchless thoroughbred; another stole off like a weasel in the night, and the third took passage on the Ship that Never Returns.

CHAPTER XXVII

THE TRIAL OF MOLL HAWK

THE trial of Moll Hawk was a brief one. "Judge" Billings, as foreman of the jury, asked permission of the Court to make a few remarks before the taking of testimony began.

"Your honour, this here jury got together last night and sort of talked things over while Mr. Benbridge and other patriotic citizens of Lafayette were engaged in organizing a number of noble and brave-hearted gentlemen into a company of soldiers to give battle to the bloodthirsty red man who is about to swoop down upon us, with tommyhawk and knife and rifle, to ravage our lands and pillage our women—er—I mean *pillage* our lands and—er—so forth. As I was saying, your honour, we talked it over and seeing as how we have all enlisted in Mr. Benbridge's troop and he sort of thought we'd better begin drilling as soon as possible, and also seeing as how this here trial is attractin' a good deal of attention at a time when we ought to be thinkin' of the safety of our wives and children,—if we have any,—we came to the conclusion to address you, sir, with all respect, and suggest that you instruct the counsel on both sides to be as lenient as possible with the jury.

"This here innocent girl's father broke out of jail and got away. As far as this here jury knows he ain't likely ever to come back, so, for the time being at least, there don't seem to be anybody we can hang for the
346

crime with which the prisoner at the bar is charged. This jury was picked with a great deal of care by the sheriff and is, I am reliably informed, entirely satisfactory to both sides of the case.

"In view of the fact that Black Hawk's warriors are reported to have been seen within twenty miles of our beautiful little city, and also in view of the additional fact that Mrs. Rachel Gwyn, one of our foremost citizens and taxpayers, has recently informed me,—and your honour also, I believe, in my presence,—that she intends to give this poor girl a home as soon as she is lawfully discharged by the jury as not guilty, we, the jury, implore your honour to keep an eye on the clock. As we understand the case, there were only two witnesses to the killing of the villain against whom this young woman fought so desperately in self-defence. One of 'em is here in this courtroom. The other is dead and buried. It is now ten minutes past nine. We, the jury, would like for you to inform the counsel on both sides that at precisely ten o'clock we are going to render a verdict, because at a quarter-past ten the majority of us have to attend a company drill. The lawyer for the prisoner enlisted last night as a private in our company, and so did the prosecuting attorney."

"This is a most unusual and unprecedented action on the part of a jury," said the Court gravely. "However, in view of the extraordinary circumstances, I feel that we should be as expeditious as possible in disposing of the case on trial. Gentlemen, you have heard the remarks of the foreman of the jury. Have either of you any reason for objecting to the suggestion he has made? Very well, then; we will proceed with the trial of Mary Hawk, charged with murder in the first degree. Call your first witness, Mr. Prose-cutor."

The little courtroom was jammed to its capacity. Hundreds, unable to gain admission, crowded about the entrance and filled the square. The town was in the throes of a vast excitement, what with the trial, the Indian uprising in the north, the escape of Martin Hawk and the flight of Barry Lapelle, hitherto re-garded as a rake but not even suspected of actual dis-honesty. The *Paul Revere,* with Captain Redberry in charge, had got away at daybreak, loaded to the rails with foot-loose individuals who suddenly had decided to try their fortunes elsewhere rather than remain in a district likely to be overrun by savages.

Moll Hawk sat in front of the judge's table and at her side was Kenneth Gwynne. Mrs. Gwyn and Viola occupied seats on a bench near one of the win-dows, facing the jury. The prisoner was frightened. She was stiff and uncomfortable in the new dress the sheriff's wife had selected for her. Her black hair was neatly brushed and coiled in two thick lobs which hung down over her ears. Her deep-set eyes darted rest-lessly, even warily about her as she sat there in the midst of this throng of strange, stern-faced men. Now and then they went appealingly to Mrs. Gwyn or Viola or to the sheriff's wife, and always they seemed to be asking: "What are they going to do to me?"

The prosecuting attorney, a young man of slender experience but chivalrous instincts, solemnly an-nounced that he had but two witnesses to examine and then he was through. He called the undertaker to the stand.

"In as few words as possible, tell the jury who it was that you buried yesterday afternoon."

"Jasper Suggs."

"Was he dead?"

"He was."

"That's all, your honour."

"Any questions, Mr. Gwynne?" inquired the judge.

"None, your honour."

"Call your next witness, Mr. Prosecutor."

"Mr. Sheriff, will you take the stand for a moment? Did you see the defendant along about four o'clock yesterday morning?"

"I did."

"State where."

"At her father's cabin."

"State what had happened there prior to your arrival, if you know."

"This defendant had had a little difficulty with the corpse, and he was dead on the floor when we got there."

"From a knife wound?"

"Yes, sir."

"Who inflicted that wound, if you know?"

"Miss Mary Hawk."

"You are sure about that, Mr. Sheriff?"

"Pos-i-tively."

"How can you be sure of that, sir, if you did not witness the deed with your own eyes?"

The Court rapped on the table.

"This is your own witness, Mr. Prosecutor. Are you trying to cross-examine him, or to discredit his testimony?"

"I beg your honour's pardon."

Kenneth arose. "We will admit that Jasper Suggs came to his death at the hands of the defendant."

"In that case," said his gentlemanly adversary, "the State rests."

"Judge" Billings was heard audibly to remark: "Give 'em an inch and they take a mile."

"Order in the court! Call your first witness, Mr. Gwynne."

"Take this chair, if you please, Miss Hawk. Hold up your right hand and be sworn. Now, be good enough to answer the questions I put to you, clearly and distinctly, so that the jury may hear."

After a few preliminary questions he said: "Now tell the Court and the jury exactly what happened, beginning with the return of your father and Jasper Suggs from a trip to town. Don't be afraid, Miss—er—Moll. Tell the jury, in your own words, just what took place between the time you first heard Suggs and your father talking in the cabin and the arrival of the sheriff and his men."

It lacked just three minutes of ten o'clock when she finished her story. It had been delivered haltingly and with visible signs of embarrassment at times, but it was a straightforward, honest recital of facts.

"Any questions, Mr. Prosecutor?"

"None, your honour. The State does not desire to present argument. It is content to submit its case to the jury without argument, asking only that a verdict be rendered fairly and squarely upon the evidence as introduced. All we ask is justice."

"Any argument, Mr. Gwynne?"

"None, your honour. The defence is satisfied to leave its case entirely in the hands of the jury."

"Gentlemen of the jury," said the Court, glancing at the clock, "the Court will omit its instructions to you, merely advising you that if you find the prisoner guilty as charged your verdict must be murder in the first degree, the penalty for which is death."

"Judge" Billings leaned over and picked up his hat from the floor. Then he arose and announced:

"We, the jury, find the defendant not guilty."

"Prisoner discharged," said the Court, arising. "The Court desires to thank the jurors for the close attention you have paid to the evidence in this case and for the prompt and just verdict you have returned. Court stands adjourned."

Later on Moll Hawk walked up the hill with Mrs. Gwyn and Viola. Very few words had passed between them since they left the curious but friendly crowd in the public square. Finally Moll's dubious thoughts found 'expression in words, breaking in upon the detached reflections of her two companions.

"I don't see why they let me off like that, Mis' Gwyn. I killed him, didn't I?"

"Yes, Moll,—but the law does not convict a person who kills in self-defence. Didn't you understand that?"

"But supposin' I wuz starvin' to death an' I stole a ham like Bud Gridley did last fall when his pa an' ma wuz sick, wouldn't that be self-defence? They put him in jail fer two months, jest fer stealin' a ham when he hadn't had nothin' to eat fer three days,—bein' crippled an' couldn't work. Wuz that fair?"

"Don't forget, Moll," said Rachel ironically, "that Henry Butts valued his ham at seventy-five cents."

"Anyhow, hit don't seem right an' fair," said Moll. "I didn't have to kill Jasper to save my life. I could ha' saved it without killin' him."

"You did perfectly right in killing him, Moll," broke in Viola warmly. "I would have done the same thing if I had been in your place."

Moll thought over this for a few seconds. "Well,

maybe you might have had to do it, Miss Violy, if them fellers had got away with you as they wuz plannin' to do," she said.

Silence fell between them again, broken after a while by Moll.

"They'll never ketch Pap," she said. "I guess I'll never lay eyes on him ag'in. I wuz jest wonderin' what's goin' to become of his dogs. Do you suppose anybody'll take the trouble to feed 'em?"

.   .   .   .   .   .

Toby Moxler, Jack Trentman's dealer, accosted Kenneth Gwynne at the conclusion of the first drill.

"Jack found this here letter down at the shanty this morning, Mr. Gwynne. It's addressed to you, so he asked me to hand it to you when I saw you."

Kenneth knew at once who the letter was from. He stuck it into his coat pocket, unopened.

"Tell Jack that I am very much obliged to him," he said, and walked away.

When he was safely out of hearing distance, Toby turned to the man at his side and remarked:

"If what Barry Lapelle told me and Jack Trentman yesterday morning is true, there'll be the dog-gonedest scandal this town ever heard of."

"What did he tell you?" inquired his neighbour eagerly.

"It's against my principles to talk about women," snapped Toby, glaring at the man as if deeply insulted. Seeing the disappointment in the other's face, he soft-ened a little: " 'Specially about widders," he went so far as to explain. "You keep your shirt on, Elmer, and wait. And when it *does* come out, you'll be the most surprised man in town."

Kenneth did not open Barry's letter until he reached

his office. His face darkened as he read but cleared almost instantly. He even smiled disdainfully as he tore the sheet into small pieces and stuffed them into his pocket against the time when he could consign them to the fire in his kitchen stove.

"Kenneth Gwynne, Esquire.

"Sir: Upon receipt of your discurtious and cowerdly reply to my challenge I realized the futility of expecting on your part an honourable and gentlemanly settlement of our difficulties. My natural inclination was to seek you out and fource you to fight but advice of friends prevailed. I have decided to make it my business to verrify the story w^h has come to my ears regarding the Gwynne and Carter families. In pursuit of this intention I am starting immediately for your old home town in Kentucky where I am convinced there still remain a number of people who will be able to give me all the facts. If I was misled into making statements that were untrue in my last meeting with your sister I shall most humbly apologize to her. If on the contrary I find that what I said to her was true I will make it my business to bring all the facts to the notice of the people of Lafayette and let them decide what to do in the matter. In any case I shall return in about a month or six weeks at w^h time I shall renew my challenge to you with the sincere hope that you may accept it and that I may have the belated pleasure of putting a bullet through your cowerdly heart. I must however in the meantime refuse to sign myself
"Yours respectfully
"BARRY LAPELLE."

CHAPTER XXVIII

THE turmoil and excitement over the Indian out-
break increased during the day. A constant
stream of refugees, mostly old men, women and
children, poured into Lafayette from regions west of
the Wabash. By nightfall fully three hundred of them
were being cared for by the people of the town, and
more were coming. Shortly after noon a mounted scout
rode in from Warren County with the word that the
militia of his county was preparing to start off at once
to meet the advancing hordes; he brought in the report
that farther north the frontier was being abandoned
by the settlers and that massacres already had occurred. There was also a well-supported rumour that
a portion of the Illinois militia, some two hundred and
fifty men in all, had been routed on Hickory Creek by
Black Hawk's invincible warriors, with appalling losses
to the whites. He bore a stirring message from his
commanding officer, urging the men of Tippecanoe to
rouse themselves and join Warren County troops in
an immediate movement to repel or at least to check
the Sacs and Miamis and Pottawattomies who were
swarming over the prairies like locusts.

The appearance of this messenger, worn and spent
after his long ride, created a profound sensation. Here
at last was official verification of the stories brought
in by the panic-stricken refugees; here was something

that caused the whole town suddenly to awake to the
fact that a real menace existed, and that it was not,
after all, another of those rattle-brained "scares" which
were constantly cropping up.

For months there had been talk of old Black Hawk
and his Sacs going on the warpath over the occupation
of their lands in Northern Illinois by the swift-ad-
vancing, ruthless whites. The old Sac, or Sauk, chieftain had long threatened to resist by force of arms this
violation of the treaty. He had been so long, however,
in even making a start to carry out his threat that the
more enlightened pioneers had ceased to take any stock
in his spoutings.

The *Free Press*, Lafayette's only newspaper, had
from time to time printed news seeping out of the
Northwest by means of carrier or voyageur; their tales
bore out the reports furnished by Federal and State
authorities on the more or less unsettled conditions.
There was, for example, the extremely disquieting story
that Black Hawk, on his return from a hunting trip
west of the Mississippi, had travelled far eastward
across Northern Indiana to seek the advice of the British commander in Canada. Not only was the story of
this pilgrimage true, but the fact was afterward defi-
nitely established that the British official advised the
chief to make war on the white settlers,—this being
late in 1831, nearly twenty years after the close of the
War of 1812. Many of Black Hawk's warriors had
served under Tecumseh in the last war with England,
and they still were rabid British sympathizers.

Amidst the greatest enthusiasm and excitement, the
men of Lafayette organized the "Guards," a company
some three hundred strong. After several days of in-
tensive and, for a time, ludicrous "drilling,"-they were

ready and eager to ride out into the terrorized North-west.

Kenneth Gwynne was a private in "The Guards."

During the thrilling days of preparation for the expedition, he saw little of the women next door. Doubtless for reasons of their own, Viola and her mother maintained a strange and persistent aloofness. It was not until the evening before the departure of the "Guards" that he took matters into his own hands and walked over to Rachel's house.

The few glimpses he had had of Viola during these busy days and nights served not only to increase his ardent craving for her but caused him the most acute misery as well. Utter despond had fallen upon him.

It was significant of her new attitude toward life that she had cast aside the sombre habiliments of mourning. She was now appearing in bright, though not gay, colours,—unmistakable evidence of her decision to abandon all pretence of grief for the man she had looked upon for so many years as her father.

There was a strange, new vivacity in her manner, too,—something that hurt rather than cheered him. He heard her singing about the house,—gay, larksome little snatches,—and she whistled merrily as she worked in the garden. Somehow her very light-heartedness added to his despair. What right had she to be happy and gay and cheerful whilst he was so miserable? Had he not told her in so many words that he loved her? Did that mean nothing to her? Why should she sing and whistle in her own domain when she must have known that he was suffering in his, not twenty rods away? He was conscious at times of a sense of injury, and as the time drew near for his departure without so much as a sign of regret or even interest on her part, this feeling deepened into resentment.

He was very stiff and formal as he approached the porch on which Viola and her mother were seated, enjoying the cool evening breeze that had sprung up at the end of the hot and sultry day. A strange woman and two small children, refugees from the Grand Prairie, had been given shelter by Mrs. Gwyn, but they had already gone to bed.

"We are off at daybreak," he said, standing before them, his hat in his hand. "I thought I would come over to say good-bye."

His hungry gaze swept over the figure of the girl, shadowy and indistinct in the semi-darkness. To his amazement, he saw that she was attired in the frock she had worn on that unforgettable night at Striker's. She leaned forward and held out her hand to him. As he took it he looked up into her dusky face and caught his breath. Good heaven! She was actually smiling! Smiling when he was going away perhaps never to return alive!

She did not speak. It was Rachel Carter who said, quietly:

"Thank you for coming over, Kenneth. We would not have allowed you to go, however, without saying good-bye and wishing you well on this hazardous undertaking. May God protect you and all the brave men who go out with you."

He had not released Viola's hand. Suddenly her grip tightened; her other hand was raised quickly to her face, and he was dumbfounded to see that she was dabbing at her eyes with her handkerchief. His heart swelled. She had been smiling bravely all the while her eyes were filled with tears. And now he knew why she was silent. He lifted her hand to his lips.

"I want you to know, Viola dear, before I go away," he said huskily, "that I can and will give you back the name of Gwynne, and with my name I give more love than ever any man had for woman before in all this world. I lay my heart at your feet. It is yours whether you choose to pick it up or not."

She slowly withdrew her hand. Neither of them heard the long, deep sigh in the darkness beside them.

"I don't know what to say to you, Kenny," she murmured, almost inaudibly.

"There is nothing for you to say, Viola, unless you love me. I am sorry if I have distressed you. I only wanted you to know before I go away that I love you."

"I—I am glad you love me, Kenny. It makes me very happy. But it is all so strange, so unreal. I can't seem to convince myself that it is right for you to love me or for me to love you. Some day, perhaps, it will all straighten itself out in my mind and then I will know whether it is love,—the kind of love you want,—or just a dear, sweet affection that I feel for you."

"I uuderstand," he said gravely. "It is too soon for you to know. A brother turned into a lover, as if by magic, and you are bewildered. I can only pray that the time will come when your heart tells you that you love me as I want you to, and as I love you."

They spoke thus freely before the girl's mother, for those were the days when a man's courting was not done surreptitiously. It is doubtful, however, if they remembered her presence.

"There have been times—" she began, a trace of eagerness in her voice, "when something seemed to tell

me that—that I ought to keep away from you. I used
to have the queerest sensations running all over—"
She did not complete the sentence; instead, as if in a
sudden panic over the nearness of unmaidenly revelations, she somewhat breathlessly began all over again:
"I guess it must have been a—a warning, or something."

"They say there is such a thing as a magnetic current between human beings," he said. "It was that,
Viola. You felt my love laying hold upon you, touching you, caressing you."

"The other night, when you held me so close to you,
I—I couldn't think of you as my brother."

Out of the darkness spoke Rachel Carter.

"You love each other," she said. "There is no use
trying to explain or account for your feelings. The
day you came here, Kenneth Gwynne, I saw the hand-
writing on the wall. I knew that this would happen.
It was as certain as the rising of the sun. It would
have been as useless for me to attempt to stop the
rising sun as to try to keep you two from falling in
love with each other. It was so written long ago."

"But, mother, I am not sure,—how can you say
that I am in love with him when I don't know it myself?" cried Viola.

"When you came, Kenneth, I knew that my days
were numbered," went on the older woman, leaning forward in her chair. "The truth would have to come
out. A force I could not stand up against had entered the field. For want of a better word we will call
it Fate. It is useless to fight against Fate. If I had
never told you two the truth about yourselves, you
would have found it out anyway. You would have
found it out in the touch of your hands, in the leap of

the blood, in the strange, mysterious desire of the flesh over which the soul has no control. You began loving him, Viola,—without knowing it,—that night at Phineas Striker's. You—"

"How can you say such a thing, mother?" cried Viola hotly. "I was in love with Barry Lapelle at that—"

"You were never in love with Barry," broke in her mother calmly.

"I think I ought to know when I am in love and when I am not!"

"Be that as it may, you now know that you were never in love with him,—so it comes to the same thing."

Kenneth's heart gave a joyous bound. "I—I wish I could believe that. I wish I knew that you are not thinking of him now, Viola, and wanting him back in spite of all he has done."

Viola arose suddenly. "I am going in the house," she said haughtily. "Neither of you seems to think I have a grain of sense. First mother says I am in love with you without knowing it, and now you are wondering if I am in love with Barry without knowing it, I suppose. Don't you give me credit for having a mind of my own? And, mother, I've just got to say it, even if it is insolent,—I will be very much obliged to you if you will allow me to make up my own mind about Kenny. It is not for you or anybody else to say I am in love with him."

"Oh, don't go away angry, Viola," cried Kenneth, distressed. "Let's forget all we've said and—"

"I don't want to forget all we've said," she exclaimed, stamping her foot. "How dare you come over here and tell me you love me and then ask me to forget— Oh, if that's all it amounts to with you, Kenneth, I dare say I can make up my mind right now. I—"

"You will find, Kenneth," broke in her mother drily, "that she has a temper."

"I guess he has found that out before this," said Viola, from the doorstep. "He has had a taste of it. If he doesn't like—"

"I am used to tempers," said he, now lightly. "I have a devil of a temper myself."

"I don't believe it," she cried. "You've got the kindest, sweetest, gentlest nature I've ever—"

"Come and sit down, Viola," interrupted her mother, arising. "I am going in the house myself."

"You needn't, mother. I am going to bed. Good night, Kenny."

"I came to say good-bye," he reminded her.

She paused with her hand on the latch. He heard the little catch in her breath. Then she turned impulsively and came back to him. He was still standing on the ground, several feet below her.

"What a beast I am, Kenny," she murmured contritely. "I waited out here all evening for you to come over so that I could say good-bye and tell you how much I shall miss you,—and to wish you a speedy and safe return. And you paid me a great compliment,— the greatest a girl can have. I don't deserve it. But I will miss you, Kenny,—I will miss you terribly. Now, I *must* go in. If I stay another second longer I'll say something mean and spiteful,—because I *am* mean and spiteful, and no one knows it better than I do. Good-bye, Kenneth Gwynne."

"Good-bye, Minda Carter," he said softly, and again raised her hand to his lips. "My little Minda grown up to be the most beautiful queen in all the world."

She turned and fled swiftly into the house. They heard her go racing up the stairs,—then a door open and slam shut again.

"She would be very happy to-night, Kenneth, if it were not for one thing," said Rachel. "I still stand in the way. She cannot give herself to you except at a cost to me. There can be nothing between you until I stand before the world and say there is no reason why you should not be married to each other. Do you wonder that she does not know her own heart?"

"And I would not deserve her love and trust if I were to ask you to pay that price, Rachel Carter," said he steadily.

"Good-bye, Kenneth," she said, after a moment. She held out her hand. "Will you take my hand,—just this once, boy?"

He did not hesitate. He grasped the hard, toil-worn hand firmly in his.

"We can never be friends, Rachel Carter,—but, as God is my witness, I am no longer your enemy," he said, with feeling. "Good-bye."

He was half-way down to the gate when she called to him:

"Wait, Kenneth. Moll has something for you."

He turned back and met Moll Hawk as she came swiftly toward him.

"Here's somethin' fer you to carry in your pocket, Mr. Gwynne," said the girl in her hoarse, low-pitched voice. "No harm c'n ever come to you as long as you got this with you,—in your pocket er anywheres. Hit's a charm an old Injin chief give my Pap when he wuz with the tribe, long before I wuz born. Pap lost it the day before he wuz tooken up by the sheriff, er else he never would ha' had setch bad luck. I found it day before yesterday when I wuz down to the cabin, seein' about movin' our hogs an' chickens an' hosses over to Mis' Gwyn's barn. The only reason the Injun give it to Pap wuz beca'se he wuz over a hundred years old an' didn't want to warn off death no longer. Hit's just a little round stone with somethin' fer all the world like eyes an' nose an' mouth on one side of it,— jest as if hit had been carved out, only hit wuzn't. Hit's jest natural. Hit keeps off sickness an' death an' bad luck, Mr. Gwynne. Pap knowed he wuz goin' to ketch the devil the minute he found out he lost it. I tole Miss Violy I wanted fer you to have it with you while you wuz off fightin' the Injuns, an' she said she'd love me to her dyin' day if I would give you the loan of it. Mebby you don't believe in charms an' signs an' all setch, but it can't hurt you to carry it an'—an' hit's best to be on the safe side. Please keep it, Mr. Gwynne."

It was a round object no bigger than a hickory nu⁼ He had taken it from her and was running his thumb over its surface while she was speaking. He could feel the tiny nose and the little indentations that produced the effect of eyes.

"Thank you, Moll," he said, sincerely touched. "It's mighty good of you. I will bring it back to you, never fear, and I hope that after it has served me faithfully for a little while it may do the same for you till you, too, have seen a hundred and don't want to live any longer. What was it Miss Viola said to you?"

"I guess I hadn't ought to said that," she mumbled. "Anyhow, I ain't goin' to say it over again. Good-bye, Mr. Gwynne,—and take good keer o' yourself."

With that she hurried back to the house, and he,

after a glance up at the second story window which he knew to be Viola's, bent his steps homeward.

His saddle-bags were already packed, his pistols cleaned and oiled; the long-barrelled rifle he had borrowed from the tavern keeper was in prime order for the expedition. Zachariah had gotten out his oldest clothes, his thick riding boots, a linsey shirt and the rough but serviceable buckskin cap that old Mr. Price had hobbled over to the office to give him after the first day of drill with the sententious remark that a "plug hat was a perty thing to perade around in but it wasn't a very handy sort of a hat to be buried in."

His lamp burned far into the night. He tried to read but his thoughts would not stay fixed on the printed page. Not once but many times he took up from the table a short, legal-looking document and re-read its contents, which were entirely in his own cramped, scholastic hand save for the names of two witnesses at the end. It was his last will and testament, drawn up that very day. Minda Carter was named therein as his sole legatee,—"Minda Carter, at present known as Viola Gwyn, the daughter of Owen and Rachel Carter." His father had, to all intents and purposes, cut her off without a penny, an injustice which would be righted in case of his own death.

It was near midnight when he blew out the light and threw himself fully dressed upon the bed. Sleep would not come. At last, in desperation, he got up and stole guiltily, self-consciously out into the yard, treading softly lest he should wake the vehement Zachariah in his cubbyhole off the kitchen. Presently he was standing at the fence separating the two yards, his elbows on the top rail, his gloomy, lovelorn gaze fixed upon Viola's darkened window.

The stars were shining. A cool, murky mantle lay over the land. He did not know how long he had been standing there when his ear caught the sound of a gently-closing door. A moment later a dim, shadowy figure appeared at the corner of the house, stood motionless for a few seconds, and then came directly toward him. The blood rushed thunderously to his head. He could not believe his senses. He had been wishing—aye, vainly wishing that by some marvellous enchantment she could be transported through the dark little window into his arms. He rubbed his eyes.

"Viola!" he whispered.

"Oh, Kenny," she faltered, and her voice was low and soft like the sighing of the wind. "I—I am so ashamed. What will you think of me for coming out here like this?"

The god of Love gave him wings. He was over the fence, she was in his arms, and he was straining the warm, pliant body close to his bursting breast. His lips were on hers. He felt her stiffen and then relax in swift surrender. Her heart, stilled at first, began to beat tumultuously against his breast; her free arm stole about his neck and tightened as the urge of a sweet, overwhelming passion swept over her.

At last she released herself from his embrace and stood with bowed head, her hands pressed to her eyes.

"I didn't mean to do it,—I didn't mean to do this," she was murmuring.

"You love me,—you love me," he whispered, his voice trembling with joy. He drew her hands down from her eyes and held them tight in his own. "Say you do, Viola,—speak the words."

"It must be love," she sighed. "What else could

make me feel as I do now,—as I did when you were holding me,—and kissing me? Oh,—oh,—yes, I *do* love you, Kenny. I know it now. I love you with all my soul." She was in his arms again. "But," she panted a little later, "I swear I didn't know it when I came out here, Kenny,—I swear I didn't."

"Oh, yes, you did," he cried triumphantly. "You've known it all the time, only you didn't understand."

"I wonder," she mused. Then quickly, shyly: "I had no idea it could come like this,—that it would *be* like this. I feel so queer. My knees are all trembly,—it's the strangest feeling. Now you must let me go, Kenny. I must not stay out here with you. It is terribly late. I—"

"I can't let you go in yet, dearest. Come! We will sit for a little while on the steps. Don't leave me yet, Viola. It is all so wonderful, so unbelievable. And to think I was looking up at your window only a few minutes ago, wishing that you would fly down to me. Good heavens! It can't be a dream, can it? All this is real, isn't it?"

She laughed softly. "It can't be a dream with me, because I haven't even been in bed. I've been sitting up there in my window for hours, looking over at your house. When your light went out, I was terribly lonely. Yes, and I was a little put out with you for going to bed. Then I saw you come and lean on the fence. I knew you were looking up at my window, —and I was sure that you could see me in spite of the darkness. You never moved,—just stood there with your elbows on the fence, staring up at me. It made me very uncomfortable, because I was in my nightgown. So I made up my mind to get into bed and pull the coverlet up over my head. But I didn't do it. I put on my dress,—everything,—shoes and stockings and all,—and then I went back to see if you were still there. There you were. You hadn't moved. So I sat down again and watched you. After awhile I—I—well, I just couldn't help creeping downstairs and coming out to—to say good-bye to you again, Kenny. You looked so lonesome."

"I was lonesome," he said,—"terribly lonesome."

She led him to a crudely constructed bench at the foot of a towering elm whose lower branches swept the fore-corner of the roof.

"Let us sit here, Kenny dear," she said. "It is where I shall come and sit every night while you are gone away. I shall sit with my back against it and close my eyes and dream that you are beside me as you are now, with your arms around me and your cheek against mine,—and it will be the trysting place for our thoughts."

"That's wonderful, Viola," he said, impressed. " 'The trysting place for our thoughts.' Aye, and that it shall be. Every night, no matter where my body may be or what peril it may be in, I shall be here beside you in my thoughts."

She rested against him, in the crook of his strong right arm, her head against his shoulder, and they both fell silent and pensive under the spell of a wondrous enchantment.

After a while, she spoke, and there was a note of despair in her voice:

"What is to become of us, Kenny? What are we to do?"

"No power on earth can take you away from me now, Minda," he said.

"Ah,—that's it," she said miserably. "You call me

Minda,—and still you wonder why I ask what we are to do."

"You mean—about—"

"We can be nothing more to each other than we are now. There is some one else we must think of. I—I forgot her for a little while, Kenny,—I was so happy that I forgot her."

"Were ever two souls so tried as ours," he groaned, and again silence fell between them.

Kneeling at the window from which Viola had peered so short a time before, looking down upon the figures under the tree, was Rachel Carter. She could hear their low voices, and her ears, made sharp by pain, caught the rapturous and the forlorn passages breathed upon the still air.

She arose stiffly and drew back into the darkness, out of the dim, starlit path, and standing there with her head high, her arms outspread, she made her solemn vow of self-renunciation.

"I have no right to stand between them and happiness. They have done no wrong. They do not deserve to be punished. My mind is made up. To-morrow I shall speak. God has brought them together. It is not for me to keep them apart. Aye, to-morrow I shall speak."

Then Rachel Carter, at peace with herself, went back to her bed across the hall and was soon asleep, a smile upon her lips, the creases wiped from between her eyes as if by some magic soothing hand.

CHAPTER XXIX

THE ENDING

AT crack-o'-day Kenneth rode out of his stable-yard on Brandy Boy, and went cantering away, followed on foot by the excited Zachariah, bound for the parade ground where the "soldiers" were to concentrate.

The rider turned in his saddle to wave farewell to the little group huddled at Rachel's gate,—three tall women who waved back to him. Rounding the bend, he sent a swift glance over his shoulder. There was but one figure at the gate now; she blew a kiss to him.

Nearly three hundred horsemen moved out of Lafayette that forenoon amidst the greatest excitement and enthusiasm. Most of them swam their horses across the river, too eager to wait for the snail-like ferry to transport them to the opposite bank. They were fearfully and wonderfully armed and equipped for the expedition. Guns of all descriptions and ages; pistols, axes, knives and diligently scoured swords; pots and pans and kettles; blankets, knapsacks and parcels of varying sizes; in all a strange and motley assortment that would have caused a troop of regulars to die of laughter. But the valiant spirit was there. Even the provident and far-sighted gentlemen who strapped cumbersome and in some cases voluptuous umbrellas (because of their extraneous contents) across their backs alongside the guns, were no more timorous than their swashbuckling neighbours who scorned the tempest even as they scoffed at the bloodthirsty red-skins. Four heavily laden wagons brought up the rear.

Kenneth Gwynne rode beside the ubiquitous "Judge" Billings, who cheerfully and persuasively sought to "swap" horses with him when not otherwise employed in discoursing upon the vast inefficiency of certain specifically named officers who rode in all their plump glory at or near the head of the column. He was particularly out of sympathy with a loud-mouthed lieutenant.

"Why," said he, "if the captain was to say 'halt' suddenly that feller'd lose his mind tryin' to think what to do. No more head on him than a grasshopper. And him up there givin' orders to a lot of bright fellers like you an' me an' the rest of us! By gosh, I'd like to be hidin' around where I could see the look on the Indian's face that scalps him. The minute he got through scrapin' a little hide an' hair off of the top o' that feller's head he'd be able to see clear down to the back of his Adam's Apple."

Historians have recorded the experiences and achievements of this gallant troop of horse. It is not the intention of the present chronicler to digress. Suffice to say, the expedition moved sturdily westward and northward for five or six days without encountering a single Indian. Then they were ordered to return home. There were two casualties. One man was accidentally shot in the arm while cleaning his own rifle, and another was shot in the foot by a comrade who was aiming at a rattlesnake. Nine or ten days after they rode out from Lafayette, the majority of the company rode back again and were received with acclaim. Two score of the more adventurous, however, separated from the main body on Sugar Creek and, electing their own officers, proceeded to Hickory Creek and on to the River

O' Plein in Northern Illinois, without finding a hostile redskin.

As a matter of fact, Black Hawk was at no time near the Indiana border. His operations were confined to Northwestern Illinois in the region of the Mississippi River. Subsequently a series of sanguinary battles took place between the Indians and strong Illinois militia forces supported by detachments of United States troops under General Brady. It was not until the beginning of August that Black Hawk was finally defeated, his dwindling horde almost annihilated, and the old chieftain, betrayed into the hands of the whites by the Winnebagos, was made a prisoner of war. And so, summarily, the present chronicler disposes of the "great Black Hawk war," and returns to his narrative and the people related thereto.

Kenneth Gwynne did not go back to Lafayette with the main body of troops; he decided to join Captain McGeorge and his undaunted little band of adventurers. Gwynne's purpose in remaining with McGeorge was twofold. Not only was he keenly eager to meet the Indians but somewhere back in his mind was the struggling hope that, given time, Rachel Carter's reserve would crack under the fresh strain put upon it and she would voluntarily, openly break the silence that now stood as an absolutely insurmountable obstacle to his marriage with Viola. Not until Rachel Carter herself cleared the path could they find the way to happiness.

He would have been amazed, even shocked, could he have known all that transpired in Lafayette on the day following his departure. He was not to know for many a day, as it was nearly three weeks after the return of the main body of troops that McGeorge and his little band rode wearily down through the

Grand Prairie and entered the town, their approach being heralded by a scout sent on in advance.

Kenneth searched eagerly among the crowd on the river bank, seeking the face that had haunted him throughout all the irksome days and nights; he looked for the beloved one to whom his thoughts had sped each night for communion at the foot of the blessed elm. She was nowhere to be seen. He was bitterly disappointed. As soon as possible he escaped from his comrades and hurried home. There he learned from Rachel Carter herself that Viola had gone away, never to return to Lafayette again.

.   .   .   .

Mid-morning on the day after the troops rode away, Rachel Carter appeared at the office of her lawyer, Andrew Holman. There, in the course of the next hour, she calmly, unreservedly bared the whole story of her life to the astonished and incredulous gentleman.

She did not consult with her daughter before taking this irrevocable step. She put it beyond her daughter's power to shake the resolution she had made on the eve of Kenneth's departure; she knew that Viola would cry out against the sacrifice and she was sorely afraid of her own strength in the presence of her daughter's anguish. "I shall put it all in the paper," she said, regarding the distressed, perspiring face of the lawyer with a grim, almost taunting smile, as if she actually relished his consternation. "What I want you to do, first off, Andrew, is to prepare some sort of affidavit, setting forth the facts, which I will sign and swear to. It needn't be a long document. The shorter the better, just so it makes everything clear."

"But, my dear Mrs. Gwyn, this—this may dispossess you of everything," remonstrated the agitated man of law. "The fact that you were never the wife of Robert—"

"Your memory needs refreshing," she interrupted. "If you will consult Robert Gwyn's will you will discover that he leaves half of his estate, et cetera, to 'my beloved and faithful companion and helpmate, Rachel, who, with me, has assumed the name of Gwyn for the rest of her life in view of certain circumstances which render the change in the spelling of my name advisable, notwithstanding the fact that in signing this, my last will and testament, I recognize the necessity of affixing my true and legal name.' You and I know the sentence by heart, Andrew. No one can or will dispute my claim to the property. I have thought this all out, you may be sure,—just as he thought it all out when he drew up the paper. I imagine he must have spent a great deal of time and thought over that sentence, and I doubt if you or any other lawyer could have worded it better."

"Of course, if the will reads as you say,—er,—ahem! Yes, yes,—I remember now that it was a—er—somewhat ambiguous. Ahem! But it has just occurred to me, Mrs. Gwyn, that you are going a little farther than is really necessary in the matter. May I suggest that you are not—er—obliged to reveal the fact that you were never married to him? That, it seems to me, is quite unnecessary. If, as you say, your object is merely to set matters straight so that your daughter and Mr. Gwynne may be free to marry, being in no sense related either by blood or by law,—such as would have been the case if you had married Kenneth's father,—why, it seems to me you can avoid a great deal of unpleasant notoriety by—er—leaving out that particular admission "

"No," she said firmly. "Thank you for your kind advice,—but, if you will reflect, it is out of the question. You forget what you have just said. For a lawyer, my dear friend, you are surprisingly simple to-day."

"I see,—I see," mumbled the lawyer, mopping his brow. "Of course,—er,—you are quite right. You are a very level-headed woman. Quite so. I would have thought of it in another moment or two. You can't leave out that part of it without—er—nullifying the whole object and intent of your—er—ahem!—I was about to say confession, but that is a nasty word. In other words, unless you acknowledge that you and Robert were never lawfully married, the—er—"

"Exactly," she broke in crisply. "That is the gist of the matter. Society does not countenance marriage between step-brother and -sister. So we will tell the whole truth,—or nothing at all. Besides, Robert Gwyn put the whole story in writing himself, as I have told you. The hiding-place of that piece of paper is still a mystery, but it will be found some day. I am trying to take the curse off of it, Andrew."

As she was leaving the office, he said to her, with deep feeling: "I suppose you realize the consequences, Mrs. Gwyn? It means ostracism for you. You will not have a friend in this town,—not a person who will speak to you, aside from the storekeepers who value your custom and"—he bowed deeply—"your humble servant."

"I fully appreciate what it means," she responded wearily. "It means that if I continue to hold my head up or dare to look my neighbour in the face I shall be called brazen as well as corrupt," she went on after a moment, a sardonic little twist at the corner of her mouth. "Well, so be it. I have thought of all that. Have no fear for me, my friend. I have never been afraid of the dark,—so why should I fear the light?"

"You're a mighty fine woman, Rachel Gwyn," cried the lawyer warmly.

She frowned as she held out her hand. "None of that, if you please," she remarked tersely. "Will you have the paper ready for me to sign this afternoon?"

"I will submit it to you right after dinner."

"You may expect me here at two o'clock. We will then step over to the *Free Press* and allow Mr. Semans to copy the document for his paper." She allowed herself a faint smile. "I daresay he can make room for it, even if he has to subtract a little from his account of the stirring events of yesterday."

"Your story will make a great sensation," declared the lawyer, wiping his brow once more. "He can't afford to—er—to leave it out."

At two o'clock she was in his office again. He read the carefully prepared document to her.

"This is like signing your own death warrant, Rachel Gwyn," he said painfully, as she affixed her signature and held up her hand to be sworn.

"No. I am signing a pardon for two guiltless people who are suffering for the sins of others."

"That reminds me," he began, pursing his lips. "I have been reflecting during your absence. Has it occurred to you that this act of yours is certain to react with grave consequences upon the very people you would—er—befriend? I am forced to remind you that the finger of scorn will not be pointed at you alone. Your daughter will not escape the—er—ignominy of being—ahem!—of being your daughter, in fact. Young Gwynne will find his position here very greatly affected by the—er—"

"I quite understand all that, Andrew. I am not

thinking of the present so much as I am considering
the future. The past, so far as we all are concerned,
is easily disposed of, but these two young people have
a long life ahead of them. It is not my idea that
they shall spend it here in this town,—or even in this
State."

"You mean you will urge them to leave Lafayette
forever?"

"Certainly."

"But if I know Viola,—and I think I do,—she will
refuse to desert you. As for Gwynne, he strikes me as
a fellow who would not turn tail under fire."

"In any case, Andrew, it will be for them to decide.
Kenneth had already established himself as a lawyer
back in the old home town. I shall urge him to return
to that place with Viola as soon as they are married.
His mother was a Blythe. There is no blot upon the
name of Blythe. My daughter was born there. Her
father was an honest, God-fearing, highly respected
man. His name and his memory are untarnished. No
man can say aught against the half of Kenneth that
is Blythe, nor the half of Viola that is Carter. I should
like the daughter of Owen Carter to go back and
live among his people as the wife of the son of
Laura Blythe, and to honourably bear the name that
was denied me by a Gwynne."

He looked at her shrewdly for a moment and then,
as the full significance of her plan grew upon him,
revealing in a flash the motive behind it, he exclaimed:

"Well, by gosh, you certainly have done an almighty
lot of calculating."

"And why shouldn't I? She is my child. Is it likely
that I would give myself the worst of everything without seeing to it that she gets the best of everything?

No, my friend; you must not underrate my intelligence. I will speak plainly to you,—but in confidence. This is between you and me. There is no love lost between Kenneth Gwynne and me. He hates me and always will, no matter how hard he may try to overcome it. In a different way I hate him. We must not be where we can see each other. I am sorely afraid that the tender love he now has for Viola would fail to outlast the hatred he feels toward me. I leave you to imagine what that would mean to her. He has it in his power to give her a place among his people. He can force them to honour and respect her, and her children will be *their* children. Do you see? Need I say more?"

"You need say nothing more. I understand what you want, Mrs. Gwyn,—and I must say that you are in a sense justified. What is to become of young Gwynne's property here in this county?"

"I think I can be trusted to look after it satisfactorily," she said quietly; "perhaps even better than he could do for himself. I am a farm woman."

"I thought maybe you had some notion of buying him out."

"He would not sell to me. His farm is being properly handled by the present tenant. His lots here in town cannot run away. The time will come when they will be very valuable, or I am no prophetess. There is nothing to keep him here, Andrew, and his interests and my daughter's will be as carefully looked after as my own."

"We will be sorry to lose him as a citizen."

"If you are ready, we will step over to the *Free Press* office," she said, without a sign that she had heard his remark.

They crossed the square and turned up the first

street to the left. "This will be a terrible shock to your daughter," said he, breaking a long silence.

"She will survive it," replied Rachel Gwyn sententiously.

He laid his hand on her arm. "Will you accept a bit of advice from me?"

They stopped. "I am not above listening to it," she replied.

"My advice is to postpone this action until you are sure of one thing."

"And what may that be?"

"Kenneth Gwynne's safe return from this foray against the Indians. He may not come back alive."

"He will come back alive," said she, in a cool, matter-of-fact tone. "It is so ordained. I know. Come, we are wasting time. I have much to do between now and nightfall. Bright and early to-morrow morning my daughter and I are leaving town."

"Leaving town?" he cried, astonished.

"I am taking her out in the country,—to the farm. If I can prevent it she shall never put foot in this town again. You know Phineas Striker? An honest, loyal man, with a wife as good as gold. When Kenneth Gwynne marches back to town again he will find me here to greet him. I till tell him where to find Viola. Out at Striker's farm, my friend, she will be waiting for him to come and claim his own."

A smile he did not understand and never was to understand played about her lips as she continued drily, for such was the manner of this amazing woman:

"He will even find that her wedding gown is quite as much to his fancy as it was the day he met her."

THE END